The Bolt

The Bolt

P. R. Shore

COACHWHIP PUBLICATIONS
GREENVILLE, OHIO

The Bolt, by P. R. Shore
© 2025 Coachwhip Publications edition
Cover: Elf-bolts, Museum of the Royal Irish Academy, 1857

First published 1929
Pseudonym for Helen Madeline Leys, 1892-1965
CoachwhipBooks.com

ISBN 1-61646-605-7
ISBN-13 978-1-61646-605-3

1

I am quite aware that I am not the kind of person who ought to write the story of what happened at Ringshall. The trouble is, I don't quite know who should.

I suppose it should be Roger Cartwright, since he was really the most active of us all (I mean, of course, of the amateurs; I am not of those who despise the police—indeed, I have a strong respect, I might almost say affection, for Inspector Grier; and I'm sure they all did what they could, and were certainly extremely active). But Roger Cartwright says he won't, though it is now, of course, quite *de rigueur* for parsons, and even, I believe, dons, to do human things like that. He says two sermons a week is enough, which is absurd, because sermons are, unfortunately, quite different, and anyhow it's generally only one. But if he won't, he won't; and anyhow I want to, partly because I really was 'inside,' and know personally a good deal of what went on, partly because they all think I can't do it, and chiefly because I want to.

Where to begin is the difficulty. Looking back over the diary which, like many spinsters, I keep spasmodically, I find that I began to keep systematic entries about the affair on 1st July; but that was only because it was not till then that I realized that things were in such a frightful tangle, and began to write them down to try and sort them

out in my mind. I must begin the story before that—in
fact, even before that dreadful 29th of June.

It was looking back through my diary, though, that
showed me how much goes on in your ordinary everyday
life that you never notice. Now that I know what happened, and how it happened, I wonder that, in those early
days of the year, I thought nothing could happen at Ringshall, and saw nothing—well, odd, at least—in the way
some of us behaved. But it's easy to be wise after the event,
and I sometimes wonder (now; I didn't before) whether all
country villages are the same, and whether in other little
places there are such storms brewing under the quiet surface. Anyhow, it's only fair to tell as much as I can remember of the things which might have helped me to guess.

We used to be a very happy little community at Ringshall. Any one who had lived there for less than ten years
was still a stranger; you must have had your roots in the
village for generations before you were really 'of' and not
merely 'in', it. This once used to annoy me; but as I got
used to Ringshall, and realized the immense age of its
rolling downs and its lonely barrows—of the wicked flint
arrow-heads that one picks up looking as if they'd been
chipped yesterday—the old, half-remembered magic, the
remains of a lost worship of forgotten gods—I came to
know that I am, really and truly, only the visitor of a day.

But I haven't always felt this, and a good many of us
never felt it at all. We wondered, some of us, at the 'secretiveness' of the villagers, and were annoyed or amused according to our respective characters. Most of us were wise
enough to keep our feelings to ourselves; only Mrs. Harrington was rash enough to try to 'educate them out of their
superstitions', and she was one of those people who are
always wrong because they believe they are always right.

I don't think any of us cared very much for Mrs. Harrington. Godfrey Harrington, the squire, of course did—

once; he was liable to short, violent fits of affection, and, before his second marriage with Mrs. Ward, as she was then, he had had more than one 'affair' which came to nothing, because the objects of his passion knew that it was temporary and simply kept him off till it was over. But with Mrs. Ward it was different. I may be a rustic, but I know enough of the world outside Wiltshire to know that. She was, no doubt, a very fascinating person, and the way in which, even as a 'nobody' in the village, she twisted us all round her fingers and organized us and generally ran us, showed that at least she had personality. She was very handsome, in a cold, repressed sort of way; also she was extremely wealthy—for Ringshall. No doubt in New York, where I understand that the average income is about £50,000 or so, she would have been a pauper; but, reserved as she was, there could be no doubt that she could have bought up any ten, or even twenty, of us without noticing she'd done it.

You have probably gathered from this account of her that I didn't care for Mrs. Ward. You are perfectly right. I didn't. When she first came to Ringshall, in pathetic black that made her lovely hair like amber, I felt sorry for her and admired her; but I shall never be one of those who are to inherit the earth, and she very soon got my dander up. I'd only lived in Ringshall for eight years, but I felt that she was more of a 'foreigner' than I, and I did dislike the way in which she proceeded to show us how a village should be run. She got hold of dear old Mr. Jukes, the vicar, and made him feel remiss about Church societies and guilds and things; she tackled Mr. Jervis, the schoolmaster, about handweaving and community singing; she started G.F.S.s and Missionary Societies and Mothers' Meetings, and even revived the dreadful custom of District Visitors; she induced the Dorcas Society, which used to be a mere excuse for pleasant gossip and pretty needlework, to sew the most dreadful garments which no one would conceivably wear if they could get woad. She was the only person I've ever known who really *bought* those bundles of haircloth flannel and shoddy serge which certain shops advertise as 'suitable for charity'—which I suppose they are, if you take Mrs. Ward's view of charity. Certainly nothing could make the recipient feel smaller. That is not a digression, though Roger Cartwright says it is. It is there to show you what she was like—a lovely, wealthy, red-haired lady who bought charity bundles. Roger writes his sermons on the logical 'one, two, three' plan, and knows nothing of more artistic methods. But, though you may not notice it at the time, practically nothing of what I put in to this account of our mystery is superfluous. It all comes in somewhere. Only I don't call it one, two, three.

We all felt that Mrs. Ward (as she was when she first came to Ringshall) was a challenge. She challenged us all, each in a different way. She challenged Lady Gervaise as our beauty and Woman of the World; she challenged Mrs. Arnold as our Lady Bountiful; she challenged me as a gardener and practical person. She made us all feel like back numbers, and showed us that we were lacking in public spirit, with which she proposed to inspire us. And she certainly did get us going. Societies of the most improving kind sprang up everywhere, and there were soon nearly, if not quite, as many district visitors as cottages.

When Mrs. Ward first came to Ringshall over three years ago, we all immediately allotted her to the widowed squire, Godfrey Harrington. We are, like all village communities, greatly given to matchmaking, and this really seemed miraculously suitable. You had on the one hand a widower, handsome, weak, poor, of good family, 'encumbered' (if you can use the word of Celia) with a very pretty and affectionate, but rather headstrong, daughter of nineteen, who could not do a single one of the things that

squires' motherless daughters ought to be able to do; on
the other a widow, still fairly young (well, not more than
forty-five, anyway), strong of character, lovely (though
carefully preserved) of face, and very wealthy, with a gift
for 'managing.' I must say the Squire did his part. He
collapsed at once, and obviously. But it took him nearly
a year to bring it off, and we all thought the fact that
he'd stuck to it so long, and persisted in his attentions in
spite of her austerity, spoke well for the permanence of the
affair.

I must say for myself that, even before she agreed to become Mrs. Harrington, I saw where the snag would come.
Celia, of course. Celia, as I said, is a girl of some—well,
self-will is a little strong, but you know what I mean. From
the first she didn't like Mrs. Ward and Mrs. Ward didn't
like her. But we all wanted the match so much that we
said, and thought we believed, that it would be all right.
We told each other that it would set Celia free to have such
a capable woman as head of her father's household, and,
if the woman had been just a shade less self-sufficient, it
would have been true. But the two were antagonistic, absolutely. Celia remembered her own mother, and idolized
her memory. She had always resented her father's facile
admiration for other women, and would have disliked a
stepmother anyhow; but to put Mrs. Ward in her mother's
place was, to her, a bitter injury, almost a blasphemy.

I suppose Mrs. Ward knew. She was no fool, whatever
else she was, and I imagine she always had her eyes pretty
wide open to her own interests. But if she thought that
Celia wasn't of enough consequence to bother with, she
made a bad mistake. Pretty girls with a taste for games and
dancing aren't necessarily butterflies entirely, and Celia
had a good deal of determination and vigour, though I'll
admit that they seldom showed. So when Mrs. Ward suddenly capitulated (and it was extraordinarily sudden) and

everybody was full of congratulations, and every person you met said how suitable and what an excellent thing, if sudden—well, I wondered.

It was soon pretty obvious. Celia and the new Mrs. Harrington were 'crossed,' as Ringshall people call it, by nature, by circumstances, by everything. And they would neither of them yield an inch. Mrs. Harrington didn't seem to understand that when a girl has had her own way entirely for nineteen years, you can't reduce her to complete submission all of a sudden. She said (and probably with truth) that it was time Celia learnt that she couldn't always have her own way, and that she was lacking not only in consideration but in prudence, foresight, and even common decency. All of which only meant that Mrs. Harrington disapproved of Stephen Earle.

I remember very well the day I first heard of that, was early in May, and I was out cutting tulips (which I grow with extreme success), when Celia lounged in, pretending she wanted to give me her Club accounts.

"I can't do accounts on a day like this," I remonstrated, with a comprehensive gesture of the scissors. "You'll have to come another time."

"Oh, any time'll do," she answered idly, picking up my trug and pretending to examine the tulips, of which she knows nothing. "What sort are these?" she went on—as if she cared!

I told her, though I knew she wasn't listening. She seemed to have nothing more to say, so I went on with my job.

"Miss Leslie," she suddenly burst out, "I want your advice."

"You mean you want to tell me what you're going to do," I said dryly.

She looked down at me doubtfully. She looked very pretty, with her short hair golden in the sun and her clouded eyes as blue as a baby's.

"I—no, I don't. I don't know what to do, quite. I—"
She broke off.

I saw she was really bothered. I stood upright and took off my gloves. My hands are one of my few good points, and I am careful of them, even if it's only cutting tulips.

"Well?" I asked. "What is it, Celia?"

"It—it's Stephen."

"Stephen? What about him?" I asked sharply.

I am very fond of Stephen, though, being my godson, he does always make me feel horribly old, and I always like to explain that I was only sixteen when he was christened. I was very glad when he and Celia took to each other very warmly. Stephen is a dear boy, and good-looking in a dark, puckish sort of way. The only thing I could see against the connexion with Celia was the extreme poverty of both, and, when you're twenty-three and clever, poverty oughtn't to be a serious bar to your attentions to a girl you love. So I didn't like to hear that Celia, standing young and fresh in the spring morning, was 'bothered' about Stephen.

Celia didn't answer me, but her pretty mouth drooped.

"What's Stephen done?" I asked again.

"Oh! *He* hasn't done anything," she replied, and a dimple trembled in her cheek.

"*That's* all right," I said, with relief. "Then why worry?"

She looked at me with brightening eyes.

"Is that what you advise?" she asked.

"I haven't advised anything," I declared hurriedly.

"Practically you have. You implied that if *he* was all right I'd no need to worry, and we could go ahead."

I considered this.

"Yes," I said then, "I think that's exactly what I do mean. Why not?"

"Whatever happens?"

"We—e—ell . . . I mean this, Celia. If you and Stephen love each other—(good girl, I didn't know girls could blush like that nowadays)—and if he's got the pluck and perseverance to make enough to marry you on, I think you ought to do it. Not immediately, of course," I added hastily, "nor perhaps for years; but some day."

"I don't want to marry just yet," she assured me. "I only—well—Stephen asked me to be engaged, and I said I would."

"Well? That seems quite reasonable. You're both a bit young, of course"—(their united ages were just three years older than I am!)—"but a long engagement's not a bad plan. It might make Stephen buck up and earn a living."

"Then—you'd advise me to carry on?"

"What's against it?"

She scowled—there's no other word for it—and dug her toe into the gravel.

"*They* are—at home."

"Your father is?"

"*Father!* You know as well as I do what father is. He'd let me do anything I liked—marry Stephen or the sweep, if I wanted to—so long as I didn't bother him about it."

This was true. Godfrey Harrington has always been criminally lax and careless with Celia.

"No, it's not father. It's Her."

This was not polite, nor even grammar, but I knew what Celia meant. I shouldn't have cared to call the new Mrs. Harrington 'mother' in her place, and as for Christian names, which I believe is the modern custom, you simply couldn't. Not Mrs. Harrington.

"I see," I said.

I did. I could see quite clearly what was probably happening in the Harrington *ménage*. Mrs. Harrington did not care for Stephen Earle, whose tongue is apt to embroil him with those who care overmuch for their dignity. She had no use for a penniless and cheeky boy, however charming, as a stepson-in-law. She probably foresaw (not knowing either Stephen or Celia properly) that she would be continually being called upon to finance the family of her husband's daughter. She had no doubt put her foot down extremely hard and extremely tactlessly, and had got across Celia (who really is absurdly easy to manage) with unusual determination. What I couldn't see was why Celia should mind.

"It's *damnable* at home," the child burst out suddenly. "She got at father before I could," she went on, "and you know father—he's like pux—patty—I mean putty—in her hands. She made him say I couldn't, and when I argued he worked himself up into a fearful state about it—"

She stopped, evidently recalling the state. She even turned pale.

"I went to him last night," she continued, with an obvious effort. "He—he—"

"Was he furious?" I asked, with interest. I couldn't imagine Godfrey Harrington having the force to quell a mouse, let alone a high-spirited girl like Celia, by his wrath.

"Furious? No. I wish he had been. I could have dealt with that. No, he was—well, I suppose it was sentimental really, but it seemed pathetic at the time. He—he *cried.*"

She gulped and blushed scarlet at the memory. Celia, like me, thinks crying a shameful deed even in a woman.

"He got into no end of a state—and you know how delicate his heart is. I got scared—really scared. He—"

She stopped again. This time it was I who nearly swore. I am sick of Godfrey Harrington's heart. It is diseased, and I suppose he can't help that, but he trades on it to a disgusting extent. He can get over poor, softhearted, honest Celia every time.

"I don't think I'd worry about that," I said, rather dryly.

"You would if you'd seen him. He turned an awful colour, and panted. . . . We had to help him to bed. She

said it was brutal of me, and I expect it was, to get him
into such a state. Only, what am I to do? I *can't* treat
father like that—he's always been so frightf'ly nice to me,
and I promised mother I'd be good and not worry him. But
it's not fair to Stephen, either, neither to be engaged nor
let him go. And I *can't* let him go."

I'd never seen Celia cry before—as I said, she despises
tears—but she was winking moisture out of her eyes then
That told me a good deal more than her words about the
kind of time she'd been having at home.

I was furious. I bent down and cut some tulips to get
a hold on myself. I found afterwards I'd ruined that bed.

"I think what I'd do would be this," I said at last. "I'd
tell Stephen exactly what's happened, and ask him to wait
six months. That's not much to ask. In that time your
father will have got used to the idea—it won't upset him
for you to mention it, anyhow—and he may give in. As
you say, he doesn't mind himself. And you'll get that long
to think over the whole affair and see where your duty
does lie. I don't believe in sacrificing love to a whim myself, but you mayn't have to—things may have changed by
then. A lot may happen in six months."

"Not in Ringshall," she sighed. "Nothing happens in
Ringshall."

I wonder if, in the light of what happened, Celia ever
remembers that she said that? I don't suppose she does.

2

It was some weeks after that, I think, that Roger Cartwright came to see me. I don't mean that he hadn't dropped
in often enough—for a curate, he is very sociable; in fact,
you'd hardly guess he was a curate if he didn't sometimes
wear a dog-collar—but this was a special visit. I knew it
at once, because he began, like a real curate, with polite
nothings, which amused me a good deal—so much, in fact,
that I wouldn't help him out, but answered just like the
real lady I ought to be, at thirty-nine, in a country village
full of Societies.

He chatted, I remember, of the Mothers' Outing,
of the new hassocks for the choir, of the unsatisfactory
attendance at Sunday school (though we couldn't blame
the children, with only dear Mrs. Arnold and Mrs. Jukes
to teach them, and Mrs. Harrington as general supervi-
sor); and I couldn't for the life of me think what he was
after, unless it was scandal, of the 'I-think-you-ought-to-
know' type (which is most unlike him), or a request for
something unpleasant.

At last I got bored. It was a hot day in early June, and
there were the first strawberries for tea, and the delphini-
ums were like bits of sky filtered through the leaves of my
beeches. I couldn't go on playing spinster to Roger Cartwright's curate. So I stopped the performance.

"Let's cut the cackle and come to the hosses," I suggested. "What are you after? A subscription? Because I'm penniless till quarter-day."

He grinned. He has a very nice grin that crinkles up his eyes and shows all his nice clean teeth.

"No, it's not a sub. this time. But I don't mind admitting that I've come for something. Advice."

I put my foot down. Really, you might think I was that terrible person known in pious books as the Village Angel (in other words, busybody) who always plays Providence and drips good counsel on every page. Whereas I don't like advice, either to give or to take, and I told him so.

"I know," he said, rumpling up his hair as much as it would—it's very short. "Let's call it a consultation, if you like. I do want to talk it over."

"That means Mrs. Harrington," I thought. But I only said encouragingly:

"Well? What's she done now?"

He looked at me.

"Do you know about it, then?" he asked.

"No," I said patiently. "I'm waiting to hear."

"Well, it's this. Mrs. Harrington is going in off the deep end about Peter's Fair."

"Why?"

"Well, to begin with, she thinks it's wrong to have a do of that sort on a Church festival."

"What bosh!" I said roundly. "What about Christmas? And Easter and Whitsun? To say nothing of football matches on Good Friday! And Peter and Paul isn't even kept everywhere. Anyhow, I think it's good religion to rejoice on a Church festival."

"I know. I said all that."

"And I suppose she then said that the Church was going to the dogs."

"Something like it," he admitted ruefully. It had clearly been a fairly strenuous interview.

"She won't stop the Fair," I said, "whatever else she does. Nothing, humanly speaking, could stop the Fair. Why, as an institution, it's older than history."

"Yes. I think she's recognized that—at last. But she's not satisfied. She's going to run it herself, to make sure that it's run right."

"I see," I said dryly.

Now to understand the full inwardness of this, you must know something about Ringshall Fair. It is held on St. Peter and Paul's Day, the 29th of June, and, I believe, was held on or about that day before Saints Peter and Paul were born. I don't mean as a fair; but archaeologists (who infest Wiltshire) have told me that there were rites held at Ringshall about Midsummer Day, when woad was the wear. It is so ancient and so firmly rooted that not even the Puritans could get rid of it. What used to take place ages ago, one (perhaps fortunately) does not know; it seems pretty certain, from old records, that it was at one time held, not in the Manor House grounds, as it now is, but on a clear, open space between the Manor and the village, called Foakes Green. The site was altered, some time in the sixteenth century, I believe, and the Manor has been used ever since.

Roger Cartwright rumpled up his hair again.

"I wish Mrs. Harrington wasn't so keen on the Good Old Merry England stunt," he remarked, with some apparent irrelevance.

"Why?"

"Why, because she's taking the line that if the Fair is to be held at all, it's to be held in the traditional style—on the old ground, with an accompaniment of folk-dances, Old English sports, and all that bunk. My fault, really, for talking about the old way of looking at it as a religious festival—that put her on to it. But I had no intention of putting all this Garden Cityish rot into her head. Everything spelt with an extra 'e' on to it. You know the kind of tripe."

"I do, well. Olde Englisshe Gifte Shoppe. But though it's a pity, I don't see that it matters."

"Not *matter!* Don't you know the feeling about Foakes Green?"

"I know people won't walk across it after dark."

"That's it. It's supposed to be—I don't know—uncanny. Foakes Green is said really to mean Folks' Green—Fairies' Green. There's that stone slab, you know—prehistoric altar or something—said to be 'dangerous'. Oh yes, I know it's tosh, but—the villagers don't think so. You and I—we'll never get their point of view. It isn't a question of reason, nor even of belief, entirely. It's a question of tradition—something unspoken, unformulated in the blood . . ."

I nodded. I'd come across this before—this instinct relic of a forgotten fear, that made people cross their fingers when they saw a red-haired woman, and made it possible for them to put herbs and milk on old Mrs. Nokes's doorstep to 'keep her sweet' to them. I don't suppose many villages still have a witch. I can't imagine Ringshall without one.

"Still," I argued, "why worry? She'll never get them to go back to Foakes Green."

"She'll make 'em. She's got Harrington to say they mayn't use the Manor grounds."

"What an ass that man is," I said pensively.

"Oh, of course. But there'll be the deuce to pay."

"I don't see why. If they want the Fair enough to hold it at all costs, they'll hold it on Foakes Green. If they're too frightened of the Green, they won't hold the Fair."

He made an impatient movement.

"They won't give up the Fair—ever. No; what'll happen (I think) will be this. They'll hold the Fair on Foakes Green, and they'll be in such a panic that they'll all get a good bit of Dutch courage. They'll all be drunk, and they'll all have it in for Mrs. Harrington."

"That'll happen sooner or later, anyway. She rubs them up the wrong way."

"She does," he assented, rather grimly. "It'd have been likely, anyway; but she doesn't understand that our folks are independent and won't be run. She will try to run 'em all the time."

"I know. Tells the mothers how to bring up their children, and likes all the children to curtsey."

"Yes. And they won't stick it. They're talking as it is."

"About Mrs. Harrington? Well, to be honest, the villagers aren't the only people to do that. You can't expect a— well, a startling person like Mrs. Harrington to come out of the blue to a village like this and not attract a certain amount of comment."

"Yes, but—it's not so much her appearance, though of course that goes against her—"

Red hair, and a tiny cast in one eye! Of course, to Ringshall that spelt witchcraft. I hadn't thought of that.

"It's—well, her history," he finished.

"Her history? What is it? Of course I knew she had a Past with a capital P, but I never heard what it was. Do be an angel and tell me."

I was quite excited. I'm not as a rule excessively curious about my neighbours' histories, but Mrs. Harrington so exactly looked the part of a Woman with a Past and I've always wanted to hear a *really* lurid story. The usual shilling shocker seems, to my depraved taste, so tame. But I was to be disappointed again. The curate made a hopeless gesture.

"I can't tell you. I've no idea what it is. Only—well you know how it is in Ringshall. Give them a hint and they'll give you a three-volume novel. And we know that there is something in Mrs. Harrington's past."

"Do we? Don't we only think there is because she looks as if there must be?"

He looked at me attentively.

"We've nothing to go on," I continued, "beyond the fact that she came here a widow, without saying where from, and that she's never said a word about her past life. Why should she? She's not garrulous, nor even sociable. As to the fuss people make about her and Godfrey Harrington—the way she refused and refused him, and then suddenly accepted him and married him within a month— well, I gather that either she'd heard he was changeable, and wanted to be sure of him before she accepted him, or else that she simply gave in out of boredom and the worry of having him always about, looking at her like a spaniel with stomach-ache."

"She's not the sort to give up her own wishes for want of persistence."

"Well, then, it was the other thing. She wanted to be sure that he really would stick to it."

"Perhaps. . . . But—" He hesitated; then he said rather tentatively, "I wonder if she gave him long enough."

I jumped. I thought that no one but myself had noticed the coming development. I looked at the curate with respect.

"Have you noticed it too?" I asked.

Again he hesitated.

"You're quite safe," I assured him. "Even if you're not thinking of the thing *I'm* thinking of, I'll keep your guilty secret."

"I know you will. You do," and I could feel myself blush with pleasure. I suppose it's because I live in rustic surroundings that I do still blush, when annoyed or when really gratified. He went on:

"Don't you think Lady Gervaise has—well, changed a little since she came home?"

"Then it *is* what I'm thinking of!" I exclaimed. "Yes, that's it. Lady Gervaise. You're right; she's got a something—a polish, a charm—since that visit to Paris. And Godfrey Harrington has noticed it—and her. I believe you're right, and Mrs. Harrington didn't wait long enough before she said 'Yes.'"

"It's a relief to talk of it," the curate admitted. "I've thought it some time—six weeks or more—but it seemed so foul I tried to think it was my disgusting imagination. I thought perhaps one had got so used to seeing Harrington fall in and out of love that one expected it when it wasn't there."

"I know. I thought that too. It did look as if he might settle down when he married again. . . . Poor Celia! It'll be horrible for her, if it's true."

He nodded.

"Loathsome brute," he muttered.

"No," I protested, "he's not that. He hasn't the force. He's just hopelessly fickle and feeble. But what will be the end of it, Heaven only knows."

"Oh, I expect it'll be all right in the end—as far as Harrington's affairs ever are all right," said he. "Mrs. Harrington has far too much vigour to let him go. Besides, she holds the purse-strings."

"Lady Gervaise generally gets her own way."

"Yes, but I'd back Mrs. Harrington against her any day. Besides, Mrs. Harrington *is* Mrs. Harrington. I don't see how they'd get over that."

Neither did I, except by divorce, for which there could be no excuse.

"You think they'll bow to the inevitable?" I asked.

"I don't see what else they can do. He'll soon forget it, anyhow."

I shrugged.

"Perhaps. But I wish Lady Gervaise would go back to Paris."

"So do I. She's not doing any good here."

"How d'you mean? To herself, or to the village?"

"Either—both. Which you like."

"She's got nothing to do," I pleaded.

"I know. That's just it. 'Satan finds some mischief still'—that sort of idea. A woman like Lady Gervaise can't just exist supinely. She's got to have an interest. I'm afraid she'll find it at the Manor House. And she's so reckless. She's been pretty discreet so far over this, but how long can Lady Gervaise be discreet? Soon there'll be talk—and worse than talk."

"What's worse than talk?" I asked cynically.

"Imitation." His tone was quite grim. "She has a great following in the village. Her family's a very old one here, and she is the last representative. She's extremely pretty. She has a way with her. She's generous, reckless, amusing, happy-go-lucky. She never preaches, because she always ranks herself among the sinners. She makes sin very attractive."

"But, my dear soul," I protested, "this is a model village. We never break the Commandments except in the mildest way. Even Mrs. Harrington can't find much to condemn."

"She'll make it, then—she and Lady Gervaise between them. She'll preach virtue till they're sick of the very word, and turn to vice for relief—with a very charming example saying all the time, 'Of course it's naughty, but isn't it fun?' Ringshall's human, Miss Leslie. There comes a time when the meekest worms turn from a rather nagging preceptress to a very attractive seductress—if there is such a word. You can't blame them."

"Not a bit," I agreed. "I sympathize heartily. If Mrs. Harrington kept telling me in season and out of season how wicked I was to spend sixpence on cider at the 'Lady and Hare,' I should get roaring drunk for a week. But she doesn't interfere with me, which is what I call so unfair. She takes it all out on the cottagers. Speaking of which, has it struck you that that's the precise effect she's having on young Joe Greaves?"

"If Joe Greaves goes completely to the bad," said Roger Cartwright vehemently, "which he very well may, it'll be Mrs. Harrington's fault and no one else's. I know she doesn't mean it, but the way she holds him up in public and scolds him for spending his own money on a drink at the 'Lady and Hare' is enough to make him throttle her. The lad works hard enough for his wages. Surely he has a right to get some fun out of his life. And even if he hasn't who gave Mrs. Harrington the right to meddle with him?"

"I suppose she's thinking of Lydia," I said apologetically.

"Lydia? What Lydia?"

"Lydia Salt—you know, the under-housemaid at the Manor. Joe's her young man. I suppose Mrs. Harrington thinks he ought to be saving for the wedding. She's always urging them to marry, which is very disinterested of her, for she'll find it hard to get another maid like Lydia—or any at all."

"If she's goes on as she's doing, Joe won't be worth having," said the curate. "And it's a rotten shame, for he's really one of the nicest lads in the place, only he won't be druv. I think all the more of him for it. And if Mrs. Harrington goes on nagging at him to get married, I should think they'd break off the match."

I wanted to tell him that, if my suspicions were well founded, that mustn't happen. But I am too old-fashioned to use the modern frankness of speech, useful and good as I believe it to be. I said nothing; but Roger Cartwright is fairly shrewd, and I think he guessed what was in my mind.

"Oh lord! What a nuisance women are in a parish!" he groaned. "Good, interfering, well-meaning, parish-working women, I mean," he added hastily. "I suppose they're too pious to be human. What a mess this one virtuous woman is making of us all! I wish Solomon had known her, and then he wouldn't have written the Book of Proverbs."

I agreed. Mrs. Harrington is exactly the kind of woman who would, as Solomon says, get up in the middle of the night and give meat to her family, regardless of their feelings.

"Isn't she!" I assented heartily. "Here we've got Godfrey Harrington ripe to make a scandal; Joe Greaves rushing to the bad; Lydia's marriage with Joe doubtful; Celia miserable. And she means so well!"

"That's just the trouble. It's these people who think they were born to reform the world who make it so much worse than it need be. I wish they'd remember that humility's a Christian virtue."

"I wish Godfrey Harrington would go away and take his wife with him," I said. "A few years abroad would be beneficial. I think I'll drop the suggestion."

"It wouldn't work," he grunted gloomily. "She'd think Ringshall could never get on without her, and would sacrifice herself, loudly, to benefit it. I wish she'd find another sphere for her activities. There must be lots of town parishes where she'd hardly be noticed among the throng of 'workers.' We could do without her extremely well."

"We could," I agreed. Afterwards I felt perfectly *awful* when I remembered that. But it was true—and how could I know what was going to come?

3

I believe the Fair Committee was an afterthought. Certainly it was created and summoned far too late to do anything except agree to whatever Mrs. Harrington (President, of course) suggested. I don't know why I was on the Committee, except that I always am,—after all, there aren't so many people to choose from—and that I always used to accept on purpose to oppose Mrs. Harrington, who was invariably Chairman or President, as the case might be. This time I was even keener than usual to oppose, because I couldn't for the life of me see why there should be a Committee to organize a Fair that Ringshall had managed to run by itself for more centuries than you could count. But it was no good. Everything had been arranged, and we were only there, like the King, to give a formal assent to what was already practically accomplished.

Mrs. Harrington was quite offensively pleased with herself. Even in the break after the formal meeting, when we all had tea and chatted amongst ourselves, you could hear her burbling:

"So *much* nicer to have it on the old ground, don't you agree? Such a picturesque setting, with those lovely old oaks all round, and the stone—altar, or whatever it was—in the middle. It will look too charming, with the stalls and booths dotted about, and the dancing—the dear old folk-dancing—going on at the wide end. I can see it so clearly in my mind's eye. I can't think why no one ever thought of moving the Fair back to the old site before."

"I can tell you that," said Miss Todd, who need not be either as ugly or as blunt as she is, but likes to be both. "It's because this is the village Fair, run by the village for the village—and the village doesn't like Foakes Green."

"*Dear* Miss Todd! *Please* don't let's go over all that again. This will be a splendid way of getting rid of the old superstition. When they've danced and played and enjoyed themselves for a whole day on Foakes Green, they'll forget its old associations, just as children would. You know, these people *are* just like children when you get to know them thoroughly."

Miss Todd snorted. Her family is one of the oldest in Ringshall. There are Todds all round the place, in every walk of life. She knew a good deal more than most of us about Ringshall folk and Ringshall ways and thoughts. She shared a good many of these last herself.

"It'll attract so much attention, too," Mrs. Harrington went on. "Quite a lot of people have written to secure sites for stalls and side-shows—nothing *vulgar,* of course, all very respectable and nice—and I think some of the County people will come to see the dancing and the Fair as it used to be. It will give Ringshall quite a lot of prominence."

We shuddered.

"Do we *want* prominence?" pleaded Mrs. Jukes, the vicar's wife.

"We want Progress," said Mrs. Harrington, with her patronizing smile. "Surely, dear Mrs. Jukes, we want Progress. And prominence is necessary to Progress."

"Oh yes. Oh, quite so," murmured old Mrs. Jukes in a hypnotized way. "Yes. Progress. Oh, by all means."

"So glad you agree," smiled the Squiress. Much it would have mattered if she hadn't! "So now it's all settled—if only the weather will be, too!"

We could do nothing in the face of such satisfaction as that. If we had gone, one by one, and told her quite bluntly that she was wrong, that she'd make trouble, that she would get herself hated, she'd only have smiled tolerantly and thought how petty jealousy flourishes in these country places. We did console ourselves by exchanging glances and shrugs, and some of us got as far as murmurs about self-sufficiency and arrogance; but it was no use except as a safety-valve to our own pent-up feelings. The atmosphere was pretty sultry, though, and most of us were grateful to gentle, ineffective Mrs. Arnold for changing the subject.

"By the way, Mrs. Harrington," she began, "is it true that you've decided to get some one new in Mrs. Nokes's place?"

"Well," smiled the Squiress, "you mustn't say *I've* decided to. As President of the Nursing Association in this district, I've very strongly recommended it, and I think I may say that the Committee will support me. It's a scandal that that *dreadful* old woman has been *allowed* to act as—er—as—"

"Midwife," said Miss Todd brutally. Mrs. Harrington allowed a visible shudder to convulse her frame, and closed her eyes for a second. "Well, of course Mrs. Nokes is a drunken old hag, and not of the best character, but she lost precious few patients."

"Perhaps," said Mrs. Harrington, with such studied patience that I'm sure we all longed to shake her. "But you must admit that her methods were—well, primitive to a degree—"

"Snuff at the critical moment," interjected Miss Todd in what she may have intended to be an aside.

"—and *most* insanitary," finished Mrs. Harrington.

"They trusted her," pleaded Mrs. Arnold.

"Yes—as a necromancer!" If Mrs. Harrington hadn't been such a perfect lady, I'd have said that she snorted. "They go to her for charms, I believe. *Charms,* in the twentieth century! That is one of the reasons why I am determined she shall go. She represents one of the worst elements in the village—I mean the element of superstition. She prepares the way for people like that horrid fortune-telling gipsy who came last autumn. Why, do you know that people actually put milk on her doorstep, as they used to do for witches long ago? It is exactly that kind of thing that I—intend—to—put—down." She looked very determined as she said that. "And then, she's a bad influence in—er—in other ways." Here she pursed up her lips and looked extremely prim.

"You mean her son?" asked the irrepressible Miss Todd. "Well, of course we all know he hasn't got an official father"—(Mrs. Harrington again closed her eyes with a shudder)—"but the village thinks he isn't human, you know."

"Not *human?*" asked the Squiress, in a tone of pained horror.

"No. They think he's a changeling. Sons of witches are never 'canny', you know."

Mrs. Harrington turned on her a face of righteous indignation.

"Is this—er—idea due to the fact that the poor lad is imbecile, or to the general feeling about his mother?"

"Both, I expect," said Miss Todd cheerfully. "Witches have changelings for sons, and changelings are 'God's fools'. If a reputed witch has a fatherless imbecile, like poor Tom, for a son, of course he's a changeling in Ringshall eyes."

"That settles it," said Mrs. Harrington grimly. "Mrs. Nokes shall go. She is incompetent and ignorant as a nurse.

If she is also the focus of such gross superstition as this, she shall go at once. At *once.*"

"'You mustn't say *I've* decided it,'" quoted Mrs. Ludlow, the doctor's wife, aside to me.

"I suppose you've already got her successor in your mind's eye," said Miss Todd, who was rapidly losing her temper. "Some one nice and pious, who'll lend them all tracts, eh?"

Mrs. Harrington wisely made no reply to this gibe; but Miss Todd pressed heavily on.

"You've got a protegée who's a nurse, haven't you? You used to go and see her a good deal at one time, I remember. Perhaps *she's* to be poor old Mrs. Nokes's successor?"

Mrs. Harrington winced visibly. Then she said in a low, constrained voice:

"She—is dead. She died in February."

I had never seen her display so much emotion before. In fact, I had never seen her display any real emotion before. I was impressed and touched.

"Oh—sorry," growled Miss Todd. "I didn't know."

But Mrs. Harrington recovered her self-possession in a second. She was, without exception, *the* most reserved woman I've ever met.

"Mrs. Nokes," she said firmly, "is, as I say, unsuitable in every way. She has done far more harm than good in the village. In fact, she's done more harm than any one can estimate."

Nobody said anything. We wanted to contradict her, of course, but the trouble was that we hadn't a leg to stand on.

"Surely you do all agree," continued the Squiress in the scornfully emphatic tone in which one addresses the hopelessly stupid, "that to have Mrs. Nokes as our village nurse is most undesirable?"

And, of course, the trouble was that we did. No one wants a dirty, drunken old harridan to mutter charms over

sick-beds, even if she, or some one like her, has done so
for centuries. That was the worst of Mrs. Harrington. She
was so often right; but she was so annoying about it that
you immediately took the other side rather than admit it.
As usual, we all left the Manor House rather ruffled, having meekly accepted all Mrs. Harrington's proposals. You
can't, if you are human, wonder that we felt vindictive.

"What I want to know," snorted Miss Todd, as she
stumped along between Mrs. Ludlow and me, "is, who is
Mrs. Harrington, that she should come to Ringshall and
manage us all like this?"

"She means well," I said feebly.

Miss Todd snorted again.

"If what they say in the village is true," she said darkly,
"her own past isn't the kind that'll bear too close investigation."

"Do tell us why not," said Mrs. Ludlow, with intense
interest. "So many people say that and never explain why."

"Well, they say," said Miss Todd, with careful emphasis
on the vague source of her information—"mind, I don't
know—but they *do* say that she wasn't really a widow when
she married Godfrey Harrington."

"Oh!" said Mrs. Ludlow, with great satisfaction. "Biga-
my. And why was it she wouldn't have him at first?"

"Goodness only knows," said Miss Todd, refusing the
responsibility of invention. "Of course, it mayn't be true,"
she added regretfully.

"I expect what it really was," I said, "was that she first
married an undesirable, and separated from him; and then
he died, and she was free to accept the Squire."

"Mmmm. Perhaps," said Miss Todd. Clearly this theory
was too tame and legal to suit her vindictive dislike of
Mrs. Harrington. "Personally, I think she's too good to be
good, if you know what I mean."

And she parted from us, with glances and shrugs that spoke volumes. I wished she had voiced her suspicions. As I said before, I love lurid stories, and I never seem able to hear a *really* purple one.

The next day—a Tuesday, I remember—I had occasion to go to Rutter's. Rutter keeps the village shop, which is also in a way the village club. That is, all Ringshall goes there to buy bacon and boots and seed and tape and toffee and potatoes and bread and oil and stamps, but also to meet friends and exchange gossip. When you go to Rutter's, you are not expected simply to buy something and go away again. If you do that, you are a 'foreigner'; and it was typical of Mrs. Harrington that this was always what she did, throwing a queer glance of mingled suspicion, wistfulness, and contempt at the gossips as she went her superior way.

On this particular Tuesday, Rutter's was full. People always run out of all sorts of things when anything special has happened in the village. They were mostly women— though, as it was after five, one or two men had dropped in, ostensibly for tobacco or snuff; and in a dark corner (which Mrs. Rutter calls alternately the Liberry, on the strength of a dozen antiquated volumes, and the Milnery, on the strength of three unchanged and unchangeable straw hats) I saw Celia Harrington, absurdly pretending to choose a book. There was some one else with her, joining in the ridiculous pretence; and though he is my godson, I immediately turned my attention to the rather flyblown picture-postcards. Though I am very fond of both Stephen and Celia, and like to believe that they are fond of me, I felt that I should be *de trop* at that moment. Their *tête-à-têtes* could not be very frequent.

It was the smell of stale cider that first made me aware of Mrs. Nokes's propinquity. Really she was rather repulsive, standing in the mellow light of a June afternoon, her dingy bonnet on one side and her grey elf-locks straggling from under it, and her grimy hands fingering everything on the counter. Mrs. Rutter would have been pretty sharp with any one else who did that—Mrs. Rutter is as fresh and clean as her own sun-bleached linen—but Mrs. Nokes was a privileged person. For a moment I felt keen sympathy with Mrs. Harrington. Certainly Mrs. Nokes, fresh (or stale, rather) from a day in the bar of the 'Lady and Hare', was not a desirable person to nurse the sick of Ringshall.

At that moment she was certainly also what Roger Cartwright calls 'half-seas-over'. She was carrying on a ceaseless grumbling monologue like a threatening thunderstorm; and its theme was—of course—Mrs. Harrington.

"'Tisn' me as should be thrust out o' door," she was muttering. "'Tis her, an' the likes o' her, furriners and intermeddlin' 'lopers as they aal be, aal on 'em. Eh, an' will be till the wormses have 'em, which may it be soon!"

A general murmur of assent to this pious wish encouraged her. She turned and addressed the crowd.

"Eh, souls, you've heard as I'm to be thrust out, have 'ee? Me, as has nursed 'ee and your fathers before 'ee, and brought your childer into the world. 'Tidn' for the like o' you to say who you'll have to put the blessed herbs by your corpses, an' the salt on the lips o' your new-born childer. No, 'tis for a furriner to say, an' you'm to touch your locks an' say 'Thankee, mum.'" She spat voluminously. An angry growl went up from the villagers.

"And what's the cause?" went on Mrs. Nokes, her voice rising shrilly to the true gipsy rant. "'Tidn' for your goods, souls, don't 'ee think it! 'Tis because I knows too much!"

She rolled an Ancient Marinerish eye over the fascinated faces before her.

"Ah! She may say as I knows nought. Me, as knows that as no one else i' the martel world can learn! She may say as I'm a wrong woman, 'long o' my poor Tom, as was born o' Hallowe'en at the dark o' the moon. Her! Her, as has a dread in her soul and a shadder at her shoulder to tell her on't—a shadder as means death! Her, as gets secret messages she shakes to hear! What's your choice, souls—her, a furriner, who goes i' dread, or me, who knows the secrets o' Rin'shall Stone and Foakeses Green? Her, who'd turn 'ee aal by the bottoms, or me, who's nursed 'ee from your mothers' wombs to the s'roud?"

She had, of course, no need to ask. There was a general murmur.

"'Tidn' her as we wants."

"'Nation take her!"

"Us won't see 'ee put out, mother."

And one louder, stronger voice:

"'Tis her as we'll put out!"

Without looking, I knew it was young Joe Greaves who said that. Mrs. Nokes turned to face him.

"Ah, an' 'twill be the better for 'ee, Joe Greaves! 'The stoat turns on the vare.' 'Tis them as has a bad spot theirselves as can see it i' other folkses."

Joe came a step forward. He was deeply flushed, and I suspected that he, too, had spent too much of his day and too much of his pay at the 'Lady and Hare'.

"She haven't—have she—" he stammered.

The hag gave a scream of eldritch laughter.

"Use your eyes, Joe Greaves—use the eyes God gave 'ee! What have she got agin' 'ee? 'Tidn' the cider as she throws up at 'ee."

So I *was* right in my guess about Lydia Salt!

"Ah, you'm a bad 'un, Joe—bain' 'ee?" chuckled the hag. "But never 'ee mind 'en, Joe. 'Tis the stoat as turns on the vare."

Could this really be the mystery, I wondered? Could there really be such a secret as Joe's in the immaculate Mrs. Harrington's past?

"Ah, you may look!" she crowed triumphantly, looking at the faces crowding about her. "You may look! I aren't the only one as knows her secrets. I tell 'ee as there's one as sends her messages as she don' like to get—one as she'll pay wi' red gold to quieten! Ah, but see, she'm a *lady*, souls. She can have her secrets and her sins. But Joe and me, we'm poor folks. Joe must do as she bid 'en, an' me—I must pack, an' never a one of 'ee shall I lay out again!"

Again came that threatening, growling murmur. I thought of the French Revolution, which is a thing that fills me with terror. To my great relief, a diversion occurred. Mrs. Rutter, who is without exception the most sensible woman I know, took the stage.

"Now, that'll do!" she declared, bustling forward. "We don't want no chat o' that kind. Mrs. Nokes, you'll step in, won't 'ee, an' bite a bit along o' we? Joe, best be off home like a sensible lad, i'stead o' stand there talkin' like a Newb'y carter. I never heard such chat, never i' all my creepin's! Get along, now, do 'ee, souls."

She swept them like a strong, fresh wind. Mrs. Nokes, still grumbling, retired into the shop parlour to be regaled and coaxed with the spice-loaf which I could smell in the oven. Joe, looking half abashed and half scared, but wholly defiant, marched off alone. The others drifted away in twos and threes, heads together. The discussion was not finished because the 'club' was deserted.

It was only then that I remembered Celia. She had been in the Liberry all the time. Much as she disliked her stepmother, it couldn't have been pleasant for her. I looked round for her, and there she was, Stephen at her side, and a book in her hand.

"I'll take this one, please, Mrs. Rutter," she said, and I admired the quiet steadiness of her voice, though the book pretence was absurd. She had a volume of Dodds's *Universal Mothers' Guide*.

"Lord-a-me, Miss Celia, was 'ee back i' there? Well now, and I'm sorry of it," said Mrs. Rutter heartily. "But 'ee mustn't take it to heart, missy. They don't mean nought. 'Tis only talk."

"Oh, I know," said Celia indifferently; "thank you all the same. Good-night, Mrs. Rutter."

And she turned, with her faithful escort, and walked out.

I joined on to them. I thought I might be forgiven if I did so now.

"Well, Celia," I said, "what a lot you've learnt. How thrilling to have a real stepmother who is haunted by shadows! I particularly liked the touch about the gold. I'd do almost anything if some one would give me red gold not to. Who do you think it is that Mrs. Harrington buys off?"

Celia said nothing for a moment or two. I stole a sideways look at her, and, to my astonishment, she was quite grave and rather pale.

"What has Joe Greaves done to annoy Her?" she asked, ignoring my flippancy.

"Oh—" I hesitated. I saw Stephen grinning maliciously at my embarrassment. Stephen, who is Ringshall born and bred, always knows the latest rumours with uncanny accuracy. "Ask her," I suggested.

"I will," Celia declared. "Joe's too nice to hate one without a good reason."

"I shouldn't tell her that Mrs. Nokes accuses her of the same nameless crime, though," Stephen put in. "It might annoy her."

"No. Nor that she is supposed to be paying some anonymous 'shadow' vast sums not to betray her," I added; and again I stole a look at Celia. She said nothing

"Celia," I cried, "do tell me—is Mrs. Harrington being blackmailed? How perfectly splendid!"

"Oh! *Don't* be silly," said Celia crossly. "She isn't a *joke.*"

And her manner was so curt that I became quite deco-
rous, and talked of Mrs. Henry Newport's newest baby all
the rest of the way. I thought Celia deserved to be bored,
and I haven't the least doubt that she was.

4

I could not make up my mind about the Fair. To be quite frank, I wanted to go. I love fairs, though I never have the courage to go on the roundabouts. Still, you can always watch other people doing it, and the general feeling—the excitement, the crowd, the gay stalls, the shouting, and the flicker and flare of the naphtha lamps as the quiet sky darkens—all seem to me romantic, almost like the beginning of an adventure.

But, to be frank again, I didn't want to go to this Fair simply because it was so much more Mrs. Harrington's show than Ringshall's. If I could only have organized it successfully, I should have suggested an embargo on that Fair. But I knew that it was impossible. Mrs. Harrington or no Mrs. Harrington, the villagers would go, every man, woman, and child of them; and in the mob of them the few I might muster—Mrs. Arnold, the Ludlows, the Vicar and his wife, the schoolmaster—would be neither here nor there. I couldn't even count on what Miss Todd would do about it, whether Ringshall ways or hatred of Mrs. Harrington would have it as far as she was concerned. Well, I thought, I at least would be proud and stiff, and stay primly at home in a haughty isolation.

June 29 dawned hot and blue—one of those miraculous jewels of days which an English June can occasionally produce, and which, I suppose, are the pretext for poems about that disappointing month. The sky soared, flawless, over the hot, shorn meadows; the scent of the new-made haystacks blended with the dog-roses. It would be very hot in the afternoon, but the morning was perfect. I was at work in the garden very early, and even in that dewy, scent-filled peace, I could hear the hammers going as the booths were erected on Foakes Green. What a day for a village fair! Arcady wasn't in it.

As the morning wore on, I felt more and more restless. My two admirable maids, Betty and Jenny, had leave for the day. They had left a large provision of cold food enough to keep a family for a week, let alone a solitary spinster for a day.

As a rule, I like a day quite alone. I have the garden, books, a piano, lots of odd jobs to do, and the time flies past. But on this feast-day of the Holy Apostles Peter and Paul, I could settle to nothing. I felt like a child who hasn't been asked to a party—left out, miserable, completely at a loose end. I told myself that there was thunder in the air, and how glad I was that I'd arranged to stay quietly at home. The heat and noise on Foakes Green would, I said firmly, be too awful. I than added, equally firmly, how nice it was to have such a day completely to oneself in a perfect garden. So it was rather inconsistent of me to jump up with alacrity when I heard some one trying to ring my ancient iron bell.

I don't know whom I expected to see—Celia, perhaps, or Roger Cartwright, or Stephen, though it wasn't like any of them even to try to ring—but I certainly didn't expect Lady Gervaise. Yet there she was, perfectly charming and deliciously cool in mauve georgette that made her skin and hair look like the ivory and ebony of Arabian Nights princesses.

"Do come in," I invited, with far more genuine cordiality than I generally have for Lady Gervaise, who always strikes me as a bit of a minx.

"I won't stay," she said; but she floated into my dim old hall like a lovely butterfly. "I only came to see if you'd gone to the Fair yet, and, if not, if I might come with you. It's so much more fun when there's two of you."

"I don't think I'm going," I said, rather uncertainly.

"Not going! Oh, Miss Leslie, but you *must!* Why not?"

I hesitated. I didn't want to tell her my real reason, partly because I was a bit ashamed of it, partly because I didn't know if she knew how Mrs. Harrington was behaving about it.

"*Don't* get ladylike!" she pleaded. "It's so heavenly to be vulgar, don't you think? I'm sure you do. I'm sure you love going on roundabouts and sucking bulls'-eyes, and having your fortune told, and winning vases at hoop-là. Now don't you?"

"I do," I confessed.

"Well, then!"

But though I do love all these things, it wasn't that that made me give in. It was rather that I felt that something was going to happen. The air was full of it—suggestions, hints, vague impressions. It was like a mental thunderstorm brewing. I scented danger somehow, to some one. . . .

Even as I laughed at myself, I gave in.

"All right," I agreed. "Will you wait for me a minute?" It didn't take me more than ten literal minutes to change. If it hadn't been for Lady Gervaise, I'd have gone in the old blue cotton, but her elegance made me feel that I must do something about it, and I was comparatively smart when I rejoined her. She had, of course, something pretty to say about my frock, and although I knew all the time that she'd have said something equally nice if I'd never changed at all, I liked it. She could always please you, even when you saw through and through her.

It was still early—only just after midday—when we reached Foakes Green, but the ground was already crowded. All Ringshall was there, as I knew it would be, and, as Roger Cartwright had foretold, most of Ringshall had fortified itself against the terrors of the place. I don't mean that there was a mob of drunkards. But the scent of cider was strong, and most people were flushed and more excited and garrulous than usual. Also, the Fair itself was slightly different. There were some new stalls, and several new side-shows, most of them the kind of horrid suburban things you see in the Birmingham district at such times— Madame Zenovas, race games, 'scenic railways,' all that sort of thing. But there were also one or two, equally up-to-date, which were not objectionable. There was a lovely new roundabout, and a sort of rifle range with airguns for weapons, and a genuine Cheap Jack. I felt the old childish excitement rising as pushed our way in among the noisy mob crowding round the new attractions.

It was blazing hot. Foakes Green seemed like a green cup, with sides of ancient oak woods, into which the radiant sun poured its golden rays. The clamour was deafening—showmen shouting, children screaming, men arguing the hoarse whistles and tinny bray of the roundabouts competing with the shrieks of the adventurers in swingboats. But even through the din I could hear Mrs. Harrington's voice somewhere behind me placidly flowing on.

"Oh yes, of course, it's a very much larger affair this year. Such a perfect site for a fair. . . . It will bring so much trade to the village. . . . Oh no, it's only excitement making them so noisy. No, it *can't* be anything else—you see, there's only one inn, and that hasn't been open long enough for people to—er—exceed. It's pure excitement."

And that was the woman who talked about 'knowing the people thoroughly'! Did she really not know about the facilities for obtaining cider at any hour?

She was in her element. There was nothing she liked so well as acting up to her part as Lady of the Manor, and it was, of course, extra nice when there was an audience to do it to. The 'County people' she had spoken of had turned up in fair numbers—on account of the weather, chiefly, no doubt—and Mrs. Harrington fairly spread herself. I could hear them cooing the appropriate replies that Mrs. Harrington's conversation always seemed to expect and (from us) never received.

"Dear Mrs. Harrington, how too wonderful you are!"

"What a perfect spot! A stroke of real genius, Mrs. Harrington."

And, in the booming bass of some local grandee:

"This is the sort o' thing the country needs, eh, Jenkins? Progress alongside of picturesqueness, eh?"

That was Sir Digby Barnet, I knew. He always had something of that fatuous sort to say. I whispered to Lady Gervaise:

"How that man would spread himself over a really juicy occasion—a visit from Royalty, or a revolution, or a murder, or even a strike!"

"Let's provide him with one," she replied in the same tone. "We could manage the murder, anyhow, and it would be quite a charity; he'd enjoy himself so."

He was, meanwhile, burbling on:

"Charmin', quite charmin'. And I s'pose you know them all, eh, Mrs. Harrington? Guide, philosopher, and friend sort of idea, eh? Well, I always say, give me a really good woman to *make* a village."

"Oh, well, I can't quite claim all that, Sir Digby! But I do know most of them, and their little troubles and worries.

I think it's one's duty, when one's been placed in a certain position, to try to do what one can."

"Quite, quite. Hullo! Who's that pretty girl comin' off the roundabout? Seem to know her face. Little beauty, eh?"

I felt, rather than heard, Mrs. Harrington's "Tch!" of annoyance.

"It's Celia—my husband's daughter," she said, vexation in every tone. "She *never* seems to acquire any sense of dignity. Fancy her riding on the horses, like any village girl! Surely she must realize that these—er—sports are for her inferiors. She *must* see that None of Us *join* in them."

Lady Gervaise drove her elbow into my side and winked.

"Come on, Miss Leslie," she said in her clear, high voice. "Let's do a show. No point in coming to a Fair if you don't join in the fun. Let's try this new rifle range."

We were just beside the booth, which, of course, was why she chose it. She walked up to the showman.

"Two, please," she said loudly, putting down a shilling. "Now, Miss Leslie, you first. Bet you don't get a bull."

"Three shots for tuppence. Try yer skill, ladies and gents. Three shots for tuppence!" shouted the man.

He was, obviously, not a local man. He had the real Midland voice and accent, and a vulgar, bloated sort of face. He was very much 'the boss,' too—doing all the talk and none of the work. All the tiresome part—the giving out of rifles, putting up of targets, and so on—was done by a little, wiry, dirty, gipsy-looking man with a black beard and earrings, just like a wicked little pirate. He'd have looked much better in the foreground than his horrid 'boss'; he really looked the part and matched the general landscape beautifully. Perhaps the 'boss' knew that his effect would be spoilt if he allowed the picturesque little assistant to be much seen, and kept him in the background on purpose.

I took the gun that the pirate handed to me and put it to my shoulder. I'd never held such a thing before, and I was flustered by Mrs. Harrington's eyes, which I could feel boring into my back. I don't mind admitting that I shut my eyes tight and jumped at the *bang* of the rifle in my ear.

Lady Gervaise laughed.

"Right off the target!" she said. "Try again."

"Not I!" I said fervently. "It's bruised my shoulder as it is. I'll forfeit my other two shots."

"That's because you didn't hold it tight enough," said Lady Gervaise.

She raised her rifle and took a steady aim. *Bang!* The target showed a black dot near the centre.

"Only an inner. This rifle isn't quite true," she said composedly, and aimed again. *Bang!*—and the shot was in the exact centre of the bull's-eye.

"Good shootin', miss," applauded the showman.

"I'll bet any one I get five bulls in six shots," said Lady Gervaise. "But I warn you all I'm pretty useful with a rifle. . . . No takers? All right, then, I'll do it for the fun of the thing. I'll have another three shots, please."

She put down her twopence, and then, almost without pause, fired her four last shots. Each one was a bull's-eye.

A murmur of applause went up from the crowd. The showman seized his chance.

"Pretty shootin', miss, very pretty shootin'," he said.

"I'll give you this 'andsome vawse as a reward for skill. Now, you lads, you ain't a-goin' to stand by and let a lady teach you 'ow to shoot? Come on, gents, try your luck. It's easy, ain't it, miss? Three shots for two pence, and 'andsome prizes for three bulls in three shots. Try your luck, ladies and gents!"

Some one slapped down twopence and took a rifle. It was young Joe Greaves, flushed and cidery.

"Go it, Joe!" the crowd encouraged him. "Show 'em your style, Joe! Good ol' Joe!"

Personally, I thought he was too much elevated to do more than equal my own ignominious score. But I forgot that Joe's father had been a keeper. Joe could shoot almost before he could walk. He could shoot straight in his sleep. *Bang, bang, bang!*—three bulls!

"Ar, you can't 'alf shoot in these parts!" said the showman. "Don't give a pore man a chawnce. Now, lads, come on, see if you cawn't level that. Don't be beat, boys."

His appeal was responded to at once. There was a general movement towards the booth, and twopences began to rain in. I was glad to see that the loathsome 'boss' had to cope with it all single-handed. The little gipsyish assistant had just departed—to his dinner, presumably—followed by a hoarse command not to be all day abaht it, and to be back by two at litest. Personally I hoped that he would be very late, and that the wretched cockney would have the hardest hour of the day to deal with alone.

Lady Gervaise touched me on the arm.

"Come along," she said in an aside. "This is too much of a good thing. Besides, I don't believe Mrs. Harrington's watching us any more. Let's find her and shock her again."

But poor Mrs. Harrington was already getting a new shock. She was quite near us still, by the fortune-teller's tent, and two people were just emerging from their consultation with the Powers of Darkness—Celia and (of course) Stephen Earle.

"Who is the handsome young man with Miss Harrington?" asked one of the attendant 'County' ladies.

"It's—I believe it's a Mr. Earle," said Mrs. Harrington frigidly. "Rather a young ne'er-do-weel, I'm afraid. . . . Celia, I want you a moment. Come here."

She spoke to the girl as if she were nine instead of nineteen. Celia advanced, looking distinctly sulky.

"Celia, it's after one," said the Squiress, in a voice that was in itself irritating. "Go up to the house and see that everything is all right for lunch; and tell Lydia that she may come down to the Fair, if she likes, as soon as she has washed up."

"That'll leave the house empty," Celia reminded her.

"You had better stay. You've had all the most enjoyable part of the time here; I don't think it will be quite suitable for you to stay any longer. It will be very hot after lunch, and the people are very excited. You'll be much better off with a nice book in the garden."

Celia said nothing, but looked rebellious. Mrs. Harrington took not the slightest notice, but went smoothly on.

"Your father may be in at any time. He wasn't sure when he would be back. But mind you're about, to attend to him whenever he comes in. The trains are in at 4.40, 7.19, and 10.12. There isn't another till very late, and I will be at home by then. The maids have leave to be out till eleven, but of course that won't matter if you're in by ten. You can be in the garden all the rest of the time."

"When will you be home?"

"I can't say exactly. I mean to walk over and see old Ben Salt as soon as I can get away from here. I shan't be very late—I shall be in by eleven."

"Why are you going to see old Ben Salt so late?"

"Don't be inquisitive, Celia. It's a horrid trait in a girl. I have to see him about Lydia, who is far from well. Now go home at once, and remember all I've told you."

Celia, looking undeniably sullen, turned to go. I followed her with my eyes—until I saw another face. Joe Greaves was still standing near the rifle range, and on his face there was the most curious expression of fear, hatred, and anger. I realized that, from his place by the booth, he could have heard every word that Mrs. Harrington said, and I saw that, if looks could have killed, the Squiress would have dropped dead at that moment. The next second he turned on his heel and swung off across the Green.

I was so intrigued (yes, a horrid word, but there isn't another) that I only vaguely heard Celia call over her shoulder:

"Sorry, Stephen, I've got to go home. See you later, perhaps."

"I'll come with you," Stephen proposed eagerly; but Mrs. Harrington wasn't going to have that.

"Miss Harrington has something to see to for me, Mr. Earle. I'm afraid she won't have any time to spare."

"Can't I help?" begged Stephen. He looked more like Puck than ever, standing merry and brown under the shade of the mighty oaks. You expected to see pointed ears sticking up through his thick dark hair.

"No," said Mrs. Harrington shortly; and Stephen laughed, showing all his white teeth. No wonder she disapproved of him! I shook my head at him and frowned, because I always feel responsible for him; and he laughed again, all over his elfish face. Mrs. Harrington turned haughtily away.

"*Do* introduce me to that *dear* old man!" cooed a tactful county dame, indicating old Tony Barton, who, if we ever are forced into being a show village, will star as the Oldest Inhabitant.

This was exactly the right note. Mrs. Harrington immediately smoothed herself into the model Squiress she always aimed at being.

"Ah, Tony, how are you? Enjoying the Fair?"

"No—o—o—a!" said Tony uncompromisingly. "That I hain't. Nor be none on us."

"What! Not enjoying it?"

"No—o—o—a."

"But why not?"

"Us can't enjy nowt on Foakeses Green."

Mrs. Harrington turned to her friends with a little gesture of despairing resignation.

"Some old superstition!" she said, with a little laugh. "Shall we go and see the dancing?"

Obviously she recognized that Tony was a very insecure prop to her reputation as liege lady of Ringshall.

They moved on in dignity. Old Tony spat.

"Ah, 'twill be well if worse don't come on it," he said to the world at large. "'Tis bad when Peter falls o' a Froiday, like he do this year, and 'tis worse when he comes at full o' the moon too. And then her goes an' puts Fair o' Foakeses Green!"

A scream of shrill laughter, which I recognized at once as coming from Mrs. Nokes, broke in.

"Look ahere, souls!" she chuckled, hobbling along after the retreating Squiress.

She paused just short of the group of aristocrats, and with great dexterity, spat on the black blob that was Mrs. Harrington's shadow. She then, with a malignant grin that was perfectly horrible to see, bent over it and cracked the joint of her thumb, muttering all the time. I could not hear a word she said, but there was something horribly blood-curdling in the weird performance, in the crowd of people, under the hot, clear sun.

Tony and his circle watched in grim silence. Then one of them said:

"Martel fooul the woman be."

"Ah. Oi wouldn' 'ave woise woman crack thumb at me, not for the goold of Ind."

"Well, souls, us'll see what us'll see. Her may goo a-prinkin' in her silks and satins now, but 'twill be her shroud as she'll be a-wearin' soon."

"Ah, that 'twill."

Silly as it all was, I felt a little shiver run down my spine. It's no good saying that it couldn't possibly affect

the span of Mrs. Harrington's days for old Mrs. Nokes to
spit on her shadow and crack her thumb at her. I know
that. But what you know doesn't always account for what
you feel.

"Come away!" I whispered to Lady Gervaise. "Let's go
and see the dancing too."

The dancing was very pretty, though it *was* Mrs. Harrington who had arranged it. It was just the place for the
simple figures that look so complicated, and the charming
old tunes seemed like echoes of the days when it didn't
need a 'foreigner' to get those same dances going under
the ancient trees. As the sun got a little lower and the air
cooled, I felt cheered and quite my normal self again and
thought how foolish heat and nervousness can make you.

I had asked a few people—Stephen and Roger Cartwright and Celia, and now Lady Gervaise—to supper after
the Fair. We had all had a very early lunch, and tea (if at
all) at a booth, and supper would be welcome. It would
only be a picnic affair, for both my maids had leave to be
out till the Fair closed at eleven; but no one minded that.
So, when the country dancing palled, I bade a temporary
farewell to Lady Gervaise, and strolled back to the Dower
House to see about the meal. As I went, I laughed aloud to
think how old Tony and his mates had scared me by their
grim hints of horror. It was a lovely evening, scented and
serene, and the garden looked beautiful. I went in, to prepare the nicest supper I could muster, with a very peaceful
heart.

5

Roger Cartwright was the first guest to arrive. He came in time to stem strawberries while I brewed coffee, which I make supremely well. I was quite glad of him, because I did want to have everything extra nice by the time Lady Gervaise arrived.

"I didn't see you at the Fair," I said to him, as I stood over my brew with a large spoon, waiting for the psychological moment to stir.

"Didn't you? I was there. I saw you at the rifle show."

"Don't be odious. I don't believe you."

"Honour bright, I did. I say, what a shot Lady Gervaise is!"

"Well," I said, a little annoyed, "she ought to be. She goes to shooting parties every autumn. No wonder she's decent at it."

"Decent, yes—but that was a wonderful exhibition. I tried the beastly guns, and not one I had was true. It's done purposely, of course. But it didn't seem to worry her."

"No. Nor Joe Greaves."

"Oh, Joe! He could score a bull with a pop-gun. I say, did you see poor Tom Nokes?"

"At the rifles? No. Was he there?"

"Rather, and old Mother Nokes treating him to shots long after the boy wanted to stop. Kept telling him he must try to beat Joe. She was tight, of course."

"Well, so was Joe."

"Yes, I know." Roger Cartwright's face clouded over. "I don't know what to do about that lad."

"You can't do anything," I said helpfully.

"No, I don't suppose I can. It's his look-out. He may pull up now that—" He broke off abruptly.

"When he's married, you mean?" I said.

"Y—yes. But you know the situation. If Lydia's father has anything to say to it, that'll be never. He'd never let them marry till Joe does better than he's doing now."

He'd like it still less if they didn't marry, was what I wanted to say. I didn't, because, as I say, I'm old-fashioned about these things. But I think the curate guessed what was in my mind.

"*Damn* Mrs. Harrington!" he said suddenly and heartily.

"Quite so," I applauded. "But why just now?"

"Because she will try to take a hand in things she doesn't know a thing about," he said, quite crossly.

As he said it, I had a sudden remembrance of a tiny episode—Mrs. Harrington telling Celia that she was going to see old Ben Salt 'about Lydia'—and Joe's expression of mingled fear and fury. I wondered what was behind it, and if the curate knew. I felt pretty sure he did.

He didn't mean to tell me, though. He seemed to think he'd said enough. All he said was:

"I've done these strawberries now. What next?"

I told him to take them into the dining-room, and then gave him a tongue to open, because whenever I use a tin-opener it turns and bites me; and then he made a quite admirable salad. Really, for an unmarried parson, he is very domesticated. Just as he finished, the telephone bell rang, and he went to take the message.

"It was Celia Harrington," he said, when he came back. "She rang up to say that she can't come to supper. Mrs. Harrington won't let her. Harrington's out, and Mrs.

Harrington has to go to see some one in the village, and she says some one's got to be there to see to Harrington when he gets in."

"What bosh!" I said roundly. "Isn't there a maid in? I suppose she guesses that Stephen's coming, and doesn't want Celia to meet him. That woman's a public nuisance. As if Godfrey Harrington couldn't have a cold meal put out for him, like anybody else!"

"I thought it was pretty thin as an excuse," he agreed. "Besides, if Harrington's gone to town, as he said he was going to do, he'll have fed on the train. He couldn't come back early. He didn't leave till about eleven."

"How do you know? I heard he was away—Mrs. Harrington said so—but she didn't say when or where he'd gone."

"He told me himself. I saw him at the Fair."

"Was he there? I didn't see him."

"No. It was early—before it was officially open. He was doing the heavy squire when I saw him."

"*What!*" I exclaimed.

"Yes. I thought it was rather a good sign, too. He hates that kind of thing, so he must have been trying to please the Squiress. Yes, he was at your rifle show—"

"Nothing to do with me," I interjected.

"—teaching the boys how to hold a rifle. He had his own Loxley airgun for them to practise with. He might have given you a lesson or two if he'd known you had a fancy that way."

"You are odious," I repeated, "and no one could ever teach me to shoot, anyway, even if they were good at it."

"Well, to do him justice," said the curate reluctantly, "Harrington is that. And he was decent to the kids, too."

"And now, I suppose," I said with resignation, "there'll be an epidemic of airguns, and we'll all go in danger of our lives."

"Harrington did warn them that airguns were risky things," said Roger Cartwright, "especially those like a Loxley, that'll take quite a big missile, and that you could quite well kill a person with one if you fired anything pointed or very hard out of one. In fact, he seemed quite sensible."

At this point Lady Gervaise arrived, and I said we wouldn't wait for Stephen. It was already a quarter past nine. We went into the dining-room, and there he was, sampling the strawberries with the greatest *sang-froid*.

"Hullo, Aunt Marion!" he said, quite calmly. I am not his aunt, but I'm tired of remonstrating when he calls me this. "Where have you come from?"

"Where have you?" I retorted.

"Through the window. I say, Celia can't come."

"I know. Have you been up to the Manor House?"

He nodded gloomily.

"Isn't it foul?" he appealed to us. "Why in he— I mean, why can't old Harrington eat his beastly food without having Celia on tap to help him do it? He said himself he didn't want any one to wait about for him."

"What?" I exclaimed.

It was utterly contrary to all I knew of Godfrey Harrington for him to say that he didn't want attention.

"Did, really. Celia told me. Said they'd all be tired, and he'd just come in and eat something cold. So why on earth Celia should have to hang about the Manor House all day and all night, I can't see."

I could, and I suppose the others could too; but we didn't like to tell Stephen so. Besides, we were all, after our scrappy meals, more interested in our own food than in Godfrey Harrington's. It quite cheered me to see how nice the table looked, in spite of Stephen's depredations, and how soon the dishes emptied.

But in spite of the food (which really *was* nice!) something seemed wrong. Roger Cartwright was more silent than usual, and I guessed that he was thinking of Joe Greaves, perhaps planning ways to get the lad back to his old steady self. Stephen was frankly sulky, brooding over his disappointment. He had, naturally, been counting on my discreet disappearance with the other guests after supper, and had looked forward to a quiet couple of hours with his Celia. As for Lady Gervaise, she was quite unlike her usual charming, if insincere, self. She was jumpy and nervous—she absolutely leapt in her chair when Stephen dropped the lid of the biscuit-box—and could not keep either mind or body steady. For myself, I was both tired and cross. I told myself that we'd all had a tiring day, but I knew that it wasn't only ordinary heat and fatigue that was making us all so horrid. I wondered if there was thunder brewing. It certainly was very hot.

"I suppose you heard about the accident at the Fair?" asked Stephen at last, when the conversation seemed on the point of expiring.

I jumped eagerly at the topic.

"No. Those horrible swings, of course."

"No, nothing like that. Only a stall bust up. No one even hurt, let alone killed. How bloodthirsty you are, Aunt Marion! You look quite disappointed."

"Well," I admitted, "I do call a broken stall rather dull. I thought you meant something exciting."

"It was quite exciting while it was happening."

"How did it happen?" asked Lady Gervaise; and somehow, as she asked, I had an odd, quite unjustifiable impression that her slow voice was exaggeratedly languid, as if to conceal a real excitement or interest.

"Oh, I suppose it was to be expected. You know what a crowd there's been round that rifle-gallery thing?—ever since you gave your display, Lady Gervaise. That chap must have made a fortune."

"He looked a perfectly horrid man," I said; but the others seemed to think this irrelevant.

"Well, the blessed thing got so popular that the chaps wouldn't queue up properly. 'Course, they were all a bit— well, above themselves, and they got a bit rough. It was great larks, seeing old Dan Gregory trying to do the heavy London bobby, and the more he ordered them about, the worse they got, shoving in and hustling. These travelling shows aren't made to stand that sort of thing, and after a bit the whole concern simply went smash. You never saw such a mess in your life! When the sides gave way, naturally the chaps who'd been shoving against them went down head first, and there was a bit of a rough-and-tumble— they weren't in a state to see reason. There were one or two quite pretty scraps going on in about two secs., and of course the stall was simply in crumbs. Old Gregory was simply priceless, trying to sort 'em out and take notes and read the Riot Act all together. I hear the showman's lost quite a number of guns."

"I don't feel any sympathy with him," I said. "He had a perfectly loathsome face. The pirate was heaps nicer."

"Did he say if he saw any one actually take the guns?" asked Roger Cartwright.

"I don't think so. He hardly could, you know, in a mix-up like that. The whole Fair closed down almost at once. I expect the other showmen thought the same thing might happen to them. But the chap may quite well find when he's picked up the crumbs, that he hasn't really lost any at all. It isn't like Ringshall chaps to pinch things like that."

"They weren't themselves to-day, though," the curate reminded him. I could see that he was rather bothered, and I had a sudden idea—did he think it possible that Joe

Greaves had taken a gun? Was he frightened of what he might do with it if he had?

"*I* think," Stephen went on, "that the person to recoup him is Mrs. Harrington. The whole mess-up of the Fair is her fault, and she's got money to burn."

I thought—but it may quite well have been my fancy—that Lady Gervaise moved uneasily when he said that. It's quite certain that she became increasingly nervous from then on, and when I proposed a move into the garden, where it might be cooler, she rose at once.

It was a little—not much, but a little—cooler in the garden. The church clock was just striking a quarter to ten as we strolled out, but it was still almost daylight. There was a faint smell of dew mingling with the heavy, spicy scent from my pinks and roses. Thanks to the accident which had closed the Fair, it was very still, so that it seemed as if you could hear the soft, melancholy note of the bell striking the hour seconds after it had really sounded.

As we stepped out on to the lawn, a big white owl, half blind in the lingering light, blundered across the garden. I saw it, I think, before any one else—certainly before Lady Gervaise; though it came, in its bewildered flight, quite close, she did not see it till it nearly touched her. Its wings seemed to sweep her hair, and its evil yellow eyes seemed to glare into hers.

She sprang back and screamed aloud. The owl hooted in derisive melancholy, and blundered away. Lady Gervaise was quite white and trembling.

"What was it—what was it?" she whispered, clutching at my arm.

"Only an owl," I assured her, and I slipped an arm round her, for I was really afraid she might fall.

"An owl?" she faltered. "Are you sure?"

"Certain. There it is—see? Against the beeches?"

She laughed, a shaky, scared little laugh.

"So it is! I thought—"

She broke off abruptly, biting her lip.

"What a fool I am!" she went on, more calmly. "It's— I think there's thunder about, don't you? I feel horribly on edge."

For a minute I wondered whether there was anything behind this most uncharacteristic confession of a very unusual weakness. I looked at her closely, but could see nothing more than might be easily accounted for by her fright. And yet—it was so very unlike Lady Gervaise to be scared by ghost or demon, let alone an owl!

"Look!" said Stephen suddenly. "There's Celia! She must have got rid of Harrington early."

Was it fancy, I wondered, or did Lady Gervaise's slight figure stiffen against my arm? I decided that it was fancy. I expected her to show some sort of emotion at the mention of Harrington's name, simply because I linked her with him in my imagination.

"So it is," I said. "Perhaps he didn't come by the 7.19. If he didn't, he won't have arrived yet—it's not ten."

And I waved to the tall white figure crossing my lawn.

6

Celia came and joined us, and we all found seats under the cedar that gives my garden so much dignity. Celia sat on the grass, with Stephen lying on his back beside her, staring up through the dark layers of cedar to the pale purple sky beyond it. Celia was so fair and slim in her straight white frock, Stephen so elfin and untamed, that they looked, under the great tree and twilight sky, like nymph and faun strayed from the timeless youth of the world.

We were all silent for a little—the night was too still and perfect for chatter; but silence was too much of a strain for Lady Gervaise. She fidgeted, and then began to make talk.

"So you managed to get away after all?" she asked Celia.

The girl nodded idly. She was engaged in sticking grasses into Stephen's thick, curly hair.

"How did you do it?" I asked. I felt that it wasn't manners to make my 'polite' guest feel embarrassed by our casual silences.

"Oh," she shrugged, "I just didn't wait."

"Has your father got to feed alone after all, then?"

"He hasn't turned up. I could have come to supper, only I thought it wasn't worth a row. Nothing was said about not coming afterwards. Dad can't be back now till about half-past ten, and anyhow he said we weren't to bother. So I left his supper out and came away."

"And Mrs. Harrington?"

"She's still out. Seeing some one in the village. She said she might not be in till eleven, she started so late."

"I see."

There was another pause, in which I could *feel* Lady Gervaise's nervousness, though she sat fairly still. I knew she was wanting us to chatter—that the peace and silence were fretting her, turning her in upon herself—and I rummaged in my mind for a topic, but could think of none, save the one central topic in all our minds. For I know we were all thinking of Mrs. Harrington—that stern and handsome autocrat who seemed to thwart us each in some special way. But, as I could think of nothing else, and something had to be said to break the silence that was straining my guest to screaming point, I used it.

"How much better Mrs. Harrington is looking," I said to Celia. "Don't you notice it? I remember I thought she was looking so ill in the spring—so worried."

"Yes," replied the girl, rather indifferently. "She's looking better now than she's done for months."

"More's the pity," said Stephen *sotto voce,* and annoyed me very much. I couldn't say anything, because I didn't think anybody else had heard; but it was a stupid and a heartless thing to say, and I meant to scold him afterwards, though it is seldom of any use to scold Stephen, who always pretends exaggerated penitence with his rogue's eyes laughing at you all the time.

"I've noticed it too," said Roger Cartwright. "All the spring, from Christmas to Easter, she looked quite ill and haggard. She looks a different woman now."

"It must be the tiny morning dose," I suggested. "Tasteless in tea. That schoolgirl feeling."

"You're mixing up two different things," said Celia. "It's 'schoolgirl complexion', and she's got that anyway." (Which was nice of her, for she must have guessed, as I did, that Mrs. Harrington's complexion was not beautiful entirely of its own accord.) "No," the girl went on, "I think something's happened—something to please her, or relieve her mind. . . ."

Her voice hesitated and trailed off, and she stole an uneasy glance around at us. I could see that she had been on the point of confiding something further about her stepmother, and had remembered that Lady Gervaise was there—and Lady Gervaise is not of our own particular little circle. I respected her loyalty. I thought the subject of Mrs. Harrington had better drop.

But I could think of nothing else to say. Suddenly, from behind the beeches, the owl hooted again—a menacing, fateful note that made even me shiver a little. It seemed altogether too much for Lady Gervaise. She rose abruptly to her feet.

"Will you forgive me if I run off to bed, Miss Leslie?" she said, and her tone was unnecessarily urgent. "It's lovely here, and I've enjoyed it all so much, but—but I have a brute of a headache, and I think, if you don't mind, that I'll be better in bed. Do forgive me, won't you? No, please don't move," she added, as the two men rose to escort her home. "I'd really, *honestly,* much rather not. It's not two minutes to Haresfoot. I'll run across alone. *Please.*"

Her voice and manner were so earnest that they accepted it. She bade us all good-night, still in the same nervous manner, half excited, half alarmed, and then flitted away like a pale moth in the gathering dusk. I caught Roger Cartwright's eye, and I could see that he liked it as little I did—though why I didn't like it I couldn't have told. Wherever you turned, mischief seemed brewing on that perfect June night, with the great moon hanging like a pearl in the deepening purple of the stainless sky.

I had walked to the edge of the lawn with Lady Gervaise, and when I came back to the little group under the cedar I found that 'the strings of their tongues had been loosed' by the departure of our polite visitor, and they were talking freely.

"—so I believe it must be money," Celia was saying as I approached. "She used to get most frightf'ly worked up, and was always cutting down expenses—you remember, Miss Leslie, how she *would not* buy a decent coat, though she looked like nothing on earth in that awful old grey, because she said it was the end of the winter? And she used to be so anxious that no one should answer the telephone but herself. She got frantic one day because I answered it, thinking she was out, and I didn't know the person speaking. And there were letters—"

"And all this has stopped?" asked Roger Cartwright.

"Yes—oh, some weeks ago. Stopped dead. She went up to town—let's see, it was on the first, I think"—(she faltered, and I guessed that she and Stephen had probably good reason to remember the date!)—"and bought simply masses of clothes. She's still very strict about the 'phone, but if she gets any calls they don't worry her as they used to. And she burns all her letters . . . D'you know what I think?" she added suddenly. "I believe she gambles."

We made incredulous noises—that is, we elders. Stephen merely rolled over and looked at her attentively.

"My *dear* Celia!" I exclaimed. "*Do* be probable. Mrs. Harrington gamble! I'd as soon expect to hear of the vicar plunging—sooner."

"Well," said Celia obstinately, "it's the only thing I can think of that accounts for it. She went in too far—horses, or the Stock Exchange, or any old thing—and lost more than she could afford. So she pulled up all round, and paid up a bit at a time; but she couldn't pay up quick enough, and kept being dunned—even blackmailed—on account of the scandal, perhaps. And now she's got square."

"Good enough," Stephen agreed. And it certainly did fit. Still, Mrs. Harrington—our organizer of religious societies, our model Squiress, a gambler. . .

"I don't believe it," I said roundly.

"I don't know," said the curate slowly. "It's possible, you know. She's such a very dark horse, people don't think it's wrong to gamble on the Exchange, for some queer reason."

"Besides," Stephen added casually, "she was a bad hat, wasn't she, before she came here?"

"Stephen!" I exclaimed, really angry with him. "How dare you say that sort of thing! You're as bad as Mrs. Nokes!"

"Yes. I got it from her," he said calmly. "She seems to know a lot about the Squiress. She knew about those letters, if you remember."

"Yes," I retorted, "and said they were blackmail, and meant death! If that's the sort of authority you go by, Stephen, you'd better hold your tongue."

"Well," he replied, quite unabashed, "how d'you know they *weren't* blackmail?"

I snorted. I really was furious with him. I can't think what makes Stephen behave like that. It can't be original sin, for he howled enough when he was christened to let out far more devils than the usual allowance.

The church clock struck, and Celia sprang to her feet.

"Half-past ten! I must get back," she said. "There'll be no end of a row if She gets back before me."

I realized, more vividly than I had for days, how galling it must be for a girl like Celia, brought up in the modern independence, to have suddenly thrust on her a stepmother who made 'no end of a row' if she was out at half-past ten

with a spinster friend. I almost—but not quite—began to
sympathize with Stephen's indignant fury with the woman.
Celia took her troubles so sweetly, so gallantly, that one
didn't realize quite what she did put up with for the sake
of peace in her father's house. But I expect she let go to
Stephen. No wonder he hated the woman.

"Well, good-night, then, Celia," I said, "if you really
think you ought to go."

I took her in my arms and kissed her. We didn't as a
rule embrace on parting, but I felt a sudden gush of admiration and sympathy, and acted on an impulse. And I
knew, from the way in which she squeezed my hands, that
she knew what made me do it.

"I'll see you home," said Stephen, rising all in one
piece, like an animal.

"And so will I," added the curate. "It'll be wiser," he
added, feeling, as I did, their disappointment.

And so, of course, it was. If there was to be a row any
way, what sort of a row would it be if Celia appeared
accompanied by Stephen Earle? Whereas a curate was a
most correct escort, and might manage to get her out of
trouble altogether. Besides, unless I was very far out in
my guess, it would be found that he had some very urgent
message to deliver *en route,* and would only catch them up
near the Manor House.

I saw them depart with a quiet mind, and turned into
the house to read for half an hour before going to bed.
I couldn't lock up till the maids got back at eleven, so I
thought I'd have half an hour's real peace first.

The house was very quiet—stiller, if less peaceful, than
the garden. I thought, as I lit my reading-lamp, that after
all things weren't so bad. We had all dreaded that 29th of
June; Roger Cartwright and I had been prepared (or I had,
and I believed he had) for something terrible to happen
on that day. It had seemed fraught with omens; nameless

terrors had somehow seemed imminent. And here we were, nearly at the close of it, and what had happened? Nothing—unless you count the accidental smashing of a showman's booth!

I laughed aloud as I went across to select a book.

"This'll be a lesson to me," I thought, "not to believe in 'dreams, omens, superstitions, and suchlike fooleries.' Of course nothing has happened. How could it? Why should it?"

Like an answer, a noise shrilled at my ear. It was only the telephone bell, but it made me jump as if it had been a ghostly reply. I actually hesitated before taking down the receiver.

I told myself, as I did so, that it could be nothing worse than Mrs. Arnold asking me about a clue in her latest crossword, or Mrs. Jukes in a flurry about some meeting or other. And all the time I knew it was nothing of the kind.

I put the receiver to my ear.

"Yes?" I said; and my voice sounded odd and strange in the silent house.

"Is that Miss Leslie?" asked a man's voice.

"Roger! I mean—what is it?" I asked. I hoped he hadn't heard me say "Roger!" in that flapperish manner.

"It's—I say, can you come over to the Manor House?"

"*Now?*"

"Yes. It's—something horrible has happened." His voice ceased abruptly; then it began again.

"Mrs. Harrington is dead. Killed. Can you come?"

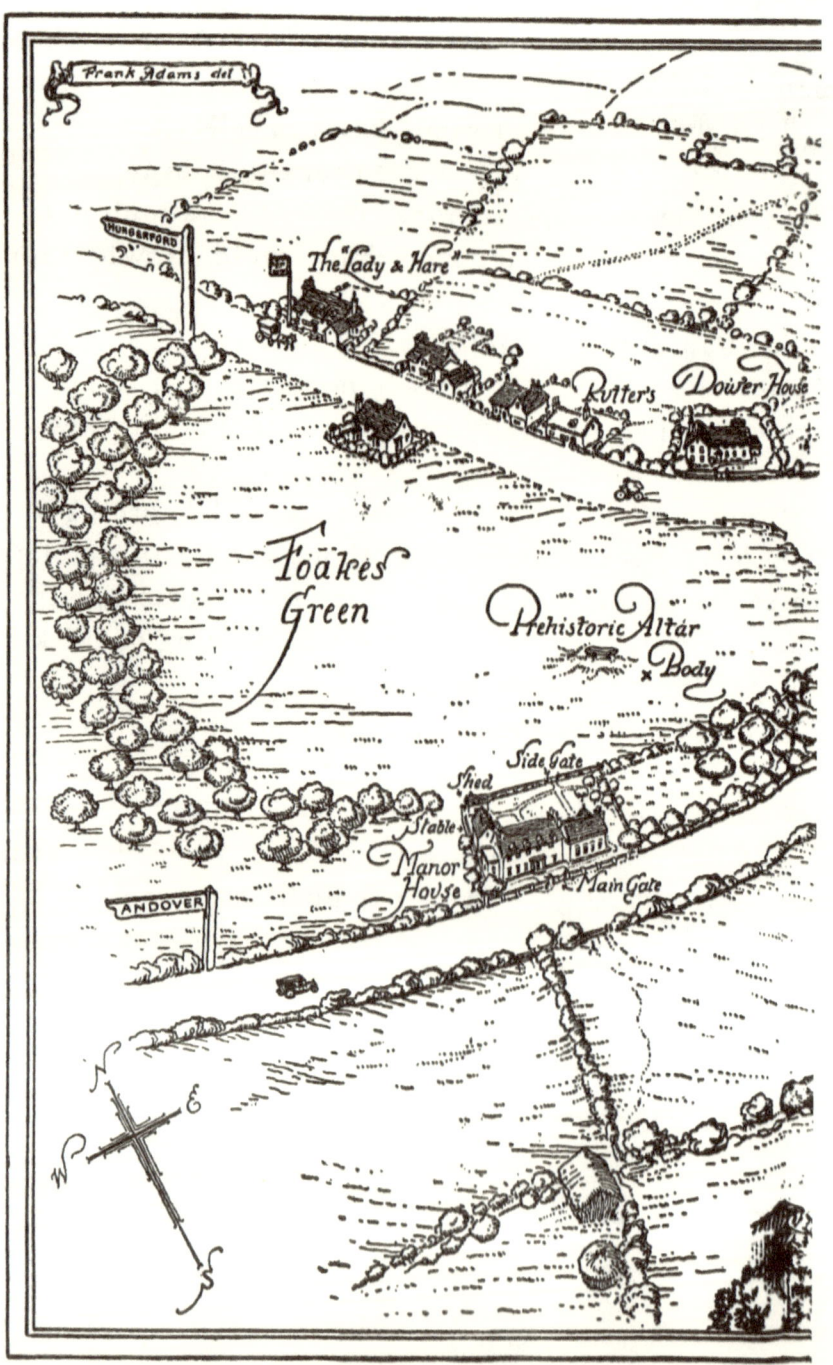

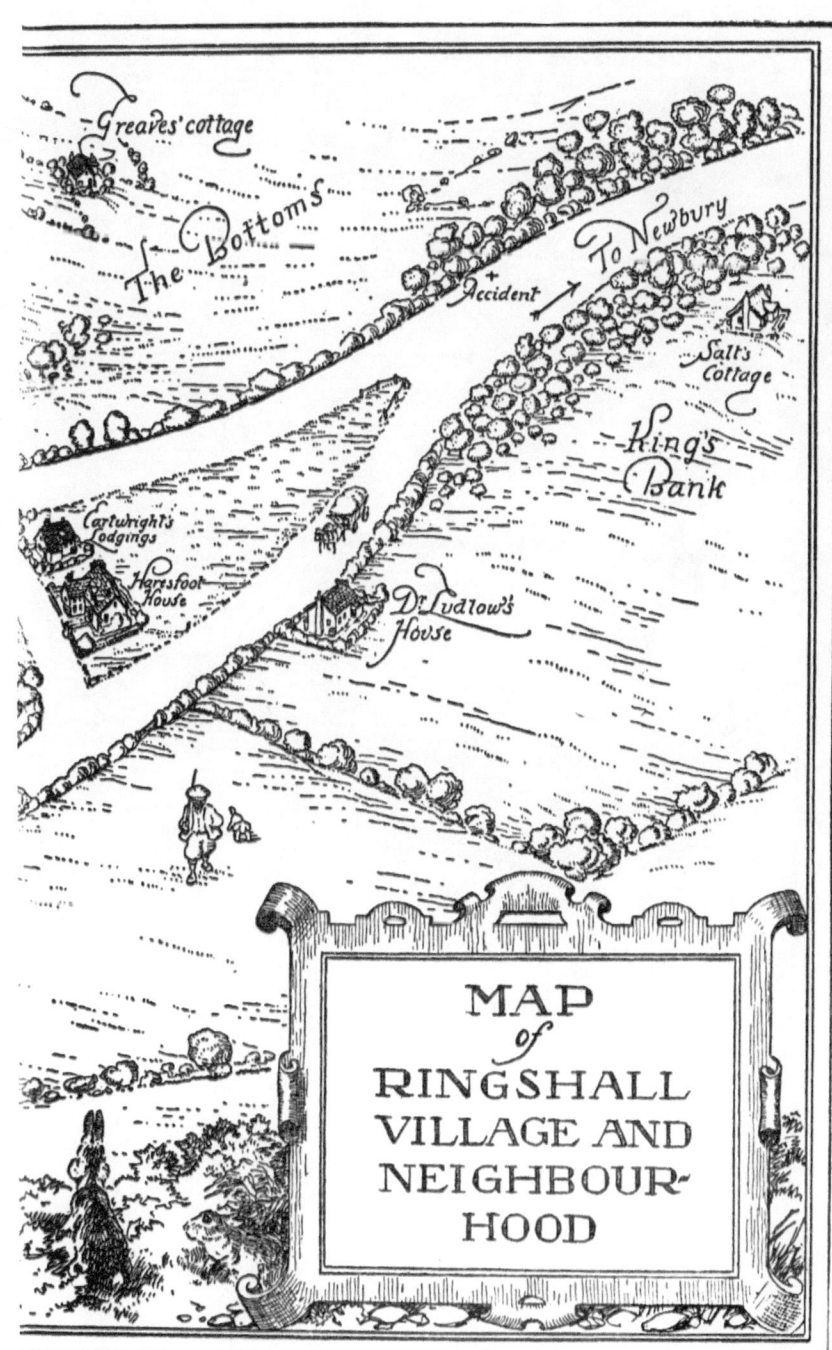

Greaves' cottage

The Bottoms

To Newbury

Accident

Salt's Cottage

King's Bank

Cartwright's Lodgings

Haresfoot House

Dr Ludlow's House

MAP
of
RINGSHALL
VILLAGE AND
NEIGHBOUR-
HOOD

7

For a moment my brain whirled. I could think of nothing. Somewhere in the back of my mind I seemed to hear "I told you so."

I pulled myself together.

"Of course I'll come," I said. "But can't you tell me a little more first? Does Celia know?"

"Yes."

His voice hesitated, and then he went on:

"She—Stephen and she—found her. She was lying on the Green. She was quite dead."

"On Foakes Green!"

"Yes."

"What made you say that she—had been killed?"

"Because she—I don't know if she's been shot or stabbed. There's a biggish hole in the back of the head—too big for a bullet, I think, but round. . . . I don't know what to make of it. . . . I say, do come. I can't talk over the telephone about a thing like this."

"I'll come at once."

I was just going to ring off when a thought occurred to me.

"Is Celia all right?"

"She's horribly upset, of course."

"I'll bring something along for her. I won't be five min-utes."

I got out a bottle of sal volatile which I've had by me ever since Jenny was hysterical once, and some aspirin. I thought Celia might need the first, and I knew I should need the second. Then I scribbled a line to the maids to say that I was spending the night at the Manor House, and went. I ran all the way; but, though it is the nearest way, I did *not* cross Foakes Green.

Roger Cartwright met me at the door.

"Thank God you've come!" he said fervently, and though I ought not to have thought of anything but the tragedy which confronted us, I couldn't help knowing that I was pleased.

"Where is she?" I asked.

He shuddered a little.

"I've rung up the police. I suppose they'll bring her here."

I felt a little sick.

"I meant—Celia."

"Oh! She's in the library. Will you go to her?"

"Just a second. Tell me—are you *sure* Mrs. Harrington is dead?"

"Certain. She was lying in the middle of the Green, on her face. Her head pointed this way. She must have been coming back to the Manor House when she was killed."

"Then she wasn't—she can't have been there long?"

"No. Her—her hand was still quite warm."

"Is Godfrey Harrington back yet?"

"No. That's why I rang you up in such a hurry. Celia's alone."

I was just moving towards the library when we heard a sound—heavy steps shuffling outside. I knew instinctively what it was.

"Don't let them in for a minute," I begged. "Let me get Celia upstairs first. She can't stand any more."

He nodded, and I went into the library. The light was on, but Celia stood by the window, staring out into the darkness. As I came in, she turned and looked at me vacantly, as if she didn't know me. She was dreadfully white, and her face looked old.

"Celia," I said, going over to her. "Celia, won't you come upstairs with me now?"

She still stared at me dully. I went up and put my arms round her, as I had done in the garden. Somehow that seemed to break through her dazed senses; I expect she unconsciously connected it with the quick rush of emotion we had both felt then. She threw her arms round my neck and burst out crying like a baby.

It was easy after that. I got her upstairs by the back way, and I don't think she heard the dreadful quiet sounds in the front hall as the police brought in their burden and laid it out in the cold, stiff room that had been Mrs. Harrington's sanctum and was now the ante-room of her grave. I got Celia, still sobbing openly, to undress, and put her into bed; then I rang for a maid.

I wondered, as I waited for some one to answer, what had become of all the maids who generally kept Mrs. Harrington's house in such exquisite order. No doubt they had, like my own Betty and Jenny, not seen why their late leave for the Fair should be curtailed because the Fair had happened to close early; but, even so, it must be long past the time fixed for their return. I rang again; and this time I was answered.

It was Lydia who came—that Lydia Salt who ought even now to be married to Joe Greaves. But I could see that she was going to be worse than useless to me. She was on the verge of hysteria, only waiting for a sympathetic word to 'give way' altogether. If my sal volatile were used, it would be Lydia who used it.

"Lydia," I said sharply, "please go downstairs and find Mr. Cartwright. Ask him if they've telephoned for the doctor yet, and, if not, ask him to tell the doctor to bring something for Miss Celia. Quick, now."

The girl stood staring at me, twisting her apron in her shaking hands.

"Oh, miss, I daren't go down to the hall, so I daren't!" she wailed. "They'm a-layin' of her out in the li'l parlour. I couldn't go past, not if it was ever so!"

"Don't be a fool!" I snapped; but even that didn't rouse her. She just whimpered feebly.

"Well, then, you stop here in case Miss Celia wants anything," I said, seeing that nothing would move her. "I'll go and ring up Dr. Ludlow myself—if he hasn't started."

I found what looked at first like a crowd in the hall. Our own constable, Dan Gregory, was there, and the gardener from the Manor House, and two other men, and Roger Cartwright. As I came down the fine old staircase, the curate was dismissing the men (who had, I guessed, come with Gregory to help him carry the dreadful burden), and Gregory was fumbling with the telephone.

Roger Cartwright turned to me as the men tramped out.

"How's Celia?" he asked.

"Better. She's crying. But I want Dr. Ludlow to see her."

"I asked him to bring something along for her when I rang him up at first."

"Good. You *are* useful," I said, with relief. "I suppose he's on the way."

"Ought to be here any minute. That's his car, I expect."

A car came dashing up as he spoke, and the next moment Dr. Ludlow was in the hall. Gregory hailed him with obvious relief. He was not used to sudden deaths—no village policeman is—and it was clearly a great comfort to him to have experts handy to advise him. He led the doctor away at once.

I knew I ought to go back to Celia, but I simply *couldn't*. I felt I simply must hear the doctor's verdict first; I must hear what it was that had so terribly-fulfilled the prophetic instinct that had haunted me all that day.

We sat silent, the two of us, listening to the tiny muffled movements in the little room beyond. I wanted to ask questions, to hear details—but I couldn't, while those small significant sounds went on. We both sat tense, holding our breath, as one would during an operation on the living.

It seemed hours that we sat there. It was, in actual time, not very long, and the dreadful business was not yet over when I heard a new sound—a second car approaching rapidly.

"The police from Newbury," Roger Cartwright whispered, meeting my eyes. "Gregory telephoned to them at once. Major Gaythorpe, the Chief Constable, is away, you know. I suppose they'll send an inspector."

And he rose and went to the door.

Just as the inspector, followed by a couple of constables, entered, Dr. Ludlow and Gregory emerged from the little room. The hall again seemed full, but this time the number of people seemed hopeful, not terrible. It now as if something were to be done, some step taken, and that is always the most hopeful thing that can happen in a crisis.

Gregory introduced the doctor to the inspector.

"I thought it best, sir, to get the doctor to make an examination at once," he said, obviously hoping for a word of commendation.

He didn't get it.

"You oughtn't to have touched the body till I'd had a look at it," said the inspector—rather he snapped it. "And now, I suppose, you've been and tramped all over the place, and got the doctor to open the body."

"I haven't done that exactly," said Dr. Ludlow, pleasantly calm and efficient. "I've made a very full external examination, but I haven't gone any further. I may say, apart from the wound in the back of the skull, I can find no trace of anything wrong."

"Thank you, sir. It's as well *some* one has some sense," said the inspector, with a withering glance at poor Gregory.

"I'm afraid it's my fault that the body was moved," put in the curate. "I was there when it was found—just after, rather—and I went and fetched Gregory. I told him he'd better bring it up here. I didn't feel at all sure that she was quite dead."

"Hm," grunted the inspector. Then he cheered up.

"Well, sir, as you were there when the body was found—"

"Immediately after," corrected Roger Cartwright.

"Who actually found it?"

"Miss Harrington and Mr. Earle saw it first. They—"

"One moment. Will you please tell me exactly your own version of what occurred?"

"I'm afraid I can tell you very little," said the curate. "I started to cross the Green with Miss Harrington and Mr. Earle, at about a quarter or twenty to eleven."

"You are sure of the time?"

"Not to a minute. But we, all three of us, had been at the Dower House to supper, and we rose to go at half-past ten. You remember, Miss Leslie?" he added, turning to me.

"Perfectly," I corroborated him. "The church clock struck the half-hour, and Celia jumped up and said she must go, and you and Stephen went with her."

"You were there, madam?" asked the inspector.

"It's my house," I informed him.

"How far is it from this lady's house to the spot where the body was found?" he asked the curate.

"Oh—five or six hundred yards, I should say. We took a minute or two to say good-bye, and then strolled over the Green. I separated from the others for a few minutes"— (Aha, I thought, I just thought you would!)—"and was not with them when they made the—the discovery. I thought I heard Miss Harrington cry out, and called out 'What's up?' or 'Is anything wrong?'—I can't remember my exact words."

The inspector was writing busily.

"Yes. . . . And then?"

"Ste—I mean, Mr. Earle—came to my gate. He called out, 'Come here—something awful's happened!' I went running, and saw them standing by a—a pile of some-thing—I thought at first it was a pile of sacks or awnings or something. And then I saw it was a—a human body." He paused again. "Mr. Earle was holding Miss Harrington," he went on, after a moment. "He said to me, 'My God, Cartwright, don't you see? It's Mrs. Harrington.'"

"What did you do then?"

"I felt the hand. It was still warm, but I thought it was not the hand of a living person."

"What made you think so?"

"I was a chaplain in France. I—I know the feel—"

"Yes. What then?"

"I told Mr. Earle to take Miss Harrington home, and went across to Gregory's cottage. He is the local police-man."

"Why did you go for him instead of for the doctor?"

"The doctor lives some distance away. I'm afraid my only thought was to get the poor lady to the Manor House, and to get the police on to the job. I could see the hole in the back of her head, and blood had trickled down her neck. I thought it was a job for the police."

"Hm. What then?"

"I followed Mr. Earle and Miss Harrington up to the house. I knew Mr. Harrington was in town, and in any case wasn't the kind of person to be very useful in an emergency. I thought I might come in handy."

"But hadn't this Mr. Earle you speak of come up already?"

"Yes; but he's only a boy. I thought I might be wanted."

"What did you do when you arrived?"

"I walked in—the door was standing open—and saw a light on in the library—that room there."

Instinctively we all turned and looked at the library door.

"I heard voices. I heard Miss Harrington telling Mr. Earle to go."

"Did she know that you had arrived?"

"No, I don't think so."

"Then why did she dismiss this young man and leave herself alone?"

Roger Cartwright hesitated. Then he said, rather doubtfully:

"I think it was—a kind of scruple. She knew that, if Mrs. Harrington had been alive, she would not have liked him to be there."

"Why not? Propriety?"

"N—not exactly. She—Mrs. Harrington—disliked Mr. Earle and didn't like him to see much of Miss Harrington."

"Oh! No love lost between the lady and this young man, eh?"

"No." The curate hesitated, and then added, "I'm afraid that was the case with a good many people here. Mrs. Harrington wasn't—well, wasn't very popular."

The inspector wrote again.

"Yes. You heard the young lady telling this young man to go. When then?"

"I went and telephoned to this lady—Miss Leslie—and asked her to come over. I thought Miss Harrington might need a woman. I then rang up the doctor—"

"One moment. You didn't yourself go in to Miss Harrington?"

"No. She—she was saying good-bye to Mr. Earle."

"Oh!" The inspector's tone told us that he had grasped that part of the situation. I could imagine exactly what Roger Cartwright had heard—Stephen pleading to be allowed to stay, and Celia firmly sending him away. It must have been pathetic. I could see the curate gently closing the door and taking the practical step of getting some one else to give to Celia a little of what she wouldn't take from Stephen.

"And when did this Mr. Earle leave?"

The curate paused.

"I didn't see him go," he said then. "He must have left by the library window. I don't think he came through the hall. I'm almost sure he didn't."

The inspector tapped his teeth with his pencil.

"Have you anything else to tell me, sir?" he asked then.

"I can't think of anything more," replied the curate.

"Thank you. I shall be able to find you later, if I should wish to ask you anything?"

"Oh yes—I lodge in the village. Gregory knows where."

"Thank you, sir. That'll be all, then. Now, sir, you please," he went on, turning to Dr. Ludlow and flicking over to a clean page of his notebook.

"You say you have examined the body externally, sir?"

"Yes."

"I take it that life was extinct when you were called in?"

"Oh yes. But she hadn't been long dead."

"Can you say at all how long?"

"Well, on such a hot night as this, it's a little difficult to be precise. I should say from a quarter to half an hour."

"Ah! Not longer?"

"It might be as much as three-quarters of an hour."

"And you examined her—when?"

"I reached the house just before a quarter-past eleven."

"Have you found the cause of death?"

"Yes. The brain has been pierced by some missile driven into it through the back of the skull."

"A bullet?"

"Well, that's what bothers me," confessed the doctor.

"The post mortem will show, of course, but from external examination I find it difficult to guess what actually did cause the wound. There is a round hole, about three-quarters of an inch in diameter, of quite a different character from the ordinary bullet-wound. The loss of blood is almost negligible. In fact, it looks more like the thrust of a pointed weapon than a shot. I could imagine such a wound in the head of a person who had fallen on to an iron spike."

The inspector considered this.

"You think, however, that the wound was actually caused by a missile which has remained in the head?"

"I—*think*—so," said Dr. Ludlow slowly. "I believe that there would have been a very much larger effusion of blood if it had been withdrawn."

"Hm. I should like you to make an autopsy as soon as possible. Could you manage it to-morrow morning?"

"Yes."

"Good. And now, can I see Miss Harrington?"

"Not to-night, Inspector," I begged. "She's absolutely exhausted to-night, and I want Dr. Ludlow to see her and give her a sleeping-draught."

"Well, I dare say to-morrow would do," said the inspector reluctantly. His tone was that of the schoolboy who has to lay down an exciting story at a thrilling spot. He shut his little book with obvious regret.

"And now, if you'll come along, Miss Leslie," said Dr. Ludlow in his nice, competent way, "we'll have a look at Celia."

We went up, leaving the inspector to chat with the constable. I felt sure he'd have to chat to some one, even a subordinate, or burst. Lots of men are like that.

8

Dr. Ludlow was an excellent man in an emergency. He had thought of Celia's probable condition of mind as well as of body, and had a supply of sensible and comforting talk, as well as a sedative all ready for her. I had always admired him, but never more than I did that night, when he dealt first with the corpse of a murdered acquaintance, then with a police inspector, then with an overwrought girl, and finally with an hysterical maid; for Lydia, who was still in Celia's room when we went in, had worked herself into such a state that poor Celia was wrestling with her, quelling her excited cries and trying to calm her down, instead of studying her own comfort and needs.

Having dosed Celia and put her back into her bed, and having removed Lydia to the nearest room and dosed her, Dr. Ludlow drew me aside.

"Where are the other maids?" he asked.

"I've no idea. They haven't come home. I expect Banks—the gardener, you know, who helped Gregory with the—the body—I dare say he met them and told them what had happened, and they won't come back. You know how all the village will take this. They'll think it's black magic. Look at Lydia—and she didn't hear a curse being laid on Mrs. Harrington."

"What's that?" he asked sharply. "A curse? What d'you mean?"

So I told him about Mrs. Nokes and the way she had behaved at the Fair, and how the old men had said that evil would come of her cracking her thumb and spitting on Mrs. Harrington's shadow.

"I see," he said thoughtfully. "So you think they won't come back?"

"Not to-night, anyway."

"And that girl, Lydia, is worse than useless," he muttered.

"I'm staying, of course," I reassured him. "Really, Dr. Ludlow, do you think I'd leave Celia alone with the maids, even if they were here and efficient? Of course I'm staying."

"Excellent," he said, with relief. Really, men *are* fools, even the best of them. What did he *expect* me to do?

"Can I go round to the Dower House and collect anything for you?" he asked then.

"That would be nice," I said gratefully. "I just dashed over, and didn't stop for a thing. Tell Betty I'm staying, and ask her to collect all I'll want in a bag. She'll know what to put."

He went off, and I went back to listen at Celia's door. I could hear nothing, so I went in to have a look at Lydia. She was better, but still in rather an alarming state, considering that she ought to have been avoiding violent excitement. I made up my mind that when the doctor returned with my things I'd get him to take Lydia back to her own home. It wasn't far, and I felt that to deal with Lydia, as well as with Celia and her father, when he arrived, would be more than I could bear. Besides, the girl worried me. I couldn't quite account for her tremendous excitement and obvious terror. It wasn't as if she'd been there when the 'witch' laid her curse on the dead woman. I told myself that a girl in Lydia's condition does get easily upset, and that the murder (for murder I was sure it was) of Mrs. Harrington was enough to account for her state. But all the time I felt that there was something more, something behind it. I almost had the impression that Lydia had *expected* the tragedy—and yet she hadn't heard the curse. I felt I could do very nicely without Lydia that night.

Dr. Ludlow, when he came back, agreed with me. The Manor House was no place for Lydia, and she was no possible use to me or Celia. He said he would take her with him and leave her at Ben Salt's.

"You won't mind being left?" he asked, looking sharply at me.

"Not in the least," I assured him. "And if I were, I don't see that Lydia would be any use. Besides, I expect the Squire will turn up some time soon. It must be frightfully late."

"It's half-past twelve," he said, looking at his watch, and I gasped with astonishment. Only an hour and a half since I'd first heard of the tragedy! It seemed impossible.

"The inspector will be over about ten to-morrow morning," said the doctor. "Will you tell Harrington, when he comes, to be ready for him then? And I'll try and get some of the maids to come up early in the morning. Goodnight, Miss Leslie. I don't know what we'd have done without you."

In spite of my bold words I felt pretty lonely as I heard the noise of the doctor's car die away. Luckily there was a good bit to be done. I went down and made sure that the door of the little sanctum was locked—why, I can't tell you, but I liked to feel sure that it was. I was vaguely surprised to see no police about. I thought, somehow, a policeman sat up night and day in a house where there had been a sudden and violent death. Perhaps they were out searching the Green for clues. Then I went upstairs again and peeped in on Celia. The drug had worked, and she was asleep, looking like a child-angel, with the moonlight bathing her face, framed in the short, soft hair. I kissed her very softly and stole out. I then proceeded to make my own arrangements.

Celia sleeps in a room opening out of a little corridor which runs at right angles to the main bedroom corridor. The chief bedrooms—Mrs. Harrington's, the Squire's, the spare rooms, and so on—are in the main corridor. In Celia's passage there is one other room, opposite hers, and I decided to annex that, partly to be near Celia, and partly because I somehow rather shirked the big, empty, important rooms which seemed to breathe of their dead mistress. It was as if the little passage, with the two smaller, unpretentious rooms, were Celia's domain. I felt I should be welcome there.

Betty had thought of everything. Hot as it was, she had even included a hot-water bottle. I made up the bed with linen from the huge old press on the landing, and then I undressed. I got into bed just as the church clock struck the quarter-past one.

I took two tablets of aspirin, put out my light, and determined to go to sleep. I could see the sky from my window, and could hear a tiny breeze just ruffling the branches of the trees outside. The sky was extraordinarily clear and pure, almost green, and the great serene moon floated in it like a jewel. The air seemed to breathe of peace. I lay quiet, not asleep, for I was conscious of the wind and the slow-sailing moon, and then, slowly, sleep came stealing over me.

I am quite sure that I hadn't been asleep more than a few minutes when I started awake. I always sleep very lightly, and that night I was, of course, on the alert in case Celia should want me. At first I could not be sure what it was that had awoken me. I thought, of course, of Celia, and sat up to listen. Then I heard it again.

It was the noise of some one moving softly about. And it did not come from Celia's room.

I slipped out of bed and put on my dressing-gown and slippers, my ears straining all the time. I felt perfectly convinced that some one was moving in the big room in the main corridor just opposite the opening of our little passage—Mrs. Harrington's room.

At first, I admit it, I felt simply terrified. I turned cold, and I felt a kind of pricking in my armpits that comes when I am really horribly scared. And then I pulled myself together.

"You idiot!" I said to myself crossly. "Of course it's Godfrey Harrington, come in without my hearing him."

And of course I knew that that explanation was as silly as my terror. To begin with, I am an extraordinarily light sleeper. Aspirin or not, I should have heard him, however softly he had crept up the stairs. Besides, Godfrey Harrington does not, and has not ever, I believe, shared his wife's room. He does not even have a dressing-room opening from it. He never enters her room at all. And if he had, this once, why should he be stealing round quietly instead of going to his own perfectly good room two doors farther on?

I pulled myself together and opened my door, holding the handle firmly and turning it very slowly. I did not want whoever—or whatever—was in Mrs. Harrington's room to hear me coming. I closed it behind me equally gently. I had not made a sound.

The moonlight poured in through the uncurtained windows of the corridor, making huge squares of silver on the blackness of the polished floor. I felt like some one in a fairy-tale—some one adventuring in a lost and secret castle, where anything might happen. . . .

I stole on, a step at a time, feeling along the wall with one hand as I went. And then, just as I reached the corner and turned into the main corridor, the moon played me false.

I don't know how I did it, but I missed my footing on the slippery boards. I stumbled, stretched out my hands wildly, and came down heavily on both knees. To my own startled ears the noise sounded appalling. I knew that if the sounds I had heard in Mrs. Harrington's rooms had been made by any one who had a right to be there, that person would come out at once to see who, or what, had fallen in the passage. I got carefully to my feet, and had to stand for a moment rubbing one knee, which had been badly bruised by the fall. No one came. The sounds had ceased completely.

I can't say how very reluctant I was to go on with my search. I was shaken by my fall, and I was—I'll confess it—very much frightened. I knew now for certain that the sounds in Mrs. Harrington's room ought not to have been there—were not made by any person with a right to be there. It was therefore, of course, my obvious duty to investigate them. But I had to scold myself as I had scolded poor Lydia Salt before I got going again.

I don't know who, or what, I expected to find. I don't know whether I was relieved or not when I opened the door. The room was in darkness. Not a sound met my ears but the tiny, almost inaudible, flicker-flicker of the curtains at the open windows. And yet I had the feeling, which I suppose every one knows, that the room was either occupied or had just been occupied. It seemed full of the presence of another person.

I snapped on the electric light, blessing all my gods that the Manor House had an installation. The room was apparently quite empty.

It looked as any woman's room might when she has left it for a few minutes and is just coming back. A chair was half turned away from the dressing-table, as if she had just risen; a pair of slippers lay near it, not placed carefully, but shaken off. The bed . . .

I turned quite cold and sick. For Mrs. Harrington had left her house before noon to go to the Fair; she had been carried back, dead. And her bed was rumpled and disturbed as if she had just risen from it.

I called up all my courage—I had very little left!—and went across to that bed. There was no doubt about it. Some one had lain there—lately. The clothes were rumpled and tossed, and in the pillow there was the unmistakable dent made by a person's head. I touched that dent with a gingerly finger. *It was still warm.*

Again I pulled myself together. I told myself wildly that it was quite possible that Mrs. Harrington had come in from the Fair for a rest during the afternoon, and had lain down on her bed. And again I knew it was rubbish. It was, to begin with, quite unlike Mrs. Harrington to do such a thing; but if she had really been overcome by fatigue, she would never, never have lain on the neat bed, all ready prepared for the night. She had a broad, comfortable sofa in her room. She was the type of woman to whom it would be literally impossible to disturb an orderly bed while there was a perfectly good couch to lie on. And as to getting right *in* to bed, it was ridiculous to think of it. Besides—I remembered it with a shudder—that pillow had been *warm!*

Suddenly I felt overwhelmed by sheer terror. I felt convinced that I was not alone, and, more than that, that the other Presence threatened me. Everything in the room seemed to breathe of their owner—that owner who lay downstairs, pierced through the brain. . . .

I turned and ran. Bruised knee and all, I ran like a hare back to the little friendly room in Celia's corridor, and locked the door behind me.

9

Safely in my own room, with complete silence all about me and the door well and truly locked behind me, I called myself every kind of a fool. One does, you know, when it's over. But I knew quite well that it would take a very great deal to make me go back into that room. If it was a burglar (as I had now persuaded myself it must have been), let him burgle. My conscience wasn't sufficiently highly developed to try to force me to stop him.

I sat down on the edge of my bed, lit a cigarette, and tried to think it over calmly. Suppose some ruffian, a hanger-on, perhaps, of one of the visiting shows which had spoilt Peter's Fair, had heard of the wealth of the Harringtons—or rather of Mrs. Harrington. Suppose he had also heard that the man of the house was away in town. Wouldn't it be quite likely that he might make an attempt at burglary? Of course it was. No one in Ringshall can go to town for the day without the whole village knowing of it. Probably the Squire's absence had been construed into a violent quarrel with his wife, and a dramatic departure for 'foreign parts' by now. Certainly it would be common talk that he was away, and that only women were in the house.

Good enough, so far. But it didn't explain the bed.

Shaken and terrified as I had been, I knew I was right about the bed. It had been disturbed and rumpled by some one other than its owner. Some one had been lying there just before I went in. Yes, only a minute before; for the pillow was cool again two minutes after I had first touched it. Fine linen, like Mrs. Harrington's, cools very fast. And I *knew* it had been warm when I touched it first.

Well, it didn't do any good to lose my hard-earned sleep over the problem. I would leave it till the morning, and talk it over with Roger Cartwright. He wouldn't laugh at my terror, but he would probably have some quite simple suggestion which would solve the mystery. I crushed out the end of my cigarette and tumbled back into bed.

I was dead tired, and I knew that I should sleep now from sheer weariness. My eyelids were heavy already. I felt that I was going to sleep like the dead.

I turned my back to the room, still flooded with silver light, and closed my eyes. And then—my heart gave one heavy, sickening *thump*. I had distinctly heard a stair creak.

I lay rigid, my heart hammering, and listened. There was no doubt about it. Some one was coming, slowly and heavily, up the stairs.

The steps came along the corridor. They stopped. Then—horrors! They turned down the little corridor. Slow, fumbling, stealthy steps, moving towards me—towards me and the sleeping Celia.

They stopped at her door.

I can't tell what I thought or feared. I only felt that something was going to go into Celia's room, where she lay asleep. . . .

I sprang up, and ran, bare-footed as I was, to the door and flung it open. And then I screamed.

My hand had touched another hand. Some one *was* there just between our rooms. As my scream rang, out— (and I blush now to think how high and shrill and terrified a scream it was)—that other hand clutched mine, and a voice said—a shocked, agitated voice:

"My God! What's that? Who is it?"

"Oh, it's you!" I said, and my voice sounded ridiculously shaky and odd. "I forgot you."

"Miss Leslie!" said Godfrey Harrington incredulously. "Why, what on earth—"

"I'm looking after Celia," I began.

"Celia? Celia's not ill, is she?"

I was pleased to hear that his voice was, for once, quite concerned.

"No—not exactly." I wondered how to tell him. "She—she's had a shock."

"A shock? What sort of a shock?"

I wondered if it was fancy, or whether his voice really sounded perturbed, alarmed, almost guilty.

"Mrs. Harrington—" I began—and stuck.

"Yes? What?"

"She's—there's been an accident."

"An accident? To my wife?"

I nodded.

We had moved out into the main corridor now, and I could see his face quite plainly in the brilliant moonlight. I watched him carefully; I was a little afraid of that heart of his. But it was not only that which made me watch. It was his immediate expression. It was surprised—yes; but it was not shocked. Not alarmed. Not even anxious. It was disturbed and—I thought—disappointed. He recovered himself in a second—so soon that I began to doubt whether I really had seen anything but the concern which his whole face now showed.

"Is it serious?" he asked.

"Very."

He took a step towards me.

"She—she's not *dead?*"

I nodded. I couldn't speak to him. There had been a look on his face . . .

"Agatha! Dead!"

There could be no doubt about his tone now. It was absolutely all it ought to be. I was furious with myself for that other impression I had had.

"How did it happen?" he asked then.

"No one knows. Her body was found on Foakes Green, the brain pierced by some weapon."

"You have—what steps have you taken?"

"The doctor has been, and the police have been over from Newbury. They are coming again to-morrow—I mean to-day—at ten."

He was silent. I still watched him intently. For I could not be sure, even now, that when he had first heard the truth, his tone, as he said "She's not *dead?*" had not been one of—relief.

"Where is she?" he asked then; and at the question I had a thrill of hope. Suppose he had come in earlier, when I was first asleep. Suppose he had gone into his wife's room—feeling ill, perhaps, and needing her. He was the kind of man who must have some one round when he feels ill. Suppose he had gone in, found the room empty, and lain down on her bed . . .

This all passed through my head in a second—so fast that, before I realized the great difficulty, that no one was there when I went in, only a minute later, I spoke.

"When did you get back?" I asked.

"Just now—five minutes ago."

"Did you go to her—to Mrs. Harrington's room?"

He stared at me.

"Just now? No, of course not. Is—is—*she*—there?"

From that question I knew he was telling the truth.

"No," I replied, half absently.

"Why did you ask?"

"I—oh, I just wondered."

I don't know why I didn't tell him. Partly, I think, it was because I was suddenly so very tired. I felt I simply couldn't say another word, let alone tell a story like that, which it frightened me even to think of.

"I was just going to see if Celia was asleep," he went on. "I was going to say—to say good-night."

Tired as I was, I knew that he hadn't meant to end his sentence like that. "To say good-night" was an after-thought. Besides, Godfrey Harrington did not, normally, bother to go, at 2.30 a.m., to see if Celia was asleep—especially not when he'd had a very long day in town and he was tired—and I remembered that the steps on the stairs had sounded very weary. Another puzzle!

"Do go back to bed, won't you?" he said then.

"Yes, I will. You don't want anything?"

For, even to my hard heart, he looked ill and haggard in the white, pitiless light of the moon. And, hate it as much as I might, he did have that heart.

"Oh no, thanks, nothing at all," he said hurriedly—too hurriedly for a selfish man. "I'll just go down and—and lock up. . . . Where did you say . . ." His voice trailed off. I grasped his meaning, however.

"In her little study. The door is locked."

"Thank you. Good-night," he said, and turned back to the stairs.

I went back to my room and lay down again. This time I felt as if I should never sleep again. It was too much of an effort to try even to do that. But my eyelid closed almost at once. As I felt the blessed mists of sleep stealing over me I heard—or thought I heard—a sound which at the time I merely accepted. But in the morning when I woke, I remembered the sound very clearly; and then it did occur to me to wonder why, and to whom, the bereaved husband of a murdered woman had telephoned at three o'clock in the morning.

I dressed with the sound of it in my head, and the thought of it suggested others. There seemed to me, looking back on it, several rather odd things about Godfrey Harrington's behaviour that night. First, it was unlike him to get back, after a tiring day in town, as late as 2.30. But it must have been quite that when I heard him first. I had gone to bed at half-past one, had slept, had been awakened, had paid that visit to Mrs. Harrington's room, had smoked a cigarette, gone back to bed and nearly to sleep again, all before he paid his visit to the little corridor. Then why had he come to that corridor at all? Not really to say good-night to Celia. Celia, like all Ringshall girls, is always asleep by midnight; and even if she hadn't been, Godfrey Harrington would never have bothered to go to her after a tiring day in town—unless, of course, he wanted something. But he declared, when I offered to get him anything he might need, that he wanted nothing. Then, had he *really* sounded relieved when he first heard that his wife was dead? It was a horrible idea; but then he was a singularly selfish, cold-hearted man, in spite of his 'affairs,' and we all knew—or thought we knew—that Mrs. Harrington no longer had the hold over him she had once had. He was tired of her energy and her imperious management of him. He was, to speak the truth, tired of her. So that might be an explanation—if I had been right, that is, about his immediate reaction to the news of her death. But—last and almost greatest problem of all—why had he telephoned? To whom? At three o'clock in the morning, who (except a doctor or the police) could have been likely to be up and give him an answer? *Was* it a doctor or the police? Had he simply wanted to corroborate my statement that both had already done what they could for the moment?

I could not help, in my own mind, fitting the two incidents of the night together. If the Squire had got in earlier, and had been upstairs, my first, and most alarming, experience was explained. But not entirely. For why, if it had been he I heard in his wife's room, had he vanished when he heard the noise of my fall? Where had he vanished to? He was quite ready to speak to me later on, when I must have startled him quite as much by that shriek. Besides, I felt quite sure that he had been prepared to hear me say that his wife's body was laid out in that bedroom. He certainly had appeared quite astonished when I asked if he had been in before.

Another idea struck me. Suppose Godfrey Harrington walked in his sleep? Suppose he had come in some time before I heard him, tired out, had sat down for a moment, and fallen asleep. He might then have come up, still in his sleep, to his wife's room and lain down.

That sounded all right till you came to the same snag— what had become of him when I went into the room? If he had been moving in his sleep, wouldn't the sound of my fall have woken him? Wouldn't he have come out and asked what was wrong, and where he was? No. Tempting as it was, I had to admit that there didn't appear to be any connexion between the visitor to Mrs. Harrington's room and Godfrey Harrington's unexpected appearance in the little corridor. I gave it up, and went down to breakfast.

10

I was alone at that rather dreary meal. The maid who had come back with daylight, laid me a small place on the vast and gleaming table in the great correct, formal room. Celia, they said, was still asleep and her father had been down early and gone out. Yet another unusual thing for Godfrey Harrington to do!—especially after a day in town, a late return, and a shock such as he had found to greet him.

I was still at table when I saw Dr. Ludlow's car approach, and I hurried out to meet him. He looked tired and worried, and rather abstracted, as if his mind were occupied, with a problem.

"Harrington back yet?" he asked, after we had exchanged greetings.

"Back from London, do you mean? Or from his walk?"

"*Walk?* Has the man gone out for a little stroll?" he asked, with heavy sarcasm.

"Doctor, that's unfair," I remonstrated. "If he had, it would be a very sensible thing to do. But he's probably gone to see the police—or you—or to look at Foakes Green—or anything."

The doctor grunted.

"P'r'aps," he admitted grudgingly. "How's Celia?"

"Still asleep—or was, half an hour ago."

"Good. I'll just go and have a look at her. She'll have to see that inspector, you know, when he comes. So will Harrington."

It was then that I noticed that the door of the little study was open.

"Oh," I cried, "have you—?"

He nodded.

"Yes. I took the body away early and did the p.m."

"Did you find . . . ?" I half whispered.

He looked at me oddly.

"If you don't mind—I think I'd better not say anything till I've seen Inspector Grier. It's—*damn* queer," he added to himself.

He went up then to see Celia. I accompanied him, partly for convention's sake, partly to see the child for myself, and partly to occupy my thoughts. Warm and fine as the morning was, I didn't want to hang idly about the house and garden, with nothing but riddles and puzzles—and unpleasant riddles and puzzles at that—to dwell on.

Celia was awake, and quite wonderfully steady and controlled. She had, of course, had a good eight hours' sleep to steady her; but she was naturally a girl of courage and good sense. She seemed to realize perfectly that she must put in an appearance at the coming inquiry, and to be prepared, though rather reluctant, to do so.

I stayed with her while she dressed, talking a little, and trying incidentally to extract, quietly, a little information. Fortunately she gave me a lead by asking after her father.

"Of course he—knows?" she said, with a just perceptible catch in her voice.

"Yes. I told him when he came in last night."

"Was he frightfully upset?"

"He took it very well," I said guardedly.

Celia said nothing. She was stooping down, fastening her shoe, so I couldn't see her face.

"He came along to see if you were all right," I mentioned casually.

"Me?" She looked up, clearly astonished. *"Father* came to see *me?"*

"Doesn't he, as a rule? If you've gone to bed when he's out or anything?"

"Heavens, no! Why should he? How awfully nice of him to bother! I suppose he thought I might be—worrying."

I didn't disillusion her by telling her that Godfrey Harrington had paid his visit to her room before he knew of his wife's death. If she could bolster up an admiration for her father somehow, I thought she'd better. It seemed to me it was going to get a shaking.

"How did father seem?" she asked next.

"He was tired. He didn't get in until after two. But he didn't seem ill." I paused, and then added, "I'm afraid he didn't sleep well. He was up very early."

She looked concerned. I went on, as casually as I could:

"Is he often restless at night? Does he dream, or walk in his sleep, or anything?"

"No," she replied, and her voice was surprised. "I've never heard that he did. And I should be sure to know if he had bad nights."

Of course she would. Godfrey Harrington being what he is, so would every one in Ringshall. Another theory gone! Luckily, I hadn't much believed in it.

At this point a maid came and knocked. I opened the door.

"Please, miss, it's the police," the girl whispered, her eyes wide and rather scared. "They want the master, miss, but I can't find him. Will you come, please, miss?"

I went down at once. It struck me, as I came down the wide stair, that the grouping in the hall was almost exactly as it had been last night—the inspector from Newbury, Gregory, Roger Cartwright (who must have been collected by the police as they passed), and another constable. Only the whole atmosphere was changed. Last night, with the moonlight mingling with electricity to produce an odd, almost weird effect, the hall had seemed a fit stage for tragedy. Now, with the brave sunlight flooding the place, and the sunlit garden showing through the open door instead of the mysterious dim trees and moonlit lawns, it looked cheerful, comfortable, even business-like. My spirits rose enormously.

"Good morning, Inspector," I said, as he greeted me. "I'm so sorry, Mr. Harrington doesn't seem to be in yet. He went out after breakfast. But Miss Harrington is up, and she will see you if you like."

"Thank you, madam. Yes, if Mr. Harrington is out, I should like to see the young lady. But I thought I left a message asking Mr. Harrington to be present?"

"You did. But, to tell you the truth, Inspector, I can't remember whether I gave it. I think I did, but I can't be sure. You see, we had a rather agitated night—and he came in very late—and I had to tell him the news . . ."

"Quite so. I quite understand, madam. He will be in soon, I suppose?"

"Oh, certainly, I should say."

I was relieved at the calm way in which he took it. I was rather scared of the police in connexion with death. From the many books I had read, they always seemed to have such enormous power and to arrest people so casually.

"Shall I call Miss Harrington?" I asked.

"Thank you. Is there any small room we could use to conduct the inquiry? This is rather—er—public."

"I can't, of course, give over any room to you," I said. "This isn't my house. I'm only a guest. But I should think you might use this little morning-room for the time being."

I opened the door, and he and his officer (who, I now saw, was something superior to the ordinary bobby) went in. Then I went and fetched Celia.

"You'll stay with me, won't you?" she whispered as we crossed the hall. She was outwardly perfectly collected, but the nervous squeeze she gave my fingers told another tale.

"I'll try," I promised. "I will, if they'll let me."

They did. They were, to do them justice, very nice, both to Celia and to me. The inspector even welcomed my rather hesitating suggestion that I should be present.

"Not that I expect Miss Harrington is going to need any nursing," he said, with quite a nice smile at Celia. "I'm not going to alarm her or worry her. Only of course it will be pleasanter for her to have a friend handy."

He set chairs for us, and sat down himself at a small table where he had laid out sheets of blank paper and a fountain-pen.

"Now first, Miss Harrington," he began, "I want to ask you some general questions about Mrs. Harrington. She was your stepmother, I understand?"

"Yes."

"Had you known her long, previous to her marriage with your father?"

"Not very long. She'd been in the village some time, I believe—about three years—but I was at school when she first came. I have only known her eighteen months or so."

"What was the date of her marriage with your father?"

"November 19, 1926."

"That is, just about the time that you came home?"

"I came home the following Christmas."

"I see. Now, don't think me impertinent if I ask you some rather personal questions. Were you very intimate with your stepmother?"

The girl hesitated. Then—

"No," she said in a low voice. "I—we—I'm afraid we didn't get on very well."

"Would you have known of it if she had any special worry—any financial trouble, say?"

Again Celia hesitated.

"Well," she said at last, "I shouldn't have known for certain—I mean, she wouldn't have told me. She'd have thought I was too much of a child. But then, I doubt if she'd have *told* any one. She was very reserved about her private affairs."

"You say she wouldn't have told any one. But you might have guessed if anything had been wrong?"

"Ye—es," she admitted reluctantly.

"And you did think so, didn't you?"

"I—no—well, yes, I did," Celia blurted out. "But I was quite probably wrong," she added hurriedly. "I—it was only guessing."

"Yes, I quite understand that. But we have to do a certain amount of guessing sometimes, Miss Harrington. Now I take it that you are as anxious as we all are to clear up the mystery of this poor lady's death?"

"Of course."

"In that case—and for that reason only—I want you to tell me what you thought was wrong, and why you thought so."

Again she hesitated.

"It—it seems so *rotten,*" she burst out then, "to pry now when she can't stop us—when she'd have hated it so—"

"But if it's to find out who—or what—was the cause of her death? Isn't that a bit different?" Inspector Grier put in gently. I liked that man, even though I knew his nice manner was all to serve his own ends.

"Yes . . . I suppose . . . After all, it's not much. I thought she'd seemed worried for some months past. Since just before last Christmas, I remember, because I thought perhaps it was just bills and bothering about parties and things for the village. But it wasn't that. It went on, and got worse. She used to watch the post very carefully. Lawson—that's the parlourmaid—had orders to bring all the letters to her as soon as the post arrived in the morning; and she would never be out at post-time in the evening, not even for a committee. She always managed to see all the letters before any one else."

"Was that all that made you think there was something wrong?"

"Not quite. She was a very rich woman, you know; but for the last five or six months—since a little before Christmas—she'd become frightf'ly careful—cut down her own personal expenses in every possible way. Even father noticed it, because I remember his saying one day that surely she needn't bother to economize when she had so much of her own."

"And what did she say to that?"

"She—well, she rather snubbed him. She said her personal expenditure was her own affair. And of course it was."

"Of course. . . . Did she have any callers—apart, I mean, from her village acquaintances? Did any stranger come to see her?"

"Not that I know of. But I think she thought some one might."

"What makes you think so?"

"Because she was so very particular about telephone calls. She always liked to take them herself, though it's really Lawson's job, of course. She was quite annoyed once when I took one which was for her, though it was quite a trivial message from a tradesman. I told her some one whose voice I didn't know was asking for her, and she was awfully ang—upset."

"Did she tell you it was a tradesman?"

"Yes. A new fishmonger."

"Hm." The inspector paused a moment, and began drawing a little pattern of dots on his blotting-paper. Then he said in a meditative voice:

"And this began about Christmas of last year and has gone on ever since?"

"No. It began about Christmas all right—rather before, I think—but it had stopped."

"*Stopped?*" He sounded very much taken aback.

Celia nodded.

"It stopped—oh, about six weeks or more ago. It made a tremendous difference to her. She altered quite a lot."

"How?"

"Well, she'd been sort of—I don't know how to put it—not cowed, that's much too strong—but *distraite,* irritable, undecided, quite unlike herself. And then she got quite all right. She got energetic, interested in things. She began to spend freely on her clothes and things. But she was still very particular about the post and the telephone. I'd have thought that was her natural reserve, only that she usedn't to bother when I first came home."

The inspector sat silent, elaborating his pattern of dots. Then he said:

"Miss Harrington, I know you can't tell me anything certain. But didn't you make any guess as to the reason for your stepmother's conduct?"

Celia hesitated.

"I'm sure you must have," he said persuasively. "Any one would. You must have made some sort of guess. Didn't you?"

"I—well, I did think about it. I—I may have thought— oh, all sorts of silly things."

"Such as—?"

"At first I thought it might be *my* correspondence she was interested in; but I soon saw it wasn't. Then I began to wonder if she'd been doing something silly—something she was ashamed of—perhaps some sort of gambling. I thought it was just possible that she might have made her money like that in the beginning, and, having done well at it, had determined never to do it again, and be very good, you know. And then she might have been drawn in again—I suppose it would be frightf'ly fascinating— and lost money—a lot of money—and been dunned. That would account for her being all right for money at first, and then suddenly being so careful, and for her being anxious, about the same time, that no one should get letters or messages meant for her."

The inspector nodded.

"I don't call that silly at all," he said. "I shouldn't wonder if you might be pretty near the truth."

There was a short silence. Then the inspector began again.

"Do you happen to know what sort of life Mrs. Harrington led before she came to Ringshall? Did she live in town? Had she many friends?"

Celia shook her head.

"I've no idea. She's never spoken to me of her past life."

"Has she friends of her own, made before she knew you?"

"I don't know."

"She hasn't had visitors? Hasn't a large correspondence?"

"She hasn't had any one to stay here. Correspondence— oh yes, she had an enormous number of letters. She had a lot of interests, you know—societies and things," said Celia vaguely.

"But not a large private correspondence?"

"I can't tell. You see, I never saw the incoming post— that is, not the past six months or so. But once—"

"Yes?" he encouraged her, as she paused.

"Once—in February, it was—I happened to go in to her study just after the post had come in, and she—she was most awfully upset. . . . It mayn't mean much to you, as you didn't know her, but she—she'd been *crying.*"

Celia's voice sounded quite shocked.

"Oh! And that was unusual?"

"Unusual? If I hadn't seen her with my own eyes I'd have said it was impossible! I was so surprised that I did an idiotic thing—I asked her what was wrong, and if I could help."

Celia flushed scarlet. I guessed at the nature of the reception of that impulsive sympathy and offer.

"What did she say?" The inspector bent forward eagerly.

Poor Celia crimsoned still more.

"She didn't want my help," she said shortly.

"Did she say so?"

"Not exactly. She said she'd had a sharp attack of toothache."

"Well?"

"Well—she couldn't have. I knew (though I don't think she knew I did) that she hadn't any of her own teeth."

"I see." The inspector's tone was quite grave, but the hand at his moustache was a little obvious. "So you thought it was something she didn't want you to know about?"

"I'm certain it was. But that's nothing to go on, you know. She was very reserved to every one, and especially to me."

"Why 'especially to you'?"

Celia moved uneasily.

"We—we didn't understand each other. She thought I was just a spoilt little girl who needed keeping in her place. And I—I'm afraid I wasn't very n—nice to her.' She bit her lip, which was trembling a little. 'I didn't l—like her marrying father. I wouldn't have liked any one to d—do that. And I resented her t—trying to keep me in order." She flushed again, that deep, tell-tale crimson.

"That was getting worse, wasn't it—your mutual dislike?"

Celia nodded.

"It does, if you have to live together," she pointed out.

"Yes; but there was a reason, wasn't there? An extra reason for your not hitting it off?"

She reddened again, but she met his eyes squarely.

"You mean my engagement. Yes. She didn't like it."

"You are engaged?"

"Not yet. But I mean to be, and I said I did."

"And that was why you thought, at one time, that it might be your correspondence that she wished to watch."

"Yes."

"She objected to the idea of your engagement?"

"Yes. She said I wasn't old enough."

"Was that her only reason?"

Celia was silent. Her flush had faded entirely.

"Isn't it the case that she didn't approve of your choice?"

The girl sprang to her feet.

"My affairs have nothing to do with this inquiry!" she declared defiantly. "Why do you ask me about my engagement? It's got nothing to do with—with my stepmother's death."

"No, of course not," he soothed her. "Never mind about that. Tell me now about yesterday. Where did you spend the day?"

Celia sat down again, looking like a sulky child.

"The first part of the morning I was in the house. My father was going to town, and there were odd jobs to do for him; and there were some people—Sir Digby and Lady Barnet, Lady Carruthers, and one or two others—coming to lunch. My stepmother was busy over the Fair, and I stayed to look after things. I went down to the Fair about eleven, or a little earlier."

"You were with these visitors?"

"At first. I didn't stay with them, I got too bored," said Celia frankly. "I joined on to first one friend and then another." She had the grace to blush as she caught my eye. The inspector said nothing, but I felt sure he had noticed the glance and guessed what it meant. "About one, my stepmother sent me home. She said that as the maids were out, some one ought to be in. So I went back. I sat about—read, wrote some letters—put in time generally. Our visitors came in to tea about five. My stepmother told me then that she wished me to be in all the rest of the day, in case my father came back. She would be at the Fair until eight or half-past, and was then going to see Ben Salt, one of the maids' father. She said I wasn't to go to supper with Miss Leslie, as we'd arranged, because she didn't expect to be in before eleven. She'd told me that before, at the Fair, but I expect she wanted to make sure that I understood. And she hadn't said before that I wasn't to go out to supper. P'r'aps she didn't know I was going."

"Did you do as she said?"

"Yes—practically. I hung about, had an early supper, and got things ready for my father. About nine I rang up Miss Leslie to say I couldn't come."

"Had you been alone all the time?"

Celia flushed again.

"Not quite. Mr. Earle came up with a message, and stopped to talk a bit."

So that was how Stephen had known that Celia couldn't come to my party.

"At what time did he come?"

She thought a moment.

"About a quarter or half-past six, I should think. He left a little after seven."

"Yes. Did you remain alone all the rest of the evening?"

"No. I got sick of it. About a quarter to ten, or a little later perhaps, I thought I'd run over to Miss Leslie's just for a few minutes. I'd been alone most of the day, and I wanted a chat. I knew my father, as he hadn't got in before, must be coming by the 10.12. It takes him about twenty minutes at least to get up to the house, so I thought if I went at half-past ten or so, it'd be all right. I stayed at Miss Leslie's until half-past ten, and then Mr. Cartwright and Mr. Earle said they'd see me home."

"Did they accompany you all the way?"

"N—not quite. Mr. Cartwright had to go in to his lodgings for something, and we—Mr. Earle and I—walked on."

"He took you right across the Green?"

Celia hesitated for the fraction of a second. A queer, obstinate look came over her face.

"Yes," she said then.

"You were together when you found the body?"

"I—I didn't see it at first. Stephen—Mr. Earle—saw it first."

"Did he call your attention to it at once?"

"Y—yes."

Again there was that hint of hesitation.

"What did he say?"

"He said, 'Celia, come home at once,' or something like that."

"Do you mean that he said that before you saw the body?"

"Y—yes."

"But how was it that you hadn't seen it, if he had?"

She said nothing.

"Come now, Miss Harrington. Isn't it the case that you were not there at all when the body was found?"

I jumped in my chair. I'd never thought of this. I couldn't think why, having been tactfully left alone, Celia and Stephen should have separated.

"Isn't it?" persisted the inspector.

"I—I'd passed it," she muttered. "I did see something, but I thought it was just a pile of sacks, or awnings, or something. I could tell from the way Ste—Mr. Earle spoke that there was something serious the matter. I don't know why, but I thought at once of that pile. I turned towards it, I remember, and he caught hold of me, and said, 'Don't look.' I said, 'What is it? Is some one ill?' He—Stephen—looked *awful*. He hates to see things hurt. He just said again, 'Don't look.' I thought I ought to go and see what was wrong, in case I could help—I've done first aid and all that—and I ran across."

She stopped and gulped.

"I—I'm rather mixed after that. Mr. Cartwright was there—I don't know when he came—perhaps he was following us—he meant to—and he told Stephen to take me home. But I said he mustn't stay—it wasn't fair to—to her. So after a bit he went. But he'd have stayed to help if I'd let him."

"Yes. . . . Well, Miss Harrington, you've given me a lot of help. I won't bother you any more just now."

Celia rose with alacrity. I was just going to follow her when the door opened, and Godfrey Harrington, looking both angry and distraught, came in.

"Inspector, what is this I hear?" he cried. "Is it true that a post-mortem examination has been made on my wife's body without my consent?"

"Quite true, sir. You were not available." The inspector's tone was dry.

"It's monstrous!" exclaimed the Squire. "I ought to have been consulted."

"We couldn't wait, sir."

"Has—has anything been found?"

"A very curious thing has been found, sir. Mrs. Harrington's death was caused by the brain being pierced by a fragment of stone."

"*Stone?*" gasped the Squire.

"Yes, sir. By what is believed to be a flint arrowhead. What they call an elf-bolt. It has been driven right through the skull. It must have killed her immediately."

11

We were all silent for a moment after that. Personally, I felt *awful*. That it should have been one of those wicked, primeval weapons of stone that had killed her seemed to me to be the final touch of horror. It linked up with the whole business of that terrible Fair—the whispers, the fear of the villagers, the mumbled curse of the 'witch.' I felt as if I had seen with my own eyes the hated woman crossing the Green—that Green haunted by a thousand fears, by the memory of nameless sacrifices—in the aloof, cold light of the mysterious moon. I could see the curse taking effect—could hear the whizz as the elf-bolt—the stone sharpened by other stones, by a forgotten race, to a point of cruel sharpness—darted through the quiet night air. . . .

I pulled myself together. This was sheer nonsense, old wives' tales. Yet I could not help a cold shudder as I thought of what had happened in the night—the silent, secret visitor to the dead woman's room lying on her bed. You might explain the bolt. I didn't yet see how, but it might be done. But I couldn't think how you could explain that tumbled bed, warm from a vanished cheek . . .

I sat up with a jerk. While I had been dreaming the inspector had been getting on with the work. Celia had gone; I dare say I was forgotten. Anyhow, no one seemed to mind me, so I stayed where I was and listened.

"—in town all day," I heard Godfrey Harrington finish a sentence.

"You started early?"

"Fairly early. I'm not an early riser."

"What train did you catch?"

"I got the 1.24 express from Savernake."

"How did you get to Savernake?"

"I walked to Dimsey, and took the 12.51 from there to Savernake. I left home about twelve, or a little before."

"And before that—before you left home?"

"Oh—I don't know—I don't think I did anything much."

"Just hung about at home?"

"Exactly."

"Didn't go out at all?"

"No. I was making small preparations for my visit to town."

Mentally I opened my eyes. I remembered that Roger Cartwright had said distinctly that he had seen the Squire at the Fair. It was so unusual for Godfrey Harrington to have bothered with the village boys that I was sure he could not really have forgotten that he'd done it. But, of course, I said nothing. It wasn't my affair. Besides, I wasn't going to draw attention to myself.

"Let's see," said the inspector, "that 1.24 gets to town somewhere about four, doesn't it?"

"Just after. Ten past, I think, to be precise."

"Rather late, wasn't it, for a business visit?"

"Not for my business. I wanted to see a friend who was leaving town unexpectedly."

"When was he leaving?"

"Last night; he was sailing by the night boat to Calais."

"Do you mind giving me his name?"

"Not at all. It was Mr. Henry Felton, of the firm of Felton and James, Solicitors."

"You wished to see him on legal business?"

"Well—partly, though it was in a private capacity. We are personal friends."

"It was pressing, I take it?"

"Well—it was like this. It would have done in a week's time, or even a month. But Mr. Felton is to be away for some time, on account of his health, and is travelling—leaving no settled address."

"Why didn't you go before?"

The Squire made a little deprecating movement.

"I'm incurably lazy," he confessed, with a little smile. "I hate going to town, and I kept putting it off. I realized suddenly that Felton was due to leave England at once, so I wired to him to expect me, and went up."

"I see. Did you wire the day before?"

He hesitated for the fraction of a second. Then he said:

"No. It wasn't till yesterday morning that I remembered that Felton was due to sail that very day. I wrote out a wire in the train between Dimsey and Savernake, and gave it to a porter at Savernake to send. But I found, when I met Felton, that he'd never got the wire. I suppose the porter shoved it in his pocket and forgot all about it."

"But you met your friend all right?"

"Yes, by a stroke of luck. I met him on the pavement, just outside his rooms. We had some tea together in a shop, and then we walked about in St. James's Park, discussing my business. It was rather absorbing, and I realized suddenly that I should only just have time to catch my train. We parted rather hurriedly, and I got an Underground train to Paddington, hoping to catch the 6.27, which would land me at Savernake in time for me to get a connexion to Dimsey that would let me catch a 'bus almost as far as Ringshall. Unfortunately I just missed the train. There isn't another direct to Savernake, so I decided to wait for the 8.47 to Newbury, and get on from there. I

had some dinner, got the train, took the 10.42 from Newbury to Savernake, getting in somewhere about half-past
eleven. I couldn't get on to Dimsey, either by train or 'bus,
and I couldn't get a conveyance so late; but it was a lovely night, and I decided to walk. I did that, and got home
about half-past two. It's only a little over ten miles."

"Did your family know that you meant to spend the
day in town?"

"My wife did. I don't know if she told the household."

"Did she know what train you meant to come home by?"

Godfrey Harrington looked surprised.

"I really don't know. I don't think we discussed it.
Why?"

"Both your wife and daughter seem to have expected
you any time after 4.30."

The Squire thought a moment.

"It's possible," he said then, "that as my wife was out so
much in the morning, she didn't realize that I'd made such
a late start. She may have thought that I'd gone a couple
of hours earlier than I did, and gone up by the 11.8. If I'd
done that, I could have got back by the train that gets in
to Dimsey at 7.19, and taken the 'bus home. But I couldn't
possibly have been back before that. I certainly told my
wife that I couldn't say when I'd be in, and that no one was
to wait up for me."

Of course, preparation for the Squire had been a mere
excuse to get Celia home. I thought I could explain that to
the inspector later, if the point interested him. Meanwhile
he was carrying on.

"Did either your wife or your daughter know what was
your business with this Mr. Felton?"

Harrington flushed a little.

"No," he said in a low voice.

"Can you give me any idea of what it was?"

"I—I'd like—I'd very much rather not."

There was something almost pleading in his voice.

"Is Mr. Felton your ordinary solicitor?"

"Yes."

"He knows your private affairs pretty intimately?"

"Yes."

"Have you made your will?"

The question was shot out quite sharply; but either Godfrey Harrington was prepared for it, or he wasn't interested in it.

"Yes. I made a new one at the time of my marriage."

"And your wife?"

"I don't know. She was very secretive about her affairs, and I—I didn't like to ask her." He flushed a little. I could see that it might be awkward, when you'd married a woman as rich as Mrs. Harrington, and were yourself chronically hard up.

"Yet it's likely that she did make one, I suppose? I understand she was a very wealthy woman."

"I can't tell you. Yes, I imagine she did. But I don't know. I don't even know who was her lawyer, though I suppose she had one."

The inspector paused again. Then he fired another surprising shot.

"Mr. Harrington, is it true that you were contemplating a separation from your wife?"

I jumped. The Squire had turned a ghastly greyish colour.

"I—I—no—no, it's a lie, a damned lie!" he gasped.

"You didn't go to consult Mr. Felton on the point?"

"I—no, of course not! I never thought of such a thing. I don't understand you, Inspector. This is a damnable insult!"

He sat up. A little colour struggled back into his face.

"You must forgive me," he went on, in a more natural tone. "It gave me a shock to hear you suggest such a thing—

with such a terrible separation as has come to us. I think I can explain the rumours you have no doubt heard. It is quite true that at one time my wife and I were—weren't—didn't seem able to hit it off very well. She was a very energetic and capable woman, and I thought she didn't make enough allowance for my delicate health and—and general temperament. That was absolutely all there was to it. You find these little—er—frictions in any household. As a matter of fact, our life—my wife's and mine—was singularly happy and peaceful. She was a wonderful manager and organizer, and I had the greatest respect and admiration and—and love—for her. I can't describe to you how overcome I was at the news of her death."

He stopped. It sounded most convincing and pathetic; and yet—he hadn't been so overcome but that he could telephone, a few minutes later, to some one . . .

A thought struck me. Suppose he *had* been trying to arrange a separation, and that he had been calling up this Mr. Felton, at his hotel at Dover or Southampton or wherever it was, to tell him that—well, that he'd got it? I knew that there had been plenty of rifts in the Harrington lute, whatever Godfrey Harrington might say about its wonderful harmony. And I think Inspector Grier thought so, too. I dare say Celia had told him more than she thought she had.

"Now, Mr. Harrington, I want you to answer this very carefully. Can you honestly say that you have never once contemplated the idea of getting a separation from your wife?"

Again the Squire went that ghastly colour. He hesitated, gasping rather painfully.

"Of course, you needn't answer me if you don't want to," Grier went on, "but it's common talk that you did, and you're sure to be asked about it at the inquest."

Harrington put up his hand as if he wanted to loosen his collar.

"I—some months ago, in a fit of foolish irritation, I believe I said some such thing," he muttered. "It was the kind of thing one; says in anger, and regrets ever after. I never, even when I said it, expected my wife to take it seriously."

"But she did?"

"Y—yes—yes, she did. She—she took things very literally always. She answered quite seriously, saying that it would be against her principles to do such a thing. Of course, I had never really meant it."

"Never?"

"Never."

"How long is it since you said this to your wife?"

"Oh—I don't know—weeks, months, perhaps. But I remember that I noticed, just after I had spoken, that a maid was passing the open door. I thought at the time that there would be a report spread that we were separating. I explained to my wife that I had never really meant it, hoping that the maid would have been interested enough to hang about and listen, and would hear me say so."

"And no more was said on the subject?"

"Not a word. We had other little—er—differences, but of late things had been much easier, and we seemed to have got on to a new and better understanding. We—we were very happy."

He overdid it that time. Personally I felt sick, and I saw Inspector Grier's face harden.

"That was fortunate," he said, with the least possible emphasis on the last word. A short pause seemed to drive the implication home.

"Now, Mr. Harrington," he went on, in a pleasanter voice, "what about your movements on the twenty-eighth,

the day before the death? What did you do on Thursday—
you and your wife?"

The Squire considered.

"Thursday? What did I do on Thursday?" he pondered.
Then "Oh, I remember! I walked over to Devizes to see the
museum. I'd heard it was a good one of its kind, and generally very quiet. I left home early, about half-past nine,
and walked gently over, taking lunch on the way, and got
to Devizes in the early afternoon. I strolled round the
museum, looked in at one or two old curiosity shops, had
tea, and came back as far as Dunstall by the 'bus. From
there I walked home."

"Quite a long day," commented the inspector. "It must
be twelve miles or more to Devizes."

"Yes, it's quite that. Oh, I can do a good day's walk
with any one so long as I'm not hurried," said the Squire
complacently. "Hurry and shock, agitation of any kind—
I'm very seriously warned against those, Inspector. But,
apart from my heart trouble, I'm not at all a weakling. If
I had been, I should have thrown up the sponge long ago."

The inspector, a little dryly, congratulated him. But I
noticed that he squashed his victim's pitiful effort to drag
a red herring across the trail.

"Did you buy anything at Devizes? From the curiosity
shops, for instance?"

"No. The tea-shop was the only one I actually entered,
and that was very full. I had to wait a very long time."

"You were alone on this expedition, I take it. What was
your wife doing that day?"

"Ah, there I can't help you, I'm afraid. My daughter
might know. But, you see, I was out all day."

"Quite."

Inspector Grier continued to embroider his little design
dots, studying it with an absorbed expression. I watched
his face and decided I liked it quite a lot. He might not be

brilliant, but he looked careful, patient, and, I thought, shrewd. I wondered whether he would laugh me to scorn if I told him of the curious episode of Mrs. Harrington's bedroom. I almost thought I'd try.

12

I could hardly hope that I should be allowed to remain where I was during all the interviews which Inspector Grier held with his various witnesses. He certainly hadn't forgotten that I was there. I hardly hoped he would, he was far too much on the spot; but I rather admired him for letting me know he hadn't, as soon as he got rid of the Squire.

"Do you know Mr. Harrington well, Miss Leslie?" he asked in a friendly, conversational sort of voice.

"Fairly well," I said cautiously.

He smiled at me, and I couldn't help smiling back; his twinkle was infectious.

"Had you heard this rumour of a separation between him and his wife?"

"No. But then it doesn't really pay to listen to Rings-hall gossip. There's too many stories without any foundation except hope."

"Wish father to the thought, eh?"

"Exactly."

"There seems to have been a lot of gossip about this poor lady," he suggested.

"Oh yes, there was. Hints at a lurid past, and all sorts of things. So there would be about any stranger who wasn't too popular."

"Why was she so much disliked?" he asked, with a pleasant air of exchanging confidences.

I saw through him, of course, but I didn't a bit mind being pumped.

"Oh, she was tactless," I said. "And—well, a bit conceited. That's enough, you know, in a remote village."

"Rather ran the world, eh? Could have made it better if she'd been consulted at the Creation?"

"Rather like that," I admitted.

"Why was she so much opposed to Miss Harrington's engagement?"

"As Miss Harrington explained—" I began; but he cut me short.

"That's exactly what she didn't do. There was more in it than pure love of interference."

"Well—she, Mrs. Harrington, didn't like Mr. Earle."

"No? Why not? He struck me as a very pleasant young man."

I wondered when they'd met, but I couldn't ask just then.

"He is," I said, "very. But he has no bump of reverence. Also he has practically no money."

"I see. . . . By the way, who is Mrs. Harrington's next-of-kin?"

"I've no idea. I suppose her husband is, if she hasn't left a will. He inherits, doesn't he, if she died intestate?"

"Yes, he's chief legatee. But it doesn't strike me that the lady was the kind who leaves things to chance. She sounds the kind of woman who'd be certain to make a will—if not several wills."

I looked at him with respect.

"That's an extraordinarily good shot," I said. "She was exactly that kind—the will-shaking kind, as Butler calls it. And she was very much the business woman, too—managed all her own investments and so on. She would be sure to make a most detailed distribution of her property."

"But if by any chance she didn't—or if her will can't be found—I suppose her husband would be pretty sure to finance his daughter?"

I got hot.

"He might," I said, "but neither she nor Mr. Earle would take it. They both know that it would be the very last thing Mrs. Harrington would want done with her money. They'd never look at it."

Inspector Grier said nothing to that. He paused a moment and then said:—

"I wonder where she would be likely to keep her will?"

"I've no idea," I said. "In that little study of hers, perhaps, or at her bank."

"Nowhere very obvious, I'll bet," he said thoughtfully. "Nowhere where it could be easily found and read. . . ."

I agreed.

"Did she ever speak to you about her affairs?"

"Never. We weren't in the least intimate. Especially lately."

"Why 'especially lately'?"

"Because I was in the other camp. I backed the engagement."

"Oh, I see." He sat silent, while I tried to summon up my courage to tell him of my fright of the night before. But in the light of day it sounded too absurd, and I have a very strong dislike of appearing absurd, and a still stronger dislike of being put down with kindly contempt as an hysterical female.

"I've seen Mr. Earle," Inspector Grier went on, after a pause. "It seems he was alone when he found the body."

"Alone?" I asked. "Why, where was Celia?"

"It seems that when they—he and Miss Harrington—were getting near the Manor House, she asked him to run back after the parson for something—some paper or other. I gathered that the idea was that she didn't want to be seen coming in with him, and thought she'd get rid of him, or that the parson would come along with him. She seems to have walked on under the oaks, and he ran back, going straight across the Green. He saw the body and at first thought it was some one the worse for drink. When he saw who it was, his first idea was to get Miss Harrington away, but she seems to have guessed that something was in the wind, and looked round to see what all the hurry was about. Why did she tell me that she was with Mr. Earle when he found the body?"

I didn't answer. I knew well enough why she had done so, and I thought it was a silly thing to have done. But I wasn't going to give her away to any inspector, however nice.

"Mr. Earle was quite open," Inspector Grier went on reflectively. "He told me that he and Mrs. Harrington had constant quarrels, and that he had practically been forbidden the house."

"I didn't know it had gone as far as that," I murmured.

"I suppose that would be entirely on account of Miss Harrington?"

"I suppose so. Though Mrs. Harrington never cared much for Mr. Earle, she had no other possible reason for forbidding him the house."

"Mr. Cartwright says that she—Mrs. Harrington—seemed perfectly well on the day of the Fair."

"Oh, certainly. Very well and cheerful. She was enjoying herself thoroughly when I last saw her, about seven or so."

"Miss Leslie, apart from this affair of the engagement, do you know of any one else in the village who had a real grudge against Mrs. Harrington? Any one who would do her an injury—who had even threatened her?"

I hesitated; then I said:

"Two or three people had a real grievance; but I don't think a soul in the village would really have touched her."

"Perhaps not, normally. But wasn't it the case that yesterday the village people were not quite normal?"

Gregory had been talking, obviously. I saw no further need for concealment. So I told him about Joe Greaves's annoyance and about Mrs. Nokes and the curse. And then, emboldened, I told him what had happened the night before.

He listened very gravely. Then he said:

"It's certainly very odd. Have you been into the room this morning?"

"No," I confessed, "not inside. I locked the door this morning, and took out the key. Here it is," and I handed it over.

"Good!" he approved. "That was a wise move. Now, I wonder if you'd mind coming up with me? It would be a very great help if you could tell me if you notice anything more—or anything different—from what you saw last night."

"I'll come, of course," I said, rising. "But I warn you, Inspector, I shan't be much use. After I'd noticed the bed, I saw nothing else. That was enough."

"Quite—I quite understand that. But still, if you don't mind—there might be something—"

We went upstairs together. As we walked, I noticed how lightly and well the man moved. He was tallish and burly, but he moved beautifully, accurately and freely like a trained dancer or gymnast.

"This is the door," I said, pausing.

"And that, I suppose, is the corridor where you and Miss Harrington sleep?"

"Yes. That door on the left is her room; the one opposite is the one I chose."

"Will you show me exactly what your movements were?"

I went down the little passage and opened the door of my room.

"I came out here," I said. "Here, at the junction of the corridors, I paused to listen. The place where I fell would be about here."

"How long do you think it would be from the time when you first heard the sounds to the time when you fell?"

I thought.

"Three or four minutes at the outside."

"And you have no means of judging how long the sounds had been going on?"

"No," I admitted; 'but I am a very light sleeper. My maid says you can wake me by looking at me. If the sounds had been going on long, I think I should have been sure to wake earlier."

"Now, before we go in, will you try to remember everything you saw in the room?"

I thought hard. Open windows with fluttering curtains, a chair turned slightly away from the dressing-table, slippers lying loosely near it, an undisturbed sofa, the bed. . . . That was all.

He unlocked the door, and we went in.

I gasped.

The bed was straight and smooth, the pillows plumped up, and all the windows were closed.

"I—I'm *sure*—" I began feebly. I had never felt such an abject fool in my life.

"What time did the maids return this morning?" he asked.

"They were late. No one called me, even. They were only just in time to get breakfast. Anyhow, they'd never have come in here. They're terrified of—of death."

The inspector walked over to the bed.

"As you remember it, was the bed actually unmade? Or was it as it is now, only rumpled?"

"Unmade, I think—I'm almost sure it was. I remember seeing the covers thrown back, the sheets rumpled. . . . Yes, I'm sure it was unmade."

"Good. That's a help," he said, with satisfaction.

"Why?"

"Because it's been made since, and we ought to be able to find out something about the person who made it."

He examined the surface of the bed minutely, and then very delicately lifted the quilt off. He repeated the process with the counterpane. Then he beckoned to me.

"Look! What do you make of it?" he asked.

I looked at the bed. The top blanket was smooth, but the next showed wrinkles underneath. The sheets were rumpled. The corners showed ends of sheet and blanket sticking untidily out.

"No housemaid made that bed," I said decidedly, "nor even a decently brought up woman. Either it was made in a tearing hurry, or else a man made it."

He nodded.

"Mrs. Harrington was very particular, wasn't she, about her household arrangements?"

"Very."

"She'd have noticed it at once if she'd gone to bed and found it like that?"

"Any one would. It would be wretchedly uncomfortable."

Then a horrid thought struck me.

"Inspector," I gasped, "do you think—did the person who made that bed know that it *wouldn't* be noticed—because—because Mrs. Harrington would never sleep in it?"

He looked at me seriously.

"It's possible, isn't it?" he said quietly. "But it doesn't follow. The bedmaker might simply have been in a tremendous hurry."

"But, look here—when was it remade?" I asked.

"Almost immediately after you left, I should think," he replied. "As soon as it was clear, from the way you ran, that you wouldn't be coming back. The person know that you couldn't be going to fetch help; there was one to fetch."

"You don't—do you mean that there was some one else in here all the time? Hiding?"

(I remembered the impression I had had of an alien presence in the room. Perhaps it hadn't been so far out.)

"Well—don't you think it's likely? You see, the noises went on till you fell. That scared the visitor. He, or she—let's say 'X'—didn't know who was coming, or how soon. There was no time to get away. Naturally, X hid—came out when you'd gone, hurriedly replaced the bed-clothes, and went. I gather that in going, the door was used, and that X closed the window he'd come in by. He—X—made two mistakes. He shouldn't have re-made the bed, and he shouldn't have closed the window."

As he spoke, he was blowing powder—'finger-print powder' I believe it's called—on the window. It didn't seem to have any result.

"Why mistakes? So long as he didn't leave prints, I mean," I said, watching him.

"Of course, X hoped that either you'd say nothing, for fear of being laughed at, or else that your story wouldn't be believed. He didn't want us to take any notice of the bed, as we'd be sure to do if it was found tumbled, as you saw it. So he covered it up, and hoped that, if you said anything, no one would believe that you had seen it un-made at two a.m. He was right not to leave it," he added, with just a touch of triumph, "though wrong in his guess about you."

He *had* found something—not much, but something. On the bottom sheet of the bed there was a purplish stain. It was quite a tiny one, but it seemed familiar somehow.

I'd seen that stain before, quite lately, and tried to get rid of it. The inspector gave me the clue by sniffing at it.

"I know what that is!" I exclaimed. "It's a poppy stain—the mark of a crushed poppy petal."

"Good for you!" said he heartily. "And, if I'm not mistaken, we'll find poppies growing not far off. X must have brought a petal in on his boot."

He went over to the windows and looked out. Immediately under one window there was a huge flamboyant Oriental poppy.

"We know his exact mode of entry now," said the inspector, with satisfaction. "I must get a ladder and have a look at that wall. It's almost impossible to climb a wall and not leave a trace. If you have any more experiences or ideas, Miss Leslie, I hope you'll give me the benefit of them," he added, drawing in from the window. "After Mr. Harrington, you're the most useful person I've met in this case."

"Mr. Harrington? I didn't think *he'd* told you much," I said.

"Oh, he told me a lot. I'm sure he'd be surprised if he knew how helpful he'd been," said the inspector reflectively.

And he opened the door for me most politely.

As I went downstairs, two things were puzzling me. First, what was it that Godfrey Harrington had told the inspector apart from his actual words? Was it his manner that had given away something? Was it what he *hadn't* said? Or had he been lying in some part of his evidence? That, I thought, I could puzzle out by thinking over what he had said. I have an excellent memory for details, and especially for conversations. I felt sure that, if I wrote it down at once, I could remember most of what had passed between Godfrey Harrington and Inspector Grier. Then I'd have to solve that puzzle by means of clues, like a good crossword.

The other thing was this. Granted that Inspector Grier was right (as I had to admit sounded likely) and that some one, man or woman, had got into Mrs. Harrington's room by the window—what was the object of that visit? At the first blush, one would say burglary. But burglary, of the ordinary sort, didn't begin to fit X's actions. The household had been disturbed till late. Surely, if X had been a normal burglar, he'd have put off his visit till a night when we weren't on the *qui vive*. On the other hand, he might have discovered, from the villagers, that the maids were away and the Squire out; but every one expected that the Squire would be in by half-past ten or so, and I didn't see how the villagers could have known that he wasn't—unless, of course, a watch had been kept for his arrival.

Then there was another point. Supposing X had discovered that Godfrey Harrington wasn't back, and had thought the opportunity for burglary a good one, why had he come to Mrs. Harrington's window (which she always kept closed in very hot weather) instead of a ground-floor one? Why climb a wall and force a window when (as I remembered guiltily) there was a library window standing wide open on the ground floor, simply inviting him in? That looked, I thought, as if X knew the house, and wanted something which he (or she) knew to be in Mrs. Harrington's room, and wouldn't risk meeting a stray bobby or some one roaming about the house. If that was so, what would that something be? Jewelry? Letters? Papers of some other kind? Could it be her will? Inspector Grier had seemed inquisitive about her will.

But finally, and most puzzling of all, why in the world had X carefully unmade the bed and made it again? Had he been looking in the bed for whatever it was he wanted? That was possible; but *why had he lain in the bed,* staining the sheet with the poppy petal from his boot, and leaving the print of his head in the pillow?

These questions would have to be solved by sheer brain. I had no clue. But I meant to do my damnedest to find the answers.

13

At the moment, however, it looked as though it was not my immediate job to get on with solving the riddle. It was, I knew, my duty to go and find out how Celia was getting on, and see if she wanted to talk to me about things. Fortunately I met her in the hall, just after I had parted from Inspector Grier, and took her out with me into the garden. The Manor House has quite a good garden. That is, it is spacious and (since Mrs. Harrington's advent) well kept, and nearly always has flowers in it. But I maintain that it is not half as nice as mine, which is smaller and not as well kept (I don't have a man and two boys to deal with mine; one man once a week is my allowance), but which has more flowers, which you can pick. However, such as it was, Celia and I went into it, and sat down under some trees, which are the nicest thing in it.

Celia looked tired and rather grave, but not overcome. I thought it would be good for her to talk for a bit.

"I like that Inspector Grier," I began at once. "He isn't a fool, and therefore he doesn't think every one else is one."

"Been patting you on the back, has he?" said Celia, smiling in a way that did my heart good.

"Yes, he has," I said stoutly. "He has a high opinion of my intelligence."

"Sort of Mutual Admiration Society," murmured Celia.

"Quite. Perhaps I've met my fate at last, Celia. Or do you think he's married?"

"Oh, sure to be. To a nice little roundabout wife who cooks chops for him and says, 'Yes, dear, how clever you are, but where did I put the salt?'" she said bitterly.

"I'm sure he hasn't got a wife in the least like that." I maintained. "He's got too much sense to marry a mere pincushion."

"He hasn't enough sense *to*," she retorted.

"I'm sure he's got loads of sense. Why don't you like him, Celia?"

She fidgeted.

"He asks such perfectly *idiotic* questions," she burst out at last. "What could it matter to him whether I was engaged to Stephen or not?"

"You can't tell," I said, with an air of wisdom which I thought suitable to one who had actually seen a detective on the trail using finger-print powder. "He had his reasons, no doubt."

"Perfectly idiotic reasons!" cried Celia, with pink cheeks. I stared.

"Just because Stephen and she didn't get on—and because he left me, and was by himself on the Green at eleven . . ." she stormed on, "and because he found it. . . . Why, *I* was by myself too—and I was alone before I came to the Dower House—and I disliked her far more than ever poor Stephen did—"

"My dear Celia," I said, "are you trying to tell me that you think Inspector Grier suspects *Stephen* of—of killing Mrs. Harrington?"

"Of course he does!" she raged. "I've seen Stephen. That man saw him first, and asked him all sorts of beastly things—about our engagement, and about whether he had been alone when he found her—and Stephen said he had, of course; but how was I to know that? I thought that rotten inspector would think something foul if I admitted that I hadn't been there, and so I said I had. And he knew all the time I hadn't. And he asked Stephen where he'd been all the evening, and Stephen said with you, and that he'd got to your house before nine. And then he remembered he hadn't been there so early, and the inspector knew he hadn't. *How* did he know if he hadn't been spying round and asking questions? And he asked Stephen if he couldn't produce some one who'd been with him before he came to you, and he couldn't, except me—"

"Oho!" I thought. But I said nothing.

"—and whether he'd been shooting at that rotten show, and—and all sorts of horrible things. As if Stephen *could!* He might just as well suspect me. Perhaps he does."

She seemed to me to be just a trifle too vehement.

"What did Stephen think of this examination?" I asked.

"Oh, pretended to laugh at it. You never know what he really thinks, he laughs at everything—or seems to. He talked a lot of bosh about the shadow of the scaffold . . ." She grew a trifle pale. "It's too *stupid! Isn't* it?" she demanded. "Why, Stephen didn't even really dislike Her, except for my sake. She hated him, of course, but he used to laugh and be perfectly charming to her. It was I who—who—"

She caught herself up. She couldn't say "who hated her" of a dead woman.

"*Isn't* it a lunatic idea?" she demanded again.

"It is," I agreed, "and I don't believe Inspector Grier thinks anything of the kind. It's his job to find out where we all were that evening, and especially between ten and eleven—and what we all felt about Mrs. Harrington. He's asking everybody the same things. It's part of the usual routine." (I didn't know this, of course, and don't now, but it seemed to me both a likely and a reassuring thing to

say.) "And secondly," I went on, like a parson, "even supposing he had—er—fixed his eye on Stephen, you've got
to remember that he doesn't know Stephen as we do. Of
course, to you and me, the very idea of Stephen committing a murder is too absurd for words."

She looked at me with eyes in which I thought I could
see hope, a little fear, and a good deal of question.

"Celia," I said firmly, "you mustn't let this horrible
business distort things. You were perfectly idiotic to try
to lie about Stephen being alone when he found the body.
Yesterday you'd have laughed at the bare idea of Stephen
committing a serious crime—*any* crime, let alone murder.
Well—it's the same Stephen."

She drew a long sigh.

"I know. Only—I'd rather let go to him that evening.
I—I got the hump, being alone all day, and thinking how—
how rotten things were. And I—I cried a bit. . . . Stephen
was awfully sick. I've never seen him really furious before,
but he was then. And he said it had got to end. 'I'll see it
does,' he said, 'and jolly soon too'—something like that.
I—he frightened me, he did really, he looked so—I don't
know, ready for anything. And so, when he told me that
she—she was dead—and he was the only person—"

"Bosh!" I declared. "Celia, aren't you ashamed of yourself? *Stephen,* indeed!"

"I know," she muttered, looking down. "Only I—I like
to hear you say so too," she added naively.

"You just hold on to that," I said. "It's perfectly, absolutely true, and it's pretty hard on Stephen to believe
anything else."

"I don't—I didn't!" she cried eagerly. "I *knew* it was
impossible. That's why I was so furious—"

"Of course it's impossible. As for Inspector Grier's
questions—as I say, they're a matter of routine. If you'd
studied the subject of crime in fiction, as I have, you'd

know that. And let me tell you, Celia, he's a very shrewd man."

"Who's a very shrewd man?" asked a voice behind us; and the Squire slumped down into a third chair.

"That inspector—at least, so Miss Leslie says," answered Celia.

Her father didn't answer for a moment. I stole a sideways look at him. I thought he looked white and ill.

"He may be," he said then, in a voice which sounded indifferent. "I haven't any means of judging. But he seems to me very officious, and a good deal more inquisitive than the circumstances warrant."

"That's what *I* say!" cried Celia.

"Also it seems to me," Godfrey Harrington went on, "that he's neglecting an obvious avenue of inquiry. One thing is certain—that poor Agatha was either killed by accident (which is quite likely when one remembers that some guns were stolen from that booth, and that all the lads in Ringshall were mad about using them); or she was killed deliberately—murdered. Myself, I believe it was an accident; but if it wasn't, it seems to me that the obvious place to look for her murderer is in her past life in the years before she came here."

He glanced at us, a furtive, sidelong look which put me on the alert at once.

"He has been trying to find out about that," Celia said; but I rudely interrupted.

"I thought you knew nothing about her past," I said.

"Exactly," he caught me up. "That's exactly what I mean. Normally, I should. If she had nothing to conceal—nothing she was afraid to have me know—surely she would have told me something of her past life. As it is, I know nothing—not a single thing. I don't even know how long she was married to this man Ward, or who he was, or how he died, or when. Surely one would expect to?"

"Did she never say *anything* about her past life?" I asked.

"Never—not directly. She did once or twice say something which led me to believe that she had not been happy. I remember once—not so long ago—when we were out here together, she said how delightful it was to be at peace. I remember she said, 'You don't know, Godfrey, you can't even guess, what it means to me to be here, safe with you.' She said it so fervently! At the time, I only thought that she meant that life is hard for an unprotected woman, and that it was good to have a man to look after her; but even then I felt that there was more in it than that."

So I should think!—unless he was improvising. From a woman of Mrs. Harrington's type, the 'poor, lonely, unprotected female' touch was unthinkable; and for any one, even of the feeblest nature, to think of Godfrey Harrington as a protector and guide was equally impossible. Either he'd invented it, to feed his vanity, or else Mrs. Harrington really had a secret which her new position as his wife made more or less harmless.

"And there were other things, too," the Squire went on—"little remarks and so on which made me feel sure that she had led an unhappy life. Sometimes only a look or a sigh, sometimes a sentence only half completed. . . . It takes unhappiness, Miss Leslie, to make a woman as reserved as Agatha was. No happy woman is so—so aloof."

That seemed to me more like the truth. I nodded.

"And she was secretive, too," Celia joined in. "There was that business about the post and the telephone—"

"Quite," nodded her father. "Yes, if Inspector Grier wants to find out who killed her, let him find out about her past."

"I thought you believed in the accident theory," I said, rather dryly.

"So I do. But this inspector doesn't. He believes in a murder."

"How do you know that?"

He made an impatient movement.

"Isn't it obvious? No country policeman, hoping for a big 'case' and possible promotion, likes to believe in an accident when there's the faintest chance of a crime. Besides, the offensive way in which he cross-examines us all shows which way the wind's blowing. Yet he neglects this most obvious line of inquiry."

"You don't know that he does," I defended the absent inspector. "He seemed to me to be very much interested in her past. Only you couldn't tell him anything about it."

He turned sharply round and looked at me.

"How do you know—" he began.

"Oh, I was there. Didn't you see me? I was in the window-seat. Inspector Grier knew I was."

The Squire appeared to me to think rapidly. Or—no, I'll be quite honest, even to him. I *thought* he appeared to, and my immediate idea was that he was going over what he'd said to the inspector to see if I should be able to spot any discrepancy between what he'd said and what I knew. Apparently he couldn't think of anything. If he'd told a lie, it was one that I couldn't know about. He sank back in his chair. And to this day I don't know whether my impression was right, or whether I only saw it because I expected to. I am not given to imputing base motives to people for what they do, but in those days following on our murder I did little else.

Godfrey Harrington passed his hand over his brow with a familiar gesture of weariness which always annoys me. So does his habit of sighing, which he now proceeded to do. I wish some enterprising government would put a tax on sighs. They are such a contemptible way of expressing pity for oneself. When Godfrey Harrington does it—and he always does, when he thinks some one ought to be informed that he needs pity—he immediately dries up all my fund of sympathy. He is so obviously capable of giving himself all the sympathy that any one can possibly need, that I don't see why he should expect any more.

"Poor dear Agatha!" he sighed now. "It is impossible to put into words what her loss will mean to me. It is the kind of blow that mutilates, Miss Leslie—that cripples and maims the soul. One is never quite the same again. Such a loss as that can never be restored."

A flippant remark, I think of Samuel Butler's, to the effect that the man who marries again doesn't deserve to lose his wife, came into my head. I didn't, of course, say it. Anyhow, I felt too sick to want to. I saw Celia steal a comforting hand into his. I didn't know how she *could* be taken in. He had got over the loss of a much nicer woman with extreme ease. Besides, horrid as I know it sounds, it did seem to me that this overwhelming grief was a bit sudden. In the earlier part of his conversation he had been far more interested in explaining how his wife had probably died than in grieving because she was dead.

Perhaps he guessed my thoughts. Very vain people are often extremely sensitive to other folks' opinion of them, I've noticed. In spite of Celia's silent sympathy, the man wasn't satisfied.

"People often think," he mourned on, "that because one says nothing one feels nothing. True grief, Miss Leslie, is generally silent."

"Yes," I agreed dryly, "it is."

He glanced at me, a look which oddly mingled reproach and inquiry.

"I think of my poor baby girl, too," he went on, covering Celia's hand with his. "Left alone, just when she needs a mother's care—"

I think even Celia felt sick at that. She drew her hand away.

"No, daddy," she said, gently but firmly. "You mustn't—I mean, I can't pretend that. She—I never thought of her as my real mother. I—you mustn't expect me to be—*terribly* upset. It's horrible, terrible, and I feel a perfect pig about her, but—"

"I think you'll regret that dreadful speech, Celia," said the Squire. "I hope you will. Meanwhile, I think I shall be best alone—alone with my grief," he added, dropping his voice to the appropriate note.

I watched him go with satisfaction. Hypocrisy I cannot endure, and sentiment I loathe, and when they are combined I am apt to forget myself. I turned to Celia, who looked very uncomfortable.

"Don't bother, Celia," I said. "You were quite right. One doesn't suddenly begin to love a person just because they've died."

She said nothing. I wondered whether she had at last begun to see through her father. If so, it would be a greater grief to her than any she had yet known—greater even than the loss of her own mother. For she would have lost, not merely his presence, but his personality. He would vanish utterly, never having existed. I felt relieved when she silently got up and went into the house. I could do nothing about it, and I hate to see people suffering.

14

I was still sitting under the trees when I saw Roger Cart-wright's figure crossing the lawn towards me. I was delighted to see him. I had a lot I wanted to say, and a good many things I wanted to ask.

"Come and sit down," I invited him, "and give me a cigarette and let's talk."

"I hoped you'd be alone," he said, obeying my instructions, and filling a pipe for himself. "I've got a lot to talk over with you."

"So have I with you."

"Have you?"

"Yes. But I want to hear your news first, please. I want to know first exactly what did happen when you and Stephen saw Celia home last night."

"I can't tell you much. I thought it would be tactful to let them walk a bit of the way together, so I remembered that I had some papers that Mrs. Harrington wanted in my digs, and asked Celia and the boy to walk on and I'd catch them up. I meant to be gone only a few minutes, just to let them say good-night, you know—"

I nodded.

"Were there really any papers?" I asked.

"Oh, rather! And I really wanted Mrs. Harrington to have them—or rather, she really wanted to have them. But

I couldn't find the beastly things anywhere, so I was longer than I meant to be. I gather that Celia thought she'd better hurry up, and that she didn't want to turn up accompanied by Stephen only, so she sent him after me as an excuse for getting rid of him. Otherwise he'd have stuck by her in case she got into a row when she reached home. Well, what seems to have happened was that they had walked along the edge of the Green, in the shadow of the oaks, but when the boy was sent to my digs he ran across the Green, which is the shortest way, of course. And he came upon the body, lying in the middle of the Green."

"What did he do?"

"He says that he turned queer—he hates the sight of pain or death, you know, in any form. Then he ran on to my digs, called me out, and told me. I told him to get back to Celia and get her home while I dealt with the accident—I didn't think, from what he said, that it was—as bad as it was. But when we reached the body, Celia was practically there. She had turned back after us, I suppose to get my support for her return home."

"So you then sent her home with Stephen, and—and did the rest?"

"Yes."

I pondered a moment. Then I said:

"About how long was it after you left them that Stephen came and told you about the death?"

"Well, I find it rather hard to say. Of course, that's what the inspector wanted to know straight away. I should say it was somewhere about ten minutes—perhaps a quarter of an hour."

"And how long had Stephen left Celia when he came to you?"

"There again, we can't tell at all exactly. She was getting impatient at his absence, you see, or she wouldn't have come after him. He can't be at all sure how long it was that he stood by the body—one can't judge of time when one's faint. I don't suppose it was very long."

"But long enough to—to make the inspector curious?"

"Exactly. He—I mean the inspector—has been here, of course?"

"Very much so. Did you get any bits of information out of him?"

"Not one bit even. I rather gather one isn't likely to."

"Quite," I nodded.

"I've also seen Gregory," went on the curate. "He was much more communicative. From what he said, I gather that there's a certain amount of attention being paid to the accident theory."

"Really?" I asked, with interest. "That's what the Squire thinks—or wants us to think he thinks. What did Gregory say?"

"He told me that they'd been inquiring into this collapse of the rifle range and the loss of the guns. It seems that this man (he calls himself Alberti, but I bet his friends know him as plain Bert) now says that only two guns are missing, but that those two are the best of the lot. Of course, he would say that, hoping for compensation of some sort. On the other hand, the police idea seems to be that the smashing of the stall may be a put-up job—that some one tried all the guns, spotted the best, marked it in some way, and then hit on this way of getting it, or them."

"He'd have had to try every gun there was, pretty well." I objected.

"Yes. But some one did do that—or very nearly. You remember how I told you that old Mother Nokes kept Tom at it?"

"But," I protested, "it isn't a bit like Ringshall people to do a cunning thing like that."

"Not like most of 'em. That's what I said. Of course, as Gregory sagely said, one will do what another won't; besides, they weren't themselves—"

"But, my dear man," I interrupted, "when a village lad gets drunk he may do stupid things, or wrong things, or cruel things, but he doesn't do a thing that's a clean contrary to his ways and his tradition. Our people are awfully straight. They don't steal. Still less do they plan clever thefts when they're drunk."

"I know. I said all that. Only, of course, it doesn't apply to the Nokeses as it does to nearly every one else. The only queer thing is that, as far as I can make out, old Mother Nokes wasn't there when the smash-up occurred. Apart from that, I only made things worse by saying that it wasn't at all like a drunken theft."

"How?"

"Well, you see—a theft when a man's drunk, and a shooting accident afterwards, wouldn't be so bad. It would be pretty terrible, of course, but not half as bad as a deliberate murder. And, though Gregory didn't say so, I guessed that the other idea was this—that the stall was smashed on purpose, the purpose being to get the gun,

and that the gun was wanted for—a particular use."

"How perfectly horrible!" I exclaimed.

"Horrible," he agreed. "And yet—I don't know that it's not more possible than the drunken accident theory. . . ."

In spite of the hot sun lying across my lap, I felt quite cold. For I could see how very possible that theory was. How possible that some one, some one who hated and feared Mrs. Harrington, whose happiness she threatened, might plan that raid on the rifle booth—might hide, with the stolen gun, in the thick oaks bordering Foakes Green. . . . Some one who had tried the guns, shot wonderfully well, knew what missile to use, how to allow for a faulty sight. . . . Some one who had openly threatened

Mrs. Harrington, and who, standing beside the rifle stall, had heard her say that she was going to Ben Salt's and would be home about eleven. . . . Some one whose face had been convulsed with rage and fear when she had said so. . . .

"That's terrible," I murmured.

"Isn't it? When I saw the way it might pan out, I shut up and plumped for a drunken theft and an accident afterwards. Though I don't believe it."

"Neither do I," I admitted. Then I said, rather hesitating:

"I wonder if you'll think me a perfect fool if I tell you something?"

"I don't expect so," he said, smiling a little.

"It's nothing definite," I went on. "It's only something in my mind which I want to get rid of. I think it'll be enough just to tell it, only there's no one but you I'd dare to tell it to."

"Dare?"

"Yes. I'm terribly afraid of being laughed at."

"I won't do that," he promised.

"Well . . . Listen, then. Some days ago—on Tuesday—I was in Rutter's shop. There were a lot of people there, all furious over the Fair. But I'm only bothering about one of them—Mrs. Nokes."

He looked at me sharply, but said nothing.

"She was drunk, of course," I said, "but—well, I had the impression that it only loosened her thoughts, that she wasn't improvising, but only speaking out what she had thought for some time. *In vino veritas* sort of idea. Well, she talked about Mrs. Harrington."

"Naturally."

"Oh, quite. But she wasn't saying the sort of thing that every one else was saying. I can hear her now."

"What was she saying?"

"She said, 'She has a dread in her soul and a shadow at her shoulder. A shadow that means death.'"

In the hot silence of the garden the words sounded terrible in my own ears.

"Then at the Fair yesterday she cursed Mrs. Harrington. She spat on her shadow and cracked her thumb. You know?"

He nodded.

"I've heard of it. I've never seen it done."

"Nor had I, before. I thought, when I heard it spoken of, that it sounded childish. But it didn't seem a bit childish when it happened. It was *beastly*. Mrs. Harrington talking away unconsciously, and that hag grimacing over her shadow. . . . It—it seemed *real*, somehow . . . dangerous. . . . I can't explain. And then—then she's killed, in moonlight, on that haunted Green, by an 'elf-bolt.' . . . I can't help wondering—though I've often laughed at charms and ghosts and magic, I can't help feeling—just a bit queer. . . ."

My voice tailed away. It sounded so feeble, so absurd! But it felt real enough to me. The curse, muttered in hot sunlight on the Green; the death in the mysterious moonlight, among moving restless shadows, when magic is abroad—death in almost the very spot where the curse had been spoken, death by a flying arrow made by hands dead centuries ago. . . . And then, later, the strange head lying on the dead woman's pillow. . . .

"Go on," said the curate quietly.

I looked at him inquiringly.

"There's something more, isn't there?" he asked.

I gulped.

"Well—yes, there is. I've told no one this, expect the inspector. No one knows. Last night, after the doctor had gone, and Celia and I were alone in the house, I heard some one moving in Mrs. Harrington's room."

He sat up with a jerk. It was almost as if my words had confirmed some idea in his mind.

"What time?" he asked excitedly.

"About a quarter to two, I should think. Or it might have been two. Between half-past one and two, anyhow."

He sank back, as if disappointed.

"What did you do?"

"I went to see what it was."

"You've got pluck," he commented. As usual, I blushed. I'm sorry to have to record it, because I like, especially in this connexion, to appear as sensible as I can. But this is a true narrative.

"I *had* to," I explained. "I didn't want to. And it wasn't pluck, because I was in a panic of the deepest azure."

"Well?"

"Well—I made a fool of myself, of course. That is, if it was a—a human sound I heard. I fell, and made a noise like a ton of bricks. I got up again and went in . . ."

I stopped. Even now I felt a cold qualm of terror as I remembered that room.

I saw, from the curate's expression, that my face was giving me away. I hurried on.

"The room was—occupied. I didn't see any one, but I *felt* some one was there. One does, you know," I appealed.

He nodded.

"And—and—the bed had been lain in. Some one had just got out of it. And—and, oh, Roger, *the pillow was warm!*"

He whistled softly.

"And," I went on desperately, "I can't help putting it all together! 'There's a shadow at her shoulder—a shadow that means death!' And the curse, and death coming, just there and just then. And the elf-bolt, shot out from among those old, old trees, killing her by the stone altar. And some one in her room, after her death, lying in her bed . . ."

He said nothing for a little. He sat smoking quietly, and somehow his silence was very comforting—far more reassuring than any pooh-poohing could have been.

"It was pretty beastly," he said then. "What did you do?"

"I ran," I confessed. "I went and locked myself in. And, about half-past two, Godfrey Harrington came in."

"*Ah!*" He sat up straight again. "Are you sure he only came in then?"

"I'm sure it wasn't he in Mrs. Harrington's room, if you mean that. I asked him if he had been in, and he asked if the—if her body was there. He couldn't have thought of that if he'd been in himself. All the same, he did behave very oddly."

And I told him the episode of Godfrey Harrington's visit to the little passage.

"Hm," said the curate. "And, to be perfectly, absolutely honest, what did you think was his *immediate* sensation when you told him about his wife's death? Surprise? Grief? Relief? What?"

I hesitated.

"Well—I've been thinking about that. But I can't be quite sure. You see, I dislike him so much that I'm apt to expect him to behave badly."

"Ah! So you think in the back of your mind—?"

I nodded.

"I'm sorry. I really do hate to say it. But I believe he was relieved."

"And startled? Surprised? Shocked?"

"Y—yes. Oh yes. Certainly surprised."

"Mmmm. Have you seen anything of him to-day?"

"A little. Quite enough."

"Well, I'm going to make a guess now, and you can tell me if I'm wrong. You'll like that. Doesn't it seem to you that he's far more interested in the possible cause of his wife's death than grieved because she's dead?"

"I did rather think that—well, that his sorrow was a bit of an afterthought. It appeared so suddenly, and was so very obviously done for effect."

"Quite. . . . Well, now, listen. I hoped I could explain the visitor to the bedroom. I can't, just yet; but I think I shall in time. I've got a theory—oh yes, just like the best detectives. And what's more, so have the police—in fact, I believe they've got two."

"And Godfrey Harrington has another," I murmured. "At least one, if not two."

"Yes. And if you look all round—not only at yesterday, but at the last few days or even weeks—you'll have one. The spook idea isn't necessary, and I think, if you work on it, you'll find so many other more attractive, and even more probable, theories that you won't need to worry about Mrs. Nokes—in the magic connexion."

I thought I could read a double meaning in the last words. I set them aside mentally to think over at leisure.

"Now, look here," went on the curate. "Do you happen to know at all what Harrington told the police about his movements yesterday?"

"Yes. I was there when the inspector was questioning him."

"Do you remember pretty accurately what he said?"

"I scribbled down the times he gave," I replied. "I don't quite know why, except that he was so glib with his time-table."

Roger Cartwright looked at me inquiringly.

"I mean," I explained, "that normally, when one's had a pretty bad shock, as we're told the Squire had last night, one doesn't remember exactly where one was at certain moments of the past two days. One has to pause and think, anyhow. Godfrey Harrington didn't pause. He had the whole thing pat."

"I see. Good for you—spotting it, I mean. May I see his time-table?"

I produced it from my bag—figures jotted down on the back of an envelope, which wouldn't convey anything to any one if I did happen to drop it.

"Here we are," I said. "'In town all day.' That is, of course, not a bit accurate. He didn't mention that he was at the Fair. Perhaps he thought his visit was too short to count. Anyhow, he said he was mooning about at home all the morning—'1.24 express from Savernake.' I suppose there is such a train?"

The curate had a time-table in his pocket. He produced it and proceeded to check my figures.

"That's O.K.," he announced. "Gets up at 4.12."

I nodded.

"He said 'about ten past.' That's all right. Well, he says that he met his friend, had tea with him in a shop walked with him in St. James's Park, tried for the 6.27 to Savernake, and missed it."

"There isn't another," said Roger Cartwright, his eyes on the time-table.

"So he said. He got a train to Newbury—the 8.47 . . ."

He nodded.

"That would be the next best," he muttered. "It gets to Newbury at 10.22."

"That's about right. He got the 10.42 local from Newbury to Savernake, arriving about 11.30—"

"11.37," nodded the curate.

"—and walked home."

"Let's see. It's between ten and eleven miles to Savernake, and Harrington doesn't walk fast, though he's a good goer if he doesn't hurry. If he left Savernake about twenty to twelve, and went at an average of three miles an hour, he'd be home somewhere about ten to three."

"Well—he was a little earlier than that, I should think. But then, three miles an hour is putting it a bit low. He walks faster than that, and it's not much, if at all, over ten miles. I should say he'd do it in three hours. And it wasn't much over half-past two when he came to the little corridor."

"Dash it all!" scowled the curate, rumpling up his hair. "That's *all* wrong."

"Wrong?" I asked, surprised. "It's just about right."

"I know. And it oughtn't to be."

I gasped.

"Surely you don't suspect—?" I stammered.

He coloured a little.

"I said it was only a theory," he muttered. "But this sends it phut."

He sat staring at the figures. Then he seemed to cheer up.

"As you said," he remarked, "one doesn't remember a rather complicated time-table like that straight off the reel, next day, after a bad shock. I wonder if it's possible . . ."

He thought again.

"The trouble is, one can't check it," he said then. "It was market day at Savernake yesterday, so the Dimsey bus would have been full, and there'd have been a bit of a crowd at Dimsey Station. Besides, Harrington hardly ever goes to Dimsey; he mightn't be recognized by a soul. And they wouldn't be likely to remember him at Savernake Station, either."

"The porter might," I suggested. "The porter who took the wire."

"What wire?"

"Didn't I mention it? Sorry. He wired to this man Felton from Savernake Station, saying that he was coming."

"Ah, now we can prove it!" exclaimed the curate eagerly. "The post office will have the telegram, with a date stamp."

I explained that the wire had apparently never been sent.

"Still, the porter would remember," I added hopefully.

Roger Cartwright shook his head.

"He'd remember it all right,' he said, 'if it happened. But I doubt if he'd own up. It was pretty bad, to take the wire and the bob or whatever it was, and no doubt a tip as well, and then do nothing about it. No, I don't quite see . . ."

He sat pondering. Then I said:

"Why do you doubt it? It's exactly the sort of thing he would do, to leave it to the last minute to see this man Felton, and then dart off like that, wiring *en route*. In fact, the glibness of the time-table is the only queer thing about it."

He said nothing.

"*Why* do you doubt it?" I asked again.

The curate looked up and smiled, rather ruefully.

"I'm afraid chiefly because it knocks out my pet idea," he admitted. Then he added, rather inconsequently I thought, "I suppose you've seen nothing of Lady Gervaise since—since Mrs. Harrington's death?"

"No. I hardly should, you know. She wasn't intimate here."

"Exactly. That's why—"

"Why what?"

"Why it strikes me as odd that she knew about it early this morning."

"She can't have!" I exclaimed. "Her house is right outside the village. Her maids must have been in before it was commonly known. She can't have known about it—"

"She did," asserted the curate. "Ludlow told me. He was taking away the body to do the p. m. It was on a stretcher, Gregory and the other bobby carrying it. They met Lady Gervaise."

"But—Dr. Ludlow came awfully early."

"I know. It was before seven."

"And Lady Gervaise was up? In the village?"

"Yes. He said she looked as if she were going for a walk—hat on, and all that. Well, she saw the stretcher. Ludlow says that she turned quite white and said, 'Oh, Dr. Ludlow, what are you doing? *Is that Mrs. Harrington's body?*'"

He paused a moment, and then added slowly:

"There wasn't a soul about. She was obviously on her way from Haresfoot to the village, and Ludlow didn't see a single person. How did she know that Mrs. Harrington was dead?"

15

We were still considering this when a maid—Mrs. Harrington's invaluable Lawson—came across the lawn to us.

"Excuse me, miss. The inspector from Newbury is here, and would like to see you and Mr. Cartwright."

"Ask him to come out here, will you, Lawson?" I said. I added to Roger Cartwright, "I like that inspector. He didn't laugh at me about the bed in Mrs. Harrington's room. He examined it with finger-print powder, and found a poppy-stain in it. I'm sure he's going to be interesting."

"Do tell me about the poppy stain," said the curate, with very proper interest; but I said I'd do that later. At the moment the inspector was imminent.

He came and sat down, at my invitation, in the chair which Celia had occupied.

"It's a stroke of luck, finding you here, sir," he said to the curate in his comfortable voice. "Perhaps, as it's turned out like that, Miss Leslie will excuse me if I begin with you. You know the village people pretty well, I take it, sir?"

"Fairly well, yes."

"Do you know a young man called Greaves—Joe Greaves?"

The curate made a little involuntary movement—of protest, it seemed to me.

"Yes."

"Know him well?"

"Yes, quite fairly well."

"Do you know why he bore such a grudge against the late Mrs. Harrington?"

Roger Cartwright hesitated. Then he said:

"Yes, I believe I do."

"Will you tell me what it was he had against her?"

Again he hesitated.

"It was this," he said at last. "A few days ago—perhaps a fortnight—Greaves married a girl named Lydia Salt." (I jumped, but managed not to show it.) "The marriage was kept strictly secret," the curate went on, "for two reasons. One was that Joe was working as an ordinary labourer for Farmer Lester. He knew that old Salt, Lydia's father, would never let his girl marry him until he had a better job than that. Ben Salt's a wealthy old chap, as village people go, and he'd set his heart on Lydia making a good match. He told her that if she married to please him he'd buy her a house—oh yes, he could do it easily—and 'see to' her generally; but, like many far richer men, he wanted the other side to match.

"Well, about a year ago, Lydia went into service in Savernake. She'd been brought up very strictly by her father, who's as stern an old Puritan as you could meet. Her mother's been dead for twenty years. Lydia knew absolutely nothing of life. Also she'd had a desperately dull existence, prayer-meetings being old Ben Salt's one idea of relaxation. Well, you can guess that happened. When you have a pretty girl like Lydia, young, ignorant, starved of interests, and put her alone in a country town where she's free from her father's inquisition, you get trouble. Poor Lydia got it.

"I gather she discovered pretty soon what had happened. She left her situation and came home, hoping, I think, at first, that things weren't as bad as she feared. She got a job with Mrs. Harrington. Then she found she was in a mess. She was terrified. Her one idea was suicide. Joe found her down by the mill-pond—just in time.

"She had to tell some one, and she'd known Joe all her life. She knew he cared for her—as she did for him, really. The other was just—an episode, an excitement, that would never have happened if she'd been reasonably happy at home. She told Joe. Well, there was only one way out— apart, I mean, from her original idea, poor child—and Joe took it. He told her he'd marry her. About a week later (I was away when they first met) he came to me and fixed it up. They were married at the end of the next week."

"But they couldn't expect to go on keeping it dark from her father," put in Inspector Grier.

"No. But there's where the other reason for secrecy comes in. Joe was hoping for a job as bailiff with a farmer called Phillips, who lives two or three miles away. It's a really good job, and Joe could do it. But Phillips won't take on a married man—lots of farmers won't, it makes the housing difficult; but Joe knew that if he once had the job, Phillips wouldn't want to lose him, wife or no wife. His idea was to get the job if he could, show what he was made of, and then, when Phillips was too anxious to keep him to object to his being a married man, to produce his wife."

"But how does Mrs. Harrington come in?"

"Like this. She'd spotted, of course, the condition Lydia was in. She knew she ought to be married, not knowing, of course, either that Joe wasn't responsible for the girl's state, or that he had done all he possibly could to put things right for her. Mrs. Harrington thought that he had deceived the girl, and she constantly threatened to tell old Salt and make him force Joe to marry Lydia. Of course, that would have dished them all round. Salt would have turned Lydia out, and the fact that he was known to be married would have prevented Joe from putting himself in a position to make the girl comfortable in the way she'd been used to. It was fatal for them to appear as married until Joe had that job—which he ought to hear about to-morrow, by the way."

"But, look here," began the inspector, "surely the girl's father could *see*—"

"Old Salt is blind," I interrupted. "He's been blind for years."

"Oh." The inspector's voice sounded very dubious. "You know, Mr. Cartwright," he went on, "this strikes me—I'm sorry, but it does strike me as a thinnish tale. I don't mean that I doubt you, of course," he added hastily, "but don't you think that they, either or both, has been—well, pulling your leg? Mrs. Harrington's version seems to me the likely one."

"I don't agree," said the curate sturdily. "I've checked it. Lydia told me the scoundrel's name—in strict confidence, of course; it wouldn't do to let Joe know it!—and I went and saw him. He admitted it—said he didn't know the girl was 'so green.' Then I know that their fears about old Salt's attitude are justified. He's told every one in the village what he'll do for Lydia if she marries a 'well-seen' man, and how he'd turn her out if she 'lowered herself' to an ordinary labourer. I quite saw poor Joe's point when he was so furious with Mrs. Harrington for threatening to put the fat in the fire—for no cause, as it happened."

"Hm. . . . But wasn't it the case that Mrs. Harrington was killed *after* leaving old Salt's house?"

"Yes, I believe so."

"Then—what's happened? Has the old chap taken drastic steps?"

The curate was clearly taken aback.

"I never thought of that," he admitted. "What a fool I am. . . . No, as far as I know, he's done nothing."

"He couldn't," I put in. "Dr. Ludlow took Lydia home last night in a state of collapse. He'd have made it pretty hot for Ben Salt if he'd bothered the girl. The village has a wholesome fear of the doctor's tongue."

"Hm," said the inspector again. He paused for a moment. Then he went on, "Well, at any rate, this much is clear—this man Greaves had a very definite dislike and fear of Mrs. Harrington."

"She shouldn't have interfered with things she didn't understand," I said.

"No doubt; but the fact remains," he said severely. "I understand, too, that Greaves is a very good shot, and that he was present when the airgun booth was smashed and some airguns stolen."

"Yes, he was," admitted the curate. "But, dash it all," he went on, rumpling up his hair, "Joe couldn't, simply *couldn't*, have shot Mrs. Harrington!"

"Why not? I don't say he did, but why couldn't he have?"

"Because it's utterly unlike him. Clean contrary to his nature."

"But he was drunk, wasn't he?"

"Not so very. But even if he had been, a man behaves more or less in character, Inspector, even when drunk."

"Not entirely," said the inspector. "A man who's borne a good deal pretty patiently may suddenly lose control when he's drunk."

"But look here," I broke in, "there's this—there wasn't the least point in Joe's doing anything *after* she'd seen old Salt. If she'd done the mischief, she'd done it, and killing her couldn't undo it."

"That's true," said Inspector Grier; "but it all points the same way—that is, that it would be done (if Greaves did it—I don't say he did, remember)—in drink. It would be an act of revenge—the kind of thing a drunken man might do, though it was too late to be of any use to him."

"All the same," said Roger Cartwright stubbornly, "I'll bet you anything you like that it wasn't Joe Greaves who fired that bolt."

The inspector said nothing for a moment; then he said:

"I don't say he did. But I do say this. He had a definite grudge against Mrs. Harrington. He wasn't in a fit state to be responsible for his actions. He had the chance to get an airgun, such as would shoot such a missile as this flint arrow-head. The very choice of missile looks to me like a villager's. But worst of all, I think, is this—very few people could shoot such a missile so accurately with a rifle that *wasn't* accurate. This man Greaves had tried the rifles and knew their faults, and I understand that he's a surprisingly good shot. From the good shooting with the bad weapon, from the choice of missile, from the motive, it looks—well, it looks as if Mr. Greaves would have a bit to explain."

I felt certain that he had altered his original words. I knew that he had been about to say, "It looks bad for Joe Greaves." I think Roger Cartwright knew it, too. He said sturdily:

"You'll find he can explain it. And, Inspector, look here—what makes you so jolly sure that the bolt was shot from one of the stolen guns?"

"Well, of course, I'm not sure," admitted the inspector. "Only it seemed, from the general interest in the show, that airguns weren't very common in the village."

"Some people have 'em, all the same," declared the curate. "Lady Gervaise has, or used to have, a good little one; and Harrington has one. You remember, Miss Leslie?"

"Oh yes. He used to let Stephen use it when he was a boy at school."

The inspector looked worried. I could see his point. There was so much too much of everything—too many people who disliked Mrs. Harrington, too many weapons, too many motives, altogether too many clues and loose ends.

"Do you happen to know the make of those other two guns?" he asked.

"Lady Gervaise's was quite a small one—an Ariel Number One," said the curate confidently, "Harrington's—I'm not sure, but I think it was a Loxley."

"An Ariel One wouldn't take that flint," said Inspector Grier positively. "But a Loxley . . . I must find out about the Loxley. I wonder if it's about anywhere in the house."

"By Jove!" exclaimed the curate, "I've just remembered. Harrington was using his own gun at that booth yesterday. I remember perfectly now. He wasn't doing anything more than practise, you know—it was before the show opened officially. He was getting much better scores than the boys, and I heard him say, 'It's probably because my gun's so much better than these. It's a very accurate one.' Then he let them try with his."

The inspector sat up.

"At what time was this?"

"Early—before the Fair opened. About ten or half-past."

The inspector said nothing, but he looked a little grim. I knew as well as if he had spoken that he was thinking of the Squire's statement, in which he had definitely said that he was at home all the morning until he left, at ten to twelve, to catch the train to Savernake. But he said nothing. He wasn't going to give himself away.

"Did you say that Mr. Earle used to use this gun of Mr. Harrington's?" he asked me.

"Yes—occasionally, years ago," I added, rather hastily. "He wasn't much good with it, and he hasn't shot since, I believe. Stephen hates killing things."

The inspector smiled at me as if he read my thoughts, which he no doubt did; but he didn't say anything. He sat looking at his boots with an absorbed air, and presently he rose and took his leave, and went off about his own mysterious business.

When he was safely out of earshot, the curate began to talk.

"You know," he said, "I was afraid of this. If you didn't know Joe Greaves, you *would* think he looked—well, suspicious. There's the motive, the ability to shoot, the practice with the guns at that beastly stall, the looting of the stall, the missile, the state of excitement he was in—and the silly fool said something idiotic, I believe—some kind of threat—"

I nodded.

"He did. I heard him."

"Well—it's not true. I'd take my oath it isn't. And it'll have to be proved it isn't pretty quick, or Joe'll lose all chance of that job at Phillips's. And that would be disastrous."

"I know. But it's awfully hard to prove a thing *isn't* so. It's much easier to prove it *is.*"

"Yes, it is. And that's what I'm going to do. I'm going to have a try at finding out—at proving, rather—who did kill Mrs. Harrington. It won't be Joe Greaves."

"You said you had a theory," I hinted.

"Yes, I have. And the more I think of it the more I believe in it."

"Do tell me," I begged.

"Well—of course, it *is* only an idea. But it does look to me as if Harrington ought to do a bit of explaining."

"You don't think he—*purposely* killed her?"

The curate looked uncomfortable.

"It sounds pretty foul," he admitted, "but just look at the facts. He says he spent all day—or what was left of it—

in town—with a man who is now out of England, address unknown. He says that he walked home from Savernake, and got in at two-thirty, or later. But how can he *prove* any of that? How can he prove that he went to town at all—that he ever got farther than, say, Newbury, or even Savernake? He might have got back quite early, for all we know. He had that Loxley gun. He could shoot more than a bit. And—he'd talked about a separation from his wife, which she wouldn't give him. He had an understanding with Lady Gervaise, too.

"Then, his conduct has been odd since he got back. Why did he come to that corridor? Why did he telephone after he heard the news of his wife's death? Why did he get up early this morning and go out? How did Lady Gervaise know about Mrs. Harrington's death, unless he'd met her and told her of it?

"My theory's this. He was tired of his wife, didn't get on with her, found her so trying that he wanted a separation. At that moment Lady Gervaise turned up, more charming than ever before, and—as we all know—captivated him. Let's put it, just for argument, that he wanted to be off with one lady and on with the other. Take it that he and Lady Gervaise were to clear out last night. What would his movements naturally be?

"I take it that they'd be something like this. He'd first fix his line of retreat. He might do that either direct or by telephone. Telephone, of course, would be quicker, but he'd have had to do the job somewhere away from home— he couldn't risk doing it from a centre where his calls might be traced. He'd probably go to some largish town where there's a good deal of telephone traffic—say Newbury. We'll be able to find out easily enough whether he did actually go to Dimsey and on to Savernake. He certainly didn't leave home before half-past eleven—a quarter-past at the very earliest. That would allow him time to get to Newbury by noon, or a little after—say half-past twelve. He'd put through his various calls— hotels, steamers, whatever he wanted to arrange—by four at the outside. He'd be back at Savernake by five, and could have been in Ringshall, even if he'd walked, by a little after eight.

"Now, suppose that all the time he'd been doing this, making arrangements for the flight, the very fact that the thing was so imminent made him want to put his relationship with Lady Gervaise on a 'respectable' basis. One's heard of similar cases often enough—cases where dwelling on an idea has made a weak man leap to a way of achieving it."

I thought that over, and I saw that it might work. Godfrey Harrington had never been thwarted in his life. He'd always got what he wanted, and he hadn't always been too scrupulous in his way of getting it. He was one of those people you find in every rank and walk of life—an instinctive and adept grabber. I could see him dwelling on his desire for union with Lady Gervaise until he would throw everything else aside to get it; and I could believe, too, that to a man of his capricious and unstable nature, he might even commit a crime to clear his way. He was just the type to lose all sense of proportion—to break the Sixth Commandment in order to keep the Seventh.

"I don't imagine," Roger Cartwright went on, "that any premeditated idea of murder would be in his mind. What I fancy would happen would be something like this. He'd get home, finish off his final arrangements, and then find himself at a loose end. He'd begin to consider the new life that was going to begin that very night. He'd get restless, hanging about the empty house—Celia was in the garden, you remember, and probably out of sight, with Stephen. He'd stray out, to be in the sight of people, if not actually among them. I make out that he'd have got out just about half-past nine—a little after the stall collapsed, when the

Fair was closing down. He'd see there wasn't any fun to be got out of hanging about the Green. Everybody was going.

"What would he do then? He didn't want to hang about indoors alone. There wasn't anything doing on the Green. Isn't it likely that he'd walk into the woods—perhaps with some sort of semi-sentimental idea of saying-good-bye-to-the-old-place sort of touch?"

I nodded.

"And, hanging about there, putting in time, he saw Mrs. Harrington crossing the Green. I can imagine how a sort of fury might rise up in him as he saw her. . . ."

I can imagine

"So can I," I agreed. "But what I can't imagine is how he happened to have a gun in his hand and a missile that just fitted it—all ready."

"The gun's all right, I think," said the curate. "He'd have appeared just after the collapse of that beastly stall. We know that some of the guns were lost. I think it's quite possible that he saw one, and picked it up idly, not meaning, of course, to make any particular use of it—he might have picked it up half unconsciously."

"He *might*, I suppose. And then, I imagine, you think that, fooling about in the wood, putting in time, he fitted a stone to it . . ."

"Yes. Something like that."

"It's *possible*, I suppose," I admitted very grudgingly. "*Barely* possible. But *most* improbable. But—he might have shot the stone out just idly and got her by accident," I added more cheerfully. "He was quite keen on the idea of an accident."

But Roger Cartwright shook his head.

"Not a real accident—not with a shot like Harrington. It was as light as day, you know, at half-past ten that night. He simply couldn't have helped seeing her."

I thought it over for a bit.

"Well," I said at last, "I suppose it is possible. I admit that it's a very great pity that one can't check his movements yesterday. Even the wire apparently wasn't sent. But your theory leaves a lot of loose ends. It doesn't clear up the mystery of the person in Mrs. Harrington's room—the person who came in by her window and lay in her bed with boots on. Also, I'm pretty certain that Godfrey Harrington did *not* know that his wife was dead when he spoke to me."

"What exactly did he say?"

"He was clearly astonished to see me. He asked what was wrong—whether Celia was ill. I told him there had been an accident to his wife. He was surprised—I'd take my oath that he was surprised."

"Hm!" he pondered.

"But then," I continued, "I can't deny that his conduct, take it all round, was, as you say, very queer. Why did he come prowling down the corridor? I don't see that the fact that he'd shot his wife accounts in the least for his doing that. And why did he telephone?"

"It works in—it *must* work in!" muttered the curate, rumpling his unfortunate hair. "It must fit somewhere."

"Because it's odd, you mean?"

"Exactly. . . . Miss Leslie, look at it square. If the Squire had *really* just got back from a tiring expedition to town, *would* he have bothered to go and see Celia, whom he never bothers with normally? Wouldn't he have fussed round for his wife and asked her for food and things?"

"Yes," I agreed, "of course he would. He'd have got her up and wanted sympathy. . . . Of course he might have been coming to rouse Celia—no, though, he wouldn't. He knows she isn't allowed to have anything to do with the housekeeping."

"And—you're *sure* it wasn't he in Mrs. Harrington's room?"

"Positive. I'm sure he didn't know that her body wasn't in there. No, I admit his conduct is queer, very queer, and I admit that he's quite probably lying about what he did yesterday, and I admit that it's possible that he might do such a thing—but I don't believe he did it. I believe the poppy-stain is the only thing that really matters."

16

The next day was Sunday. We had a terrible time at church, as you may guess—poor dear old Mr. Jukes has no taste or tact, and the hymns were terrible and the sermon harrowing. I decided that, correct or no, in the afternoon I would take Celia for a walk. The weather was still hot and fine, but a touch of sultriness was coming into the summer heat. I felt 'on edge'; I hated hanging about the house, and especially I hated that corridor with the empty room that had been visited by the mysterious stranger. I wanted to get out of the Manor House atmosphere, and I thought Celia ought to get out of it too. It wasn't good for her to sit about, brooding over the possible or impossible connexion of Stephen Earle with her stepmother's death.

I collected Celia and told her that I thought we ought to go and ask after Lydia, who had been restored to her home by Dr. Ludlow on Friday night—or rather Saturday morning. She had been, it seemed to me, quite unnecessarily agitated and terrified, and somehow I didn't think it was all due to her physical condition. I did, quite genuinely, feel anxious about the girl, but I'll admit that I also had a hope that a little sympathy and a hint that one knew her story and was on her side might make her tell what she knew—if she knew anything—of the happenings of the night before.

I didn't say this to Celia. After all, poor Lydia's secret was her own, and it didn't seem fair to tell even Celia, unless Lydia gave up all hopes of privacy and let the world into her secret. We walked in silence for some minutes, but we were both, of course, occupied with the same question—the puzzles surrounding Mrs. Harrington's death. And so I didn't need any elucidation when Celia suddenly began.

"Miss Leslie—do you think it's possible that she was *really* afraid of some one—some stranger?"

"I don't know," I replied. "You ought to know more about it than any one else. You seem to be the only person who really had any idea of such a possibility."

"Not quite," said Celia slowly. "Mrs. Nokes knew."

"So she did! Or was she just talking metaphorically, do you think? I mean—I'm not particularly superstitious, you know, but—well, Mrs. Nokes is a bit uncanny, isn't she? And I wondered whether, when she said that about 'a stranger at her shoulder that means death,' she was sort of prophesying, you know—second sight or something?"

"I don't think so," said Celia, wrinkling her pretty brows. "That remark about 'messages she shakes to hear' fits in much better with my theory of some one who was in communication with her—some one she didn't want any one to know about."

"Yes," I agreed, "it does."

We were walking in the shade of the trees now. The sun, filtering through the heavy foliage of the oaks, and the scent of the undergrowth, gave us that sort of hushed feeling that you nearly always get in woods, especially in high summer; but I didn't agree with Celia when she said it was 'like church'; I thought the stillness and heat felt haunted. I shouldn't have been in the least surprised to see a goatlike creature with a pipe. I felt—well, 'haunted' is the only word. I quite jumped when a twig snapped behind us, even though I knew, before Celia said so, that it was probably a squirrel dodging in and out and waiting for us to pass.

"I say," said Celia a little shyly, "I've been wondering—I know it's rotten to pry where you're not wanted, but—don't you think things are a bit different after a person's dead? I mean, though you wouldn't think of reading their private papers when they're alive, isn't it a bit different . . . ?"

"You mean one might find a clue to this mysterious stranger in her papers?"

"Yes. Wouldn't that be a bit different? You see, it might give us a clue as to who—killed her."

"It might. Yes, if it were to do that, I do think we'd be justified in reading her papers. But you know, Celia, we won't have the chance. The police have put seals on all her drawers and desk and things."

"Not quite, they haven't," said Celia slowly. "They couldn't find them all."

"What do you mean?"

"Well, she was very secretive, you know. That was one of the things the servants—and I—didn't like about her, the way she kept everything under lock and key. And she didn't keep her most private papers in her desk at all, I suppose she knew that locks on things like that are very easy to open."

"What did she do with them, then?"

"I don't know for certain; but I think I can guess. One night—oh, weeks ago now—I had a sudden bad go of toothache. It's a thing I never have as a rule, and I hadn't anything for it. So I went along to her room to ask for something out of the medicine chest. There was a light under her door so I tapped and went straight in. And as

I opened the door I could see quite clearly a little sort of cupboard thing in the wall over her bed. I wasn't surprised—the house is full of secret cupboards and things, you know—but she was awfully upset. She jumped up as I came in, and I think she must have pushed it shut as she moved—she got between me and the hole. I pretended I was too frantic with pain to have noticed anything; I felt I just *couldn't bear* one of those endless rows. But I saw where the hole was; I could find it again easily. It was let into the wall in the panelling just over that *pieta* picture— the door just cleared the frame. She had to kneel up in bed to reach it. And I'm sure she had papers in her hand."

"I see. And you think she probably kept her very private papers there—perhaps some of those mysterious letters she was so alarmed about?"

Celia nodded.

"I feel sure of it," she said.

"But look here, Celia. She was an excellent business woman. If she had anything very precious to keep, she'd have sent it to her bank."

"No—that's just what she wouldn't have done. She once had had some private papers destroyed in a fire in a country bank somewhere, and she'd never send papers to a bank again. Father used to tell her that things are safe enough now, and there are fireproof safes and everything, but she wouldn't listen. Miss Leslie, I feel *sure* the clue to the murder is there—in the papers hidden in the little cupboard over her bed."

"Well," I said, "perhaps you're right. But don't you think in that case we ought to tell the police?"

"No—not till we know what's in them. It may be something that hasn't to do with her death at all. And anyhow, what I feel is this—I'm sure there are papers there, very private papers; and I feel pretty sure that they have some connexion with her past life. But I think it's quite likely that she'd even rather that her murderer got off free than that the police should know her secrets."

"Yes, I agree that's quite possible. Also, as you say, they might not have anything to do with her death at all. Yes, Celia, I think you're right. When we get back we'll try to open that safe. And when we do, we'll have to decide whether what we find—if anything—ought to be shown to the police or not."

Celia said nothing, but I could see from the obstinate set of her lips that she didn't intend to help the police one atom. I saw that diplomacy would be necessary.

"If we could find anything that would set them on the track of a mysterious stranger," I said thoughtfully, "that would be much the best way of diverting their attention from poor Joe Greaves."

"And from Stephen," said Celia, voicing with a brutal frankness what I intended should be merely delicately implied.

"If they're on him," I amended; and then we were at Ben Salt's cottage, and no more could be said.

Old Salt was rather reluctant to let us see Lydia, but he had no real reason why we shouldn't, and in the end we mounted the steep little stair to her room. I couldn't make out, from his manner, whether he'd guessed what was wrong with the girl or not. He knew that she was, or had been, very ill, and told us not to "work her up"; and when I saw her I was really shocked, she looked so distraught and so desperate.

I made up my mind instantly that this should be a mere 'parochial' visit, such as I hate both in theory and in practice, and that I would not attempt to find out whether Lydia knew anything of Joe's movements on that fatal night of the twenty-ninth of June. But she wouldn't let it go at that. She knew, I suppose, that I wasn't of the district-visiting kind, and that normally I should have left it to Mrs. Arnold or Mrs. Jukes to go and see her if they felt some one ought to. Presently she gave herself away utterly.

"Is there a lot of talk in the village, miss, about the poor mistress?" she asked suddenly, in answer to a harmless question as to whether she liked wine jelly. Then, without waiting for an answer, she rushed on:

"They'll say anything in Ringshall, won't they, miss? Set o' gossipin', intermeddlin' lopers as they be!" (She had quite forgotten, in her distress, the carefully learnt 'nice' pronunciation that Mrs. Harrington was so particular to instil into her maids.) "There's naught as they won't say, if so be as they can make a taale out'n en. . . . There'll be a lot o' talk about the poor mistress."

"No doubt," I said, "but I haven't been into the village, so I haven't heard any gossip."

That silenced her for a minute; then she burst out again:

"Is it true, miss, as the police is up at the House?"

"Oh yes, of course. We've all been questioned and cross-questioned."

I tried to make my voice sound light and amused.

"Lot o' foouls!" stormed the girl. "That Gregory, he'm a-tryin' to lay it on Joe! Why, Joe weren't to home for Fair. He'd gone over to Phillipses to see about a job. He went earlyish, an' he said to me, 'I'll likely be back late, Lyd,' he said, 'so I wun't see 'ee again to-day,' he said. An' he were away aal day, not next nor nigh Fair, nor he wudn' 'a gone, not wi' Her a-runnin' of it—nobbut what Joe liked the poor mistress well," she added hastily.

"Oh, Lydia, that's a mistake," said Celia, in spite of my signals to her to hold her tongue. "Joe was at the Fair. I saw him at the rifle booth—"

"No, you never did, miss!" shrieked Lydia. "'Twere some other lad as you see—Joe weren't there, he weren't next nor nigh the place, so he weren't . . ."

It was a long time before we could soothe her, and then it was only by saying that perhaps we were mistaken. I felt the Recording Angel would be looking the other way, for he can't possibly want you to tell the absolute truth to a girl whom it might kill to hear it.

We left the cottage feeling rather perturbed—at least, I was. Of course Lydia was lying, and lying idiotically. Every one knew that Joe had been shooting at the Fair, and shooting extraordinarily well. Every one knew that he both hated and feared Mrs. Harrington. Several people knew that he had said publicly that she ought to be got rid of. When Lydia was stronger, I decided I'd tell her that she was doing far more harm than good by her stupid and patent lie.

17

The walk in the heat, and the talk to Lydia, had taken longer than I thought. It was five when we got in, and I, at least, felt that I neither could nor would do another thing till I had had my tea and a peaceful cigarette. We told Lawson to bring tea out to the garden, and were just settling down when we saw two figures approach.

Now I am, I really do think, a sociable person; but I felt that I'd had enough. People (then) meant discussion, and if there was one thing I did *not* want to do just then, it was to discuss Mrs. Harrington's death. But it was too late to retreat. We had been seen.

Luckily, it was only Roger Cartwright and Stephen. One need not be polite to them. I told them they could come and have tea if they liked, if they would promise not to say a single word about our mystery; and Stephen said morosely that he was sick of it anyway, and Roger Cartwright said that he wouldn't say a word till I began it. So we had tea, and then Stephen asked Celia to come and show him Juno's last litter—an absurd pretext, which he didn't even try to make appear probable—and the curate and I were left alone under the trees.

"All right," I said resignedly, when the children had disappeared in the direction of the stable which Juno, the setter, is allowed to use as a lying-in hospital. "You may as well tell me. It's pathetic to see you trying not to."

"Well," he admitted, "I do rather want— Have you got that time-table of Harrington's movements still?"

"Of course I have. All the same, you're barking up the wrong tree if it's him you're after."

I never remember until after I've said it whether it's 'he' or 'him'. Many curates would have told me, politely; but this curate wasn't the kind that worries about grammar, ever, and now he had something else on his mind.

"Have you got it here?"

I had. I produced it.

"Here it is," I said, "but I won't give it to you till you tell me what you want it for."

"All right. I'll tell you. I want to."

He lit his pipe, which had gone out (as men's pipes do, when neglected for a moment), and, slowly drawing at it, began to tell me.

"You know I thought there was something fishy about Harrington's explanations," he said. "Well, I thought I'd try to find out what it was. And I think I've found it.

"After I left you yesterday I walked over to Dimsey and went to the station. No one remembered seeing Harrington on the 12.51 to Savernake—but, of course, that doesn't mean anything—so I took a 'bus over to Savernake to see if I could pick up anything at the station there.

"I thought, as I was there, I might as well go and see if there was a chance that the blighter who got poor Lydia Salt into her mess would speak up if necessary; so I asked the conductor to put me down at the Risewell turn. He didn't know the route, he said—he was new on the Savernake line; so, more to make talk than anything, I asked him what route he'd been on before. He said Devizes. I asked which he liked best, and he said this, because there was more doing. 'You mightn't believe it,' he said, 'but on the Devizes route we'd often run a day and have half a dozen passengers. I only changed yesterday,' he said, 'and on my last day on the Devizes route we'd only had one passenger on the outward journey, and that was Mr. Harrington, the gentleman whose wife's been murdered.'"

I sat up.

"Did he mean that he'd been on the Devizes bus on the Friday?" I asked.

"Yes. I asked, to be sure."

"He must have been wrong."

"That's what I thought. That's why I asked again. So I asked him how he knew Mr. Harrington; and he said that when Harrington was on the Commission he—this conductor—had been hauled up on some charge or other. 'You don't forget the look of the beak,' he said."

"Then he'd got the day wrong," I declared.

"I tried that, too; but he was very positive. To begin with, it was his last day on that route, so he remembered it pretty clearly; and besides he remembered that he'd had an unusual number of passengers going the other way, to Ringshall Fair; and he remarked to the driver that it was queer that the Squire should be going out on the Fair day."

"Well," I said, after a pause, "even so, it doesn't matter very much. He went to town from Devizes instead of from Savernake, that's all."

"But why should he do such a thing? It's the same train, only it leaves Devizes a good half-hour earlier and Devizes is much farther. If he was in a hurry to get to town, why on earth didn't he go to Savernake? And why did he say he did if he didn't?"

"I've just remembered," I cut in. "He *did* go to Devizes. He said he did. But it was on Thursday, not Friday. He went to see the museum."

"I don't believe that conductor was wrong about the day. He'd every reason to remember—the last day on that route, the comparative crowd going to Ringshall, and the single passenger going the other way—and that passenger noticed particularly, because it seemed odd that the Squire shouldn't be at the Fair."

"Perhaps he left something at Devizes—in the museum, or a shop," I suggested rather feebly.

"Then why on earth didn't he say so?"

"I don't know. . . . What do you make of it?"

"This—that he didn't go to town on the Friday at all. He went (if he went at all) on the Thursday, when he said he was at Devizes; and on Friday, the day of the Fair, he only went to Devizes, from where he could have got home almost any time he liked."

I considered this.

"Well? What did you do?"

"I hopped off at Savernake, and got the 11.42 to Devizes. I thought it was possible that he'd used that as a telephoning centre. But I saw at once that it was much too small a place; he'd have gone for a bigger town. I thought Newbury was the likeliest, so I went on there.

"I went to the General Post Office, and asked the girl to get me the number of the cross-Channel steamer lines, either from Southampton or Newhaven. I thought it was probable that, since he hadn't gone to town direct, he was planning to go abroad."

"You took it for granted that he was going to—to—"

"To cut? Well, I had to start somewhere, and I admit that seemed the most probable idea. Anyhow, I thought it was worth a chance."

"Well?"

"Well, the line was engaged, so I went out for a bit to wait. The inside of a post office is no place to wait in on a day like Saturday."

He paused to relight his pipe. What pipes must cost a year in matches alone is a solemn thought.

"Go on," I said impatiently.

"Well, as I had to put in time, I went into a shop for some baccy. The place was fullish, so I stood just inside the door. And as I was standing there I saw—our friend Harrington."

"*What?* In Newbury?"

He nodded.

"You *must* have been mistaken."

"I wasn't. It was Harrington—carrying a large suitcase."

"What time was this?"

"About half-past twelve or a quarter to one."

Certainly the Squire hadn't been in to lunch. . . .

"What did you do?"

"What *does* the sleuth do on these occasions? I trailed him, of course."

I drew a long breath. This was, I felt, The Goods.

"He seemed in a hurry," Roger Cartwright went on, "and he was going quite a pace. I noticed that the case, though it was a fairly large one, swung in his hand. It was either empty or had very little in it.

"He was making for the station. When he got there, he slowed up—he'd done the walk in better time than he hoped, I suppose—and I had to do some dodging behind the taxi rank, for he stopped and looked up and down, as if he were on the lookout for some one."

"He was expecting somebody to join him?"

"No, I don't think so. He just looked about sort of—of furtively. He's about the world's worst criminal."

"Oh, come!" I protested. "Criminal's a bit strong."

"Wait," said he grimly.

I shut up with my usual docility.

"He looked about," the curate repeated, "and was obviously relieved when he saw no one he knew. He went into the booking-office, and I joined the queue a little farther down—just far enough to hear his station, and not too near for him to spot me. He booked to Southampton.

"The train was in. I kept behind him, and got into the next compartment. When we'd got going I walked along the corridor. He had a paper open and was hidden behind it. If I hadn't seen him get in, I'd never have spotted him there.

"It was easy to follow him at Southampton. Obviously he thought he was safe. He took a taxi, and I was able to hear the address—the Lymington Hotel. So of course I went there too. But I told my man I was in the dickens of a hurry, and by judicious bribery I got there first.

"I walked into the lounge and sat down, well concealed behind a paper, as if I was waiting for a friend—which, as a matter of fact, I was. In a minute or two he rolled up. He went straight to the desk. I tried my best to hear what he said, but I could only get a word or two: 'Parcels' was one, and 'Harris, George Harris' and something, about a telephone, and 'postponed'. The clerk seemed sympathetic, but she said something to which he answered, 'Of course I'll pay.' He did pay something—with paper—and then he got a hotel porter and went off upstairs.

"I ordered a drink to have a good excuse for hanging on. In about a quarter of an hour he came back. The porter was carrying his case, and I could tell it wasn't so very light this time. He looked at his watch, asked the porter to fetch him a taxi—said he was in a hurry—and cleared out."

"With you on his trail," I murmured.

"With me on his trail," assented the curate. "I nearly missed him, though. I couldn't dart out after him too obviously. I had to stroll up to the desk, pay, say it didn't look as if my pal was coming, chat to the girl, and so on; so I had to guess where he'd gone. All I had to go on was the direction his taxi'd taken; and that was away from the docks. So I guessed that he'd either gone to some office or bank, or to a second hotel, to cover his tracks, or to the station. As he said he was in a hurry, I risked the last.

"I asked the hotel porter when the next train for London left. He said at 4.10—loads of time. So he must have been going home again. I got a taxi, drove like the dickens, and hopped into the Savernake train just as it was moving. I got out at the next station and moved down the train. I thought I spotted him, but I couldn't be certain, so I stuck to the train, and at Savernake I saw him get out. He went to the cloak-room and left the case. And as he left the place I saw him carefully destroy his cloak-room ticket."

If I could whistle, I should have done so then. It seemed the only appropriate comment. As I can't, I said nothing.

"What did you do?" I asked, after a pause.

"I stayed where I was. I'd seen all I needed to. But when I got out at Dimsey I rang up the Lymington Hotel and asked whether a Mr. George Harris had booked rooms there for himself and wife."

"And wife," I murmured.

"Yes. I thought it likely. . . . Well, it came off. I pushed off some tale about having an urgent message for Mrs. Harris, and believing that she and her husband were there; and the clerk—I'd taken her measure—she was most sympathetic. She said that they had booked rooms for the night of the twenty-ninth, and had had a lot of parcels sent to the hotel, but they'd never turned up till to-day, when he appeared and said he'd had to put off coming owing to his wife's sudden illness; so he paid, took his parcels, and went."

18

We sat silent for a bit. Then Roger Cartwright said:

"Well? What do you make of it?"

"What do you?" I retorted. "I suppose you make something."

"I'm bothered if I know!" he said, rumpling up his hair. "One thing's plain—that he meant to clear out, with a woman who was not Mrs. Harrington, on the night of the twenty-ninth. But why, in that case, did he turn up at home at half-past two in the morning? Why on earth wasn't he at Southampton then? And why the parcels, and why did he destroy the cloak-room ticket?"

"If," I said slowly, "you're right in assuming that the woman who was going wasn't his wife, the answer to the first question is clear enough. He came back to fetch her."

"Why shouldn't she have gone with him in the first place?"

"Well, perhaps it was like this—he went ahead to prepare everything, cover tracks and so on, so that the elopement should go perfectly smoothly. She, meanwhile, was putting in time in camouflage. We're both thinking the same thing, so let's assume that the lady was Lady Gervaise."

He nodded.

"Well, she put in her time in the best possible way, if an elopement was really in the wind. She appeared very much in the public eye, apparently quite at her ease, diverting any possible suspicion. She'd know quite well that if she, as well as he, was missing from the Fair, Mrs. Harrington (who was, as we know, a very jealous woman) would smell a rat. So he goes to the Fair, stays as long as he dare, and then clears out to make arrangements—take tickets, secure berths, and so on; while she remains, nothing apparently further from her thoughts than a hurried departure.

"But she was, you remember, very nervous as the day went on. She was horribly on edge that evening, and she went home as soon as ever she could. My belief is that she had to pack and get her car ready for a longish and very rapid journey. Then there's another thing. You know how odd we all thought it was that he'd been so particular to say that no one was to wait in for him? And Mrs. Harrington refused to have that? Well, I believe that was because she guessed that there was something in the wind. She wanted to be sure that he *did* come in, *did* go to bed. That was partly why, she insisted on Celia going home and staying there till her father arrived. And she was right, because, as I see it, what he meant to do was this—not to come back to the Manor House at all; to fix things up for the departure, come back and pick up Lady Gervaise, drive straight to Southampton, go to the hotel to collect the new things he'd bought—he couldn't pack, you see, or take any of his own stuff without Mrs. Harrington knowing of it—and then clear out. And I believe he purposely picked the twenty-ninth because he knew that his wife would be out practically all day, and would have her mind occupied, and that the house would be empty, so that no one would know that he hadn't come in and gone to bed. He may even have left some written message to say he had, which he afterwards destroyed. We weren't in a state of mind to look for it, if he wrote such a thing. That accounts for most of the queer things he did—his unusual consideration, his visit to the little corridor, his behaviour on Saturday—everything."

"Yes," he said, and he sounded a little disappointed. "It fits all right."

"Of course," I admitted, "it washes out any hope of his being the murderer."

"Exactly. . . . And why do you say that it accounts for his going to the corridor when he did come in?"

"Why, because, though he doesn't bother to say good-night to his daughter, even Godfrey Harrington might want to say good-bye."

"Ye—es. Yes, I suppose that's true. . . . But why on earth do you think that they left it so late? Why didn't they cut hours before?"

"I think they meant to. I think that was why Lady Gervaise was so jumpy. But something happened to delay him. He's a rotten manager, you know."

"Yes." He paused. "I can't help thinking," he went on, "that there's another possibility—two more, in fact. You see, what Harrington has been out for, in this story of a visit to town, has been to fix the time of his return home as late as possible. Now to me that suggests that he really got home a good deal earlier than he admits. If he booked his rooms at the Southampton hotel by telephone, as I originally thought, he could have been back much earlier—by half-past nine, anyhow. (Dash it, I wish I'd thought of finding out whether he took those rooms personally or not, and if so, on what day!) Well, if he got back to Ringshall as early as that, a lot might have happened."

"For instance?"

"Well—I don't say this is sound; I haven't thought it out yet, and you're certain to spot about a dozen snags—but let's say something like this.

"To begin with, he'd booked the room for the night of the twenty-ninth. If your theory's right, and he only got back to collect the lady at 2.30 a.m., he wouldn't have got to Southampton again before 4.30 at the very earliest—probably later. He'd rouse comment at once, if he turned up at that hour. Why do it? He can't have mismanaged his trains to that extent."

"I expect he could. Trains from Southampton are very awkward indeed. As to the reason for taking a room at all, as I said, he had to have a depot for the clothes and things to be sent to, and that depot had to be a place he could pack in. And, if they were making an early start, their boat would have sailed by the time inquiries were started in Southampton."

"I suppose that's so. But there are other solutions. This, for instance. Suppose he'd arranged to get back by 9.30 or so, meet Lady Gervaise, and get off about ten or soon after. That accounts for her fidgeting—she had to meet him very soon after she left the Dower House. Now, they couldn't meet either at Haresfoot or at the Manor House. He wouldn't risk being seen at Haresfoot, and she, although it would be all right for her to turn up at the Manor, had to pack, get her car ready, and all that. Well, where would they meet? I say they'd have a rendezvous in the wood. It's near both houses, and also it's near the Fair, so that they could appear to be on the way to or from it. When they'd met, and he'd told her that the way was all clear, she'd go home, collect the car and her stuff, and pick him up along the Southampton road. Well, suppose that, before they parted, Mrs. Harrington came along on her way to Ben Salt's, and—"

"And made a row?"

"Yes. As you say, she was horribly jealous. The very fact of finding them together in the wood would be enough."

"Yes, I admit that."

"Well—isn't that good enough?"

"Nothing like," I said briskly. "To begin with, Mrs. Harrington was not shot in the wood, nor in any secluded spot, but right in the middle of Foakes Green, where anybody might pass at any moment."

"Not at night," the curate pointed out. "No one crosses Foakes Green at night if they can help it."

"No, but even so it isn't a likely place for a secret tryst, especially as no one thought the Fair would come to an end when it did."

"True. But, look here! The actual row might have taken place in the wood, and then, when she'd left them, and was marching off ready to make the worst kind of scandal—"

"One of them shot her?"

"Yes."

"Well, of course, they're both excellent shots, and the moon was bright as day. But you've overlooked one thing. Why should either of them have brought a gun to the meeting?"

"Ah, I know. That's *the* snag," he admitted ruefully. "They wouldn't, of course."

"Otherwise," I admitted handsomely, "it's not bad. There's the opportunity, the motive, the sudden temptation as they saw her, a clear mark in the moonlight, and knew that she'd destroy their happiness. And it explains most of Godfrey Harrington's behaviour, too. The telephone would be to the hotel—though it doesn't now explain why he came to the corridor. Only—the weapon's wanting."

The curate had been thinking hard. He was obviously very loth to give up a theory which involved the man he'd trailed like the best sleuths in fiction, and which accounted for so many things.

"I say," he said suddenly, "that stall—the one that was smashed. Suppose some one, some one not quite responsible, a bit tight or—or imbecile—pinched one of those guns, and then chucked it away in a funk into the nearest cover. Suppose, before the row, he—Harrington—saw it, and picked it up—"

"And fitted a flint arrow-head to it for a joke?" I asked, with scorn.

"No—I suppose not. . . . And yet, it *is* possible. Suppose he was early at the tryst, and had to wait some time, and while he was waiting he saw this thing and picked it up. It would glitter like fun in the moonlight, you know. If he had time to put in, it *is* possible that he'd fool about with it, fitting missiles and so on. And then, after the row, he'd have it at the back of his mind, half unconsciously . . ."

"But," I said, "even supposing you're right—which I don't for a single second suppose you are—what happened then? If all this happened at 10.30 or so, why was it that he didn't come home till nearly three?"

"Getting over it, perhaps," he suggested feebly.

"No. I tell you, when I saw him in the passage he didn't know it had happened. I'm sure he didn't."

"Well, then, there's only one other theory—and it lets out Harrington. The beginning part is the same; but let's say now that the lady was the first to arrive. She was afraid of being late, which accounts for her restlessness, and went straight to the wood, which accounts for her refusing to be seen home. She's early after all, and has to wait. In the wood she meets Mrs. Harrington, on her way back from Salt's. Mrs. Harrington is suspicious, and Lady Gervaise is on edge; to get rid of her, she says something purposely rude. They have a quarrel, and the whole thing flares up—suspicion, perhaps admission. You know how perfectly reckless Lady Gervaise is. Mrs. Harrington declares she'll stop it, and goes off. Lady Gervaise, beside herself, sees her chance of happiness going with her, and—and shoots.

"Let's say that she does it in a fit of madness. As soon as it's done, she's appalled. She rushes off, anywhere She's terrified, beside herself, forgets the careful plans and everything else till hours later, when she steals home. But Harrington, who knows nothing of all this, has waited and waited for her; when she doesn't appear, he thinks she's made a mistake about the place, and spends hours searching for her. He only gives it up when it's hopelessly too late—about half-past two, in fact. He goes home, dispirited, dead beat.

"That accounts for nearly everything—for her nervousness, her knowledge of the death, his lie about going to town, his late return, and even, if you admit the possibility of the stolen gun and the fitting of the stone, for the missile and weapon. And remember that Lady Gervaise had used those very guns, and had got five bulls in six shots with one."

"I think it's possible that you're right about the gun," I admitted, "but not about the missile. I don't think it's a bit likely that she would mess about fitting flint arrowheads to a gun while she was waiting to meet the man she was going to elope with."

"I admit that's a very weak point. But as far as I remember, your nice theory about the movements of those two doesn't account for the murder at all."

"It doesn't," I said. "It isn't meant to, because I don't believe their movements have anything to do with the murder. I haven't got a theory about that yet, only a vague idea. But one thing I *am* sure of, and that is that the bed and the poppy-stain come in. And you haven't begun to account for that."

He looked at me quizzically and was just (I'm convinced) going to say something rude; but he didn't, because just then the two children returned over the lawn. It had taken them over three-quarters of an hour to examine Juno's puppies.

"I say," said Celia, "I've been telling Stephen about that little cupboard."

"What little cupboard?" asked Roger Cartwright.

"One Celia knows of, where Mrs. Harrington kept her private papers," I explained. "Well?"

"Well—why don't we go and look in it?" asked Stephen.

"We will, if you like," I said, rising. "Celia and I agreed that it might be a good plan some hours ago."

She had the grace to blush, though he hadn't. To divert my attention she said hurriedly:

"Oh, and I say—what do you think we found at the back of the stable—right at the very back, nearly hidden by sacks and things?"

I didn't ask her why they had thought it necessary to retire right to the very back of the stable among sacks and things in order to admire the puppies who live in the front.

"What?" I asked.

"Why, one of dad's best suit-cases! The very biggest. If Banks wasn't Banks, I'd think it had been hidden there, ready to be quietly removed."

"I expect it was," I said, thinking of the curate's story.

"It can't have been. Banks isn't that kind," said Celia indignantly.

"Perhaps it wasn't Banks. Was there anything in it?"

"Not a thing. That's what's so odd. It was quite empty."

"There'd been another," Stephen put in, "a slightly smaller one, but quite large, lying on the top of the one that's there now. You can tell by the dust. But that one's gone."

"I think I know where that one is," said the curate; and though his voice was casual enough, his glance at me was significant.

"Oh, never mind the beastly thing," said Celia impatiently. "Let's go and look at that cupboard. I'm sure we'll find out all we want to know if we can once get that open."

We all moved across the lawn towards the house. None of us had anything to say, except that, just to make quite sure, I did ask Celia whether they had made any plans for the holidays. It struck me that we were perhaps going too fast in taking it for granted that the Squire's companion was to be Lady Gervaise and not, say, Celia, or even his own wife.

She shook her head.

"We weren't doing anything, as far as I know," she said. "I don't suppose we will now."

"Wasn't your father thinking of having a day or two away?"

"Oh no. He'd have known about that suit-case if he had been. But he won't ever go at this time of year. He says Ringshall's too good to miss in June."

That was that. The departure *was* a secret.

We went straight up to Mrs. Harrington's room. Everything in the receptacle line was, as we knew, sealed. Celia took the lead. She walked up to the bed.

"Bother, they've taken down the picture," she remarked. "Still, I ought to be able to get it. She was sitting up in bed, and it was by her shoulder—"

The girl got on to the bed, lay down to get the right position, and then sat up.

"It should be about here," she stated, laying her hand on the wall.

"That's right—here's the mark of the nail the picture hung on," said Stephen, examining the moulded panelling closely. He tapped the place where Celia had laid her hand. Certainly it did sound hollow.

I admit I was excited—not only by the discovery of the place of the safe, but also by something else that had come into my head as I saw Celia's way of finding the right spot.

"Here we are," said the curate.

A tiny hole—so small that you would never have noticed it in the carved panelling if you hadn't been searching for it—had caught his eye.

"Shall we force it?" asked Stephen, taking out a knife; but before any one could answer, Roger Cartwright said, a little grimly:

"There's no need. Some one else has done that."

It was quite true. As he slipped the point of the knife into the tiny hole, the whole door swung loosely out. The lock was a wreck.

"We're late for the fair," said the curate, putting his hand into the space behind. "I don't know if there ever was anything in here—but there's nothing now. It's absolutely empty."

19

It wasn't till next day that we were able to talk over this new development. We were too late, that day, to do much real work on it; besides, what I wanted to do was to collect Stephen and Roger Cartwright and, with their aid, to talk out *all* the possibilities, and it's a bit awkward to discuss the chances of a man having committed a murder when his daughter is there. Not that I thought, or ever had thought, that Godfrey Harrington had killed his wife, and this discovery of the rifled safe seemed, I thought, rather to let him out than anything; but I wanted, as I say, to talk over all there was to go on, and work out all the theories that any one held or could hold. And he certainly was a theory, if a poor one.

I did as I wanted to. I generally do. I caught Stephen and the curate walking together the very next morning, and I could have betted my last penny that they were talking over the bearing of the opened safe on the problem of the murder. I didn't waste any time. As soon as we had greeted each other I began.

"I suggest," I said, "that we three depart to some retired and privy spot, such as my garden, and get a lot of paper and pens and things, and make out a neat table of possible criminals, with pros and cons for each. I feel sure that's what really good sleuths ought to do. Besides, it clarifies the brain."

They agreed; so we strolled across to the Dower House, leaving a message for Celia to say that I'd be back in time for lunch.

I established the two men in the garden and went into the house for paper—lots of it—and every other accessory of the business man's desk, as they say in the catalogues. But, needless to say, I had the greatest difficulty in getting them to attend properly when I returned. I don't know why it is that men *will* stray from the point if you leave them to themselves for a second. They shut up, rather guiltily, when I reappeared, and I should have been willing to take another handsome bet that what they had been discussing was not clues nor crimes—in a word, not murder but matrimony.

I was rather stern with them. I sat down, arranged my paraphernalia, and gave what I considered to be a lifelike imitation of a chairman.

"Please attend, both of you," I said severely. "First, let's have a list of possible suspects."

"Isn't she enjoying herself!" murmured Stephen; but I ignored him.

"You back Godfrey Harrington," I said to the curate, "or, failing him, Lady Gervaise. Who's your choice, Stephen?"

"I haven't one yet," said Stephen, "though no doubt I'll hit on some one soon. But the police think it's either me or Joe Greaves."

I wrote these names down.

"Now yours," said the curate. "Who exactly is it that you have in your mind's eye?"

"We'll call him X," I said, with relish. "The Unknown."

"Oh, the mysterious Man from the Past," said Stephen, with an impish grin.

"Exactly. Now, is there any one else?"

"You're out of it," said Stephen, "more's the pity. You'd be a perfectly splendid criminal. But you've got a perfectly good alibi, and so has Roger. Celia hasn't. Do you include Celia?"

"No, I don't," I said crossly. "I said *possibilities.*"

"Well, then, there's nobody much left. Oh yes, there is, though. There's the girl—what's her name?—Lydia Salt."

"Lydia. Yes, I suppose there's Lydia. And there's Mrs. Nokes."

"And Tom Nokes, if you come to that," said the curate.

"Yes. Oh, heavens, what a list! That's seven—eight, if you count Lydia. . . . Well, let's start with the clergy."

I took a fresh sheet and wrote at the top 'G. H.' Under this I put at the top left-hand side 'Pro,' and on the right 'Con,' and divided the sheet into two columns. I felt most pleasantly efficient.

"Go on, padre," said Stephen. "You're invited to contribute your ideas first, in consequence of your calling. Why do you think the Squire is a murderer?"

Roger Cartwright (of course) lit a pipe.

"First," he said, drawing at it, "there's the motive. A *crime passionel,* in a way. We've gone into that, and we think—don't we?—that, given the opportunity and the weapon, he might easily have done it. Then we know that he was an excellent shot—could shoot straight in almost any light, with almost any weapon. We know that, in spite of what he says, it was possible for him to have been on the spot at the right time, and we know that he lied about what he did that day—that he wasn't in town at all, but was fixing up a flight from Southampton. Then, when he was told of the death, his immediate reaction wasn't one of grief."

"But if he'd killed her it would have been," Stephen pointed out. "He'd have been prepared for it, and he'd have shammed sorrow if he didn't feel it. He certainly wouldn't have let you think he was relieved."

"Well, an impression like that is rather slight grounds to go on one way or the other," said the curate. "But even if he did show relief, it might have been because he'd cleared out as soon as he'd fired and had a fear afterwards that he'd only wounded her, and that he was in horrible danger of her speaking."

"Weak," said Stephen firmly. "Very weak."

"But possible," I suggested.

"Mmm—well, yes. Barely possible."

"What else?" I asked.

"Well, his proceedings after he had been told were so odd. Why did he telephone, for instance, and to whom?"

"I believe it was to the hotel," I said, "to say that he'd been prevented from coming. I don't see that that comes into the murder business one way or the other."

"No, neither do I," Stephen agreed.

He was clearly very reluctant to admit the possibility, even, that Celia's father could be guilty of the crime.

"Let's put down your theory in outline," I said. "The idea is that he only went to Devizes or Newbury—Southampton at farthest—got back at nine or a little after, went to meet Lady Gervaise in the wood. He had to wait, and then got the chance to find and to try the gun. He then met his wife, had a tremendous quarrel with her, and she departed, threatening divorce or something. He shot her in a fury, and then rushed off in a panic, and only got in at 2.30. He learnt from me that he had actually killed his wife, and then—what?"

"Rang up Lady Gervaise—not the hotel—to tell her to lie low," said the curate.

I wrote down the theory, and then proceeded to put reasons in the 'Pro' and 'Con' columns. In 'Pro' I put:

1.—Had motive.
2.—Probably had opportunity.
3.—Created a false alibi.
4.—Was an excellent shot.
5.—Had not seemed distressed on first hearing of death.
6.—Rang up some one, possibly L. G., on hearing.

"And now the Cons," I said. I wrote:

1.—The lack of a gun.
2.—Improbability of his using such a missile even if he had found the gun lost from the stall.
3.—I feel certain that he did not know of any accident to his wife when I met him at 2.30.

"More Pros than Cons," commented Roger Cartwright.

"Yes," I admitted, "but I don't see how you dispose of the Cons, especially the last one. I'm positive about that."

"Well, how do you dispose of the Pros?"

"I don't have to," I stated. "I haven't got to disprove your theory—you've got to prove it."

"Hear, hear!" applauded Stephen, "That's the spirit!"

"You be quiet," I snubbed him. "Your turn's coming. Now for Lady Gervaise. What about her?"

"The theory's much the same," said the curate, "except that the last 'Con' doesn't apply. The 'Pros' are all same, plus one more—that is, that if it was the gun from the stall that was used, she'd had practice with the very type of gun that same afternoon, and done wonders with it. Then there's her early knowledge of what had happened—unless it was she that the Squire rang up or unless he met her when he was out that morning, how did she know? And then—there's another very strong point. There's her point of view."

"What d'you mean by that?" asked Stephen. He was clearly far more ready to believe in this theory than the last.

"Well—roughly, her complete lack of a moral standard, or even convention. She doesn't care tuppence for man or god or devil. She'll break any law that gets in her way—or says she will."

"Quite," I said dryly. "If she said so less often I'd be more ready to think she meant it. Still, I admit that her 'point of view' puts her more in the running than, say, Celia."

"It also makes it possible," said Stephen slowly, "that it wasn't altogether—unpremeditated."

We looked at him, but he wouldn't meet our eyes. He stared at the ground, looking stubborn and rather embarrassed.

"It's like this," he went on. "She knows, as we all do, that Harrington's an uncertain sort of blighter. She might quite well guess what would probably have been the truth—that if he'd cleared out with her, as they planned, his conscience might have been always at him till he went back to 'respectability.' She might have determined to prevent that by making their—affair—legally possible.

"She's dare-devil enough for anything—we all know that. If she really loved Harrington (and, incredible as it seems to all of us, I believe she must) I do believe that it's possible that she'd do *anything* to get him. If that's so, it makes the whole thing much easier.

"She knew, of course, that Harrington was away, and wouldn't be back for hours—for though it's possible that he could have got home early, we haven't proved that he actually did. She'd have, let's say, three or four hours to do it in. She left us at half-past nine or so—a little later, I think—and left in a very queer, excited, state. She knew that Mrs. Harrington was going to Salt's, and would be coming back latish—Celia said so, you remember, in her hearing. Isn't it quite possible that she *planned* the thing?"

"What a beastly idea," said Roger Cartwright, rather hotly.

"Oh, beastly enough—but possible, all the same, both from what we know of her and what we know happened. It gives you the motive, the opportunity, it accounts for her having a gun—"

"Hold on," said the curate. "An Ariel One, like hers, wouldn't take that flint."

"She only *possesses* that," said Stephen. "She could have got hold of another easily enough—the Squire's Loxley, for instance."

"I suppose so. Well?"

"Then there's the pellet. She wouldn't possess any herself of the right size, as her rifle's so small; and it wouldn't have been easy for her to get a regulation airgun pellet to fit the larger gun at a moment's notice. If she had, it very likely wouldn't have been—effective. But, like every other kid brought up in the village, she's quite familiar with the idea of using a flint arrow-head as a missile. We've all, times and times, shot them out of catapults at birds and rabbits, and we all know how straight they fly and how deadly they are."

"That is," I said slowly, "none of the Cons, which applied to the Squire apply to her."

"Exactly. And there's one thing more. I haven't said a word to any one, because I'm not absolutely certain, but I'm pretty sure that just before I found the—the body that night, I saw Lady Gervaise."

"*What?*" we cried simultaneously.

Stephen nodded.

"Where?" asked Roger Cartwright.

"Well—that's the rum thing. I thought I saw her run across the Green, from the side gate of the Manor House."

"How could you tell?" asked the curate. "That side of the Green was all in shadow from the oaks."

"I know, and that's why I say I can't swear to it. But she—the person I saw—had on a light dress, and I knew the run. I'd know Lady Gervaise's run anywhere. As I say, I won't swear to it; as a matter of fact, I'd forgotten about it till yesterday—I was put off my stroke, you know when I found the body—but it's a very distinct impression, and I'm almost sure."

"So that's your theory," I said. "Lady Gervaise."

He nodded.

"I plump for that," he assented. "A premeditated murder."

"I call it a rotten theory," said Roger Cartwright, with heat—too much heat, I thought. He said it as I would have said it if Celia had been the lady in question, and I don't mind admitting that I felt a distinct pang. Lady Gervaise is so very attractive! But I was, at that moment, not a woman but an investigator. I wrote down Stephen's theory, with all the Pros.—motive, opportunity, possibility of weapon and missile, her early knowledge of the death, everything.

"If you're right," I said, as I finished, "we'll have to find out how she did get hold of the gun, and where it is now."

"I'll do that," said Stephen confidently. "I feel sure that that's the solution."

"I'm not," I said bluntly. "I'm sure it's wrong."

"Hear, hear!" applauded the curate. It really did amuse me, the way those two cheered me whenever I said that the other was wrong.

"Why?" asked Stephen, with surprise. He was clearly astonished that anyone *could* disagree with such a beautiful theory as his.

"For one thing, because of something Lady Gervaise herself said. When we were at the Fair, we heard Sir Digby Barnet holding forth in his usual style, and she said, 'What a charity it would be to provide him with a murder'—something like that. Is it likely that she *could* have said that if she'd actually been planning one?"

"She mightn't have been planning it then," said Stephen. "Those very words might have put it into her head."

"Rubbish!" I exclaimed. "Besides, it leaves out too much. It doesn't account for the visitor to Mrs. Harrington's room, or for the forcing of the safe."

Stephen wrinkled up his forehead.

"The last may come in somewhere," he said, thinking hard.

"I'm sure it doesn't," I said. "I'm sure it's connected with the visit to the room, and those two fit on to X."

"Oh yes, X," said Stephen, with a kind of amused tolerance that made me long to shake him. "Let's hear about X."

"Not yet," I stated firmly. "We'll get all the other theories out of the way first—and then you'll find that X is the only one that fits everywhere."

"All right. Let's take the police ideas—Joe Greaves and me. I'll do my own *dossier* first.

"Motive—only that she blocked my engagement, and we disliked each other. Not very good. It would account for her murdering me more than for my murdering her. Opportunity—I suppose I *could* have got it in on two occasions—first, before I came to you to supper, though that would have been a bit of a rush. Did I seem very much flurried?"

"You did not," I said. "You were discovered by me, in my dining-room, eating my strawberries and in a very bad temper, about five minutes after the very earliest possible time of the murder. If you're a criminal, you're very hardened."

"Aren't I just!" he grinned. "Well, my only other chance was in those few minutes when I left Celia under the oaks and chased off after the padre. I admit that I was quite alone then, and that no one was there when I said I'd found the body. If I'd planned it, and had a gun handy, and knew the exact moment at which she'd be crossing the Green, I might have brought it off then."

"Rather a lot of ifs," I murmured,

"Yes, but we may be able to clear some of 'em up. What next? Oh, weapon. Where did I get that, now? The looted stall, I suppose. I was there when it was smashed, you know. Missile—I know all there is to know about shooting flint arrow-heads. Good, isn't it?"

"Not very," I told him. "The time's the difficulty. Even if Dr. Ludlow had been wrong about the time of her death, and it really happened as soon as the Fair closed down at nine, you'd have had to *sprint* up to get to my house when you did. And I'll swear you hadn't been running when I found you stealing my strawberries—though of course that in itself shows a criminal disposition. The other chance— the later one—is far more possible, only as you said, it presupposes too much that you'd planned it all tremendously carefully, and knew exactly when she'd be coming, which nobody could."

"True; but the police think nothing of that," said Stephen cheerfully. "It's good law, you know, to suspect the person who finds the body. All good police do it in novels. Still, if you don't like it, we'll try their other theory—Joe Greaves. You do him."

"Motive, fairly good," I said, "though, as a matter of fact, it would have been far better if the murder had happened before it did—say about eight. It was too late to be of much use when she'd done the mischief. Still, as some one—Inspector Grier, I think it was—said, revenge might be quite good enough. And if Joe was *hors de lui,* as we know he was, it might have done."

"That's right," Stephen struck in. "If you were a bit tight, you might slay a person who's put you absolutely in the soup, even though it was too late to stop 'em. I should myself."

"And the weapon and missile are possible," I went on. "Joe's shooting with those rifle-stall guns was wonderful. And, as you said, every Ringshall child uses flint arrow-heads with catapults. Then there's Lydia. She swore blue that Joe wasn't at the Fair at all, and that he liked Mrs. Harrington and wouldn't touch her for the world. That's an obvious lie, of course, and just the idiotic sort of lie she'd tell if she was afraid that Joe had really done it."

"Also," put in the curate rather gloomily, "there's the fact that Joe had spoken threateningly about Mrs. Harrington, and that he left the Fair early in a very excited state of mind."

"Drunk, of course," commented Stephen.

"More or less. Not incapable. Most of 'em were a bit gone," said Roger Cartwright.

"Well, that's not a bad theory," said Stephen. "For the police, I call it quite a good one, though too obvious, of course. It looks as if Joe would have to rake up an alibi."

"I expect he can," said the curate; but I thought he sounded a little uneasy. "Anyhow," he added more briskly, "I'm sure it's wrong. I'm sure Joe isn't the man we want. I'd rather back the Mrs. Nokes theory. She's capable of anything."

"Well, it isn't a bad case against her," I put in. "Motive, revenge on account of her dismissal, and her general hatred of Mrs. Harrington. Look at the way she cursed her that very afternoon. And *she's* got no moral standard, if you like. She's a real heathen. It was she who kept on

encouraging Tom to try the rifles. She knows all there is
to know about flint arrows. It's perfectly possible—even
probable—that if any guns really did disappear from the
stall, the Nokeses had one at least. . . . It seems to me that
she's as likely as any one."

"The only trouble is," said the curate, "that she has an
alibi, of a sort."

"How do you know?" I demanded.

"Because I thought of her first. I thought the place and
the missile looked so very like her. And I remembered how
she'd made that lad go on and on—trying the guns. Why
did she do that, if she hadn't a special interest in them?
But I found out—quietly, of course—that she left the Fair
with Mrs. Rutter, about six, and was at the Rutters' till
eight, when she went straight to the 'Lady and Hare,' only
leaving at closing time. She was then seen home by Tom
Slater, not being fit to go alone."

"And what about Tom Nokes?" asked Stephen.

"I don't know. No one ever knows where Tom is at any
given time. But I doubt Tom. He'd never have thought of
such a thing on his own, and I doubt whether old Mother
Nokes would have trusted him to go through with it,
if she'd instigated it. He talks too easily. Besides, she
wouldn't have risked getting him into a mess of that sort.
She's devoted to him, after all."

"Of course," said Stephen, "we may all be barking up
the wrong tree. The thing may have been an accident."

"Of course," agreed the curate. "Any one of the lads
might have pinched a gun, if they'd been a bit tight—as
they mostly were; and any one who did would be quite
likely to fit a flint to it—he'd done it with a catty often
enough—and might have just let fly."

"Getting Mrs. Harrington?" I asked.

"Yes."

"I don't believe it," I said, after a moment's thought.

"Oh, neither do I," said he readily.

"No one does," said Stephen. "A murder's heaps more fun. Look how Aunt Marion's enjoying it! You wouldn't want to fob her off with a mere accident, would you? And I say, Aunt Marion, do tell us about X."

"All right," I said. "Give me a cigarette—no, *not* a Turkish one, Stephen, you know I hate them—and both of you sit still and listen. If you don't agree I'm right, I'll never try to teach either of you anything again. Now listen carefully."

20

I don't know why it is that, as soon as I'm really ready to display my powers, something always happens to prevent my doing it. Here was I, having made the others put their ideas first, so that I could deal with their more obvious errors, all ready to give them a most romantic theory which would account for the poppy-stain, the visitor to Mrs. Harrington's, room, the rifled safe, and (of course) the murder in all its details; and just as I was going to start I was interrupted. Jenny came out and said that Inspector Grier wished to see me.

"Oh, bring him out," I said, with resignation. Then I cheered up. "He *may* have something to tell us that we don't know," I said to the others encouragingly.

The wretched man must have been right on Jenny's heels. I could tell, from the twinkle in his eye as he bowed to me, that he'd heard what I said.

"We're just discussing the murder," I said, uncomfortably conscious that I was blushing. "Do sit down. Have you any news?"

"Nothing that you don't know, I expect," he said, smiling. "With such very accomplished amateurs about, the professionals haven't a chance. Really, sir" (turning to Roger Cartwright), "your trailing of Mr. Harrington was very creditable—very creditable indeed."

The curate stared at him.

"I haven't been eavesdropping," the inspector assured him. "Only, you see, it occurred to me, too, that the gentleman's movements—both past and present—required a little investigation."

"Were you there all the time?" asked Roger Cartwright in a tone of unwilling admiration.

"Oh no—not personally. But one of my men was. He said you did it quite well."

I really felt sorry for the poor man. But he rallied well.

"Were you just shadowing him as a matter of routine, or were you trying to trace his movements on the twenty-eighth and twenty-ninth?" he asked.

"Both. I had two men on the job."

"I say," said Stephen, with interest, "did you happen to discover whether he took those rooms personally or by telephone?"

"Yes. He did it personally. I expect you found out most of his movements, didn't you, sir?"

"A certain amount," said Roger Cartwright guardedly. "But I was too much occupied in seeing what he was doing at the moment to trace his past movements as much as I'd have liked to."

"Do be an angel and tell us exactly what he did," I begged.

He hesitated for a fraction of a second, and then a little gleam came into his eye. I felt sure that he'd just thought of something rather satisfactory. If he had, it decided him to do as I wanted. He began like a lamb.

"Left Ringshall about 11 a.m.," he said, reading from a note-book. "Walked to Dimsey and caught the 1.5 bus to Devizes, arriving at 3.20. After that, his movements are uncertain for a few hours; but he arrived at Southampton between 6.30 and 7."

"How is that known?" asked the curate.

"Because he turned faint on the platform—excitement, I expect—and was taken into the refreshment-room by a porter. The porter looked at the time to see whether it was possible for him to get a drink, or whether it was still too early. So I expect he came by the 6.37 from Newbury. The porter—a man named Lister—remembers him very distinctly, because he refused to stop for a drink, and told the man to get him a taxi. Lister called one, and told the driver to keep an eye on his fare, because, as he said to my chap, he looked so ill that he thought he might collapse in the cab. So it was easy to get on to the driver.

"Mr. Harrington seems to have gone first to Cook's agency (where we find that he booked two singles, first-class, to Dieppe). He then visited several shops, and ended up at the Lymington Hotel. He returned to the station, telling the driver he must catch the 7.15.

"Now, there isn't a 7.15 from Southampton to any-where, but there is a 7.19 to Salisbury, and I've no doubt that that was what he wanted. You know the bad traveller's dodge of giving a cabman too early a time for a train, so as to be sure of his being in time. The 7.19 reaches Salis-bury at 8.16. I haven't got his movements, though, until he turned up again at Savernake—the only passenger to alight—on the 11.21; so I take it that he was trying to cover his tracks by changing from one train to another, finally landing at Newbury in time to get the same train to Savernake that he would have caught if he had been com-ing from town. From Savernake he set out on foot, and I can't trace his getting any kind of conveyance along the way. He probably walked the whole distance, and in that case, if, as he says, he is a decent walker but a bit slow, would have got in about 2.30."

I looked triumphantly at Roger Cartwright.

"I *said* he didn't know," I murmured; and I gently drew my pen across the sheet headed 'G. H.'

The inspector looked at me inquiringly.

"Suspects," I said, with a wave of the pen. "Everybody who is suspected by any one. Now he seems out of it."

"Your choice, sir?" asked the inspector, grinning at the curate.

"Yes, he was," answered Roger Cartwright. "And I still think he's a better shot than yours."

"And who is mine?" asked the inspector suavely.

"Joe Greaves—isn't he?"

"And suppose he were (though, mind you, I don't admit that he is), why do you think that so bad—as a guess?"

The curate picked up the sheet headed 'J. G.'

"Pro." he read. "Motive—of a sort. Poor, though, I consider. Could shoot well. Had tried guns at booth. Knew that flint arrow-heads were good missiles. Wasn't himself on day of Fair. Had threatened Mrs. H. when drunk. Rotten, I call it."

"And Con.?" asked the inspector pleasantly.

Roger Cartwright chucked down the paper.

"Oh, the chap's whole character, tradition, everything!" he exclaimed impatiently. "You don't know him, inspector. I do. I'd suspect almost any one sooner. He's incapable of it."

"All the same," said Grier, "that statement of yours isn't complete, you know. There's more than that against him."

We looked at him inquiringly.

"I see there *are* a few details you haven't discovered," he said, twinkling at me. "You ought to add to both sides of that paper, sir. First, as your *Pros* are a bit weak, let me tell you that he has an alibi—of a kind."

Roger Cartwright hit the table triumphantly.

"I knew it!" he cried. "I knew Joe couldn't be the chap we were after."

"Just a minute, sir. I said 'of a kind'," said Grier quietly. "He states that he first went to the Fair shortly before noon, and was there until a few minutes after one. He then

went to the Manor House to see his young lady, who had
been left in charge there—a maid, I suppose. At two, or
thereabouts, he left her and went over to see the farmer,
Phillips. After this he returned to the Fair, was there for a
short time only—though he admits that he was there when
the rifle range collapsed—and then went to the village inn,
staying there till nearly closing time. He left, feeling 'a bit
muzzy', and went for a stroll to clear his head. He says he
was walking about the part they call Kit's Park for about
an hour, and there met a keeper named Simms. He chatted
to this man for a few minutes, and then went home.

"Now, though the alibi between four and six is a very
weak one—for, of course, no one would notice when he
came and left the Fair—that part doesn't matter. We can't
be sure one way or the other whether he really was there
or not when the stall was broken. The barman at the inn
swears that Joe Greaves was at the inn until half-past nine
at least, and thinks he didn't go until later. But Simms
hedges. He 'can't be sure to a minute or two', either of the
time when he met Greaves or how long they talked, and
obviously thinks it was earlier than Greaves says. Both
Greaves and Simms admit that they weren't talking for
more than ten minutes at the outside, probably less.

"Say, then, that Greaves left the inn at a quarter to ten.
He'd reach Kit's Park before ten—say five to at the latest.
Give him ten minutes before meeting Simms—that's his
own estimate—and say that he talked to Simms for ten
minutes, leaving him at a quarter-past ten. That gives him
lots of time to get to Ringshall Oaks before the time of
the murder."

"Still—" began the curate; but Grier held up his hand.

"Just a minute, sir. There's a good deal to go on the
other side of the account. First, though Simms was very
cautious, I have no doubt whatever that this man Greaves
was talking to him about the harm Mrs. Harrington had

done, or was about to do, him by telling old Salt what she believed to be the case about Greaves and the girl Lydia. Simms was fairly easy to pump, and I have no doubt that Greaves talked pretty strongly. Also I gathered that he had heard him speak so before—as no doubt most people had—but that he thought that Greaves had some additional cause for anxiety or anger that night. Of course, we know that he had. He knew that she really was going to act that night—might have actually done so. Simms seemed to me to have been quite alarmed at Greaves's tone. Then there's another thing.

"I dare say you know that a good many of the showmen arrived the night before the Fair, in order to get good sites for their stalls the next day. Well, it seems that this man Alberti, the owner of the rifle range, did this. He sent his assistant down on the Thursday, and this chap spent a good deal of his time in the bar of the inn, working up interest in his show. It seems that our friend Greaves was there, and took a great interest in the specimen rifle which the assistant had had the sense to bring along."

"Half a minute," interrupted Roger Cartwright. "How did you find out all this? I mean, though Joe is a general favourite, there might be some one who'd be so keen on catching a murderer that they'd turn the most innocent conversation into a plot."

I knew that he was thinking of our local bobby, Gregory. He certainly was extremely anxious to get what cream there was to be had out of his first really exciting case; and I think the inspector guessed what was in the curate's mind.

"Oh, I'm not going by any one person's report," he said quietly, "I know my job, sir, when it's a question of getting information out of people without their knowing I'm doing it. Greaves not only borrowed the rifle—he sighted it, asked how it carried, and whether it would take any missile except the regulation pellet. Alberti's man said that it would, of course, shoot anything that would fit the bore, but added that airgun pellets were far the safest thing to use. But I suppose he scented a possible customer in Greaves, because" (here the inspector produced a notebook and read from it), "'he added that "anything was safe if the shooting was good." Greaves thereupon produced a pointed stone and asked whether that would do.'"

Grier paused. We exchanged uneasy glances.

"'Belloni' (that's Alberti's man) 'replied'" the inspector went on, "'that it certainly would if the bore would admit it. Greaves then said that he had only asked because he had found such a stone very effective in a catapult for killing rabbits, and thought that, if it were possible to shoot it from an airgun, it would save pellets in shooting rooks.' Now, I call that a poor excuse," said Grier, looking up. "If he'd used them with a catapult, he'd know for himself whether he could or couldn't kill a bird with one."

"No, he wouldn't," put in Stephen, "I've shot those flints from catties often enough, and I've used an airgun plenty of times, but I've no idea how the difference of propulsion would affect the flight. I know you can't shoot a rook with a bolt shot from a catty; but then you couldn't with an airgun pellet shot from a catty. It's the force behind the missile that does the job."

The inspector looked at him with great interest.

"I see," he said, as if this had never occurred to him before and he really was learning something. "Have you ever shot one of these flints out of an airgun, sir? Do you know how it does affect the flight?"

He did it very well, but I saw through him; also I guessed that this was what much of the conversation had been leading up to. I don't believe it *would* be very easy to pump a woman who was on the alert, whatever Inspector Grier may say. What I was afraid of was Stephen's answer.

"Let me see," he said slowly, but with the impish look I knew so well in his eye. "Have I? On the night of the twenty-ninth of June—oh no, though, I didn't. Sorry Inspector, but I don't really think I ever have."

The inspector took no notice of his impudence.

"There's one more point," he said, returning to his notebook. "Before leaving the inn, Greaves 'made a mark on the stock of the rifle, saying that he would then know it again and would be able, when he went to the Fair to pick out a gun that would shoot straight.' That gun" (here he closed his book impressively)—"that gun is among those which are missing from the booth."

Again we were silent. Then Roger Cartwright said:

"But that doesn't go for anything. If the bar was pretty full (as I've no doubt it was, on the night before the Fair, with the visiting showmen there), every man there would have kept his eyes open for the gun Joe marked. Even Ringshall bumpkins know that most of the guns *don't* shoot straight."

"Yes, sir. That's quite true," said Grier blandly. "We have no proof that young Greaves took the gun—or that any one did. It's just the conjunction of circumstances that looks—well, odd, to say the least of it."

And we had nothing to say; because, you know, the worst of it was that he was right. It did.

21

We looked at each other rather blankly. It was a bit of a facer, that conversation of Joe's in the 'Lady and Hare.' But we had no time to raise any objections or make any comments, for Jenny approached again.

"If you please, miss," she said to me, "do you happen to know where the Squire is?"

"No, Jenny. Who wants him?"

"Well, miss, there's a person come to the Manor wanting to see him particular. Lawson just run over to see if he was here. The man says as it's very important—something to do with the poor lady, miss."

"He knows she—Mrs. Harrington—is dead, then?" asked the inspector.

"Oh yes, sir, I think he do. Lawson said as he wanted to see Squire 'about his late wife,' he said, sir."

"Does the maid—Lawson—know him by sight?"

"No, sir. She said as he was a stranger, and she didn't much like his looks, she said, sir."

The inspector rose.

"I think I'll see him myself," he said. "Tell this maid Lawson to try and find her master, will you?—and say I'll talk to the man till he comes. Will you come with me, Miss Leslie?" he added, turning to me. "I should like you to see this man."

He spoke in rather a significant voice. Of course I was delighted to go. Inspector Grier seemed to me to be worth attention. He had, as he said, certainly discovered things we hadn't. Besides, he was the only person who had the intelligence to recognize the importance of the poppy-stain.

As we walked over to the Manor House, I told him of the business about the cupboard over Mrs. Harrington's bed. I thought it was simply foolish to conceal a thing like that, which might be quite important, from the professional investigator, especially as it wasn't giving away any of Mrs. Harrington's secrets to do so. But, to my disappointment, though he was interested, he wasn't thrilled. It was almost as if he had expected it. I began to wonder whether he knew more than he let on about that cupboard and its emptiness; but then I thought that if it had been he, or his minions, who had searched it, they wouldn't have wrecked the lock. They'd have taken their time, and opened it neatly, by legitimate means.

We found the visitor waiting in the big hall. Lawson may be an untrained, or only partially trained, maid, but she does discriminate with some acumen between the different visitors to the Manor House. She wouldn't trust this man in the drawing-room, or even in the morning-room. Personally, I wouldn't have trusted him as far as I could throw him, as they say. Yet I couldn't say why. He was swarthy, with the chin of a very dark man who ought to shave twice a day; but he had shaved, at least once, that day, so you couldn't call him dirty. He looked at you straight enough, but with a sort of half-defiant, pseudo-frank air which I thought more untrustworthy than shiftiness. He was obviously a foreigner of some kind, and I am honest enough to admit that this may have been the root of all my dislike and distrust. I try frightfully hard not to be insular, and not to mistrust all foreigners, but I simply cannot help it. This man held a child by the hand, and that child gave me a considerable shock.

She was a girl of eight or nine—she was evidently precocious, and it was difficult to tell her exact age, but certainly not more than nine. She was thin and rather ugly, but her face had the promise of quite extraordinary good looks; and she had the most lovely hair—hair of that peculiar and beautiful shade which most people associate with Titian, but which I—and, I suppose, all Ringshall people—associated always with Mrs. Harrington The child's features were not formed enough to bear much resemblance to the strong, handsome features of the dead woman, but there was certainly a likeness, which the rare shade of the hair strongly emphasized. As soon as I saw the child, I guessed at what was coming.

"You are Mr. 'Arrington, no?" said the man, as the inspector walked in.

"No, I'm not," said Grier, "but I more or less represent him. I understand that you have something to tell him concerning his wife's death?"

"With her death, no I learn that by chance only. I see it here."

He produced a sheet of newspaper—one of those peculiarly vulgar and stupid papers, composed almost entirely of photographic libels, which appear to be unfailingly popular. There, displayed on the front page, was a large and quite recognizable portrait of Mrs. Harrington, together with a flaring headline about the "murder mystery", and, under the picture, a horrid little summary of the tragedy, in which it was mentioned that "the dead lady's past was shrouded in mystery" and emphasis was laid on the fact that no one knew where she came from or who she really was.

Inspector Grier grunted quite crossly, but he said nothing. He handed back the paper.

"Well?" he asked. "What about it?"

"This," said the man. (I shan't attempt to reproduce his accent; our alphabet couldn't be made to do justice to his vowels, let alone the gutturals and nasals.) "That lady is not Mrs. 'Arrington. She is Signora Lagardi. She is my wife."

He said it quite quietly, but it might have been the explosion of a bomb, it startled me so.

"Oh, nonsense!" I exclaimed. "I knew Mrs. Harrington quite well. I was present at her marriage. This is certainly her portrait."

The inspector interrupted.

"Just a minute, please." He addressed the man Lagardi. "You say that this is a picture of your wife. What makes you say that?"

"I will tell you. I will tell you it all. That lady I met in Paris just after the war, in the end of 1918. She was not then *grande dame* at all; she was what you call *aventrice*—gambler, *fille de joie*—understand, yes?"

Grier nodded.

"I like her. I have great respect for her brains. We join, collaborate, isn't it?"

The inspector nodded again.

"I do not at all wish to 'ide what we do. We were not respectable, no. We live by our head, and her head, it was best. We make money, do well, yes."

"You married her?" asked Inspector Grier.

"Not then, no. But soon she tell me there will be a child. She wish to marry. For me, I—" He shrugged.

"You didn't want to?"

"No. It is not always convenient, see, for people who live like that. But she ask and ask me always, and at last I marry her. I have the paper."

He produced a bulgy pocket-book and selected a paper, which he handed to the inspector.

"And the child?" asked Grier.

"She was born the next year, in April."

The inspector was turning the paper over rather dubiously, I thought.

"Well?" he asked suddenly and sharply. "Why did you part, and when?"

The man spread out his arms in a vague gesture.

"We were not—what you say?—compatible. She was wilful, perhaps I too. She wish always to be master, boss, eh?—and I, I have spirit. We quarrel, not once, but often, always. And then there came trouble.

"There was a young man I meet, a fool, a pigeon for us to pluck, eh?—a rich young fool. I become his friend. He stay with us—you know the game?" he appealed to the inspector.

"I can guess," he nodded, rather grimly.

"I think how clever she is, how she fool and fool him. But, see! It was me that she fool. She take a liking to this boy—he was a boy, no more. One day—she vanish, and he with her!"

He paused in a dramatic sort of way, and then went on:

"I have many friends. I get on her track at once. I pursue her. But I have an ill fortune—bad luck, isn't it? There was an accident on the railway. I am injure, hurt very bad, very serious. I am invalid, twelve, thirteen month, with my back. When I recover, I have lost her trail. But I hear soon, and it is a sad tale that I hear.

"I find that she is alone. Her man—her count, that is his station—is dead, dead in a shooting accident. It is her gun that has shoot him—not kill him at once, but a deadly wound. He die in her arms. And she, she is beside herself. They say she was near mad. They think she will turn Catholic and enter a convent. Then she vanish. I hear no more. I know she have his money—he was rich, but rich!—and I think she have endow some Order and is doing penance in a cell for her bad life and for his soul.

"I cannot find her, not a trace. But then I find that she is not turn Catholic, no. She go back to the Church of her own country. She go into retirement and do good works, and her money, the wage of her sin, that she spend for the poor, isn't it?"

"How did you find this out?" asked the inspector.

"The affair of the man's death, it was known everywhere. It is here, in a journal of the place."

He drew out another newspaper, obviously a German one, and handed it over. It contained pictures—one certainly of Mrs. Harrington, another of a black-haired young man with an odd, high forehead and a full yet weak mouth—the kind of face one associates with *crimes passionels*. A third was of a group of people all in the most magnificent attire—royalties, apparently—among whom the two single portraits were prominent; another of a second group, also containing the two portrait heads.

Inspector Grier nodded.

"I remember," he said. "His name was Czenowsczi— Otto Czenowsczi; 1921, wasn't it? Of course! I thought her face was familiar, but I couldn't just think where or when I'd come across it before. So *that* was Mrs. Harrington!"

The visitor nodded vigorously.

The inspector pondered for a few moments; then he said:

"Well?"

Lagardi (if that was his name; I doubted it, as I doubted every single thing he said) again spread out his hands.

"That is all," he said, with an odd, sidelong look at Grier.

"I don't see what you gain by raking up all this scandal about a dead woman," I broke in. "Why shouldn't she go to her grave as Mrs. Harrington, even if—if she hadn't a real right to the name?"

"Oh, for that, but yes! I have not wish to make public the affair—unless it is necessary."

Again he threw a cunning, appraising look at the inspector, who still said nothing.

"How could it be necessary?" I asked impatiently.

"Only if Mr. 'Arrington is foolish. See, I have proof, many proof. She is my wife, and this is our child. She has appeared a rich woman. If she get her money by a *liaison*, that is not our affair. But it is our affair that it is her child who is the heritor—what is it?—the heir."

"If she died intestate," said the inspector, "her husband is the chief legatee, not the child. But she may have made a will."

"You do not understand," said Lagardi, with an assumption of immense patience. "It is in the paper, all the story, for any one to read. It is not so simple as you think. What has happen is this—she have not tell the world that Maria-Antonia is *my* child No, she have say that she is marry to Czenowsczi, and that the child is his. She have had it arrange that the child is recognize as his heir. You see? She is afraid that if she is discover to be his mistress she will get none of his money; but there a child can be heir of a man even if it is not lawful—not legitimate, isn't it? All the family have recognize Maria-Antonia as Czenowsczi's child and as his heir. It is so in law. The money is hers, not Agata's."

"Then, did the child go with them when they eloped?" asked the inspector.

"Yes, that was necessary to Agata's plan. But when the child has been recognize and acknowledge as the heir, that is enough. She put her in a convent. But I, I love the child. She is mine, not Czenowsczi's. I do not know about the law and the money, it have not strike me that the child is to be rich; but I want her. I am alone, see, unhappy, I trace her, and I take her to my home. I bring her up. But a friend—a man who live in 'Ungary, near the estate of the Czenowsczi, he tell me how the law stand. It is the law that my child have the money of Count Otto Czenowsczi, since he have had her recognize as his heir. It is no matter that she is not his child; she has been made his heir. And Agata, she has had the money all these years as a trust for the child. She have deceive every one. They do not know that she have lost the child. And me, I know nothing of it until lately. I think that it is Agata's right to 'ave the money. But now I know it is my child's right. I claim it now for her. I will not have the money that Count Czenowsczi have left to her scatter among the relations of Mr. 'Arrington."

Again the inspector pondered. I went over the man's story in my mind, referring meanwhile to the German (or whatever it was) paper he had produced. It certainly seemed accurate. There was, as he had said, a mention of the rather curious fact that Count Czenowsczi and his wife had agreed that their only child, a girl named Maria-Antonia, should be formally recognized as his heir, and that this had been duly done. It was also said that the child had been sent to a convent on account of her health, which was delicate, while her parents were at the big shooting-party in Salzein—that party which had ended in the tragic death of Count Otto. It certainly looked as if it were the child Maria-Antonia, and not her mother, who ought to have had the vast fortune which apparently had been left by Czenowsczi.

"There may be a will," the inspector suggested again.

"It do not matter if there is a will," Lagardi pointed out. "The money is not hers, but the child's."

"And you say that you have had the charge of the child for some time?"

"But yes. As soon as I can get about. I hear that she—Agata—have disappear after her Count's death, but the convent where she place the child, that is known, and it is not so hard to find her. She have been my comfort since."

"Does she speak English?"

"A little. She have not much, Me, I do not like the English."

"You've educated her, I suppose?"

"But yes! I have spent on her—oh, but much She is all I have."

I suppose, I thought, he's going to put in a claim for her maintenance from the Harringtons. It was, of course, true that, if he wasn't lying, there ought to have been ample funds to pay for the most expensive possible education; and it did seem a bit hard that somebody else should have had to pay for it when the child was possessed of a vast fortune. But I hoped, all the same, that he wouldn't get a penny.

"Have you sent her to school?"

"No." (Was it imagination, I wondered, or was there really a rather cunning gleam in his dark eyes as he answered—a look as if he had been on the point of being trapped, and had escaped by his quickness of wit?) "No, I have teach her myself. I do not wish to part with her, and I am a very poor man. She is delicate, and all I can give is gone to the doctors. But she is well taught."

"She can read and write, eh?"

"But certainly."

"I'd like just to see her write her name."

If he hoped to catch Lagardi out by this, he failed. The horrid little creature actually beamed with pleasure.

"But certainly!" he exclaimed again. He spoke to the child in Italian. I don't know Italian, so I don't know what he said, but she nodded vigorously, and said *"Si, si."* So

I suppose he was asking her if she could, or would, write her name.

The inspector put a chair for her, with a cushion on it, and laid out some paper.

"Have you got a pencil?" he asked Lagardi.

The Italian produced one, and handed it to the child. She took it, and he bent over her, settling her hand in the true old-fashioned writing-master way. She transferred the pencil to her left hand, and wrote, carefully and laboriously. I watched breathlessly to see whether she would fall in with a theory I had formed. But she didn't. She wrote, with extreme care, and in the wonderful flourishy hand that they still teach in France and Italy, 'Maria-Antonia Lagardi.'

I saw Lagardi cast a look of triumph at the inspector. It was as if he had said in words:

"You thought she couldn't. Well, look there!"

It was, I thought, more than the triumph that a proud father shows when his child performs a successful feat. But I wasn't sure; you can never tell what proud parents may not do where their children are concerned.

"You've taught her well," commented the inspector.

Again I couldn't be sure, but I thought there was a rather meaning tone in his voice. It was exactly as if these two were speaking in a code which consisted entirely of tones, not of words; I felt as if there was something going on underneath it—something implied, hinted, but of the greatest importance—and, try as I would, I couldn't guess what it was.

"Oh yes," replied Lagardi. "She is well taught. Is she not my only hope now that my Agata is dead?"

"Hm. Well, Mr. Lagardi, you know you'll have to produce proofs of identity—papers, you know, to show that you are the person you say you are."

"Oh, I have proof!" said the man confidently. He lugged out his pocket-book again. "See! Our marriage certificate—Giuseppe Lagardi and Agata Lumley, October 1919. The certificate of the child's birth—Maria-Antonia, April 1920. A letter from Agata when she leave me. You know her hand, yes?" I glanced at the paper he held out. Yes, I would have recognized that handwriting anywhere. How often had I not seen it on notices of committee meetings or notes of invitation! "A letter from my friend, Bamberger, who trace the child for me. The account of the death of Czenowsczi you have already see. What more do you wish?"

"Yes, yes," said the inspector, rather impatiently, "but how do I know that you are the Lagardi spoken of here?"

"Oh, for that! What do you wish? I have friends, isn't it? They will speak. Ah, and I have this."

He put his hand up to his neck and hauled out a chain.

"See! It is Agata as a young girl. Her name is on it—'Agata Lumley, 1898.' You see how the child is like."

I looked at the handsome, red-haired portrait. There certainly was a resemblance between the living child and the miniature—not a very strong one, but then miniatures are apt to flatter; besides, there is a great difference between what one looks like at eight and at eighteen, the child might be very like the portrait when she was ten years older.

"Well," said the inspector, "if you'll take my advice, you'd better put the matter in the hands of a good solicitor. You can't do much by yourself. Mr. Harrington may give in at once—she may even have said something to him—or he may produce a will and contest your claim."

"A will will be no use," Lagardi pointed out, "for it will be sign 'Harrington,' and her name is not that but Lagardi. If she sign it 'Lagardi,' she would get no one to witness it."

"Well, that all depends on whether your claim goes through," said Grier. "If you can prove that you are the man who married this lady, of course you're right—no will made in her new name will stand; but you have to prove that first, and as I say, your best plan is to consult a good solicitor."

And he handed him back his papers and bowed him out.

22

I must admit that I was a little disappointed by the inspector's handling of the affair. It was, I thought, so dull as to be stupid. Also his manner gave me the impression that he was thinking about something else all the time; in fact, I was so sure of this that I went so far as to charge him with it.

"You weren't a bit thrilled," I reproached him. "You had something else in your head all the time."

He looked at me with a twinkle in his eye.

"Well, yes," he admitted meekly. "I had."

I gazed at him more in grief than in indignation.

"Miss Leslie," he said suddenly, with a complete change of tone, "have you ever seen that man—or any one like him—before?"

"What, our friend Lagardi? No. And yet, there was something—not exactly familiar; but I've a feeling as if I'd met somebody lately—*en passant,* you know—who was like him—gave me the same sort of general impression."

"Lately, you say?"

"Yes, fairly lately. . . . I don't know. It's an impression, that's all. I might have travelled in a train or a 'bus with a man rather like him. Not this man himself, you understand, necessarily. It's all very vague."

"And do you think it *was* while travelling that you met such a person?"

"It can't have been," I said slowly, "for I haven't travelled for at least a fortnight, and it's more recent than that. And yet it's just that fleeting sort of impression that you get when you meet an unpleasant person in a public place like a train, and hope they'll get out soon. But I can't place him."

"Perhaps you will soon, when you're thinking of something else," suggested Grier.

"I might. But it won't be Lagardi himself, you know—only some one of the same horrid type."

"Oh, quite; I quite understand that," said the inspector, rather absently, I thought.

"What did you think of his story?" he asked then. "Does it fit in with what you knew of Mrs. Harrington?"

"Yes, quite well," I admitted. "And, though naturally he said nothing about that part, it fits in with what Miss Harrington told us about her anxiety—why she was hard up, watched the post, and so on."

"You mean he was blackmailing her?"

"Yes. He's just the type who would," I said. "Besides, all that bit about the child is true, isn't it?"

"It's quite true that Count Otto Czenowsczi did get a child recognized as his heir, and that she was in a convent—a sort of health place, as far as I remember—when the accident happened to Czenowsczi. But there's one queer thing—if this man Lagardi was blackmailing Mrs. Harrington, why did she relax all her precautions and so on about six weeks ago?"

"Perhaps she got some written agreement out of him that he'd stop bothering her for a lump sum down," I suggested.

"Would he ever keep such an agreement? Would she ever believe that he would?" asked the inspector quietly.

"Well, no, he wouldn't, of course—unless she threatened to prosecute him for blackmail if he broke it."

"Which she couldn't afford to do," he pointed out, "or she'd have done it long before."

"Well, then, I can't guess, unless—" I paused. A sudden idea had struck me. But I thought I'd do a little fishing before I said anything, just in case it was possible to get the inspector to give me some help. "Can you?" I asked.

"I'm not sure. If only you could remember when or where you saw the person who resembled Lagardi, I think we'd be on velvet."

I gaped vulgarly.

"Do you mean that you'd have solved the whole mystery?"

"Well, I think I'd be pretty near it. If only you could remember." He spoke most persuasively.

"I would if I could, and I've no doubt that I'll remember in time. I can't do it to order," I remonstrated. "But look here—are you trying to impress me when you say that, or is it the sober truth?"

"Oh, very sober truth," he assured me, smiling a little.

"Then I'll find out why you say so or die in the attempt!" I vowed.

"Do," he said, "but if you locate that man—"

"I'll communicate with you instantly," I assured him solemnly.

I walked back to my house wrapped in thought. If I could, I would have doubted every word that that little horror Lagardi had said; but I couldn't do that; it was too well documented, and fitted in too well with what I knew of Mrs. Harrington. The best hope appeared to me to lie in the fact that, as Inspector Grier had pointed out, he hadn't really any proof of his identity with the man named in the marriage certificate and as the child's father on the birth certificate. That, together with what had come into my head *apropos* of the cessation of the blackmail (if it had been blackmail) gave me material to work on.

My new theory was something like this. The documents were genuine enough, and Mrs. Harrington had been blackmailed by means of them; *but the real Lagardi had died about six weeks ago.* Mrs. Harrington had then, somehow or other, got possession of the papers, and, believing herself to be rid of him at last, had begun to spend freely and to relax her vigilance over the post and telephone to some extent—but not wholly, because she knew, or feared, that some crony of Lagardi's knew of her secret and might threaten scandal, even though he could now prove nothing. She would not, of course, pay him a penny—she now possessed the precious documents—but she would not care to have his letters or telephone messages made common property. No doubt either the real Lagardi or this choice friend of his had been down to Ringshall, to find out what there was to pick up about Mrs. Harrington, and had sounded Mrs. Nokes, who had put two and two together, with the cunning of her kind.

Then came Mrs. Harrington's death. On hearing of this, this friend of Lagardi's came down to Ringshall; by judicious spying or bribery he found out where the papers were kept, and stole them, with the idea of passing himself off as Lagardi. That accounted for the inspector's insistence that he must prove his identity—he had some notion that this man wasn't the real Lagardi; and perhaps that, or some offshoot from it, was the hidden something that had (I thought) lurked behind their words when the inspector had spoken that single sentence and the Italian had replied.

Then I remembered something else. When Celia and I had been to see Lydia, and she had told me of the existence of the safe, I had had a very distinct impression of the wood about us being peopled. Suppose it had been? Suppose this horrible little man had been lurking there, and had followed us, on the off-chance of hearing us say something about the dead woman? I remembered that a twig had cracked, and that we had put it down to a squirrel. . . . He had suspected the bed before—it is, after all, the place where women do most often hide things—and it was he who had lain in Mrs. Harrington's bed on the night of the murder, trying, as Celia had done, to find the place where the papers were hidden, by means of the lying position. . . . He had failed, because he didn't know about the safe; as soon as he got on to the track of that, he returned and forced it—and no doubt got what he wanted.

That was, I thought, a pretty good theory. Only it had a flaw—a bad flaw. The burglar had entered the room to steal the papers on the very night of Mrs. Harrington's death—only two or three hours after it happened, in fact. He could not possibly have known of it, or that his opportunity for the impersonation had come, unless he had actually been living in Ringshall—and that I was sure he had not been. There was only one other supposition—that the sham Lagardi was himself the murderer.

At first I thought that was excellent. He murdered the lady, stole the papers, and retired. But that was absurd. You don't steal papers in order to blackmail a person whom you have just murdered. And yet, without the papers, the blackmail was useless. I felt sure that those papers that he had just produced were the ones that had been stolen from the safe. But, if that were so, why on earth had Mrs. Harrington kept them? When they had, by some miracle, been returned to her, why hadn't she burnt them at once? Whichever way I turned I seemed to be brought up all standing. If the burglar had wanted papers for purposes of blackmail, he couldn't have committed the murder. If he hadn't, how did he know that Mrs. Harrington was dead? And, worst of all, why, why, why did those papers still exist?

I was so absorbed in these ideas that I walked straight past my own house. I didn't realize what I had done until I found myself in the wood beyond the Green; it was the coolness and shade of the shadowed depths after the hot glare across the Green that brought me down to earth again.

I stood for a few moments under the trees; and as I paused I saw Tom Nokes, the 'witch's' imbecile son, coming through the oaks. I waited. It seemed to me a Heaven-sent opportunity to do a little private sleuthing on my own. My luck seemed to be in that day, and I was going to make the most of it.

"Well, Tom," I said in a casual tone, "been after rabbits?"

"No—o—oa. I been a-shootin' croas wi' ma catty."

He held it in his hand—a powerful little catapult.

"You can't shoot crows with that," I said. "You want a gun for birds."

"Ah. But Oi ain' got noo gun."

He gave me a cunning look as he said this. I wondered why—whether it was that, with an imbecile's hopefulness, he thought that I might give him one, as I used to give him sweets; or whether it was because he was lying and he *had* got a gun—a gun stolen from the broken booth.

"Can't you get one?" I asked.

"Oi moight. But they costes a lot, they guns do, in pellets."

"You could shoot stones, just as you do out of your catty."

He looked at me with an impish grin, and I went on, as casually as I could:

"People do, you know. They say Joe Greaves does. But it might be too hard for you."

That pricked him, as I hoped it would.

"'Twouldn' be too 'ard, so! I've seed it done, bolt shot out o' gun, an' 'tis soo easy as poy. But I never let un see I a-watchin' of un."

"Who was it? Joe?"

"No—o—o—o—a!" The scorn in his voice defeats expression. "'Twere *he.*"

"Who's 'he'?"

"'Tidn' chancy to speak o' he," said Tom, lowering his voice to a gabbling mutter, and rolling his eyes. "He be *he,* that's aal."

I remembered all the village stories of Mrs. Nokes and her traffic with the dark mysteries of the Oaks and the Green, and I felt a tiny shiver creep down my spine. I had a momentary vision of the weird old beldame and her gabbling idiot son meeting under the shadows of these very trees with some dark being, whom the chequered moonlight only half revealed. . . . It was gone in far, far less time than it takes to tell. It was like a flash of feeling, no more.

"And had he got a gun to shoot bolts from?" I asked.

Tom nodded vigorously.

"Does he live here?" I asked, almost in a whisper.

Tom also lowered his voice to a mysterious undertone. "He be one o' *They,*" he whispered. "One o' the Good Folk."

"How do you know?" I whispered back.

"'Twere a elf-bolt as 'a shot," he gabbled, "an' when 'twere shot, 'a buried gun *there*—by the thorn, see?— where the Good Folk meet. An' the Folk have took his gun, 'cause 'twere theirn. I seed where 'a hid it, though he never seed I, an' I thinks, thinks I, I'll have en when 'a's gone. But when I come an' digged, 'twere gone, though I weren't but a little time."

"What did he shoot with it?" I asked, still in the mysterious voice in which we had always spoken of the Good Folk.

But I had gone too far. Tom Nokes leapt back, a clean spring of two or three yards, with an eldritch scream of laughter that rang out weirdly in the silent summer wood.

"Nowt!" he shouted. "'Tis loys as I've telled 'ee, aal on en!"

And he took to his heels and raced off through the trees.

I walked home quietly. Between Lagardi and Tom Nokes, I was in a complete whirl. Because, whatever he might say now, I felt quite certain that what the idiot had told me had *not* been "all lies." Whether he had really seen anything, I could not, of course, tell; but I did not believe that it was entirely imagination, or delusion, or just malicious fibbing. What *had* he seen? And did it, whatever it might be, fit in with the man who called himself Lagardi? Or were they two quite separate issues? I felt I had plenty to work on, anyhow, when I finally did reach my own house.

23

Eleven o'clock on Thursday, 5th July, was the time fixed for the real inquest. Of course the formal one, with its inevitable adjournment, had taken place almost at once. I had promised to be on hand in time to take Celia, who would, of course, be wanted as a witness. So I hadn't much time that morning to think over Tom Nokes's cryptic utterances and try to fit them on to the story told by Lagardi and on to the facts of the murder.

Celia was still pale and grave, but seemed quite calm and steady, though she admitted that she rather dreaded the coming ordeal.

"I don't mind talking about the way she looked when we found her," she said—but she flushed a little, and I knew that she hated having to admit that she wasn't actually there at the time when Stephen made the discovery—"but what I loathe is having to talk about her habits. I don't know how much to say about that business about the letters and telephone and the money and all the rest of it."

"Perhaps you won't be asked," I said hopefully. "But if you are, I should just answer as shortly as you can. Don't say a word more than you need, but don't hedge. When you can, just say Yes or No."

The inquest was held in the Market Hall, which is now never used for its original purpose, as we no longer have a market of our own. It was cool and dark and somehow rather mysterious in the dignified old hall, though there were reporters and a lot of strangers there, hoping for a thrill. But, in spite of them, there was none of the vulgar excitement that one gathers is often the accompaniment of a murder inquest.

Dr. Ludlow gave technical evidence of the nature of the wound in the skull, and added that there was nothing else to account for the death. The stone had penetrated the brain, and death had been instantaneous. Then Stephen was called.

He was rather pale, I thought, but he spoke quite clearly. He told how he, with Celia and Roger Cartwright, had left my house just after half-past ten. It might have been twenty-five minutes to eleven before they actually left the grounds. They had started to walk together across the Green, and then the curate had remembered that he had to turn into his lodgings for some papers he wished to give to Mrs. Harrington. He had told the others to walk on, and he would catch them up, and they had done so, walking rather slowly.

"But I understood you to say that Miss Harrington was in a hurry to reach home, and that was why you left the Dower House so early?" the coroner put in here.

"Yes, sir, but she—we both wished Mr. Cartwright to be the one to accompany her into the house."

The coroner looked as if he wanted to go into this, but a glance at Inspector Grier, who was near him, decided him not to.

"Well, let's get on then. You and Miss Harrington went across the Green, walking slowly."

"Miss Harrington and I didn't walk across the Green. We skirted it, on the east side, walking under the trees there. You see we didn't want to go too fast, and the quickest way is straight across the Green. We walked for some minutes—"

"How long?"

Stephen thought.

"I don't know; might have been five, might have been ten."

"Did you hear the church clock strike the quarter to eleven?"

"No. I—I wasn't listening."

Stephen coloured a little as he said this, and I saw a sympathetic smile steal round the court. He was such a boy, and so very good-looking and so ingenuous.

"Well?"

"Miss Harrington remembered that she'd been asked by her stepmother the day before to get some papers from Mr. Cartwright—something about a missionary exhibition, I think—and had forgotten to do so. Mrs. Harrington had been too busy over the Fair to remember to ask for them, but Miss Harrington knew that she was sure to do so next morning, and would be annoyed if she found they'd been forgotten. So she asked me to run after Mr. Cartwright and ask him to bring them along with the others. I went,— straight across the Green this time—and I noticed what I thought at first was a heap of lumber—awnings or something—on the Green. I remembered that that had been the place, more or less, where a rifle-range had been destroyed during the Fair, and, when I saw a glitter at one end, I thought it would be one of the rifles that had been said to be stolen. So I went over to have a look."

"In spite of the fact that you were in a hurry?"

"It wouldn't have taken me half a minute, if it had really been a rifle," said Stephen. "It was almost in my way, and anyhow I didn't stop to think. I just swerved a bit out of my line and—and looked."

He went rather pale.

"It was Mrs. Harrington," he said simply. "The glitter was the buckles on her shoes."

"What did you do?"

"I—I'm afraid I was a bit of a fool. It turned me queer, seeing her like that. . . . There was blood on the back of her neck. I—I don't remember very well what I did, or how long I was standing there. When I got steady again, I ran as hard as I could lick to Mr. Cartwright's. I met him just at his gate, and told him. He said I'd better go and get Miss Harrington home, and he'd see to—to Mrs. Harrington. He knows I'm no good over things like that."

He then told how he had found Celia, who had turned back to meet the men, impatient of their delay, beside the body of her stepmother. He was subjected to a strict cross-examination about the time he had taken between leaving my house and parting with Celia, and between his leaving her and meeting with Roger Cartwright. But he couldn't answer positively to any of this. It was quite evident to me that what was behind all this was a desire to find out whether, supposing that he really had found one of the missing weapons, it would have been possible for him to have shot the fatal bolt. It was a question of time only. He would have had to find the rifle, commit the murder, get rid of the gun again, and go on to Roger Cartwright's lodgings. If the time fitted, it was a fairly sound hypothesis, for it was certainly quite possible that one of the missing guns might have been left among the litter near the site of the booth.

Stephen, however, was unsatisfactory about the time. He had no idea how long he had been strolling with Celia under the dense shadow of the oaks; he couldn't say how long he had stood beside the corpse. The coroner dismissed him and called Celia.

Her evidence tallied with Stephen's, so far as that went. Her only idea was that they had been at least ten minutes under the oaks, because, she said naively, she had the time on her mind more than he had.

"It didn't matter to him if we were in at midnight," she said, "but it did to me; and I was afraid we were going to be late, and that was why—partly—I asked Mr. Earle to go back for Mr. Cartwright, though I did really want the papers too."

"And how long were you alone?"

She thought.

"I don't know—perhaps another ten minutes, perhaps less. Time seems so long when you're anxious."

"Yes, of course it does. Did you hear the church clock strike?"

"I don't—*think*—so. It would have startled me, I think, because it would have been eleven it struck, you see, and that would have been horribly late."

"It was after the quarter to eleven, then?"

"Oh, it must have been. It must have struck the quarter to when Ste—when Mr. Earle and I were walking under the oaks."

"And at what time did you find the body of Mrs. Harrington?"

"I don't know. It must have been just before eleven, I suppose. It hadn't struck the hour before I found her, or I should have noticed it. I was too much—upset, afterwards, to notice whether it struck or not. But it can't have been far off."

The coroner paused. Then he asked her an unexpected question:

"Had you any reason to fear that Mrs. Harrington might die suddenly or mysteriously?"

Celia stared in frank amazement.

"Not the very least," she replied firmly. "Her death was a tremendous shock to me—to us all."

"She had never said anything to you which suggested that she had an enemy, or any reason to fear any one?"

Celia hesitated.

"She never said anything. But of course, now that she is dead—like that—one knows that she must have had an enemy."

"But you wouldn't have guessed it before this happened?"

Again the girl hesitated.

"I don't think I could have known of it," she said then. "We weren't intimate."

I noticed, of course, and I suppose the coroner did, that this was no answer. He hesitated, as if he were in two minds as to whether to press for a real answer; but he decided not to, after a glance at Grier, and told her that would do "for the present".

Roger Cartwright came next. All he was asked for was evidence about the time at which he had left Stephen and Celia, and the time at which he had met Stephen at his gate. He put the time of their parting at twenty to eleven, more or less; he said it was before the quarter to, because he had glanced at the time as he entered his rooms, having noticed that the clock had stopped; and his watch had made it thirteen minutes to. He had spent some minutes in his room, writing a couple of postcards, and looking for the papers for Mrs. Harrington; he hadn't noticed whether the church clock struck or not, and he hadn't himself noticed the time; but he knew that Miss Harrington didn't wish to be later than eleven in reaching home, and also that she wished him to accompany her there, so he hadn't been unduly long. It couldn't have been more than eleven when he met Mr. Earle at the gate of his lodgings.

He was then asked how Stephen had seemed, and said that he looked very pale and distraught, and his manner was agitated. In answer to other questions, he said that he didn't think this at all unusual when one remembered what Stephen had just seen, and that he was one of those people who turn faint at the sight of blood. He insisted on this rather too much, I thought, as if he thought that it needed emphasis. As I said before, his methods are logical rather than artistic.

After the curate, Godfrey Harrington was called. He looked wretchedly ill, with the ghastly bluish pallor that people show who have heart trouble. He was also, you could see, extremely nervous.

After a few preliminary and more or less conventional questions, the coroner opened fire.

"Before your marriage with her, had Mrs. Harrington been married?"

"I believe so," said the Squire.

"You believe so? Don't you know?"

"I can't swear to it. She bore a widow's name."

"Did you never ask?"

"I—I—she never—she didn't care to speak of her past life. I didn't press her. I understood that she had not been happy."

"I believe she was known, before her marriage with you, as Mrs. Ward?"

"Yes."

"Did you ever make quite certain, before you married her, that her first husband was really dead?"

A most extraordinary expression passed over Harrington's face. It was (I thought) first one of consternation; then it changed to one of enormous relief; then to regret. But you know how quickly expression, reflecting emotion, alters. I can't swear to these different changes; they are only impressions I got, so rapid and so transitory that I myself doubted them the next second.

"No," he said in a rather bewildered voice. "I never doubted that she was a widow."

"Would it have been possible, then, for her even to be in communication with this first husband without your knowledge?"

"I—I can't say. I never thought of such a thing. She might have written to or heard from any one without my knowledge."

"Hm. . . . Well, now, Mr. Harrington, I want to ask you some questions that you certainly can answer. Will you tell us exactly where you were and what you were doing on Thursday and Friday, the twenty-eighth and twenty-ninth of last month?"

Harrington passed his hand nervously over his mouth.

"I'll try," he said, in a voice hardly above a whisper. "On Thursday I walked over to Devizes and visited the museum there. I spent practically the whole day over the expedition, and got in shortly after eight. I dined with my wife and daughter, and went to bed early."

"Did you meet any one you knew, either in Devizes or on the way there or back?"

"No."

"Did you sign the register at the museum?"

"Oh yes, of course I did that."

The coroner's eye caught the inspector's. Grier nodded just perceptibly.

"And the next day—the Friday?"

Harrington gave a glib—almost too glib—repetition of the time-table he had given to the inspector. He seemed quite at his ease while he reeled off times of trains, connexions, and other details of the expedition. The coroner, a little dryly, commented on this.

"I've been questioned about it before," explained the Squire, "and I've thought it over since. It's perfectly clear in my mind."

"And you are, of course, quite sure of the day?"

"Oh, of course. Quite certain."

"Hm. That's very odd. . . . Just step down a minute, please, Mr. Harrington. Call Edward Butler."

A young man replaced the Squire. He was, it turned out, the 'bus conductor whom Roger Cartwright had met in the Savernake 'bus. He swore quite positively to having seen the Squire on the Devizes 'bus on the Friday, not the Thursday. No amount of questioning could shake him.

He was followed by Albert Lister, porter, who swore to Harrington's presence, at Southampton station, at 6.30, "or as near as makes no matter", on the Friday, and by Richard Carter, taxi-cab driver, also of Southampton, who was equally positive that he had driven him about Southampton, to various shops, to the Lymington Hotel, and finally back to the station, on the evening of the twenty-ninth. Both men were very closely cross-examined as to the day, and the porter wavered under the ordeal; but Mr. Carter was certain, because he worked late on Fridays and took Saturdays off, and he knew it was his late night—also the shops would have been closed if it had been a Thursday.

After this evidence Harrington was recalled.

"You have heard what these last witnesses have sworn?"

"Yes."

"Do you still swear that you were in London between four and half-past seven on the twenty-ninth of last June?"

"I do. And I've just remembered—I can prove it."

He felt in his waistcoat pocket and produced a railway ticket. "You see—the return half of my ticket to town. I came back, as I said, by a different route, and didn't use this half. I meant to claim for it from the railway company."

The coroner examined the ticket closely. He seemed rather disconcerted. But he rallied well.

"Of course," he said, "this ticket might have been bought by any one. I can't consider it as a real proof that you were in town on the twenty-ninth because you happen to have the return half of a ticket to Paddington issued on that day. It is not, to my mind, comparable to the evidence given by the last two witnesses. What reply can you make to their evidence?"

"Mistaken—some one else—can't be expected—remember every passenger—ridiculous—mistaken, quite mistaken. . . ."

He was almost inaudible as he babbled this reply.

"Can you bring any independent witness to prove that you visited Devizes Museum on Thursday the twenty-eighth, and went to town on Friday, the twenty-ninth?"

"The visitors' book at the museum . . . the ticket," muttered Harrington.

He really was pitiful. Pressed, of course he could not produce any real proof that what he said was true. I saw the reporters' pencils racing, and the significant glances that passed between the various members of the audience. But the ordeal was not over yet.

"Is it the fact that you were intending to separate from your wife?"

Harrington turned a livid face towards the coroner, and, with a kind of choking cry, burst into a flood of speech.

"It's a lie! It's a damned lie! I've denied it once, and I deny it again. You've no right to bring up all the absurd scandal talked by a lot of old women in a country village. I, separate from my wife! It's an absolute lie! Such a thought never entered my head."

He stopped suddenly, and then, in a calmer voice, went on:

"You must forgive my heat, sir. It is harrowing to me to have these insinuations made. There is absolutely no foundation for them beyond the fact that once—months ago—I did, in a fit of ill-temper which I regretted very deeply afterwards, say to my wife that as we didn't seem able to agree—it was on some trifling detail—we might be better apart for a time. I merely meant that we should each see the other's point of view better for a short holiday away from each other. 'Separation', in the legal sense of the word, never entered my head."

"Did you take any steps to carry out this idea of a holiday apart from each other?"

"No. As I say, it was months ago now."

Silly ass! I thought; there was a chance for you if you'd only seen it—a good excuse for those arrangements to go abroad without Mrs. Harrington.

"What was the cause of this disagreement?"

"I really forget—some mere trifle. Every one surely knows how, especially in spring, when one is a little out of sorts and irritable, a tiny thing will sometimes cause an explosion of ill-temper. I fancy this was some difference of opinion on some parochial matter. I really have no clear remembrance of it beyond the fact that I did use some such expression as 'We would be better apart for a time,' or 'We had better try what a separation will do'—something quite trivial like that."

"Am I right in suggesting that Mrs. Harrington was of a jealous disposition?"

Harrington shot a wary glance at his questioner.

"We both were," he said guardedly. "We were still—almost lovers."

I felt physically sick. The man was positively loathsome—and silly, too, for it couldn't possibly have deceived any one who knew the Harringtons personally.

I believe the coroner took it for what it was worth. He dismissed Harrington—rather dryly—after this touching declaration, but told him to remain in court. He then called Joe Greaves, and I sat up, all attention. I very much wanted to hear what Joe had to say.

24

You could hardly have a more different pair of witnesses than the Squire and Joe Greaves. Joe's manner was civil enough, but stolid and dogged, and almost desperately quiet. He gave me the impression of a man who knows that he is in a tight place, but who is determined not to alter in the least degree from what he had intended to do or say. He answered in a steady, if rather low, voice to the questions that were asked him.

He was first questioned about his engagement to Lydia Salt. He told, quite simply, of her father's objection to the match on account of his ambition for his daughter, and how, in spite of it, Joe had determined to raise himself to a position when the marriage would be not only allowed but even smiled on.

"We knowed as he'd give us a bit if he were pleased," he said naively. "That were all as I were waiting for the last two year, to get a plaace as'd please him."

He went on to tell the story of Lydia's disastrous visit to Savernake, and of how he had found her on the verge of suicide, had rescued her from that fate, and had married her secretly only a short time ago. He told it all in the dogged, matter-of-fact way in which he might have described a day's work on the farm. He was, of course, closely questioned as to why he had kept his marriage a secret when Lydia's good name was involved, and he answered simply enough. In a few days' time after the marriage, his year's engagement with Farmer Phillips would be settled. It was only a question of waiting those few days, and his position would be assured. Lydia's father would give his consent to his daughter's marriage with a bailiff (as Joe would be then), and all would be well.

"'Twere only a matter o' days," said Joe, but it made aal the differ to we 'atween a labourer's job at a labourer's wage, an' no hope o' nothing better, an' a bailiff's job, wi' a snug bit from her father, an' maybe a house. We thought as it were worth it to wait. It don't mean much to you gentry, maybe," he went on, with a quiet gravity that impressed me enormously, "but it's like the differ 'atween a steady, good living for yourself and your childer, and a hand-to-mouth life, never sure as you'll be able to pay rent and buy enough bread an' boots. It meant *that* much differ to we."

"But it was bound to come out," suggested the coroner.

"Ah, but, see, not afore I knowed about this here job. 'Tis a year's engagement, an' I'll lay as he wouldn't 'a turned me off at end o' year, married or none."

Joe drew himself up. He had, quite rightly, a high opinion of his value on a farm.

He went on, still in his stolid, impassive manner, to give an account of Mrs. Harrington's discovery of Lydia's condition, her immediate suspicion that Joe was responsible for it, and her threat to force him to 'make an honest woman' of her.

"And if she had made this known to the girl's father, it would have seriously affected your future?"

"If she'd spoke afore I got job up to Phillipses, it would. Arter I had that, I did'n' care—we was goin' to tell as we was married then."

Then followed questions about his talk in the 'Lady and Hare' on the night before the Fair. He admitted everything—didn't try even to hedge. He had tried the guns, had fitted an 'elf-bolt' to one, had marked on the stock the one that he knew shot straight. He owned up to being drunk on the afternoon of the Fair itself, but qualified this by saying that he was "not mad drunk, nor even silly drunk, on'y loud an' a bit muzzy loike," and that he had a perfectly clear remembrance of all that he had done both in the afternoon and in the evening.

He had been there when the rifle-range stall collapsed, but neither saw any one take a gun nor had himself taken one. Yes, he thought he would recognize any of the guns again if they were produced. He repeated what Inspector Grier had told us about his actions on leaving the Fair, and admitted quite frankly that neither the barman at the 'Lady and Hare' nor the keeper Simms could possibly swear to the exact times that they had seen him, nor when he had finally left Kit's Park. He also admitted that he had no real alibi for the time from half-past ten to half-past eleven, since he declared, that he had been alone in his solitary cottage after leaving Simms in Kit's Park.

"Now I want you to look at this."

Some official handed up an object to Joe. A thrill ran round the court. It was a gun.

"Do you recognize this gun?"

"Ah."

"Where have you seen it before?"

"'Tis as I told 'ee—I seen it twoice. Oncet at 'Lady and Hare,' o' Thursday noight, and oncet at Fair o' Froiday."

"How can you be sure that this is the same gun?"

"Whoy, see, when chaap were a-showin' of it o' Thursday, I put a mark on stock soo's I should know 'un again.

See, how 'twere—this'n shot straight, an' I reckoned as 'tothers moightn't, soo I marked 'en as I should know 'en when I come to shoot at Fair."

"You're quite positive that you know the gun?"

"Positive sure. I heard tell as 'twere this'n as was stole when range were broke."

"Never mind what you 'heard tell.' You swear to the gun?"

"Ah."

"Do you know where it was found?"

"Noa, that I doan't."

"It was found tied along the limb of a tree—in your garden."

There was a sort of sighing rustle. I suppose that's what the papers call 'Sensation in Court,' only it was far less impressive than that sounds. Joe looked utterly taken aback, but not in the least alarmed or perturbed.

"Do you know how it got there?" persisted the coroner.

"Noa, sir, that I doan't," Joe repeated sturdily.

"Sure you don't?"

"Certain sure."

"Very well. You may stand down. Recall Mr. Harrington."

Godfrey Harrington reappeared in the box. He looked better, steadier, and more composed. I suppose he felt safer now that he saw poor Joe becoming involved.

"I understand that you possess an airgun, Mr. Harrington?"

"I—yes—I have one—or used to."

"What make is it?"

"It's a Loxley Three."

"Ah, quite a powerful gun. A large bore, I believe?"

"N—no—not especially large."

"Can you produce it?"

"I—I'm afraid I can't."

"Can't? Why not?"

"I—I've mislaid it."

"Mislaid it? Since when?"

"Oh—some time. I can't say exactly."

"When did you last use it?"

Harrington was rapidly becoming that horrible bluish colour.

"I—I can't be sure."

"Isn't it the case that you used it for practice on last Friday—the twenty-ninth of June?"

"I—I may have done."

"Don't you *know* that you did?"

"I—yes."

"Where is it now?"

"I tell you I don't know. I've mislaid it. I put it down somewhere, and I can't find it."

"Have you ever lent it to any one else?"

"Sometimes."

"To whom?"

"Mr. Earle used to use it sometimes, some time ago now; and I have occasionally lent it to young Greaves when he did shooting of vermin on my property."

"But on the twenty-ninth you used it yourself?"

"I—I—yes, I did."

"Hm. . . . Have you a new Loxley Three there, Inspector?"

"Yes, sir."

"Have you examined it?"

"Yes, sir."

"And does it admit such a pellet as that found in brain of the deceased?"

"Yes, sir; it fits exactly."

Again that whispering sigh went round the court.

"And the other gun—the one identified by the last witness. Does that take the stone, too?"

"Yes, sir, though it's a bit loose. But it fits. The stone could be shot by both guns—both the Loxley and the one found in the last witness's garden."

"I see. Thank you. You may stand down, Mr. Harrington."

The coroner then addressed the jury. He was, I must say, pretty fair to every one. As he dealt with each person's evidence, one felt that, if one knew nothing of them personally, one would have suspected three people in turn—Stephen, Godfrey Harrington, and Joe Greaves. Of course, I myself put Stephen out of it at once; and yet one had to admit that there was something amounting to hatred between him and Mrs. Harrington, that he had passed over the very spot where the rifle booth was wrecked, and might quite well have found the missing gun. Granted that, and admitting that he might have been standing on the Green with the gun in his hand when he saw the hated Mrs. Harrington close to him, one had also to admit that the time did permit of his having committed the murder. Then there was the evidence against the Squire—his undoubted lies about his movements, the fact that his gun took the pellet, that that gun was missing, that there had been quarrels between him and his wife, due probably to jealousy. Besides, his whole manner was dead against him. And finally there was Joe, whose whole future was threatened by the dead woman, who had used the gun with a flint arrow, in whose garden the gun had been found, and who had no real alibi for the time between ten to and ten past eleven. On the whole, I thought the facts were worst for Joe, and the impression made by the witnesses worst for Godfrey Harrington.

The jury must also have found these various theories of about equal importance, for they were ages and ages before they brought in a verdict. I thought they would never come, as I sat, Celia's hand clutching mine, watching he

faces of the three men. Stephen seemed calm enough, but
I could tell, from the way he moved and the way in which
his colour rose and fell, that he was really none too happy.
Joe looked stolid as ever. The Squire was pitiable in his
nervous efforts to make conversation with people he knew,
and to arouse some kind of expression of sympathy. And
the minutes crept on and on, and still nothing happened;
and then, quite suddenly, the jury returned, and Celia's
hand turned icy cold in mine.

"Gentlemen, have you considered your verdict?"

"Yes, sir. Murder against a person or persons unknown."

I admit it was a relief. I didn't like Godfrey Harrington,
but I have a passion for the truth, and I didn't want a verdict to be brought in against him. No man who was such
a complete fool could possibly bring off a murder. As for
Stephen, it was of course simply absurd; and so it was to
suspect Joe. They were quite right—the murderer was, I
felt sure, a person unknown—as yet. Yet, as I watched
Inspector Grier's face as we filed out into the hot sun-
shine, I wondered—was he (or she) unknown to us all?

25

I got Celia back to the Manor House as quickly as I could. Though she had said nothing at all, either during the evidence of the other witnesses or afterwards, I could tell well enough what her feelings were. She is, as I have said, extremely fond of her father, but she also has plenty of sense; she must have known that he came out of his examination very badly. She may even have feared (as I half did) lest the verdict should not be as vague as it actually was. Anyhow, I thought that she would be the better for a complete rest; and for myself I felt that I simply *could not* meet Godfrey Harrington on ordinarily polite terms for a little. He might or might not be a murderer—on the whole, I didn't think he was—but he was most certainly both a hypocrite and a liar, and, I believed, a perjurer as well. I took Celia up to her room and told her I'd send her up a tray. Though there had been a lunch interval, none of us had taken much advantage of it.

But luck was against me. Coming down from her room to give the order, I walked straight into her father—looking more distracted and—yes, *terrified*—than I'd ever seen a man look.

As soon as he saw me he clutched at me like a frightened child. Much as I disliked him, I simply hadn't the heart to shake him off. His hands trembled violently and were icy cold, and he caught at mine as if he were drowning.

"Miss Leslie," he gasped, "oh, Miss Leslie, I—it—"

His voice failed him. He could only stand and gasp. I was very much alarmed. He hadn't been like this when Celia and I left the court. What could have happened since?

"What is it?" I asked anxiously; then, seeing that he simply could not speak, I got him into a chair (fortunately the hall at the Manor House is well furnished) and fetched him a brandy-and-soda. The colour came back a little into his face as he drank it, and he began to look more normal.

"Now, tell me what's the matter," I said, taking the tumbler from him. "What's happened *now?*"

"I—that inspector—I asked him to have a drink with me—after that terrible inquiry—and he—he *refused!*"

His voice failed again, and he shuddered violently.

"Well?" I said.

"*Well!* Don't you know what that means? The police may never drink with—with a—a suspected criminal."

He brought the words out with a jerk.

"Oh, Miss Leslie, you don't think—say you don't think that they—that I—"

"Don't be so foolish," I said sternly. "The inspector probably had a lot to see to. He couldn't waste time with you. Besides, he may be on duty. Policemen on duty can't go casually taking drinks at village inns. You know that."

I didn't know it myself—in fact, Inspector Grier had had some of my very best Madeira before now without the faintest scruple—rather the reverse, if anything—but I thought it sounded probable; and Godfrey Harrington is the kind of fool that will allow himself to be cheated, and even cheat himself, with the greatest alacrity if it is comfortable. His face now cleared like magic.

"I—what an ass I am!" he muttered, wiping his forehead. "It's that damnable—I beg your pardon—that terrible raking up of old sorrows that's unnerved me. I think I—I'll go and lie down."

"You'd better," I agreed; and I ordered two trays to be sent upstairs instead of one, and ate my own meal in peace. But all the same I wondered—was Godfrey Harrington's terror really entirely unfounded? Had the inspector really refused his hospitality for the reason he thought? Or was it his own guilty conscience that made him fear the official attitude? And in connexion with this, I wondered why he had looked as he did when it was suggested to him that Mrs. Harrington's first husband (who was, I supposed, the man Lagardi, or a friend of his) was not dead. And I also wondered what were the contents of the dead woman's will—if she had made one.

The rest of that day passed quietly enough. I spent a good deal of time in thought, trying to piece out a really satisfactory solution from the various scraps of information I had collected. But there were so many—and you never knew whether they were connected with each other, or whether, by following up one clue, you were being led off on a false scent and neglecting the really important lines. One of my favourite detectives in fiction is always impressing his Watson with the fact that the great secret of successful detecting is never to ignore *any* fact. Well, I ask you! If I concluded every fact I knew about the various people who were even remotely connected with Mrs. Harrington's death, where should I ever make a start? And now I couldn't even trust my own intuitions. X, my X, the man (I had no doubt) of the poppy-stain, had probably materialized—and I couldn't make *him* fit, not all over. I had, I thought with some dejection, probably been plumping for X simply because I had a personal interest in his conduct and that particular episode. I felt very much like giving it up. And then the memory of Inspector Grier spurred me on. He, I felt sure, thought that he was on the edge of discovering the whole thing. He had pretty well said so. I might—*perhaps*—be induced to play the admiring Watson to a brilliant amateur, a Holmes or a Hanaud or a Poirot; but I simply *would not* be a Watson to the Holmes of the country police. It was too degrading. I would get *something* out of it. And it was with this noble resolution that I finally went to bed.

I was tired, and fell asleep almost at once. I had the most satisfactory dream, in which I had discovered a clue—a definite thread that you could hold in your hand—which would, I knew, lead me straight to the criminal; and I was following this up, pretending to Inspector Grier, who as rather eccentrically riding about the hall of the Manor House on his motor-cycle, with a glass of brandy-and-soda in one hand, that this thread was part of some fancy-work that I was doing for the next Fair. I was very much thrilled at being so near the solution, and very much amused by my deception of the inspector, when unfortunately my thread caught in the leg of a chair and snapped—and I awoke with a start.

At first I thought I had been awakened by one of those jumps you do get when you're in bed, and which, I believe, somehow prove that we are descended from monkeys. But I was, at that part of my life, prepared for anything, and so I lay still and listened, instead of simply turning over and going to sleep again.

And then I heard a sound—just the faintest rustling, tapping sort of noise—somewhere outside.

I had left my door open, so that I should hear Celia if she wanted me; but the noise was not from her room. It was more distant. I lay and listened. It sounded, I thought, furtive—dangerous. And I believe I knew at once what it was.

I felt the most enormous reluctance and at the same time a burning anxiety to find out what it was. This time

I would make no mistake. I stole noiselessly out of bed, slipped on my dressing-gown, and crept out.

The little passage was empty. The moonlight showed me that, but I had known that it would be. I stole into the main corridor and listened again.

I had not a doubt left. The sounds—tiny, faint, indescribable sounds—came from Mrs. Harrington's room.

I admit that I was horribly frightened. Whoever—or whatever—was there, it, or he, certainly had no business there. Whether it was ghost or man, X or a spirit, or even Godfrey Harrington, I did *not* want to encounter it or him. And yet I had to do something. I didn't know how long the intruder had been there. He might vanish at any moment, and my clue with him. And here, I felt certain, *was* the clue to the whole thing—the clue that I had dreamed of, and which really would be mine, and mine only, if I had the courage to pick it up.

With my heart simply hammering, I crept along the main corridor to the door of Mrs. Harrington's room. With infinite precautions I turned the handle. It made only the faintest click as I pushed the door open, inch by inch.

I knew at once that some one was there—or had just been there. There was that same feeling there had been before of a second presence in the room. The moonlight threw fantastic patches of light and shade—deceiving and tricky patches. I stood holding my breath, staring into the room. It looked empty—and I *knew* it was not.

I made up my mind—all this, of course, took only a few seconds in reality and put out my hand. The electric light snapped on.

There were two electric lights in that room—one over the bed and one before the mirror. The one I had switched on was that over the bed, and instinctively I looked, with a kind of shrinking I find it impossible to describe, to see whether again the pillow was dented and the bed rumpled.

It was not. The bed stood stark and smooth between its old curtains of rose damask. Vaguely, but greatly, relieved, I looked round the room.

At first I thought that there was nothing to be seen—that nothing had been touched in the great quiet room whose owner would never sleep in it again. And then I saw that I was wrong. The pretty dressing-table, always so exquisitely neat and dainty, was somehow different—disarranged.

Still moving very quietly, I stole over to it. And then I *knew* that I was right. Some one *had* been there—had touched the dainty trifles that lay still on the table. And, in a flash of pure panic, I knew that that person was still in the room—there, close to me, hiding. . . . I must have help.

I screamed—shouted for help as I have never shouted before or since, for I knew that the criminal, the murderer, was there in that room with me, silently lurking. . . .

My scream sounded ghastly as it shrilled in my own ears—and then, quite suddenly, darkness fell. *The light had gone out.*

I had no personal fear left now. I was only terrified lest the intruder should escape. I rushed across to the switch by the door and pressed the button. Nothing happened. Frantically I tried the other. Still darkness.

And then I was simply, purely terrified. I could see the switches from where I had stood by the dressing-table. I knew no human hand had touched them. Somehow that failure of the plain, everyday light which had been so clear only a second ago seemed to plunge me back into horror and mystery as vague as the moving shadows and gleams of light in the room itself. I threw open the door, calling again and again—and I saw a figure move at the far end of the corridor. I rushed to meet it—and I simply can't say what a relief it was to feel a human hand meet mine!

"Miss Leslie!" It was Godfrey Harrington's voice, and even in my terror I heard relief as well as blank amazement in it. "Was it *you* who screamed like that?"

"Yes—come—quick—he's there, in Mrs. Harrington's room!" I gasped like a maniac, tugging at him.

"Who? What? I don't understand."

I—left him and tore back, with him pursuing me.

"He's here!" I cried. "The murderer!"

That stirred him. We were back in the big room only a few seconds after I had left it.

"Turn on the light," he cried to me as we dashed in.

"I—I—can't—it won't!" I gasped.

Of course he wouldn't believe me, and spent another precious second in fumbling at the switches. Then a breeze fluttered my hair, and I knew we were too late.

"The window's open—he's gone!" I cried.

He just had the sense not to rush over and look at it and finger the glass. Instead, he dashed downstairs (with me at his heels, of course) and went round to the outside of the house. He stopped just short of the bed below Mrs. Harrington's window—the bed where the poppies grew. He pointed at it.

"Footprints!" he hissed in the most dramatic manner.

"Yes," I agreed, "quite so; but meanwhile he's escaping."

"Well, we can't chase him," said Godfrey Harrington, with some reason. "He's got a good start, and we're both barefoot. All we can do is to get the police on to it at once, and make sure that he leaves a heavy scent. I'll stay here and see that no one disturbs these footprints, and you go in and ring up that man Grier, tell him what's happened, and make him come *at once.*"

The energy and sense of the man perfectly astonished me. I obeyed quite meekly. It's surprising, I thought, as I ran back into the house, how hope will infuse sense into the most blithering of idiots; and in the presence of this intruder Godfrey Harrington saw, I have no doubt, the greatest reason for hope, the best sort of refutation of any suspicion that any one might have against him. No wonder that he volunteered to stand barefoot and in pyjamas in the garden on the off-chance of protecting those precious prints—or even to catch the villain in the act of returning to erase them. Mentally I scratched 'Godfrey Harrington' off my list of suspects. More than ever I plumped for X.

26

I ran upstairs and locked the door of Mrs. Harrington's room and took out the key; then I made a bee-line for the telephone. I knew the inspector's number, and thought that, at that hour of the night (2.5 a.m., I noted half mechanically, looking at the hall clock), I should get on to him at once. I steadied my voice to a pretended calm, and Exchange, for once, seemed to understand what I wanted at the very first time of asking.

The minutes crawled by. Nothing happened. I nearly danced with impatience as I thought of the criminal—*my* criminal—getting farther and farther away. . . .

Then, at last, there came a voice.

"I can't get an answer," said Exchange. "Are you sure the number's right?"

"Perfectly sure. . . . Oh, I tell you—ring up Newbury Police Station, and say that Inspector Grier is wanted urgently—most urgently—on the telephone."

Again I waited for several hours.

"Are you there?"

I suppressed the obvious retort.

"Newbury Police Station says that Inspector Grier isn't there. His number is—"

"Oh, I know his number. It's the one I gave you at first. Try it again, will you, please?"

Exchange must have been thrilled, for she certainly did her best, but presently her voice came again:

"I'm very sorry, but it's no good—I can't get an answer."

"Damn!" I said distinctly.

And then I had an idea. Was it possible, I wondered, that the inspector was at this very minute on the trail? He certainly knew something that I didn't. Could it be possible that he knew that X might come that night—was lying in wait for him, and was even now in full cry after him?

"Shall I call the number again?" asked Exchange's disembodied voice.

"No—never mind. But put me on to the Newbury police again, will you, please?"

She did, and I got a deaf moron (or so it seemed) on the wire. After several attempts to make him understand something of what had happened, I at last contented myself with a message to Inspector Grier to the effect that he was wanted at Ringshall Manor as soon as possible on account of new developments. And I then rang off in a very bad temper.

I went back to the garden, and found the Squire very little, if at all, pleasanter than myself. Of course he thought (as all men, even the best of them, do on these occasions) that I had somehow muddled it, and that it was, in some undefined way, my fault that Inspector Grier hadn't immediately materialized and got to work.

"Anyway," I said, rather snappishly, "it's no good standing about here. . . . The question is, what had we better do about it?"

"We *must* keep guard here," said Harrington. "It would be simply fatal to risk any one spoiling these footprints."

"Quite," I agreed, "but we can't stand here in airy *déshabille* all night on the off-chance of some one coming to disturb them. I tell you what—I'll wait here, if you think it's necessary, while you go and dress and fetch Dan Gregory. After all, it's his job, not ours, to catch criminals."

He went off, quite pleased to be released from his job as sentry, and I stood and waited and thought and planned.

One thing was, I thought, quite obvious—namely, that this nocturnal visitor was the same that had come before, on the night of the murder—X, in short. And that seemed to me to make another point clear.

X was after something in Mrs. Harrington's room. That first visit had been made with the object of getting it, but had not been successful. He had then, somehow, either by listening to what Celia and I had said, or by some other means, found the little safe in the wall over the bed, and had robbed that—and had still failed to find what he wanted. This was his third attempt. The great question, of course, was—What did he want? And had he got it this time?

The trouble was that this continual burgling of that room upset all my theories. I hadn't, I admit, been very clear about the exact way in which the previous burglaries fitted in with the murder, though I thought it likely that the object of those thefts had been the papers that the man Lagardi had produced for the inspector's benefit. Now, of course, that seemed hopelessly wrong. He had the papers—I had seen them myself, and both the inspector and I had felt (at least I had, and I thought that he had) that they formed a pretty strong case, though I was still perfectly unable to see why on earth, if they had been stolen from the Manor House, Mrs. Harrington had kept them. Still, whatever her motive, Lagardi had them now. What on earth could he be after now? Her will? As he had himself pointed out, it was very doubtful that she had made one, on account of the difficulty of getting it witnessed if she used her true name, Lagardi, instead of the one she was known by in Ringshall, Harrington.

I then had another inspiration. Were there *two* X's—the real Lagardi and another villain who intended to pass himself off as the original husband of Mrs. Harrington? Had this second one not known that the first one had found the papers and produced them, and was he still engaged in searching for them?

I thought that a most attractive idea, full of possibilities. On the other hand it was also, unfortunately, full of difficulties. It was possible that one of the X's had found out which was Mrs. Harrington's room, and made straight for it; but it wasn't credible that the other had been able to do the same thing—unless, of course, he had spied on the first one, in which case he would have known that he probably had the precious papers. Reluctantly I abandoned that theory, and returned to the idea of a single X. What, then, was X after now? It must, I thought, have been a will. There was almost nothing else for it to be. But even then I couldn't make it fit in with the murder.

I was so occupied with these thoughts that I hardly noticed how the time was passing, and was quite startled when Godfrey Harrington appeared, fully clothed, with Gregory at his heels.

"Piece of luck," remarked the Squire. "Gregory was up—after a hen-thief or something. He'll stand guard till they come from Newbury. I've rung them up again, and said that they simply must send some one responsible over at once. Come in and wait, Miss Leslie."

I was glad to. I discovered, now that the first thrill was over, that I was chilly. I went and got some clothes on, and then joined Godfrey Harrington in the hall, where we lit cigarettes, and waited.

We had not very long to wait. I was only half-way through my second cigarette when we heard the sound of a car approaching rapidly. We hurried out to meet it.

There were three men in it. One, the first to get out, I identified at first sight as the moron I had got on the telephone. (I was wrong, as it turned out. The moron was lively and engaging compared with this person.) This official—one can't say 'man' of a creature like that—was in plain clothes, and so was the second. A young policeman in uniform was acting as page or train-bearer or Black Rod or something.

"Well, well, well? Urrrh?" said the first of these persons. He looked and sounded exactly like a sea-lion when it comes up to blow. "What's all this? what's all this? Eh?"

"There's been a burglary," began Harrington.

"Well? Well? Isn't there a local constable? Eh?"

Harrington looked at me in a bewildered kind of way, so I answered:

"Yes, there is. He's outside now."

"Well? Who rang us up? Eh?"

"I did, in the first place," I said.

"You did, madam?" He faced round on me, and his walrus moustache positively bristled with fury, "Why did you do that—?"

I felt I couldn't bear it if he said "Eh?" again. I cut hurriedly, "I explained to the officer who took the call—" I began.

Here the second plain-clothes man spoke. I recognized his voice at once as that of the moron. There couldn't be two policemen in one station with voices like that.

"That's right, sir. Something to do with the Harrington murder case, I understood, sir."

"But that's Inspector Grier's case," fumed the Walrus. "I can't possibly—eh?"

"I can't get Inspector Grier. I've tried all round the place. And there's no time to lose."

I said this in my sternest voice. To my relief the Walrus succumbed.

They listened quite quietly to my statement, the Walrus writing it all down very busily all the time. Then he actually took steps.

"Wilberforce, you'd better go along to this flowerbed and see if you can find any traces. If so, follow them up. Report to me here."

The moron vanished.

"Now, madam—if you'll kindly show me the room."

I led the way upstairs. As I went, I could not help thinking how different I had felt when I took dear Inspector Grier up, and we found the poppy-stain. It wouldn't be the least use showing this man anything short of a bloodstain of a large size. Even then he'd probably demand a whole corpse before he really did anything.

I'd had the sense to collect an electric torch as I went. I flashed this on as we entered Mrs. Harrington's room, explaining as I did so about the lights.

"Went out, eh?" snorted the Walrus. "Turned out, you mean?"

"No. It won't go on again now."

"Wire cut?"

"I shouldn't think so. I shouldn't think there was time. I was standing here"—I moved over to the dressing-table—"looking towards the door, like this."

The Walrus went over to the same spot.

"Hm. Two lights, I see. Were both on?"

"No. Only the one over the bed."

He went across.

"You're wrong," he barked in triumph. "It can't have been. There's no bulb in it."

"It *was*—I'll swear it was!" I exclaimed, following him. And then I saw, on the bed, a real clue.

"Look!" I cried. "On the cover—see? He stepped on to the bed and took the bulb out."

The Walrus glared. I suppose I ought to have let him make that discovery. But I was far too excited to bother about a whole Zoo-ful of walruses.

"And here's the bulb," I finished in triumph, fishing out a little bulge just under the sheet. "He must have been hiding behind the bed."

"Hm. But that doesn't account for the other light going out—eh?"

"It wasn't on. It may be fused," I said. I went over to the dressing-table again, and, standing on a chair, took out the bulb. I shook it, and heard a familiar rattle. "It is," I said.

"Hm, hm. But you'd have seen any one who stood on the bed."

He obviously nourished the deepest suspicions of me.

"No, I shouldn't," I retorted. "Not from here. The curtain hides all the bed except the very foot. I can't see you from here."

"Hm. Well, Miss—er—Mrs.—er—madam, all I can say is—"

I don't know what was the only thing he could say. Probably either "hm" or "eh?" But we were interrupted by a knock at the door.

"Well? Well? Who's there, eh?" demanded the Walrus.

"Me, sir. Jackson. Please, sir, there's a message come through. It seems that Inspector Grier is ill, sir—very dangerously ill. An accident of some kind. Will you come, please, sir?"

The Walrus bustled to the door.

"Accident, eh?"

"Yes, sir—or an attack on him. They didn't seem quite sure."

The Walrus lumped downstairs. I followed as unobtrusively as I could. Wild ideas galloped through my head—

Inspector Grier pursuing a mysterious man, who turned and attacked him . . . X . . .

I slipped into a deep arm-chair, where I was sure that the Walrus, at the telephone, could not see me. I knew that if he did he would send me away lest I should hear official secrets. And I wanted to hear very badly indeed.

"Who's that? Yes, Belcher speaking. Picked up, eh? Where? *Where,* did you say? Oh! Then where is he now? Oh. What's the doctor's name? Oh—I'll spell it after you— L-u-d-l-o-w. That right?"

I started violently. Ludlow! So it *was* near here, then. I listened again, with all my ears.

"Who found him? Gray? Oh—Greaves. *Ohhhh!* Indeed. The same chap who— Yes. *Really?* Yes, I'll see him at once. Yes, I'll carry on here. Good-bye."

He rang off. I sat, my thoughts in a whirl. Inspector Grier attacked, while X escaped—and Joe Greaves just happening to be on the spot! I thought of the gluttonous satisfaction with which the Walrus had spoken of Joe, and my heart sank.

27

The Walrus sounded frightfully pleased. Whether it was because, now that poor Inspector Grier was out of the way, he would have the handling of the 'Harrington Case,' or whether it was because he thought that he would now have a chance of bullying some one into confessing to a whole lot of things he hadn't done, I couldn't be sure. I sat and tried to piece together all the things that had happened, and watched the Walrus thinking what he would do next.

What he did eventually do was to go out into the garden. I slipped along the little side passage that leads out to the servants' quarters. It runs immediately under Mrs. Harrington's room, and has windows at intervals along it. None of the passage windows is immediately under the windows of that room, but, by opening one of them a crack, I could hear quite well all that passed a few yards farther on, where the patient Gregory still did sentry-go under Mrs. Harrington's window.

"Here—you—constable—what's your name?"

"Gregory, sir. Dan Gregory."

"Gregory, eh? Well, Gregory, Inspector Wilberforce been here, I expect—eh?"

"Couldn't say, sir."

"What? Hasn't he been here? Eh?"

"A inspector have, sir. Whether 'twere him as you mentioned, I couldn't take on me to say."

The Walrus gulped audibly.

"Where is he now, eh?"

"Couldn' say, I'm sure, sir."

I could have kissed Gregory, the Walrus sounded so wild.

"Are you a fool, man?" he shouted.

"Dare say I be, sir," Gregory said pacifically.

"Where did he go? What did he say?"

"'A never said nought, sir. Took out a pocket rule, 'a did, an' measured they footprints, sir, an' maade a li'l draa-ing very pretty, sir; an' then 'a sort o' grunted like, as you might saay, an' off 'a went. Right off," Gregory added reminiscently.

"Hm. Well, you stop there till you're relieved. See?"

"Very good, sir."

Gregory still sounded calm and amiable, which must have annoyed the Walrus even more. He stumped off, leaving Gregory to continue his vigil, and I ran up the back stairs to my own room.

It was broad daylight now, and the birds were making a heavenly clamour in the dewy trees. I certainly couldn't go back to bed when everything was awake and glorious. . . . And then I had an idea. I thought that I, too, would do a little sleuthing of the same approved sort as that practised by Roger Cartwright.

I went silently out of my room, ran down the back stairs, and slipped out of the Manor House grounds. I knew, from the very sound of his voice, that the Walrus would be up to mischief in the next hour or so. I wanted to find out exactly what had happened before he made it impossible for me to do so.

As I approached Joe Greaves's cottage, I could see a tiny feather of smoke upright against the profound blue of

the sky. Good! I thought; he's at home; and I went round
to his back door.

It stood open, and I could see Joe inside, bending over
his fire.

"Good morning, Joe," I said. "May I come in a minute?"
Joe looked round.

"Come in and welcome, miss," he said, getting up. He
seemed to see nothing odd in my calling on him at five
a.m. He had the true courtesy of country folk. "Maybe
you'd take a cup o' tea?" he went on. "Kettle be just a-goin
to boil."

"I'd love one, thank you," I said fervently. I was beginning to realize that I had spent rather a hectic night.

Joe went over to a cupboard and got out a cup. I noticed
(as most women would) that his room was most beautifully neat.

"Joe," I said, plunging into my subject at once, "what's
this about Inspector Grier?"

Joe laid down the cup and looked at me—a queer, slow,
heavy look, such as Ringshall people give you when you
puzzle them or when they don't want to speak out.

"How did 'ee know about 'en?" he asked.

"We had more bother at the house last night," I explained rapidly, "and I rang him up. The Newbury people
had heard from Dr. Ludlow that something had happened,
and that you knew what it was."

"Ah?" said Joe non-committally.

"*Do* tell me, Joe," I begged. "What's happened?"

Joe appeared to consider. It was as if he were going over
the details in his mind before speaking.

"Whoy," he began at last, "I were out las' noight, latish."
(I wondered why, but thought it wiser not to ask.) "I were
comin' down King's Bank, thinkin' to cut oover to t'other
soide o' Newbury Road an' get hoame across the Bottoms.
When I comed through they trees along Newb'y Road, I

see summat black on edge o' road, on t'other soide, loike. I thought as 'a looked queer, so I went an' looked."

"And it was the inspector?"

Joe nodded. "Ah," he said briefly.

"What had happened?"

"Looked as if 'a'd failed off'n his motor-boike. 'Twere aal o' a mash, loike, the boike were, and the man seemed more dead nor quick. Covered wi' blood, 'a was. I felt in's coat, an' his heart were a-beatin', but very slow an' fainty-loike. I didn' think as 'a'd live long. Soo I up an' off for doctor. 'Twere a job for he."

"They've got a perfectly horrible man in his place," I said. "An Inspector Belcher. He's out to bully us all and—and try to make out he knows everything."

I looked at Joe closely as I said this. I hoped it might convey a warning to him.

"Be 'a, now," Joe responded politely. He seemed uninterested.

"He's sure to think that he can find out who killed poor Mrs. Harrington in two minutes," I went on.

At that Joe did look up.

"Whoy, what do 'a think—" he began; and it was at that very moment that we heard a hammering at Joe's other door—the front one, that only strangers use.

"Reckon that'll be him," said Joe quietly. "You'd best slip off, miss. Reckon if 'a be the soort as you say, 'twon't do 'ee no good for he to see 'ee a-chattin' along o' me."

As he spoke, he deftly replaced my empty cup in the cupboard.

I knew it was the truth. I knew exactly what Inspector Belcher would both think and say if he thought I was trespassing on, or even approaching near to, his preserves. I slipped gently out by the back door as Joe opened the front one.

But I did not go far. I stood just outside and listened.

I recognized the Walrus's voice at once—the Walrus stirred to action, the Man of Power.

"You are Joseph Greaves?" he began at once in his most Prussian manner.

"Ah," Joe agreed, after thought.

"I understand that it was you who informed Dr. Ludlow of the—ah—*accident* to Inspector Grier?"

He laid a horrid, sneering emphasis on the word 'accident.'

"Ah."

"Give me your account of what happened."

"I were a-crossin' Newb'y Road an' I seed 'en on the edge."

I could tell by his very tone that Joe's independent blood was roused by the Inspector's hectoring manner.

"What time was this?"

Joe paused.

"Reckon 'twould be gettin' on o' two," he said at last.

"Two! Two in the morning, do you mean?"

"Ah."

I would give anything to be able to say "Ah," as Ringshall people can say it. They can make it a question, an assent, a denial, or an ejaculation of pity, anger, or scorn. This time it was scorn, and I didn't wonder.

"And what were you doing on the Newbury Road at two a.m.?"

"I were a-crossin' from King's Bank to Bottoms."

"What for?"

"To get homealong," said Joe patiently. He allowed a touch—the merest shade of pity and wonder to sound in his voice.

"No impudence!" snapped the Walrus. "What were you out for at all, at that time of night?"

"Reckon 'tis my business," said Joe doggedly.

(As I listened to this interview, and noticed how easily Joe kept upsides with the Walrus, my admiration for the diplomatic powers of dear Inspector Grier waxed apace. *He* had got every single thing he wanted to out of Joe without the slightest difficulty.)

"You'd better be careful!" breathed the Walrus, with a kind of heavy malignity. "It won't do you any good to insult the Police."

Joe said nothing. They seemed to have reached a deadlock.

Then the Walrus began again.

"What did you do on seeing the body?"

"Feeled his 'eart."

"Well? Well?"

"I seed as 'a were pretty poorly, so I went for doctor."

"Well? Get on, man, can't you?"

"I fetched doctor along, and helped 'en to put the soul in's car. Then I comed homealong."

"How long have you been in?"

"Reckon 'tis the best paart o' two hour."

The Walrus paused. He obviously wanted to take a Strong Step and didn't know whether he dared.

"You stop at home to-day," he said at last. "You may be called on to tell *all you know.*"

He really was very funny, he tried so hard to be official and alarming.

"Caan't tell 'ee noo more'n what I have telled 'ee," protested Joe. "If I stops to home, what'll goo wi' my job at the faarm as I starts on to-day?"

The Walrus paused. He clearly wanted to give Joe as much trouble as he could, but didn't quite dare go so as to make him rebellious or alarm him too much.

"Well," he said at last, very grudgingly, "you can go to work. What's the address? I may want to see you."

"Phillips, the man's name is. Honours Mead Farm, 'tis caaled, over to Witton way."

The Walrus shut his book. I could hear the snap, he did it so viciously. I knew that I should learn no more, so I skirted my way carefully through Joe's garden, taking cover from his fruit trees and bushes, and slipped back to Ringshall across the fields. I got in before seven.

How I did miss dear Inspector Grier that, day! He might not have told us exactly what was happening, or whether the moron had done anything about finding my burglar, but he would have realized that after all he was *our* burglar, and he'd have been nice about it, and I'd have known that he would tell us what he could. As it was, that insufferable Walrus hung about the house on and off all day, doing mysterious things in Mrs. Harrington's room (to impress us, I'm sure; I feel convinced that he did nothing useful), worrying the maids, badgering poor Godfrey Harrington and me for further details which we couldn't give, bullying Gregory and the other little police constable Jackson, constantly using the telephone, and generally making himself objectionable. He wouldn't even tell us how poor Inspector Grier was. But I found that out for myself, by ringing up Dr. Ludlow from my own house, and learnt that the poor man had concussion and a broken arm and collar-bone. Dr. Ludlow added that he must have "come a terrific purler," and it was a wonder that he hadn't broken his neck. And I think it wasn't till that moment that I began to wonder how it was that the inspector, riding along a perfectly—well, fairly good high road in bright moonlight, had come that cropper. I thought it over, and decided that a little reconnaissance might help me to find out.

This happened earlier in the day than I have made it appear. I had a very early breakfast (I wanted it, in spite of Joe's tea) and rang up the doctor about eight. I then

strolled out by a rather circuitous route to the thick bushes that grow on the lower slopes of the King's Bank. I
could take cover among these, if necessary, for nearly a
mile along the road. As it happened, I didn't need to.
My path brought me out almost opposite the place where
a constable, with the help of one or two labourers, was
collecting the scattered debris of a motor-cycle and pil-
ing it on a truck. I crouched down and waited till they'd
finished, and the cortège moved solemnly off. I knew that
they couldn't mess about looking for the traces of the accident on the surface of a tarred high road. And they didn't.
They were right out of sight in a quarter of an hour.

I had no very clear idea what to look for. All I knew
was, first, that there was at least a chance that Inspector
Grier had actually been on the track of X when he had his
accident; and secondly, that there was no reason for an
accident to have occurred. As I said, to search the surface
of the road for footprints was impossible. But I hoped that
the edges, which were grassy, might hold tracks—that is,
of course, if there were any tracks to be seen. The only
hypothesis I had to go on was that some one had caused
that 'accident'—some one who particularly wanted Inspector Grier out of the way. And I hoped that that some one
might prove to be my old friend X. Whether X did or did
not = Lagardi I could not make up my mind; but I very
much hoped that he did.

I thought at first that I was doomed to disappointment.
The ground at the edge of the road was grassy, as I said,
and there had been a heavyish dew the night before; but
the heat of the last few days had baked the earth so hard
that, as I saw at a glance, there was no hope of real footprints. But even without these there might be something
else—flattened undergrowth, snapped twigs, even the traditional tobacco ash or thread of cloth on a thorn—something to indicate the presence of X. I felt that a matchbox

with an Italian inscription would meet my requirements very nicely.

I moved very cautiously. I didn't want to disturb any traces which might be there; also, I did not want to be seen if the Walrus, or his friend the moron, should take it into their heads to come investigating too. But I soon saw that I might have good hunting.

First I saw, quite clearly, the marks of some one's passing through the undergrowth and grass behind the belt of trees on the King's Bank side of the road. These traces—crushed grass, a heel-mark in an ant-hill, a broken spray of leaves here and there—led right from the Bank itself to the road; and I decided that these must mark Joe's passage, for they continued right to the edge of the road, where they were lost on the hard surface.

I tracked them (at a respectful distance) to the road, then I started to work my way along, parallel with the road and about two yards in from it on the King's Bank side. I knew I should not have much of a beat lengthways; if Inspector Grier had really been attacked, I need only go about five yards along, and not much more deep, on both sides of the road. And very soon I was rewarded.

As I said, the traces of Joe's descent from the King's Bank were clear. His path came out nearly opposite the place where the smashed bushes and flattened grass on the other side showed the spot of the inspector's fall. What interested me was that, about three yards to the south of this line (that is, nearer to Ringshall village), there were two flattened patches of lush grass under a thick whin bush. They were not very large patches—I could cover each with my hand—but they were very flat. It looked exactly as if some one had laid two flat-irons there, about eight inches apart.

I was very careful not to disturb them. I stood about a yard away from them. But I have very sharp eyes, and I felt sure that if there was anything more to be seen I should see it. But I had no luck. There were no burnt matches or dropped buttons or any of the things that ought to have been there in accordance with all the rules of detective fiction. The two little patches were all that I could see.

As I have said, the road is bordered by large trees. Many of these have ivy climbing up their trunks. I suppose it was because my eyes were searching the ground that I had at first missed the clue I got on my second effort.

It was a broken piece of ivy, about nine inches from the ground, that caught my eye. It had not been cut or broken off cleanly. It was fretted through, the stem worn right through to the tree, and the lichen on either side of it was rubbed away. On the other side of the tree-trunk, the side next the road, ivy and lichen were intact.

I guessed what it meant. I walked straight across the road, and came out about three feet behind the place where the inspector's cycle had been picked up. And I was right. On a tree exactly opposite the first, at about the same distance from the ground, there was a similar mark. And here there was something else as well. There was a molehill quite close to the tree; and in the loose earth of it there was a print—not a footprint, unfortunately, but something nearly as good. It was the clear print of a twist or plait—in fact, of a rope.

That made me certain. Inspector Grier's fall was *not* an accident. A rope had been stretched across the road on purpose to trip him as he raced along on his motor-cycle. It had chafed through the ivy on the trees to which it had bee tied. The question then was, of course—who had done this? Obviously some one who knew that he would be riding along that particular road on that particular night at about that time. And the answer to that question, I thought, depended on another. Where was the rope? It had certainly vanished now. Had the police found it and taken

it away? Or—was it hidden somewhere near, somewhere
where the man who placed it originally would be likely to
hide it when its job was done? I sincerely hoped the last.
If it was hidden, and I could only find it, I might really
have a clue to the person who had been at the bottom of
all our thrills from the murder downwards.

28

I dared not stay any longer. I was sure that it would occur even to such an one as the Walrus to come and make
personal investigations sooner or later, and I particularly
did not want to come into contact, especially contact of
an acrimonious kind, with him—at least, not yet. Later
on, when things were ripe and he had made a complete ass
of himself (as a man like that was bound to do, sooner or
later) I should not at all mind being in a position to score
off him in a freezing and dignified manner. But that would
not be yet. There was a lot of spade work to be done first.

I made a bit of a detour to get back to the Manor
House, so as to avoid meeting Belcher or any of his minions. The hot weather still held, though the sky had that
hard, heavy look, more like a roof than sky, that means
thunder coming; and the heat and my short night made me
tired, so that I moved slowly. It was well after ten when I
reached the Manor House.

No one was about. I thought it was a good opportunity
to go up to my room and either think out my discovery or
have forty winks, according as the spirit moved me.

The heat solved that problem. No one could think in
that sultry, airless sort of weather; besides, I had a headache coming. So I took fifteen grains of aspirin and lay
down on my bed. I was asleep in ten minutes.

I was awakened by a knock at my door. I sat up hurriedly—I have a real Victorian prejudice against daylight, especially mid-morning, slumber, and wished to conceal my disgraceful lapse. I went over to the chair by the window, lit a cigarette, and called out "Come in!"

Celia poked her head round the door, and I could see with half an eye that I needn't have bothered to camouflage my nap. She was not thinking about me at all, except in so far as her errand went.

"Aunt Marion!" (Celia had slipped into calling me this, instead of the more formal "Miss Leslie," since I had come to be a sort of vice-stepmother)—"Aunt Marion, can you come down to the garden? Mr. Cartwright's there. He's got some news."

News!

"About the burglar?" I asked, springing to my feet. "Has the moron actually *done* something?"

"The man who stole the papers from the safe?" As she said it, I realized that she knew nothing of the excitements of the past night. "No—at least, I don't think so. He looks worried, not a bit braced."

I threw a rapid glance at myself in the mirror, hurriedly passed a brush over my head and a powder puff over my nose—(yes, but so would any woman)—and went down.

I needn't have bothered about my appearance. I saw at a glance that the curate was far too worried to notice what I looked like.

"Well?" I said, without any formal greeting. "What's happened? Celia says you've got some news."

"I have," he answered gravely. "Belcher's made an arrest."

"An arrest? What for—the burglary or the murder?"

"The murder. He's arrested Joe Greaves."

"*What?* He *can't* have?"

"They have, though. They took him this morning."

"Why? Is there any fresh evidence?"

"It seems that they think that it was Joe who set on poor Grier. The theory seems to be that Grier was on his trail, and that Joe led him a chase, and lay in wait for him and got him as he passed."

"What bosh!" I said roundly. "If he'd done such a thing, why did he go for the doctor?"

"I suppose the theory is that he—Joe—thought it would take away from any suspicion. You see, their idea is that Joe would act like this—he'd realize that he'd probably left marks of his presence, and would want a good way to explain them. He'd have the usual layman's belief that a detective knows by instinct, almost, if you've been at a place or not. It's no good trying to get rid of traces of your presence, because you always overlook something. So Joe didn't try to conceal his, but let on that he'd just happened by and found the inspector—in which case, of course, his normal course would be to go for the doctor."

"Bosh!" I said again. "To begin with, it's far too subtle. In the second place, if Joe really was afraid of what the inspector knew, he'd never risk letting him recover. He'd make certain that he was safe never to speak again before he went for any doctor."

"I know. That's what I said at once. If Joe did attack Grier, there was no point in getting the doctor unless Grier was beyond his help. In that case, it would have been quite a good move. But I don't mind admitting that I'm worried. I'd been over at Honour Mead Farm this morning, and happened to see Joe. I—well, the truth is, I do believe that Joe does know something about the Grier business. . . ." He stared at me disconsolately as he said it. Then he changed his tone. "But, as a matter of fact, I understand that Belcher and Co. aren't saying anything about the attack—if it was an attack—on Grier. It's the murder of Mrs. Harrington he's arrested for."

I stood in shocked silence thinking it over. The curate began again.

"Of course, we know that it's absurd. Still, you know, as we said before, they have a certain amount of reason for thinking that it might be Joe. There's his hatred of Mrs. Harrington, his talk to the showman about the gun and the stone fitting it, his careful marking of the gun, his very weak alibi for the time of the murder, his skill as a shot—and then the damning fact of the gun being found in his garden. . . . And of course it *is* possible that Grier had something else to go on—something we don't know of—which he'd communicated to headquarters."

"That's all frightfully weak," I stated. "It's nearly all purely circumstantial. Besides, it doesn't begin to cover all the facts. What about the double—no, triple—burglary? Where does any motive for stealing come in at all? Joe had no possible reason for burgling Mrs. Harrington's room."

"I suppose the idea is that it *doesn't* come in—that there's no connexion between the two crimes. And, you know, it *is* just possible that some one else, not Joe at all, found it very necessary to get hold of certain documents belonging to Mrs. Harrington, whether she was dead or not. Such a person might either know of her death—might even have witnessed it—or might just have risked an ordinary burglary, and, failing to get what he wanted, have tried again. . . ."

"*Bosh!*" I repeated. "It's too much of a coincidence to ask me to believe that whenever Joe goes out to attack a person, somebody else seizes the opportunity to burgle Mrs. Harrington's room. No, the attacks on Mrs. Harrington and on the inspector are connected with the burglaries. I'm perfectly convinced of that."

"Well, then, there's another theory—ridiculous, of course, if you know Joe, but Belcher doesn't seem to take any notice of a person's character. It is that the burglar was in league with Joe—that he wanted these papers, whatever they were, and either paid Joe to commit the two attacks, or else took advantage of Joe's own intention of committing them to do a job of his own at the same time. Oh, of course it's utterly ludicrous. You needn't bother thinking out a good way of telling me that I'm a fool. I'm only trying to see what Belcher's big idea is, in order to circumvent it."

"Of course," I said, "Joe will have to explain what he was doing on the King's Bank at two a.m. Poaching, do you think? Or meeting Lydia? Anyhow, he's sure not to be able to prove what he says. But he never attempted to kill the inspector. You can see his traces, coming clean through the trees and bushes in a straight line from the bank to the road. If he'd been wanting to slay the inspector, he'd have been lurking by the road, in cover of a bush or something—"

I broke off short. That was exactly what he would *not* have been doing. If Joe were responsible for the inspector's fall, he would have had no need to lurk. On the contrary. He would have fixed the rope and gone off; and when he heard the sound of the motor-cycle and the crash—clear enough they'd sound in the silence of a summer night—all he'd have had to do would be to come straight down from his vantage-point of the King's Bank, remove the rope, and call the doctor as proof of his good faith. Hadn't he admitted that he didn't think that the inspector would live?

"What is it?" asked Roger Cartwright curiously. "You look as if you'd had an idea," he added.

"I have," I admitted. "A particularly beastly idea."

And I told him all about my discovery about a rope stretched across the road.

He whistled softly.

"I say!" he said. "D'you suppose Belcher's got on to that?"

"Heaven knows," I said.

We stared dumbly at each other for a moment.

"What did you say the marks under the bush were like?" he asked then.

I described them as well as I could.

"Have you any idea what could have made them?" I asked.

"I don't know—unless—could it be marks of some one squatting there on their toes? You say the marks were close together?"

"Yes," I said, after thought. "It could, well. The person who fixed the rope, hiding, perhaps, before crossing the road to fix the other end. . . . But it's so *unlike* Joe!" I cried then, in a kind of despair.

"Oh, of course it is. It *can't* have been Joe. Only one's got to face up to what the police will say . . ."

"I say," I cried, with a sudden inspiration, "if I'm right about its having been a rope—and I'm sure I am—where is it now? Mightn't it give us some sort of a clue?"

"It might," said the curate doubtfully. "Anyhow, if a thirty or forty foot length of rope, broken short at one end, were found in Joe's cottage, it might be very serious for him."

"Let's go and look," I suggested hopefully.

"It'll be under guard," he demurred.

"Well, let's have a shot, anyway. We can but try. And of course, since Joe's innocent, we sha'n't find a thing. Still—"

The curate agreed. I suppose we both were taking the same line in our hearts—of course Joe hadn't done it; but just suppose he *had*.

We set off together. It was breathlessly hot, and the sky was now a horrible purplish grey.

"There's going to be a storm in a minute or two," said Roger Cartwright. "Hadn't we better wait a bit?"

"No," I said. "This is Strategy. We won't get too near till the storm breaks. It's going to be a ducker. No policeman with a heart could refuse to give us shelter. There's nowhere else to go. And Joe's cottage only has one room."

"What a general you are!" he grinned. "Pity you didn't take up crime as a profession. You'd have done well as a female crook."

"I could have got the better of the Walrus, anyhow," I retorted—and at that moment lightning rent the sky across. There was a second's pause, followed by a crash of thunder and a deluge of hissing hail.

"Run!" cried the curate, taking my arm; and we ran across the few hundred yards of space between us and Joe's cottage in record time.

An evil wind was shrieking, the lightning blazed in dazzling forks, the thunder crackled and crashed almost incessantly, and the hail streamed and leapt about us. We hammered at Joe's door—and Gregory, our own Gregory, opened it.

"Mr. Cartwright, sir!" he exclaimed. "Come in, do 'ee, sir, and miss too. It be a good ole storm, idn' 'a?"

We stood gasping and mopping our streaming faces. Gregory, with true country hospitality, immediately turned his thoughts to tea.

"'Tis maybe a bit irregular," he said half apologetically, "but, lard, it can't do no harm to nobody, an' Joe, he'd be glad to do it for 'ee, poor chap, if so be as 'a was here."

We sat down. Gregory—dear, unsuspicious Gregory—never saw how fidgety and inquisitive we were. We fingered everything, had our eyes everywhere. No rope was to be seen in that little orderly cottage, in which there was only one room to conceal anything in. My hopes rose again.

The tea was cheering, and Gregory was delighted with praise of it. The storm slowly subsided, and as we finished the sun was coming out. I rose and went to the back door to look at the sky. And it was then that I thought of the little tool-shed.

Joe kept all his odds and ends there. If the rope was his, that was where it would be. But how could we make an excuse to go in and look? Gregory was doing his polite best to get rid of us now that the storm was over—he clearly dreaded a surprise visit from one of his superiors—but I thought that by a stratagem I might manage to explore that shed before we had to go.

By the greatest good luck (though I had by no means regarded it in that light at the time) I had that morning found that the petticoat I was wearing, a particularly nice slip, was in need of a small mend. I had been in a hurry, and had put on an old-fashioned 'waist' one. It was quite easy to untie the string through the thin cotton frock I wore. Very soon a white frill became visible below my frock; the rest of the petticoat soon followed.

"Bother!" I said, in a voice of rather embarrassed annoyance. "Just wait a minute for me, Mr. Cartwright. I'm going to use Joe's tool-shed as a dressing-room."

And without waiting for a word from either of them, I bent down, gathered my fallen petticoat round my knees, bundled across to the shed, and half closed the door. Gregory, I saw, with true male delicacy, closed the door of the cottage. He would certainly not even look in the direction of the shed till I emerged.

I dared not be too long. The least suspicious of males must have some idea of the way in which a petticoat is kept up, and would realise that it could not take more than a few minutes at the outside to fix it. I had to work hard.

There was a pile of old hampers at one end of the shed, and I went there first. And I had a nasty shock.

Inside the second one I touched there was rope—a long coil and a short one. And each had an end broken—frayed, not cut clean through. Together they would measure nine or ten yards.

I had no time to examine them further. The snapped ends were enough to decide me to do a little burglary on my own. I lifted my skirt and wrapped the rope round and round my body like a lifebelt. I then put on my maligned petticoat, dropped my skirt, and emerged from seclusion.

"I'm ready Mr. Cartwright," I called out.

The back door opened, and the curate appeared, followed by Gregory.

"Don't look at me," I commanded. "I've managed to get it on, but I'm horribly bulgy round the waist."

I liked that *double entendre*. I wished I could explain it to Roger Cartwright.

"Good-bye, Gregory. Thanks so much for the tea," I went on. "We're thankful we found you here, and not one of the Newbury men."

(The curate got that one. He winked at me with the eye furthest away from Gregory.)

"That's a' right, miss. Glad o' the comp'ny," said Gregory; and we walked away, leaving him in sole possession. I have seldom felt better pleased with myself.

29

"I've got it," I said to Roger Cartwright, as soon as we were safely in the middle of open fields, with no one in sight.

"Got—not the rope?"

I nodded with great satisfaction.

"How?"

I explained the ruse of the petticoat.

"It's here," I said, tapping my chest, where the bulge began, "coiled round me. I feel like Grace Darling. I want to have a good look at it presently, and then we'll think of the best place to hide it. It would be fatal if the police found it and connected it with Joe."

"Yes," said the curate in a queer sort of voice. Then he burst out: "But, hang it all, it *is* connected with Joe! What's it doing in his shed? What's it all about? Joe *can't*—"

"No," I agreed, "he can't. But we'll get that put straight soon. I feel we're just on the edge of it."

"Do you?" he said despondently. "I feel farther off than ever."

"We'll go to my house," I said, ignoring his gloom. 'I will remove the wretched rope, and we'll examine it hand in hand, easily discovering the criminal in the process. You wait in the morning-room, and I'll bring it down."

It didn't take me long to get the rope off and put it into a large attaché-case. I rejoined the curate inside of five minutes.

There were, as I said, two pieces of rope—one about twenty-five feet long and the other about eight or ten. Each of them had one broken end and one cleanly cut, and each had a very clumsy-looking knot about three or four feet from the end. It was obvious to me that the two joined together, would be just about long enough to stretch across the road, go about three or four feet beyond over the grass border and tie round a tree. The only other thing I could spot was that, to judge by the position of the knots, the rope had been cut off the trees. Joe or whoever it was that unfastened it, had not had time to undo the complicated knots.

But the sight of the rope seemed to fill the curate with joy.

"By Jove!" he exclaimed. "One thing's certain—Joe never fixed that rope."

"Why?" I demanded.

"Why? Look at the knots! Joe knows how to tie a rope. The person that fastened this could no more make a decent knot than fly."

"But—if it wasn't Joe—"

"Why was it in his shed, you mean?"

"Exactly. Because the accomplice theory's bosh, you know—utter bosh."

"Of course it is. . . . I believe you're right. I believe we *are* on the edge of it—and once we find out who tied those knots, and why Joe concealed the rope—if he did—we'll get it."

"We shan't know about the burglar," I objected. "What *can* he have been after, do you think? A will?"

"He's missed the 'bus, if that's what he wanted," said Roger Cartwright. "A will has been produced."

"What? Who had it?"

"The Squire. Apparently he gave her that desk in the study—you know, the one she used so much—and he remembered that it had a secret drawer. The will was there."

"Nothing else?"

"Apparently not."

"And what was in the will?"

"As far as I can make out, she left everything to the Squire."

Our eyes met. I think we both at that time suspected the Squire of all sorts of evil.

"Was it signed?" I asked them.

"Ordinary signature—'Agatha Harrington.' It was witnessed by Banks and Lawson."

"Hm. . . . Well, then, what *was* the burglar after? Did he want to destroy that will? Or did he hope to find another? Or was it something quite different he was after?"

"Goodness only knows. . . . Hullo, there's a ring. Better put the rope back."

We shut the attaché-case just as Betty came tapping at the door.

"Please, miss, can you see Dr. Ludlow?" she asked.

"Dr. Ludlow!" I exclaimed. "I wonder if Inspector Grier—"

I hurried to the door.

"Come in, Doctor," I said eagerly. "Come and tell us all about it."

"It's you who've got to do the telling," said he, following me into the little morning-room. "What have you done with Lydia Salt?"

"Lydia Salt!" I exclaimed. "I've done nothing. What's happened?"

"She seems to have got up—against my orders—both last night and this morning. She hasn't come back since she went out this morning. She said something about seeing you."

"I haven't seen the girl. Doesn't her father know where she is?"

"Apparently not. He says that she got up yesterday evening, latish, saying that it made her 'nervous' to be in bed all alone. She seems to have gone for a stroll—to meet young Greaves, I expect—and came back very upset and queer. Her father sent her back to bed; but she was up very early, for when he went in to see how she was, somewhere about six, she wasn't in her room, and was out of the house. She turned up again a little later, saying that she'd had a headache and been out for a stroll. Now it's my experience that when a village girl feels 'queerish' in the morning, she doesn't get up and go out for a stroll. That would be the last thing she'd do. She'd have a strong cup of tea and sit over the fire, whatever the weather."

Roger Cartwright nodded.

"She would," he agreed.

"Salt said she seemed much better when she came in," the doctor went on—"quite cheerful, in fact. But she seems to have been thoroughly restless, all the same, for she went out again about ten. Her father told her not to, as he'd sent for me to come and see her during the morning, and she was to wait in; but a blind man hasn't a chance against a determined young woman, and she gave him the slip. He says she hasn't turned up again yet."

The curate seemed to be thinking; I could see the light of comprehension dawning on his face.

"Miss Leslie," he said, turning to me, "would you mind ringing up the Manor House and asking if she's been there? If she hasn't, try my digs."

"She won't have gone to the Manor House," I stated positively. "She's shy of the other maids."

"She won't mind that," he said, equally positively. "She wants to see you, and failing you, me; and she's been all the morning trying to find us."

"I don't believe it for a moment," I said; but I reached for my desk telephone as I said it. "Still, just to satisfy you—"

I had hardly put through the call, when Betty came again to the door.

"Oh, I beg your pardon, miss," she said, as she saw me with the receiver at my ear. "But when you're disengaged, could you speak to Lydia Salt for a minute? She—"

"Is she here?" cried Roger Cartwright, leaping to his feet.

"Yes, sir. She's been before twice, only the mistress was out, and I told her she was staying at the Manor House now."

"Send her in here," I said, replacing the receiver. Exchange must have been infuriated, but that was the merest nothing to me.

Betty hesitated.

"If you please, miss—if you'd just come out and see her alone? She—well, she's very queer, like—"

"Never mind. We all want to see her," I said.

Betty departed.

I turned to the curate.

"Why are you so keen to see her?" I demanded.

"Because of the rope. She'll tell you herself," he replied; and the next second she came in.

She ignored the two men and made a dash over to me.

"Oh, miss! Please, miss, I want to tell—I want to tell 'em!" she gasped, with wild eyes.

"Tell who?" I asked ungrammatically. "What do you mean, Lydia?"

"Oh, miss, they've took Joe! They've took my Joe, an' 'twas me as done it!"

I sat petrified. She babbled on, clutching at me in a horrible, snatching, drowning sort of way.

"'Twas me as done it. All as he done was to help me after. He never did nought bad. Oh, miss, I want to tell 'em as 'twas me."

"Be quiet, Lydia," I said sternly. "Sit down over there and blow your nose and talk quietly. I can't understand a word you say."

I thought to myself that this was another burst of hysteria such as I had witnessed before, when Lydia swore that Joe hadn't been at the Fair. Now, as then, she was talking the sheerest nonsense simply to try to get him out of trouble. For, though I admit that I was startled, a second's reflection showed me that it was rubbish to suppose that a girl of Lydia's upbringing and in her state of health could have brought off such a shot as that which killed Mrs. Harrington.

She obeyed me to the letter, as hysterical people do if you deal with them severely. She sat down, sniffed, and wiped her eyes.

"Now then," I said sternly, "what's all this about? Begin at the beginning and tell me straight."

For answer she put her hand into the front of her frock and drew out a paper—much creased and worn along the folds, and rather dirty. It looked as if she'd worn it inside her corsets; in fact I've no doubt that she had.

"'Twere this as made me do 'en," she said, rather sullenly.

It was a sheet of bluish paper, ready ruled with faint lines which had failed towards the right-hand edge. It was exactly the kind of paper that you get in very cheap writing-pads—common, ordinary, impossible to trace. On it some one had scrawled in pencil: "The Inspecter is after Jo. He is going to get his last prove tonight. If you dont stop him J. will be arest for the murder of Mrs. H, but if you stop him no one will know what he was after. This is from a Freind. The Inspec. will be going to Newbury after 12 tonight. If you Tie a rope accros the road by the bend near Kings Bank it will through him off his motor and he will be stuned and Jo will have time to Run. So no more at Preasant from A Freind. N.B. this is his only chanct. If he misses it he will Hang."

"Who gave you this?" demanded Roger Cartwright, who had read the missive over my shoulder.

"I don' know, no more'n the dead!" declared Lydia. "It were in my parcel from Rutter's."

"How do you mean?" I asked.

"I gets aal my drapery an' grocery from Rutter's, see, an' since I've been took bad Mrs. Rutter sends it up. It come las' night, an' Dad, he brought 'en up to me. This were under the string."

"Who brought the parcel?"

"She gen'ly astës Tom Nokes to bring 'en, but whether 'twere him this time, I doan' know."

"And you believed this rubbish about Joe?" asked the curate.

"I never believed as he done it, for well I know as he never could 'a done such a thing. But the police, they'll taake an' hang a chap so soon as look at 'en."

"And you really thought that if you got rid of poor Inspector Grier that Joe'd be safe?"

"It says so, doan't 'en?"

Lydia, like most country folk, evidently had an implicit belief in *litera scripta*.

"So *you* fastened that rope across the road?" I asked.

"Yes—yes, 'twas me! 'Twasn't never Joe—"

"But Joe knew that you'd done it," said the curate.

"Surely 'a did, for I had to tell 'en to run, like the paper said. I went out to see 'en so soon's I got paper, but I couldn't find 'en. 'Twere latish then, so I went homealong an got rope an' went down to road, where 'twere said in the paper. There weren't nothing went by. When 'twere near on twelve I tied rope fast an' went backalong to Joe's and told 'en. But 'a wouldn' move, so 'a wouldn'. 'A said as 'a'd done nought, an' 'a wouldn't run like a thief. And 'a went straight back to take rope down."

"And what did you do?"

"I went back homealong. Joe said as I'd done too much as 'twere, an' I were martel tired. But I couldn' sleep for thinkin' o't aal, an' I got up early an' went down over Bank." (So those traces were Lydia's. I might have known that an expert woodsman like Joe wouldn't leave a track like that.) "I seed rope were gone, an' I never thought but Joe'd got there in time. So I went back home. And then I thought to go to Mrs. Rutter's and see if her knowed who'd sent the paper; so I went down village, but I never got so far's Rutter's, because they—they telled me as the inspector were dead an' Joe was took up for killing of 'en. I didn' know what to do then, for 'twere no more use to tell Gregory as 'twere me than it would've been to tell the cows. So I thought to myself as Miss Leslie were thick wi' them police chaps, an' she'd tell 'em for me. An' I've been a-lookin' for 'ee ever sin'," she finished, turning reproachfully to me.

"But, my dear girl, Joe hasn't been arrested for what happened to the inspector," I said.

She gaped. Then it dawned on her.

"Why—then 'twere true what the writing said! They *have* got summat agin' him! Oh, why wouldn' he run when I telled him?"

She got up and flung herself on me.

"Oh, miss, 'tweren't Joe, so 'tweren't! I never meant to tell, so I didn', but 'tweren't Joe, an' I'll never keep quiet while they hang 'en to death. 'Twere Squire's gun as shot that bolt!"

30

Roger Cartwright sprang to his feet in excitement.

"What do you mean?" he demanded. "Why do you say such a thing as that?"

"'Tis the truth," she insisted. "I didn' mean to say nought, for Squire's squire when aal's said, but I won't stan' by an' let my Joe suffer, not if 'a were' a score o' squires."

"But how do you know anything about it?" persisted the curate. "You'll have to tell us what you mean if you want to get Joe off, you know."

"'Twere thisaway, then. Aal the others went to Fair early, like madam said they might. I was alone in the house. Well, Joe comed in to see me, at one, maybe, or maybe a bit earlier." (I remembered that it was just on one when I last saw Joe at the Fair, listening to Mrs. Harrington with that expression of hate and fear.) "He wanted to tell I about the job at Phillipses and how 'a thought 'a were sure of 'en if only madam wouldn' force 'en to wed afore 'twas settled, like. Well, we was in the side passage a-taalkin', an' when Joe were going he sees Squire's gun in passage. 'Squire's been a-shootin', then,' he says, and 'a took up gun an' squinted along 'en. Then 'a said as twere a won-nerful good carryin' gun. 'I could fire a pellet into any one o' they bedrooms,' 'a said, squintin along 'en. 'Which

be madam's room, Lyd?' 'a said, silly-like. So I showed 'en
which 'twere, but I telled en as 'a'd have to shoot through
glass to get to hern, for her al'ays kept her windows shut
i' the heat; an' I telled 'en how particular she were about
her room, al'ays maakin' her own bed an' aal. Then 'a
taalked some more about the gun, an' how Squire did ought
to look after 'en better. "A didn' ought to leave 'en mucky
that away,' 'a said. 'Give us a rag, Lyddy, and I'll clean 'en
for 'en,' 'a says. So I got 'en a piece o' rag, and 'a cleaned
'en proper, an' put 'en back where 'twere. Well, then I
waalked out wi' 'en to side gate, and 'a went off. I never
thought no more on it till I were locking up side door an'
then I thought on the gun. 'Twere gone—it weren't there."

She paused to take breath.

"Well?" I said, as she said no more. "What else? The
fact that the gun's not to be found doesn't prove that Mrs.
Harrington was shot with it."

"Ah, but *'tis* found!" cried the girl triumphantly.

"It *is* found?" echoed the curate. "Where? Who found
it?"

"'Twere Joe as found 'en. Look, 'twere thisaway. After
I went homealong—when doctor took me—I had to meet
Joe. I had to hear how things was wi' en. Faather'd never
let me come next nor nigh Joe, for 'a said as I weren't to
have naught to do wi' a common labourin' chap. So I telled 'en as I'd got to go downalong to the House for some
o' my things as I'd left there, an' Joe, he met I in the li'l
potting-shed—you knows 'en, miss, 'tidn' used now, an'
the door stands open."

I knew it—a tumbledown little shanty, long disused, at
the far end of the Manor House garden.

"'Twere saafe to meet there, see," Lydia went on, "for
Joe, he traps rabbits for Squire, an' 'a keeps traps there;
an' no one wouldn't wonder if they seed I i' the Manor garden. So we met there, an' I were just a-thinkin' as 'twere

time to go, when Joe, he catched sight o' Squire's gun aal in among the peasticks. Joe, he took 'en in's hand, and 'a says to me, 'He's been used sin' I cleaned 'en, Lyd,' 'a says. An' 'ashowed I a scratch on barrel. 'God help us, 'twere Squire as done it,' 'a says, aal white an' shaky-like. And then 'a telled me as I wasn't never to tell a martel soul, an' a cleaned gun aal over again, and 'a put 'en back among sticks. An' I wouldn' never have telled, on'y they've took my Joe, an' he so innocent as the moon!"

We sat silent, dumbfounded at this news. And I think the thing that was chiefly present in my mind was the picture which Stephen had put there days ago—the picture of Lady Gervaise running across the moonlit Green from the side entrance of the Manor House garden, just before the body of Mrs. Harrington was found. . . .

"If *only* Inspector Grier were still on the job!" I sighed. "He'd so much more sense than this idiotic Walrus. Oh, Lydia, *what* a fool you were to believe that note! Inspector Grier's the only man who could get us out of this mess—"

"Which is, of course, exactly why he was put out of the way," put in Roger Cartwright quietly. "If we can find out who wrote that note to Lydia, we've got the murderer."

We sat, all of us, in silence. I was working furiously on this new material; Dr. Ludlow was simply looking, with bright, alert eyes, from one to the other of us; Lydia watched us, as if she hoped for a miracle. Roger Cartwright was obviously doggedly working out a train of thought.

"Well?" I said at last. "What are we to do now? Tell this perfect idiot of a Walrus about the gun?"

"He'd only say that Joe put it there," said the curate, with gloom. "He's that kind. Once he gets an idea into his head, everything he hears is simply a confirmation of it. Nothing short of dynamite would dislodge it. No, I don't think we'll tell him just yet. . . . If only we could find out—tactfully—how that note got into Lydia's parcel!"

"Well, we can, surely," I said. I turned to Lydia. "Look here, Lydia," I said. "There's one chance, and only one, of clearing Joe; and you've got to do it."

"Oh, miss! I'd do anything—I'd give the eyes out o' my yead—"

"Don't be a fool!" I snapped. "If you're going to talk like that, you'll make me think you're too stupid to do this. Now listen.

"Don't say a word to any one about the Squire's gun. As Mr. Cartwright says, the new police officer would simply think that Joe put it in the potting-shed. What you have to do is this. Go to Mrs. Rutter and tell her there was a mistake in your grocery, and you think you've got the wrong parcel. Ask her who she sent with it. If it was Tom Nokes, see him and find out whether he brought it himself or gave it to some one else; or whether he met any one on the way—stopped to talk, or put the parcel down where any one else could get at it. Don't scare him—just lead him on to chatter. And if he *did* meet any one, or gave anybody the chance to get at the parcel, let Mr. Cartwright or me know at once. But whatever you do, don't let Tom know that you're trying to get anything out of him."

Lydia stood up. Now that she had a definite job to do—a real step to take towards establishing Joe's innocence—she was a new creature. She was the reliable, quiet girl whom Mrs. Harrington had so admirably trained.

"I quite understand, miss," she said. Her very voice was changed. "I know how to do it—I know the lad well. I'll let you know at once. Good afternoon, miss. Good afternoon, sir."

And she left the room with the determined, quiet manner of a sensible woman who means to do a job efficiently.

"She'll manage it," said Dr. Ludlow, speaking for the first time for minutes. "You're an acute psychologist Miss Leslie. It's exactly what she needed."

"And exactly what *we* need, which is more to the point for us," said Roger Cartwright.

"Now, as I (and you, I expect) have missed lunch," I said, "what about a large and leisurely tea? I'll just ring up the Manor House and tell them I won't be back just yet. You'll stay, doctor, won't you?"

"Afraid I can't. I must get back and look at my patient."

"The inspector?"

He nodded.

"How's he getting on?"

"Oh, he'll do—he'll do well," he reassured me. "He's tough, and Lydia didn't bring him quite such a cropper as she was evidently intended to do. Still, it's lucky Joe arrived on the scene when he did. He didn't waste any time, fortunately."

The doctor then departed, and I gave orders for a really unbridled tea. I looked forward to a large and peaceful meal, during which the curate and I would unravel this last knot and solve the whole mystery. I then rang up the Manor House, meaning to say that I would be over there at half-past five or so, and should not want tea. And it was then that I was blighted.

"Oh, please, miss," said Lawson's prim voice at the other end of the wire, "do you happen to know where Mr. Cartwright is? Gregory said that you and he had been out together, and the inspector wishes to see him. He's been asking for him for some time, miss."

Lawson's voice, and the confusion of her pronouns, told me more than her words. She sounded harassed, especially as she said, "He's been asking for him for some time."

"Does he want to see him *now?*" I asked.

"Oh yes, miss. He seems very anxious."

"Then he can come round here," I said peevishly. "Tell him Mr. Cartwright is here, and we're both having tea. He's not going to rush over to the Manor House just because Inspector Belcher happens to want to chat. Tell him I'm here, too, and we're both very much exhausted, but if it's anything really urgent we'll see him."

"Very good, miss."

I had an idea.

"Lawson!"

"Yes, miss."

"Ask him if it'll do if Mr. Cartwright speaks to him on the telephone."

"Very good, miss. Will you hold the wire, please, miss?"

I held on. A minute later—

"Is that Mr. Cartwright? This is Inspector Belcher speaking. I want to see you at once, sir."

"This isn't Mr. Cartwright," I said. "It's me. But he can come if that'll do."

"I wish to see Mr. Cartwright, madam. Immediately."

"You'd better come round, then," I said. The man's very tone was infuriating. "We're just going to have tea. You can join us, if you like, or we'll come over when we've finished. Just as you like. But we can't possibly miss our tea."

He snorted. It was clearly most upsetting to his dignity both to be asked to tea and to be asked to wait till we had had ours. As to being asked to come to see us, instead of our meekly trotting over to see him, it utterly disgusted him. But I suppose he realized that he really had no right to demand our presence, or to starve us.

"Very well," he said grumpily. "I'll come over at once."

"To tea?" I asked sweetly.

I really wanted to know. The tea, which was to have been on a sumptuous scale anyhow, would have to be increased if we were to entertain the Walrus. But he seemed to think the question impertinent. Anyhow, he rang off without any reply except another snort.

So the prospect of our pleasant meal was dashed. I could only hope that he had something really interesting to say, or illuminating to ask—something which, with our new clues about Lydia's note and the Squire's gun, would really help us in elucidating the problem.

He appeared, very pompous and ruffled, about five minutes later.

"I have had a great deal of trouble, Mr. Cartwright, in trying to find you," he began. "I heard that you were out, and your landlady *seemed* to know nothing of your movements."

He was evidently trying to show that not only we, but everybody remotely connected with us, was probably lying.

"She often doesn't," said the curate quietly. "I can't keep her posted as to my route whenever I go out."

"I was told that you were seen with Miss Leslie."

"Yes, I was. I mean, I was with her. Didn't it occur to you that we might have ended up at her house?"

"You were not here when I rang up at 11.40 and again at 2.5," he retorted. "And the maid declared that she had no expectation of seeing you. At least, so she gave me to understand."

"Quite true," I said. "I don't need to tell my maids whenever I wish to go out or come in, or have a friend to tea."

"May I ask where you have been?"

I nearly said that we had been out to commit a murder. Fortunately Roger Cartwright prevented me.

"We went out for a walk. Oughtn't we to have? I'm so sorry. I didn't realize that we were doing anything wrong."

Belcher looked at him suspiciously, but the curate's meekness disarmed him. I suppose it didn't occur to him that any one *could* be so rash, so profane, as to try to pull his leg—especially a parson.

"I wished to ask you whether you have ever seen such a handwriting as this," he said, extracting from his pocket-book a small sheet of paper. He held it folded, so that we could only read two lines, and not all of one of them. It was a cheap paper, bluish in colour, with ruled lines. On lines was written, in a very awkward, uneducated sort of hand:

"... as soon as you get this to 12 Reddings Row, Newbury, where news of the child ..."

The writing was in pencil. And I noticed at once that the printed lines with which the paper was ruled had failed towards the right-hand edge.

The paper was the same as that on which Lydia's note had been written. There was not the smallest doubt of that. But the writing was not the same. Her note had been written in a hand fairly easy and fluent. This was extraordinarily clumsy, ill-formed writing, as if done by some one who had hardly ever held a pen.

"I don't think so," said the curate cautiously.

The Walrus looked a little annoyed.

"Never? Not even—say a matter of some weeks ago?"

"No, I don't think so. Have you any reason to think I might have seen it?"

"I have. Think again, Mr. Cartwright. A note asking you to fix up a wedding ..."

"Oh! Oh, this isn't Joe Greaves' handwriting, if that's what you mean. Not in the least like it. Joe writes quite a decent hand."

"This has been written with the left hand," the Walrus explained, with a kind of heavy patience.

"Then I'm afraid I can't help you. I'm not a handwriting expert. I couldn't tell my own writing, if it was done with the left hand."

The Walrus grew quite ratty.

"This is a serious matter, sir," he snapped. "This is the note which was sent to decoy Inspector Grier to his death."

"Oh, I guessed that," said the curate gently, "but it doesn't help me at all, since, of course, it wasn't Joe who tried to do that."

The Walrus snorted—of course. I think he really wanted to tell us that everything we said would be taken down and used in evidence against us; only even he hadn't got quite to that stage yet. He got up to go.

"*Sure* you won't have some tea?" I asked hospitably; but he pretended not to hear. He simply walked over to the door.

"Has the mor—I mean, Inspector Wilberforce—been able to trace the burglar at all?" I asked then.

I wasn't pulling his leg. I really wanted to know. But that man was so suspicious that he smelt a rat in the most innocent remarks.

"I am not in a position to make any statement on the subject," he said stuffily. And then he went away.

31

"Well," I said, when he'd gone and tea was once more pursuing its interrupted course, "we've got a lot more to go on. We've got Lydia's story about the gun having been moved and used after two in the afternoon. We've got the two notes, written on the same paper, and probably by the same person, with the aim of getting Grier out of the way. When, or if, Lydia finds out how hers got delivered, we ought to be able to fit the whole thing together."

"What's your idea about the notes?" asked Roger Cartwright.

"Oh, X, of course," I replied promptly. "And X *must* be our friend Lagardi. You can tell that by certain words in the letter to Lydia—'arrest,' for instance, when he means 'arrested.' He wanted to get Inspector Grier out of the way while he burgled. I do wish I could think why he wanted to burgle. You see, if X is Lagardi, and if his story is anything like true, the will motive isn't good enough. Even if he didn't know that her will had been found (and he well mightn't know—I didn't, till you told me just now), it isn't good enough. If Mrs. Harrington wasn't really Mrs. Harrington, no will signed 'Agatha Harrington' could stand, so it certainly wasn't worth his risking a theft of it; and if she signed it 'Lagardi,' who would she get to witness it? I say!—do you happen to know when that will of hers was made?"

"Yes. It was quite recent—only a short three weeks before her death—9th June, I believe."

"I wonder if she'd made another one, before that?"

"Goodness knows. If she did, it wouldn't matter, what would matter would be if she made another one after it."

"If she'd done that, she'd have destroyed this one. She wouldn't risk not having her money used as she wanted it. I do wish I could make it out . . ."

"I say," said the curate, "did you gather that Lagardi had had charge of the child ever since the mother ran away with the nobleman with the name like a sneeze?"

"Not all the time. She took the child, I gathered, and then put her into some kind of nursing-home run by nuns. She seems to have behaved rather oddly about that, I thought. If she thought the child was delicate, I wondered why she didn't send her to some sort of place like the convent before she ran away. Also, it did strike me as a bit odd, if you were eloping from your husband with another man, to take the child of your real marriage with you."

"Perhaps she thought Lagardi would neglect the kid."

"In that case, why not get her fixed in the nursing-home, or whatever it was, first? He seems to have got hold of the child easily enough afterwards. And, to do him justice, she didn't seem to be a bit timid of him. He spoke to her very nicely."

"You didn't care for the chap's looks?"

"Hated him on sight," I said succinctly. As I said it, the memory of Lagardi's unpleasant face came before me very clearly. Where *was* it that I'd seen some one rather like him before? "I'm sorry for any child brought up by him," I went on. "She didn't look too pleasant a child, but you can't wonder."

"And you feel pretty sure that Lagardi is X—the burglar?"

"I can't think who else it can have been. Godfrey Harrington is the only other possibility—or Lady Gervaise.
Yes, I'd never really thought of her. . . . I say—look here!—
can it have been Lady Gervaise? Could she have had some
inkling of all this Lagardi business, and—and wanted to
destroy some evidence of his existence, so that, if Mrs.
Harrington died, her money would certainly go to her
husband? You see, neither the Squire nor, of course, Lady
Gervaise, would know that there was a will."

"You mean—in that case, the murder would have been—
intentional?"

I felt myself grow hot.

"Not necessarily," I began; then I threw away pretence.
"Yes, I suppose so. You see," I went on, anxious to justify
myself to myself as well as to the curate, "things do look
bad for her now, don't they? Godfrey Harrington's gun
could, we know, take that very missile that was used. That
was proved in court. It vanishes—while he's away, mind—
and is found, used and hidden, the next night. Stephen
saw—or is almost sure that he saw—Lady Gervaise leaving
the Manor House grounds by the side gate, the one near
the potting-shed, just before he found the body, which was
then still quite warm. Isn't it at least possible that Lady
Gervaise was replacing the gun she had just used? And, if
that were so, she would know that she *must* destroy any
evidence of an earlier marriage if—if Godfrey Harrington
were to get the money—"

"Yes, but how should Lady Gervaise know of this earlier
marriage—if there really was one?"

"I don't know," I admitted, "unless—could the black-
mailer (who, I suppose, was Lagardi) have tackled Godfrey
Harrington? He might have found that she—Mrs. Harrington—wouldn't give him any more, and tried to bring
pressure on the Squire. Godfrey Harrington would never
be able to keep a thing like that to himself."

"Possible," said the curate grudgingly, "but not at probable. Every one knows the Squire's as poor as church rat.
Mrs. Harrington was the one who had the money—"

"Look here!" I cried, struck by an idea. "*This* is possible—that Godfrey Harrington got hold of a letter or message by accident. Mrs. Harrington's precautions mayn't
always have worked. If he had, he'd have told Lady
Gervaise, because, if Mrs. Harrington was really married
already, his marriage with her would be invalid, and he
could marry Lady Gervaise whenever he liked. Then it
might have struck them both that they hadn't a penny to
bless themselves with, and—and—one of them—thought
of this way of getting hold of a very large fortune. They'd
see that if Mrs. Harrington died intestate, Godfrey Harrington would be accepted as her heir; and they'd see, as
we did, that she couldn't have made a will on account of
the signature difficulty."

"But she did make a will."

"I know. But we don't know yet that it's a valid one."

"It's a good theory," Roger Cartwright admitted, "only,
you know, I don't see Godfrey Harrington planning a crime
like that, let alone putting it through."

"No. But—Godfrey Harrington was out of the way, at
Southampton—"

"And *she*—"

"Yes. Rather like Lady Macbeth, carried a step farther.
And—look here!—that clears up other things too. Suppose the Squire didn't know that this was planned. She's
got twice—ten times—his head and his determination.
She got him out of the way, purposely. *She*—did the job,
using his gun, and replacing it in the shed till it would
be safe for him to collect it and put it away in its proper
place. She was the burglar. She was looking for some exist-
ing evidence of Mrs. Harrington's first marriage, in order
to destroy it. That explains Godfrey Harrington's quite

genuine surprise when he heard of Mrs. Harrington's death; it explains Lady Gervaise's knowledge of the death, early next morning; it also explains why he was so anxious that the police should inquire into her past, and find the criminal there, and how it was that the burglar went direct to Mrs. Harrington's room—"

"But does *not* explain the notes to Grier and Lydia," put in the curate. "Say what you like, those notes were not written by Lady Gervaise."

"No," I admitted, "I don't believe they were. She could never fake her writing to look like either of them—hers is so very characteristic. . . . But do the notes matter so much? Mightn't they have been done by some one who was afraid of Inspector Grier—some uneducated person who thought he had his eye on him . . . ?"

"Who? It certainly wasn't Joe Greaves. He'd never have risked getting Lydia into a mess; besides, his whole conduct over Grier would have been absurd. Equally certain it wasn't Lydia."

"Mrs. Nokes?" I suggested.

"She can't write at all; nor can Tom."

"Well—I don't know. But does it matter? Doesn't my theory work just the same, whoever wrote them?"

"*Everything* matters, I believe," said Roger Cartwright. "I believe the whole thing hangs together. . . . I'll tell you what. I've a jolly good mind to tackle Harrington and Lady Gervaise, if we can. Tell them about the gun and ask them to explain."

"Right," I exclaimed, rather thrilled. "Let's. Which one first? Harrington? Or do you think we could go back to the Manor House, and you hold him in idle chat while I ring her up and get her to come over?"

"That would be best," he agreed. "Let's go and do it."

I left a message with the maids, in case Lydia Salt turned up while I was at the Manor House, asking her to follow me there; and then we went over to the Manor House together. I felt more really, pleasurably, thrilled than I had for days and days. I felt that we really were getting somewhere.

Our scheme acted like a charm. Godfrey Harrington was in, mooning about uneasily, only too glad to have some one to moan to. So the curate listened to him moaning (after all, it's the clergy's duty to do this) while I escaped and rang up Lady Gervaise. She was in, but didn't seem too keen about coming round to the Manor House, until I dropped a mysterious hint about the Squire getting himself into a mess. Then she was only too ready to fly over, if she could have done it. I reflected, as I hung up the receiver, on the extreme oddness of people. I would have flown equally readily to escape from rescuing Godfrey Harrington. She must have really and truly *loved* the man—and how any one *could!* Especially a woman like that, pretty, charming, devil-may-care. . . . You simply can't account for these things, I thought platitudinously.

She turned up within a very few minutes, a little pale, and very bright-eyed. She reminded me exactly of a mother-bird of a pretty and exotic sort, who thinks that her nest is threatened.

We went into the little room next to the library, which the Squire likes to call his study—though what he studies there, except his own health and comfort and woes, no one knows. I could see by Roger's face that he couldn't have borne much more undiluted Godfrey Harrington. We were none too soon.

"What's all the excitement?" asked Lady Gervaise, as I opened the door.

Really Godfrey Harrington must be the world's worst conspirator. The very way he sprang up when he heard her voice would have given him away gratis to any one who wasn't a blind imbecile.

"Fé—Lady Gervaise!" he stammered.

She was much better at it. She came in, sat down composedly, and helped herself to a cigarette from the open box on the table.

"Now tell us all about it," she commanded. "You said, didn't you, Miss Leslie, that there was some new development?"

"I did," I said—and stuck. For the life of me, I didn't know how to go on. It's easy enough to think that a person is a murderess (though I'd never have guessed *how* easy!) but it's most extraordinarily hard to tell them so.

"Well? What is it?"

She was quite cool. She might have been settling a squabble between two naughty children.

"It's this," said Roger Cartwright. "Harrington's gun has been found."

"*What?*" cried the Squire, spinning round to face him. "Found? Where?"

I admit that I was a bit scared. I didn't at all want to have the man collapsing on our hands. So I hurried on with the tale.

"It was found in the potting-shed at the end of the garden," I said, "and—there's not the faintest doubt that it had been used."

"It had—it had!" cried the Squire. "I used it myself at that damned booth."

"Can't you remember at all where you left it after that?" the curate asked him.

"I think—I can't be sure—but I believe I left it in the side entry. I came in that way from Foakes Green. I was in a hurry to get my train. I didn't stop to clean it—I'm sure of that—I just put it down."

"It was cleaned, though," said Roger. "Joe Greaves cleaned it for you." And he told him the story we had heard from Lydia.

Lady Gervaise had listened without a word; but now she spoke, and her voice was as I'd never heard it—hard, metallic, cold as steel.

"And what have we to do with this?" she asked sneeringly. "It seems to me that this only involves Joe Greaves a bit more deeply. After all, he did use that shed, and no one else did."

"That's exactly why we're sure that it was *not* Joe who left it there," said Roger quietly. "Suppose that he did shoot that gun, and slipped it out of sight in a hurry, it's obvious that the first thing he would do would be to conceal it in a better place; he would never risk it's being found there. I admit that a really subtle criminal might— just *might*—do such a thing; but Joe isn't subtle."

"No, he's not," Lady Gervaise admitted. Her voice was normal again now, quite level and friendly. "I like Joe," she went on, "and I'm quite sure that he had nothing to do with this business. But I don't quite see why you've dragged me into this discussion."

"Because we thought that you ought to know," said the curate quietly. How I did admire his pluck! "You see," he went on steadily, "there's an idea that you were in the Manor House grounds, Lady Gervaise, just about eleven o'clock that night."

"*I!*" She sat up, her colour slowly fading. "*I!* What do you mean, Mr. Cartwright? Do you mean to suggest that *I* shot Mrs. Harrington?"

"I'm suggesting nothing," he said doggedly. "But we feel that with this man Belcher in charge, anything may happen; and you can guess the kind of construction he'd put on it if he were to find out that you'd practised with an airgun in the afternoon, left Miss Leslie's early, and were seen leaving the Manor House grounds just before the murder was discovered, and that you knew of her death before any one else in the village. You see, the police

already know about Mr. Harrington's movements at Southampton on the twenty-ninth. They know that he was *not*
in London on that day, and that it wasn't his wife who was
to accompany him when he sailed from Southampton. We
thought you ought to know—both of you—about the discovery of the gun."

Lady Gervaise said nothing, but her eyes met the Squire's
in a kind of wordless consultation. Then she spoke—and
her voice was hard again, and, in an odd way, hopeless.

"*You've* made up your minds, anyhow, both of you," she
said, with a little mirthless laugh. "It's a pity to have to
blight you, but you're off it—miles off. Neither Godfrey
nor I had a hand in the murder. I'll tell you the whole
story, and you can believe it or not, as you like."

32

"Féo!" the Squire broke in agitatedly. "My dear—do you think it's wise?"

She laughed again, shrilly.

"They seem to know all that matters, anyhow," she said, "and they're happily engaged in building up a scaffold for us out of what they imagine to be the rest. . . . Yes, I think they'd better be told. Scaffolds aren't pretty erections, even when they only exist in the minds of your—*friends.*"

I winced at the tone in which she said "friends." I began to feel extraordinarily small, and loathsome beyond words.

"We *had* planned to run away that night," she went on, in her new, hard, bitter voice. "We'd loved each other for months, and of course *she* wasn't the wife for Godfrey. We believe that love is the only thing that makes a marriage— and ours was to be a true one, legal or not.

"We had it all well planned. Godfrey went to town on the twenty-eighth, and drew all his available cash out of the bank, realized his War Bonds and so on. On the twenty-ninth he went to fix things up at Southampton."

"One minute," I interrupted. "What about the Devizes Museum? And the return half of the ticket to town?"

She laughed scornfully.

"Oh, of course he went there on the way to South-ampton on the twenty-ninth," she said impatiently. "No

P. R. Shore

one ever looks at the Visitors' Book in those dead-alive museums. He simply wrote '28th' instead of '29th.' As for the ticket—I bought it. I ran over to Savernake in the car earlyish on the Friday, just in time for the 9.11, which is always crowded on Fridays, and got a return ticket. I threw away the London half, and kept the return—just in case it happened to be needed as an additional proof. I gave it to him in the interval between his giving his evidence."

"I guessed that," said Roger. "But wasn't it a bit risky for Harrington to draw his money out like that? The police were sure to find out that he had."

"How were we to know that *this* would happen?" cried she. "We never expected any police bother at all. We thought we'd be away hours before any one made any inquiries about us. As a matter of fact, that horrible man Grier had found it out—about the cash being drawn out, I mean. But it didn't, of course, have any connexion with the—the murder."

"He thought it had, though," Harrington broke in, speaking for the first time for minutes. "He—he made some terrible insinuations—"

"Never mind that now," said Lady Gervaise impatiently. "Let me get on.

"The plan was that Godfrey was to fix things up at Southampton and return for me. He aimed at getting back by the 10.12. That was, you see, because we knew that *she*—Mrs. Harrington—was horribly jealous, and if he'd been later than that she'd have begun to be suspicious and make inquiries. If only we'd known that she meant to be out seeing old Salt, of course Godfrey would never have had to come back at all; he'd have stayed in Southampton, and I'd have joined him there. As it was, we didn't dare risk his not getting back at a reasonable hour. The idea was that he was to get home, put in an appearance, say he was frightfully tired, and would go to bed early; then he'd join me. I was to have the car ready, meet him in the Manor House stable, to make sure that all was well, then return home, and say to the maids that I'd been for a stroll, and that, as the night was so lovely, I'd go for a spin in the car—I often do, you know. Then I'd pick him up and drive to Southampton. We meant to arrive about one, and have the excuse of a breakdown.

"Well, I left your house, as you know, Miss Leslie, about half-past nine. I'd attached myself pretty firmly to you all day as a kind of guarantee of respectability, in case Mrs. Harrington wanted to keep tabs on me. When I left you, I went home, put my luggage in the car—I'd packed in the morning after the maids went to the Fair—and then I went round by the woods to the Manor House. I must have got there a little after ten. I waited until nearly eleven, and still he didn't come—and then I guessed that something must have gone wrong, and he hadn't arrived by the 10.12. I was afraid the maids might get back before I did, and find my things missing—I'd had to pack up all my night things, you see. So I ran home, meaning to look up trains and find out when he could come. I kept to the dark side of the Green as I went. I saw two people—I know now they must have been Celia and young Earle—as I started, but they seemed very much occupied, and I didn't think they'd seen me."

"And then?" I prompted her.

"Then—nothing! I waited and waited. I knew he could only get back by some horrible cross-country way. And the next thing I heard was—he rang me up from the Manor House, to say that Mrs. Harrington was dead."

"And the gun?" asked the curate.

"I know no more than the dead. I've no idea what, or who, had anything to do with that."

"Then—it *wasn't* you who was in Mrs. Harrington's room that night?" I asked.

She stared frankly.

"Oh, lord! Have I been accused of that, too? Burglary, as well as murder? Not guilty. Why should I be?"

Whatever else she might be, she was honest. I felt sure of that.

We all sat silent for a few minutes. Then the curate said: "And you, Harrington? What were you after that day?"

Harrington hesitated; then he said:

"Well! I suppose there's no point in keeping it dark now. But I haven't much to add to what Féo's told you.

"I went to town on the twenty-eighth. While I was there I learned by the merest fluke, that Felton was sailing for the Continent the next day. I happened to meet a man we both know, who told me about it—Felton's breakdown, the rest of it. That was a piece of pure luck—about the only piece I had.

"I had a pretty busy day, one way and another—you see I had to sever all connexion with London . . ."

"One second. How did you go to London?"

"Walked to Dimsey and took the Savernake 'bus."

"Right. Sorry to interrupt."

"Not at all. Well—as I was saying, there was the deuce of a lot to do—you can guess the sort of thing. I got through fairly well, though, and managed to finish in time to get home a little before eight. The next day, the twenty-ninth, was of course the critical day. We'd settled on that day because we knew that my wife would be so much occupied with the Fair that she would be less—watchful than usual. I was very anxious to keep on good terms with her, all the same, because I knew that, if she were annoyed, she—she might—might guess that there was something in the wind—jealous people can be horribly acute—and—and interfere seriously with my arrangements. So when she asked me to go down to Foakes Green and see that everything was all right, I had to agree to go, though I was very anxious to be off to Southampton. I told her that I'd had an unexpected call to town on business, but would be able to do as she wished for a bit. She looked at me very oddly, I thought, when I said that I should be away that day. She was a most extraordinarily suspicious woman." (He said this in an injured sort of way, as if she had no possible excuse for being anything of the sort!) "So, quite casually, I suggested that she might get some other lady to help her out, and said that I was sure that Fé—that Lady Gervaise—would be glad to do anything she could.

"That quieted her suspicions, as I thought it would. She said that she would find out if Lady Gervaise was going to the Fair, and would be ready to stand by if she were needed for anything."

"Not that she'd ever have asked me to help, of course," interpolated Lady Gervaise. "It was far too much her show for her to stand any one else's interference. But she wanted to be quite certain that I should be there, not with Godfrey. So she rang me up."

"Well," Harrington continued, "I needn't go very fully into what I did. I took the 'bus to Devizes. It was a piece of the purest ill-luck, my being noticed by that conductor. I went to the museum, which was empty, of course—no one takes any interest in it, though it's quite good of its kind—and I knew the caretaker would never notice if I dated my signature wrong; so I put 'June 28.' I then went by tram to Newbury, changed there, got a 'bus to Andover, and from there a train to Southampton, arriving about half-past six."

"The idea being, of course, to cover your tracks if any one got on to you by any chance?"

"Exactly. Unfortunately, I was taken ill at Southampton, as came out at the inquest—"

"Yes, we were there," I interrupted. I really couldn't bear having to hear a recital of his symptoms. He looked at me with a kind of pained reproach, but carried on:

"I ordered berths on the boat sailing at eight the next morning, and booked rooms for the night at a small hotel. I had to have a *pied-à-terre* to send things to—I couldn't pack any of my own things—and also for us to wait at till the boat sailed. We expected, you see, to reach Southampton soon after one."

"But why did you arrange to leave Ringshall so early?" I asked.

"Two reasons—first, because it's daylight so horribly early now, and we had to start before that. Secondly, we hoped to be off before the Fair ended. I thought that, with all the cars about that the County people had come in, we should be able to slip off without being noticed; and I knew that, if I came in a little after ten, said I was too tired for supper and would go straight to bed, it would be perfectly easy for me to meet Féo, tell her everything was ready, and slip off to join her near the Fair, where there would have been a crowd of cars all day. But it isn't dark till after ten, and the moon rises about a quarter past; so we thought that as soon after ten as we could manage would be the best time to start.

"Unfortunately, my attack of illness at Southampton delayed me. I missed the train I had intended to get. I didn't know what to do. I didn't dare risk a wire to Féo— you know what country post-offices are—and I knew she wouldn't be in if I rang her up. And one thing I had to do was to arrive at Ringshall *as if I were coming from town*. We had decided that. You see, if my wife were in, as she well might be, she would expect that; and if she were not, she would think, when we were missed, that London had been the place I was at, and would think that I had been fixing

up our departure from town. So, though I could have got
back a little earlier by coming direct from Southampton,
it seemed wiser to delay, if by doing so I could appear to
be coming from town.

"I bought a Bradshaw and mapped out a time-table.
The last stage—the stage from Savernake to Ringshall—I
really took, only instead of getting to Savernake as I said,
I got there *via* Salisbury and Andover. I reached home, as
you know, Miss Leslie, about half-past two. That was because I ran it too fine, and missed the train at Andover. I
went straight to the Manor House, just in case Féo should
still be waiting. Of course, she wasn't; so I thought I'd go
across to Haresfoot and get off at once. Only, as I was at
home, I thought I'd just say good-bye to Celia—my baby
girl—before I went out of her life for ever."

I suppose he thought that was pathetic. Some people
will swallow down anything in the way of what the films
call 'sob-stuff.' But we were far too well used to Godfrey
Harrington to pay any attention to this little effort to get
sympathy.

"Was the idea to carry on with the elopement even
then?" asked Roger.

"Oh, certainly. I meant to go straight over to Haresfoot. I knew Féo, my loyal little Féo, would be up, waiting, ready for me. And then—I heard of—Agatha's death."

We sat silent for a minute.

"And the gun—the Loxley?" Roger asked then.

Harrington made a gesture of despair.

"I haven't the smallest idea. That is the absolute and
honest truth. I believe I left it in the side entry. I haven't
touched it since."

Again there was a pause. Then Roger Cartwright said,
speaking rather slowly:

"I suppose you never had any idea that—that Mrs. Harrington might not have been free to marry you?"

Harrington brought down his hand with a slap on the table.

"*That* was it, was it?" he cried. "Was *that* her secret? Was she married to some one else?"

"We don't know," said Roger. "We're only guessing. We hoped you might know."

"I don't," said the Squire, and he said it so regretfully that I knew he didn't. So there we were, almost exactly where we'd been days ago. It's funny how disappointing clues are. The better they seem the less they appear to lead you anywhere.

"X," I murmured to the curate, as our conference broke up. "X. It *must* be X! There's simply no one else left for it to be."

"I don't believe in X," he said, quite crossly.

So that was that.

33

I didn't return to the Dower House again that evening. I rang up Betty and reminded her about Lydia, and then retired to my room to dress and think things over.

The problem was, it seemed to me, even more complicated than it had been a few days ago; and yet in a way it was simpler, for I did think that at least three possible suspects—Joe Greaves, Lady Gervaise, and Godfrey Harrington—knocked out. And yet—were they? After all, I only had their word for it, in the last two cases. I thought that Lady Gervaise's story had rung true. I couldn't help acquitting her in my own mind. And yet I wasn't anything like so confident now as I had been a few days ago that my instinct about people was infallible. She had looked, and sounded, straight enough—but she was, and always had been, a clever woman. And yet—

"No!" I said to my reflection. "I don't believe she was lying. She's too reckless, she wouldn't have minded giving herself away to me or to Roger. She knows it wouldn't go any further."

But I didn't feel so sure about the Squire. Though Lady Gervaise might not lie on her own account, she might—and would—on his. I began to consider it from this point of view.

Suppose she was telling the truth as far as the place
where she said that she went and waited in the Manor
House stable; but suppose that he *had* got the 10.12, as
he'd meant to; that would have given him time. . . . And
yet, it seemed pointless. Why should he hold up things
like that? The flight was planned, everything was ready.
Could it have been, as I'd thought before, a kind of queer,
perverted morality that had urged him to "be off wi' the
old love before he was on wi' the new"? Or was my other
theory right—that the idea was that Mrs. Harrington
should die intestate? The first theory I did *not* believe. It
was all too improbable—you had to fit together an endless
number of unlikely happenings to make it fit at all well.
Besides, I was pretty sure that the news of the whereabouts
of the Loxley rifle *was* news to him, and that he had not
put it in the shed. But who had? That was still a puzzle.

Then the burglary—or rather, burglaries, for there
were three of them now—those didn't seem to fit in anywhere if Godfrey Harrington were the criminal, unless my
idea was right about an attempt to suppress evidence of
a first marriage. But he had seemed flabbergasted when
Roger had asked him if there were a possibility that Mrs.
Harrington's first husband might be still alive. Besides,
though he might have been the person who rifled the
safe—he'd have been sure to know of its existence—I was
pretty certain that he was not the person I'd heard in Mrs.
Harrington's room on the night of the murder, and I knew
he wasn't the visitor on that last occasion. He'd come running from his own room, and the window had been opened
while we spoke in the corridor. I felt more and more convinced that *all* three crimes—the murder, the burglaries,
and the attack on Inspector Grier—were the work of one
person, and that that person was X.

I began again, taking this hypothesis. X was connected
with Mrs. Harrington's past. He was either Lagardi, or a

friend of his. He knew some secret—probably that at the time of her marriage with Harrington she was married to some one else, either himself or a friend. Very well. But why murder her? If it was he who had blackmailed her, as no doubt it was, he had been doing very well out of her. It seemed the silliest sort of thing to do, to kill the goose that had laid the golden eggs.

And yet, it mightn't have been so silly. Suppose it was something like this: Suppose he'd begun the blackmailing without knowing that she was rich in her own right. Suppose he thought that she was using Harrington's money to pay him. And then he learnt, somehow or other, that it was *she* who was the wealthy partner. Wouldn't it then pay him better to get rid of her and claim all her money, since he could prove his marriage with her, and knew that she must die intestate on account of the difficulty of signing a will with her true name?

And there I stuck again. For it was obvious, from his own story, that he must have known weeks ago that she was rich in her own right. What beat me was, why he killed her *now?*

It was at this point that Lawson came to tell me that Lydia Salt was at the door, asking for me. I went down at once. Perhaps now I should get a clue as to the identity of X. For if Roger was right, and the notes to Lydia and Inspector Grier were parts of the puzzle, the person who delivered Lydia's note was probably the burglar—and the murderer.

Lydia looked tired and white and rather discouraged. She rose as I came in, carefully shutting the door behind me.

"Well, Lydia?" I asked. "Any luck?"

She shook her head.

"Not much, miss. Mrs. Rutter says as she gave my parcel to Tom Nokes, same as I thought she would, an' there weren't no one else in the shop when she gave it him. So I found Tom—an' he took a deal o' looking, too. And he says as he brought my parcel straight up, and never stopped nor spoke to no one. And I think as he's speakin' truth, miss; he's a noticing lad in some ways, and he's sense enough, if you go along right way with 'en."

I sat silent, deeply disappointed.

"But the note *must* have got in *somehow,*" I protested at last.

"Yes. . . . There's just one thing, miss, as I thought. I asked father what time it were when young Tom brought the grocery, and he said, "Twere just on five when he brought 'en,' he says, 'for it hadn't but just struck when he come back in.' 'What did 'a come back for?' I asked 'en, but father, he said as he didn't know; he never said nothing, just stepped back in an' straight out again. Now you know, miss, father's blind, and he were round at the chicken-pen, back o' the house. He'd heard Tom's step, an' caaled out to ask who 'twere, an' Tom said as 'twere he wi' grocery; so when he heard a step come back in, he never thought but 'twere Tom come back in. But I've seen Tom again, an' he declares as he never come back. He went straight off down lane, so 'a says, an' never seed no one."

"So you think—?"

"I think, miss, as some one may have been hid about, watching for a chance to speak to me about Joe. But I were in bed, see; an' 'twouldn' be safe to leave note loose about in kitchen, for I mightn't never have seed it. But I were safe to open parcel from Rutter's, seein' as 'twere drapery stuff as well as grocery; so when Tom left parcel, this 'un seed his chance, an' slipped in an' put note under string."

"That's extremely likely," I said. Indeed, it did seem to me the most probable solution. X was wise in counting on Lydia to get rid of Inspector Grier for him. Joe had too much sense; besides, you mightn't risk doing a thing like

that on the chance of saving yourself from arrest; but you
might, and if you were an hysterical, love-sick girl, you
would do it on the chance of saving some one you loved,
especially if you knew, as both Lydia and Joe did know,
that there was real danger of arrest and even conviction.
And Lydia was probably right, too, about the reason for
putting the note under the string.

Yes—but *who was X?*

"Lydia," I said, after meditating some time, "I suppose
you haven't seen, or heard of, any strangers being about
Ringshall lately?"

"No, miss, not since Fair. Of course there was a lot
about then."

"Yes, I know. But not since?"

"I don't think so, miss, But I've not been about much."

"No, of course not. I wonder if Joe has? Or Mrs. Nokes?"

Lydia's eyes suddenly filled with tears.

"Joe can't tell 'ee aught now," she murmured.

"Oh, he'll be out in a day or two, don't you fret," I assured
her. "There's nothing against him really. Besides, people
can see him, and we must find out if he's seen any stranger
about the place since the Fair. If any one did, Joe would.
Now, what about Mrs. Nokes? Do you think she'd know?"

Lydia shot a half-scared glance at me.

"She'd *know,*" she half whispered. "They do say as she
knows aal as goes on i' Ringshall. But 'tis ill to ask 'en
about strange men, miss. See, they do say as she has One
as she meets—a dark man—"

A familiar, in fact! Or perhaps the master of all familiar
spirits. Absurd as it was, I felt a tiny thrill run through
me, even as I wondered what Mrs. Harrington would have
said to this confession of faith on the part of her home-
trained house-parlourmaid. I couldn't help remembering
a certain talk, under Ringshall Oaks, with the son of the
witch. . . .

"I don't mean anything so silly," I snapped. "I mean a real, live, flesh-and-blood *Man*—a man who leaves notes in parcels."

Lydia turned perfectly white.

"Oh, miss!" she whimpered. 'Sure you don't think as she sent *he* to me wi' that paper?"

"He?" I asked.

"Ah. Her—her—"

"Oh! Not a devil, or a spirit, or a fairy, if that's what you mean," I said.

I got up. I saw that there was no more to be got out of this interview; I also saw that Lydia, what with the excitement of her confession, the hunt first for me and then for Tom Nokes, and her present alarm, had had more than was good for her. I told her to go to the cook for some tea, and then sent her home in a car which I ordered from the one and only 'garage' in Ringshall. It's a horrid car, but I'm sure Lydia didn't mind. She didn't have to pay the bill.

34

Stephen Earle was in to dinner at the Manor House that night. Who had invited him—if any one—wasn't very clear. He just appeared, and, apparently, meant to stay.

Personally, I was glad. Godfrey Harrington was in a very jumpy, nervous state, and I felt that I wanted some one who would just be natural and, at the same time, more or less amusing. Besides, I thought that it was rather hard on Celia that her scruples should cut her off from Stephen just when she must have wanted him most.

Stephen was of the greatest use. He chatted rather absurd, pleasant sort of nonsense most of dinner-time; and then, when we took our coffee out on the verandah afterwards, he began to tell us bits of news.

"You know, that chap Wilberforce is great fun," he said suddenly.

"The moron?" I asked.

"I suppose he might strike the unobservant like that," Stephen assented equably, "but he's really not half as bad as he seems. Do you know that he's found the boots that jumped on to the garden bed from the window last night?"

"No! Has he?" cried Celia.

"Whose are they?" asked her father—not anxiously, I noticed, but with just ordinary curiosity.

"Whose do you think? One guess each."

"Go on, Aunt Marion," said Celia.

"Of course, they belong to some one we know?" I asked.

"Oh, yes. You couldn't guess if they didn't."

I thought.

"Joe Greaves," I said then.

"Wrong. Your turn, Celia."

"Yours," she said promptly.

"No. Oh, lord, what fun if they had been! Jam for poor old Grier, wouldn't it have been? Pity. Go on, Squire."

"Oh, I don't know—who is there? Not Cartwright's, obviously—"

"Go on, dad, guess!" said Celia. "Any one—the wilder the better."

"Oh—well—Gregory."

Stephen looked at him with immense respect.

"How—on—*earth* did you guess?" he asked.

"Oh, I don't know—perhaps I'm not quite such a fool as you thought, eh, Stephen?"

"Dad! But did you *really* think it might be Gregory?" asked Celia, in open-eyed admiration.

Godfrey Harrington said nothing. He merely smiled in a superior way that infuriated me, since I knew that it had merely been the wildest shot at the least likely person.

"I expect he trampled on the bed while he was supposed to be watching it," I said brutally.

"Oh, no," said Harrington indulgently. "I placed him myself, you remember. The footprints were quite clear on the earth."

"But, dad"—Celia's voice was full of both admiration and bewilderment—"*Gregory* can't have been the burglar?"

"Why not, my dear? It's often the most unlikely person, you know, who turns out to be a criminal."

"But—*Gregory!*" Celia protested again; and I was so fed up with the Squire's pretence at a well-considered theory

The Bolt 341

that I was just going to say something really rude when (fortunately, perhaps, though I was disappointed at the time) Stephen interrupted:

"From what I heard there's no chance of Gregory having been the burglar, or even being taken for him—worse luck. I wish there was, it would be so original. But he's lost his boots."

"Ah! *That's* more like it!" I said, with satisfaction. "And not even the Walrus can say that Joe Greaves took them. He's under arrest."

"Ah, but they were pinched before that," said Stephen, with his usual impish delight in scoring off me. "Gregory's been pouring it all into my sympathetic ear. They were pinched on the very same day as old Grier got done in."

"Oh, Stephen!" breathed Celia. "Surely they don't think that it was *Joe* who burgled us?"

"The Walrus does, of course," I said bitterly. "He just *licks* up whatever he hears and turns it into evidence against Joe. What does Gregory think, Stephen?"

"Gregory," said Stephen, with relish, "thinks as it were one o' they cat-burglars what pinched 'em. He hadn't only but just stepped out to meet his missus by the 'bus, and when he come back what should catch his eye but a letter a-layin' on the table like. Right in the centre like, it were. And it said on it 'Inspector Grier—Urgent.' So Gregory thought as it were his jooty, him being in an official position like, to take it along to the station. Which he done. But when he was a-getting into his uniform to go, he couldn't find his official boots. Not nowhere he couldn't find 'em. So he says to his missus, 'Missus,' he says, 'where've you been and gone and put them boots?' And she up and says as how he'd got of 'em on when *she* went off—which was true enough, as he then recollected. So without it were one o' they cat-burglars, well, he don't know what to think."

"And did the cat-burglar also leave the note for Inspector Grier?" I asked.

"I don't know. Gregory hadn't thought out that part of it. It doesn't seem probable, somehow, does it? And yet, as Gregory says, with them sort o' chaps there ain't never no telling."

"X," I murmured. "X, without a doubt. But *what* a brilliant scheme to pinch the bobby's boots to make footprints with! I'm getting quite an affection for X."

"But," said Celia, "have you any idea what he keeps on burgling us for?"

"No," I admitted. "At least—yes, I've an idea of sorts, but it never seems to fit in everywhere."

"Of course," said Stephen, "it's very hard on the chap the way you keep on interrupting him, Aunt Marion, every time he tries to go through the room efficiently. He only once got a real chance at it, and that was the time when you and Celia went to see Lydia, and he found the safe. And even then he can't have got what he wanted, poor chap."

At this point Godfrey Harrington said that there was a heavy dew and he felt chilly and would go in. I thought he was, really, sulky because his *eclat* over the matter of the footprints had fizzled out so dismally. But we were all too much interested in discussing X the Cat-Burglar to bother whether he stayed or went.

"I say," said Stephen suddenly, "how'd it be to do a bit of this burglary ourselves?"

I nearly said that I had already committed one burglary, very successfully; but I didn't want to speak of that rope business just yet, so I held my tongue.

"What of?" asked Celia, practically, if ungrammatically. "Boots?"

"Why, that room, of course. Go through it thoroughly—the seals are all off now, aren't they?—and see what we find."

Celia looked at me doubtfully. It was quite obvious that she very much wanted to, and wasn't quite sure if it was the game. But I had no such scruples.

"Good idea," I said briskly, getting up. "It's the only thing to do, if we want to keep the secret from falling into the hands of the enemy." I rolled the words round my tongue in sheer delight at their glorious sound. "If we don't get it now, X will, some day," I added, to clinch the matter.

At that Celia rose with alacrity.

"Of course," she said, with relief. "I hadn't thought of that. Come on."

So we trooped upstairs, going pretty quietly, because we didn't want either the servants or any of the Walrus's minions to guess what we were after.

I have never, before or since, searched a room—scientifically, I mean. Of course, when you lose things . . . But that's different. I only know two things about it. One is that the thing you're looking for, whatever it is, is always in the obvious place, like Poe's paper-rack; the other is that the police (in American stories, anyhow) remove the floor in sections, and, I believe, the walls and ceiling too. I didn't propose to do this, myself. Stephen might, if he wanted to; but, though the Manor House is very old, with a priest's hiding-hole in the attics, and this little concealed safe in the panels over Mrs. Harrington's bed, I somehow didn't think it likely that there would be another secret hiding-place in the same room.

Stephen disagreed. He believed whole-heartedly in the hidey-hole idea.

"I admit," he said, "that there should be a cipher directing us how to find it. But we mustn't be greedy. We know the rules. You begin by tapping the walls to see if they sound hollow."

"You may," I retorted, "if you *will* be so old-fashioned. I'm nothing if I'm not modern. I'm going to look in the obvious places."

Stephen (with Celia to help, of course) began to tap the walls solemnly with a hairbrush. I turned my attention to the furniture.

There wasn't much. Mrs. Harrington had good ideas about furnishing, and she had in her room only what was necessary; but what there was was really good. Her bed was lovely—a seventeenth-century French one—though she'd had a spring mattress fitted. There was a sort of writing-table-cum-bureau, a dressing-table of real Sheraton to match, a Flemish press for a wardrobe, a chest of drawers to match the table, a broad couch, and a chair or two. Her bathroom opened out of the bedroom, and I determined that it, too, should be well and truly searched before we gave up our rivalry with X.

I tried the press first. I took out and examined all the clothes that hung there. Fortunately, modern clothes don't need much examining, there's so little of them. I tried the sides and the floor for false bottoms. I looked in the two or three hats that were in the only drawer. I looked on the top, and was moved with admiration to find that there was no accumulation of hat boxes and brown paper there as there is on nearly all wardrobe tops. The press yielded nothing.

Nor did the bureau. I hardly hoped that it would; it was too obvious a place for papers to be. I then turned my attention to the dressing-table; and I must admit, though I hate having to, that I had a double curiosity about that dressing-table. Mrs. Harrington was, without any exception, the best 'preserved' woman I have ever seen (I know it sounds like a grouse moor), and I'd always wondered just how she did it. Not that I needed to know just yet, but at thirty-nine you feel that you soon may.

I tried the table itself first—drawers, legs, tops, even the mirror. No luck. There wasn't much in the way of what shops call 'appurtenances.' Brushes, hand-mirror, a rosewood tea-caddy which now held pots and sachets and bottles; a manicure set. I took up the tea-caddy.

"What a jolly thing!" I said, looking at the inlaid pattern running round the edge.

"Yes, isn't it?" said Celia. "She kept her face-creams and shampoos and things in it. She said once it was her most precious possession!"

Now, though I've not by any means got the lovely Titian sort of hair that Mrs. Harrington had, my brown has, I like to think, got rather nice reddish tints in it. I'd always wondered what Mrs. Harrington used to bring out the colour of her hair. And I'm ashamed to say that this curiosity for the moment overcame my interest in the search for X's secret. I sat down with the caddy on my lap and began to turn over its contents, to find the shampoo Celia had mentioned.

I soon found it—an ordinary brand enough; one, as a matter of fact, that I sometimes used myself. I was horribly disappointed. I put it back. But as I shoved the envelope back among the little jars and tubes, it struck me that it felt much thicker than the sixpenny worth I'd got when I bought the same brand.

"Perhaps she added something," I thought; and, feeling quite absurdly guilty, I opened the wrapper to see.

I sat quite still for a moment. Then I said, in a most creditably casual voice:

"Stop making that silly noise, Stephen. I've got it. We've foiled X. Here's the secret!"

35

I can't explain why, but I just *couldn't* go through those papers, hidden so cleverly in a packet of shampoo powder, in the very room of the dead woman whose secret it was. By common consent, we adjourned to my room down the little passage, and there sat down to examine them.

There were several of them—a letter or two, two official-looking documents, a small photograph, and some kind of statement, written on very thin paper, in Mrs. Harrington's unmistakable hand. On a separate slip was written very large: "Only to be examined after my death."

I took up the statement first. It was dated 30th May 1928—only just over a month ago.

"To those whom it may concern," he began. "I am the true and legal wife of Godfrey Harrington, Esquire, of the Manor House, Ringshall, Wiltshire. Before my marriage with him I went through the form of marriage with Giuseppe Lagardi, of no fixed address. I now know that ceremony to have been illegal, since Lagardi had a wife living when we went through the form. That is the first important point—*I never was Lagardi's legal wife.*

"In April 1920 I left Lagardi with Count Otto Czenowsczi, with whom I had had relations, and by whom I had had a child, Maria Antonia, who of course accompanied us. This child was Count Otto Czenowsczi's, not Lagardi's. *I never had a child by Lagardi.* This is the second important point.

"We travelled to Obstadt, where we were formally recognized as man and wife, and our child was declared the legitimate heir of the house of Czenowsczi. We insisted on this, saying that the fact that the Count had married a foreigner made us anxious to regulate the position of the child. The truth was, of course, that we wished to have her made his legal heir so that, if ever it should come out that her father and I had never been married, she would still be his successor. We opposed any State ceremony of marriage, since I believed myself to be already married to Lagardi, and Count Otto had very strong opinions concerning the marriage ceremony, which demands a solemn oath of legal ability to marry. Of course, had we but known it, we could have taken such an oath with perfect truth; but unfortunately we were ignorant of this, and refused to go through the ceremony. We agreed to keep secret the fact that I had ever lived with Lagardi—and we succeeded. We knew that Lagardi would try either to upset this arrangement of ours, and force me to return to him (for I was useful to him in many ways) or to blackmail us by holding over us the threat of exposure. But we hoped and believed that we should be able to persuade the Court that his story was false, and that he was unhinged. Fortunately, we had no trouble in this respect. In following us to Obstadt, Lagardi was in the railway accident at Kroningen, and was seriously injured. I understand that his back was affected. He was, at any rate, temporarily completely disabled, and for a long time either unconscious or

delirious. This, of course, was of great advantage to
our plans. It would be all the easier to discredit whatever he might bring up against us if we could show
that for months he had been out of his senses. In any
case, he was totally unable to take any active steps,
either in following or denouncing us, for over a year.

"In June 1921 Count Otto Czenowsczi was killed in
an accident. I need not go into the details of this. Maria
Antonia was his heir, formally declared so by the Obsterland Court of Law; and I was now declared her trustee,
together with the Dowager Countess Czenowsczi.
Maria Antonia had always been a delicate child. She
had for months been in a convent nursing home,
and it was now arranged that she and I, together
with a specialist, Doctor Salfeld, should travel for
her health. It was also legally settled that in case of
her death (for the doctor knew that her health was in
a most precarious state) I should inherit the personal
fortune of her father, which had descended to her.

"We travelled about for over three years. We remained incognito, at my desire—my aim, of course,
being to conceal our whereabouts from Lagardi.
Late in 1924 the doctor decided that a life of travel
was now too exhausting for the child, and we settled
in England, on the coast of Dorset.

"I then heard from a source which I need not
name, but which I could entirely trust, that Lagardi
was on our trail, and that the only safe course was
for our party to separate. I could not, of course,
explain this to the Dowager and Dr. Salfeld; so it
was I who had to leave the party—with what sorrow
I need not try to express. I travelled about England
for over a year—I dared not go further on account
of the child's health, which was now extremely precarious—and early in 1926 I found what seemed an

ideal place to stay in, near enough to Dorsetshire for me to see my child constantly, but very secluded and retired. I settled in Rings-hall and lived there in great seclusion. Here I made the acquaintance of Godfrey Harrington, for whom I felt an immediate and almost irresistible attraction.

"I must here make a reference to my personal feelings, though I had hoped to avoid doing so. I had loved Otto Czenowsczi very deeply. His death came to me as the greatest shock. It seemed to me to be a direct punishment for my guilty relation with him that he should die at my hand. I was overcome with remorse, and also by fear. I determined to lead a life thenceforward which would atone for my past—to devote myself entirely to my child and to good works. When I saw that the first of these was impossible—that I should, for both our sakes, be compelled to leave my child in other hands—I took that as a clear indication of what was wanted of me. It would have been too easy to devote myself to my child. The way of the penitent is not easy. I decided then to live with and for the poor and ignorant—to uplift, teach, and help them. And I determined that I would never again, however great the temptation, enter into immoral relations with any man. Therefore, much as I now loved Godfrey Harrington, and though I felt certain that he had real need of me, I would not listen to his proposals of marriage.

"But in November 1926 I heard of the death of Lagardi. It seemed to me to be a direct sign that I had won pardon for my sins. I accepted Godfrey Harrington, and married him late in that very same month. My only grief was that I could not have my child with me; but I could not, obviously, suddenly produce her in a society which had never heard of her, and in which I was striving to reinstate myself as a Christian woman. Maria Antonia's health was now failing very rapidly, and I used to go and see her constantly, making the excuse of the illness of an old nurse. She lingered for a year. In February of this year she died."

Celia looked up at me.

"*That* was the news that upset her so, then, that day when I found her crying," she said softly.

I nodded. I remembered how, on the day of that Fair Committee meeting, she had winced as she spoke of the death of her old nurse. I went on reading.

"Before Maria's death, in November 1927 I had a letter which alarmed me very much. It was from Lagardi, and threatened me with exposure. It was quite clear to me now what had happened. He had planned that I should hear of his death, so that I should be lulled into a false security, and then, when I had relaxed precautions, and he had got certain knowledge of my whereabouts, to threaten to expose me. For months he had me at his mercy. Here I admit that I acted foolishly. I could not have him arrested for blackmail, for I simply dared not let him tell his story. Even if I had been believed when I denied it, in a place like Ringshall mud that is once thrown sticks for ever. But I should have let him believe that it was difficult, even impossible, for me to get large sums of money to buy him off with. He did not know that my child was dead, and that I had become her heir in February, and, as such, was now the possessor of the great Czenowsczi fortune. But my freedom with money, especially after February, must have given him a clue to this, and his demands became exorbitant. I was at my wits' ends to know what to do. Finally I wrote to a safe friend—the same who had before told me that Lagardi knew where I was—and asked advice. It was due to the efforts of this friend that the truth was discovered—that Lagardi never had the smallest claim on me, since his marriage with me was bigamous. I have copies, which I will enclose with this of the certificate of his first marriage, and of the lady's death in 1923.

"This discovery entirely freed me of any danger of threats from him. I was, naturally, still anxious that he should not make public the story of my past life, but he no longer had (as I had previously feared that he had) any legal claim on me. I now knew that I was, and always had been, the true and legal wife of Godfrey Harrington; and I was able to do, after some consideration, a thing which I had long wanted to do—that is, to arrange that my entire fortune should be his in case of my predeceasing him. To make certain that this should be so, I made a will to that effect, which is in the secret drawer in the writing-desk he gave me.

"I now have only one fear left, that is lest, if I should predecease my husband, Lagardi may attempt to claim my fortune. I have therefore prepared this document, together with other proofs of the truth of what I say, and am hiding them in a secret place. I am anxious that my husband may indeed inherit the fortune of my first love, Otto Czenowsczi, that we may thus be all three united. I have no more to say."

This curious document was signed "Agatha Harrington." A few lines beneath the signature had been added.

"I have reason to fear that the hiding-place I had selected for this—viz. the hidden cupboard above my
bed—has become known. I am therefore putting the
papers in a new place. I have given a hint of this to my
step-daughter, Celia Harrington, and trust that she
may remember it."

"She never did!" Celia exclaimed. "I never had the foggiest
idea—"

"She did," Stephen cut in. "You said so yourself. She
told you that that box held her most precious possessions.
So it did, if her chief wish was that your father should
have the money instead of Lagardi."

"I suppose," I said, "that she must have feared this,
you know—I mean, that Lagardi would kill her and try to
claim the fortune. That was why she had to hide the papers
where he would never think of looking for them. Because,
of course, friend Lagardi's story just goes phut now."

"Isn't the whole thing like her!" said Stephen in a low
voice. "You'd recognize her hand in that statement anywhere."

"Rather," I agreed. "The semi-legal beginning, the reserve, the cut-and-dried telling of the story, her obvious
desire not to show her feelings—the very clichés—"

"'Lulled into a false security,' for instance," he nodded.
"Yes, it's Mrs. Harrington all over."

"But, look here!" said Celia in a bewildered voice. "She
says that the child died in February, and that fits in with
what she herself said and did in February. But in that
case—who's the child that man had with him? She was like
Her, you know. I met them in the drive, and I noticed it
even then, though I didn't know that She had ever had a
child."

"Is it possible that the child *didn't* die?" asked Stephen.
"This Lagardi may have got hold of her—"

"The doctor and the old Dowager lady wouldn't have let that happen," I pointed out. "They, especially the doctor, would be on the look-out against adventurers. Besides, even if you take a wild theory, and say that they were in with Lagardi—that he made it worth their while—(which is absurd, of course, of people in such a position)—what was the idea in telling her mother that she was dead? They'd simply be making a present of the money to Mrs. Harrington. Besides, they must have proved the child's death to her. She was obviously devoted to the poor little thing. She'd never have taken it for granted that she was dead without any sort of proof. And even if the doctor wangled that part of it, why should they want to hand over that fortune to Mrs. Harrington? No doubt they, or at least the doctor, were drawing handsome salaries for looking after the child. I can imagine that they might pretend she was alive after she had really died, but not that she had died when she was really alive."

"P'r'aps there's some help among the other papers," suggested Celia.

We looked them over. The two official-looking papers were French—one, the copy of a certificate of marriage between Giuseppe Lagardi and Louise Victorine Marnier, in 1913; the other of the death certificate of Louise Victorine Lagardi, in Paris, in 1923. But the most interesting thing among the documents, bar the statement, was the photograph. It represented Mrs. Harrington—unmistakably—sitting with a child of five or six on her knee. The child was a little like Mrs. Harrington, and unfortunately reproduced her mother's slight cast in the eye, only it was more pronounced in the child. She had a high, rather oddly shaped forehead, and a full, mature mouth. Her hair was apparently dark and very curly. She was, in short, very like the photograph that Lagardi had produced of Count

Otto Czenowsczi, plus a resemblance to her mother increased by the cast in the eye.

"There's no doubt at all whose child *that* is," I said. "I saw the portrait of Count Otto. But what a sell for Lagardi!"

"I wonder how he knew that these proofs existed?" asked Stephen. "It's obvious that they were what he was after."

"I expect she told him," I said. "Probably, when she found that she wasn't, and never had been, married to him, she wrote and said that she had certain proofs that he had no claim on her, and would produce them if necessary."

"Of course, it decides the whole question of the murder," Stephen went on.

"Of course," I agreed. "Didn't I always say it was X, the Man from the Past? The idea obviously was to kill her and claim her fortune for a fictitious child; and he *had* to get hold of these papers, or the whole thing went phut."

"Then," said Stephen, "your theory is that this chap Lagardi came down to Ringshall on purpose to kill Mrs. Harrington and get those documents; that he found his chance on the day of the Fair, seized the opportunity, killed her, and immediately tried for the papers."

"Something like that," I agreed. "You see, he'd have to kill her first and get the papers afterwards, because, if she found them gone, she'd simply replace them. His idea was to kill her, suppress the evidence that her marriage with Harrington was legal, and claim all her property. It would, of course, go to her husband—her legal husband—if she died intestate."

"But what I don't understand," said Celia, "is why he produced a false child."

"Don't you see?" I cried. "He knew—he said so to Inspector Grier—that the money had been Czenowsczi's originally. He knew, though the Obsterland officials didn't, that Mrs. Harrington had never been married to

Czenowsczi, and that she had no claim on his money. But it was common property that the child had been accepted as Czenowsczi's heir, and that, *whoever she was,* the Czenowsczi fortune was now hers. His idea was to claim that she was not the Count's child at all, but his (she was born, you remember, before Mrs. Harrington left Lagardi), and that, her mother being dead, he was her natural guardian and trustee. Her birth certificate will, of course, be in the name of 'Lagardi,' not 'Czenowsczi.' If the Count chose to get Lagardi's child accepted as his heir, that was his affair; but Lagardi and her mother would be the child's legal guardians, and, if the mother was dead, Lagardi only. If he couldn't produce the child, there might be all sorts of difficulties; but if the child was there, and he could prove it was his, he was all right."

"But what about the people who'd had charge of her—the old Countess and Dr. What's-his-name?"

"I suppose, once they'd handed over to Mrs. Harrington, they would take no further notice of what happened. Why should they? They would probably never hear of all this. We shouldn't, in this country, if a similar thing happened in, say, Czecho-Slovakia."

"Bit of a risk, though," commented Stephen.

"Such a small one that I suppose he counted it wouldn't be worth bothering with. Or he may have known of something that made that part of it fairly safe. Certainly you must admit that once these two (who had no personal interest in the thing beyond seeing that the child was properly cared for, and that her mother didn't slay her to get her money), once they knew that the poor little thing was dead, and her mother had the money, they'd take no further interest in Mrs. Harrington and her affairs."

"No, I suppose not. And so Lagardi hunted up some child who had a kind of superficial likeness to Mrs. Harrington, and produced her as a proof of his *bona fides.*"

"That's what I believe. It would be safe enough, you know. We none of us knew that Mrs. Harrington had ever had a child. Personally, I never for one moment doubted that she was Mrs. Harrington's child."

"Did Grier?" asked Stephen suddenly.

"I don't know. I never thought of it. Do you think . . ."

"I wondered if he'd been making inquiries about the kid and scared this chap Lagardi."

Then I remembered the line of writing that the Walrus had displayed. "News of the child" had been promised by that writer on the blue sheet of paper.

"Oh!" I cried in delight, "it *all* fits in now! Everything! Oh, didn't I say it was X? Why *didn't* I take a bet on about it?"

36

Isn't it extraordinary how, when you get one stroke of luck, others simply pour in? I've often noticed it with cross-word puzzles—you find some quite impossible word, like 'axolotl' or 'talipot' or 'bycocket,' quite by accident, and the rest simply falls in. It was like that now. I'd just decided that we simply must, in fairness, tell Roger Cartwright of our discovery, and was about to ring up and tell him that it was all solved, when I was myself called up by Dr. Ludlow.

"That you, Miss Leslie? I thought you might like to know that your pal Grier has recovered enough to talk. Wilberforce is with him now, and I rather gather that things are moving."

"Oh, Doctor! *Can't* I see him?" I begged. "I've just made the most *frightfully* important discovery; it solves the whole thing. Do just tell him that I've found the thing that X was looking for in Mrs. Harrington's bedroom."

"Hold on a minute," said the doctor.

I stood for hours and hours, listening to the little fizzling and plopping that goes on at the other end of a telephone wire. It must be getting latish, I thought, and really to waste time like this was maddening. Would the man *never* come back? I nearly danced with impatience and rage.

I was so occupied with listening to nothing on the telephone, and with the thought that I might get dear Inspector Grier to arrest Lagardi at once, that I never heard Roger Cartwright come in. He simply appeared at my elbow. But I wasn't surprised. I felt that nothing could ever startle me again.

"Sit down and wait," I hissed. "The mystery is solved. I'm hoping to go round and tell Inspector Grier about it. He's better."

He grinned at me. He obviously thought I was getting excited over nothing.

"X, I suppose?" he said gently.

"X indeed," I retorted, "and X is no longer the unknown. We have him on the hip."

Here the telephone rang.

"That Miss Leslie?" came Dr. Ludlow's voice. "Inspector Grier can see you, if it's *really* important. Only you simply *must not* let him get excited. If you do, I won't answer for the consequences. If it wasn't that he thinks you may just have got the one last thing he wants to make an arrest, I wouldn't let you near him."

"I have; I'm sure I have!" I cried. "It's frightfully important, Doctor. I'm extremely fond of Inspector Grier, and I wouldn't hurt him for the world, but I'm sure it's worth the risk to tell him. I'm coming round at once."

I hung up the receiver to prevent further discussion, and caught up a wrap. It was half-past ten, and the dews were heavy. I didn't know what had become of Celia and Stephen, and I didn't care. They were by now probably discussing other things of more personal interest than the doings of Lagardi.

"Come along, too," I said to the curate. "The inspector will let you hear, I'm sure."

I said it very kindly, but he merely grinned. Ah, I thought, you little know what a thrill you're going to get.

The poor inspector looked very ill, as was natural—but he still had his nice twinkle, and the relief, after the Walrus, was so great that I nearly kissed him.

"Sit down here, Miss Leslie," said the doctor, who had let us in, "and don't let the inspector talk much. I'll have to stay, you know—can't let you go upsetting my prize patient."

Something in the way in which he said those last words made me realize that it must have been really touch-and-go with the poor inspector. My heart warmed to him more and more.

We all sat round—it looked rather like the levee of a monarch in reduced circumstances—and I began.

Inspector Grier said nothing. He lay taking it all in with bright, shrewd eyes, and every now and then giving a tiny nod, as if I'd verified some idea of his.

"Have you got the papers there?" he asked in a queer, weak sort of voice when I'd finished.

I handed them over.

He looked through them attentively, and then heaved a sigh.

"That's got it," he said. "That's the last link. I'd no idea that she hadn't been married to Lagardi. He's safe now, all right."

"*Safe?*" I asked.

"Yes—safe for the gallows, I mean. Only hope they've got him where they want him by now."

"Did you know this all the time?" I asked, with deep respect.

"Most of it. Trouble was, I couldn't trace the child. The old Countess is dead—died a few months ago—and Salfeld died under very suspicious circumstances about three weeks ago. It was supposed to be a political crime, but—I wondered. I got on to Lagardi, of course, as soon as he left that day—had him shadowed. I'd noticed the names of the trustees of the child in that rag he showed us, and, when I remembered about Salfeld's death, I got wondering. I looked it up in the Obsterland papers, and didn't get much—only that he and the Dowager had taken sort of official charge of the child (there was a very anti-British passage there, hinting that it wasn't safe to leave her in the hands of her grasping mother), and that she was having her health attended to. That fitted in with Lagardi's story of a convent nursing-home. But after all, that was years ago. No one seemed to have any idea what had become of either the child or her mother. The Dowager Countess had died abroad; Salfeld had been done in—though they let on that it was a normal death. Tracking Lagardi didn't seem to get me anywhere.

"I felt all the time that it was the kid that was the solution. I expect you noticed the mistake he made about her. He said she'd lived with him all her life, and that he educated her, and that—but he didn't know that she was left-handed. It was pretty clear that he'd never had much to do with her, or he'd have known that. So I began to follow up the kid. Tried to find out when she'd appeared, where she came from, and that . . ."

"And did he spot that you thought she wasn't the right child?"

"Must have. He thought he'd settled that, though, when she knew what her name was supposed to be. He didn't spot what I was after in that writing business. I saw she was left-handed by the way she held out her left hand to shake hands with us, when we first came in. But then I thought that might have been just a chance, so I fixed up the other way."

"And I suppose his idea was either to do you in completely, or at least to get you out of the way while his claim went through?"

"The first, if possible," grinned the inspector. "You see, he didn't know how tough I am. Though, as a matter of fact, a good long illness would have done him quite well. I'd nothing definite to go on, you see—not enough even to report on, let alone ask for a warrant. The kid was my one hope. His idea was to get me out of the way and shove it on to that chap Greaves. Of course it looked bad for Greaves any way. Any one who didn't know him personally" (here he grinned at Roger Cartwright) "thought he was the murderer. I did myself for quite a time."

Of course, if Lagardi was out to push it on to Joe, a lot was accounted for. It accounted for the gun being planted in Joe's cherry-tree, for the attempt to connect Joe with the attack on Inspector Grier (killing two birds with one stone, that was), for the notes—everything. Well, no—not quite for everything. Not for the discovery of Harrington's gun in the potting-shed.

"What beats me," said the curate, after a few minutes' silence, "is how he got on to Joe at all—how he knew he had a grudge against Mrs. Harrington, had talked that rubbish about her, had tried the bolt in the show gun on the night before the Fair—"

"Oh!" smiled the inspector, "hadn't you got that? Our friend Lagardi was the showman's assistant—the little gipsyish man."

The pirate! *Of course* that was who he was!

"That was how he seemed familiar to Miss Leslie," the inspector went on. "Of course, his beard being shaved off put her off spotting him when he turned up at the Manor House. It makes a tremendous difference, especially if you've only seen a man casually and haven't taken much notice of him. But I spotted that there'd probably been a beard there not very long ago . . ."

He stopped. His voice sounded very weak.

"Just one thing more," I said, refusing to catch Dr. Ludlow's eye. "How did Mrs. Nokes know that about the letters?"

"That was Lagardi's one bad break," replied Grier. "He came down to Ringshall in the late autumn, got up as a gipsy pedlar. The idea, of course, was to spy out the land—to make sure that the woman he had his eye on really was the right one. He'd lost her, you see, for a good while, and he couldn't risk blackmailing her till he was quite certain she was the right woman. I got most of this from the woman who keeps the shop—Mrs. Rutter. She was very much annoyed by this peddling business—said all the village girls were spending their savings on him instead of waiting to do their Christmas shopping at her place. He seems to have done a bit of fortune-telling—posed as a gipsy—"

"I remember," I murmured. "Mrs. Harrington was frightfully annoyed about it. Superstition again. You remember?" I added to the curate; "he went to the maids at the Manor House—"

"Rather, I do," he assented. "Mrs. Harrington tried to get the vicar to get the police to interfere."

"That's it," nodded the inspector. "Well, he seems to have got on to Mrs. Nokes then and done a bit of pumping; and the whole thing got her thinking. . . . And the maids seem to have talked about Mrs. Harrington's secretiveness about the letters, and given the old hag another hint . . ."

"They did," I agreed. "Celia told me that both she and the maids resented the line Mrs. Harrington took about correspondence."

"There you are, then. A strange man, interested in the lady—the lady's secretiveness about letters—a bit of work done under the guise of fortune-telling—the lady's hatred of fortune-telling—that's enough."

"Quite enough," I agreed. "After all, Mrs. Nokes's hints were of the vaguest kind. She just had an idea of a secret . . ."

At this point the doctor interfered and turned us out. But we didn't mind much. I—and I think Roger Cartwright too—wanted to finish piecing it out ourselves.

It was a lovely night, warm, scented with hay and dew, with the old moon only lately risen, though it was after eleven. It was much too good a night to go in, especially when we wanted to talk; so almost without words we agreed to stroll about out of doors and finish tidying up the last ends of our problem.

"What a fool I was not to spot that man!" I said, as we turned out of the doctor's gate. "It might have put me on the right track at once if I'd remembered where I saw him before."

"I don't see how you could expect to," he said consolingly. "He wasn't in evidence at the Fair. It wouldn't have suited him to be too noticeable."

"I wonder what gave him the idea—of acting as showman, I mean?"

"I expect he got the wind up over her refusal to pay him any more, and came down to this part of the world—not to the village, but somewhere near—Dimsey, perhaps—to spy out the land. He'd hear about the Fair, of course—it's talked about all round the country, you know, days and weeks before it's due—and he'd see that the excitement, having strangers about and all that, would give him excellent cover; so he put off his little effort till the day of the Fair itself."

"And in the interval, I suppose he got the idea of attaching himself to a show. Yes. That'll be about it."

"What I wonder is," said Roger, "whether he picked the rifle show on purpose, or did he just see, after he got the job, how well it might suit his scheme?"

"I don't see that it matters which it was. It might be either. But he must certainly have got the notion of shooting with an elf-bolt, and of perhaps being able to push it on to Joe Greaves afterwards, from that talk the night before in the 'Lady and Hare.' I expect, if we could know all that was said there that night, we should find that our friend Lagardi put a good deal of what was said into Joe's head, if not into his mouth."

"Yes—sure. But, I say, you know the chap must have had the most miraculous luck. How could he know that Mrs. Harrington would be on the Green at 10.30, and that the Fair would be over?"

"Oh, I've got it!" I cried. "I remember perfectly. It was while we were just beside that rifle-booth that Mrs. Harrington told Celia that she was going to see old Salt, and would be back a little before eleven. All he had to do was to find out where Salt lived—easy enough—and get a good place *en route*. And, if the Green was clear, that would be an excellent place—she'd make a perfectly splendid mark, and he could hide among the oaks. . . . I say! He must have been there still when Celia and Stephen passed. They must have been within a few yards of him."

"Yes; and Tom Nokes must have been hiding there too. Of course, he does haunt the oaks at night, especially in full moon. Just think—if Tom had only spoken, we should have had the whole thing days and days ago."

"But how did Lagardi know that the Green wouldn't be full of people when Mrs. Harrington was crossing it?" I asked. "Unless—I say! Do you think he organized the smash-up of that stall?"

"That's it! Of course he did," cried Roger, "and pinched the rifle himself—the same rifle he'd got Joe to mark the night before."

"Then—did he use that gun, do you think?"

"Why not? Oh, the Loxley, you mean?"

"Yes. What about that?"

He considered a moment.

"Mightn't it be something like this?" he said then. "Did this chap get any time off, do you know, during the day?"

"He got his dinner-hour. I saw him hand over to his boss."

"Well, then—suppose he used that time to go up to the Manor House. He might have gone there for one of two reasons—either to look for those papers, or to get the Squire's gun. You see, he was in charge while the Squire was messing about at the booth in the morning; he'd have seen what a powerful gun it was. He might have wanted to have it in case anything went wrong with his plan for getting the other one, the one Joe had marked. But I expect he really went to have a look for those papers. He'd guess that the house would be more or less deserted."

"He *knew* it was," I broke in. "Mrs. Harrington said so in his hearing. I remember distinctly. She said so when she told Celia to go up and tell Lydia she might go to the Fair."

"Well, that's clear then. He went up to the House, keeping under cover, of course. He'd go by the nearest way, by the side gate, and he'd probably take cover for a bit to watch for Lydia leaving and to see where Celia went. Her mother advised the garden, you said, which would have suited the burglary plan excellently. Now, coming by the side way, where would he hide?"

I thought for a moment.

"In the furnace-house," I said, almost at once. "He'd see what it was by the chimney, and he'd know that the furnace couldn't be going on a roasting hot day, with everybody out."

"Just what I thought, too. And the furnace-house is very near the side door into the house. He'd be able to spot Lydia going out. It would be an ideal place for him.

Well, what happened, of course, was that Joe turned up to see Lydia, and, as she told us, obligingly pointed out the Squire's gun, which Harrington had left, as he thought he had, in the side entry; and also, by a wonderful stroke of luck for our friend the murderer, Joe indicated which was Mrs. Harrington's room."

"Oh, of course," I breathed. "The windows—"

"Yes. The only room with the windows shut. Well, Joe and Lydia then strolled down the garden—taking their time, no doubt—and left the coast clear.

"But the only unkind thing that Joe and Lydia did was that they took so long over their otherwise useful chat. Friend Lagardi no doubt had to be back at his job early-ish—"

"At two," I murmured. "I heard Bert tell him."

"Quite. So he couldn't look for the papers then. He hadn't time, and Celia might have been about somewhere. All he had time to do was to pinch the Squire's gun and clear out."

"I don't quite see why he bothered with the gun," I objected.

"Why, because he knew perfectly well that only one or two of the guns on the stall would shoot straight. He especially wanted to use the one Joe had marked, and to use it with an elf-bolt, so that he could saddle it on to Joe. But, you see, that one gun might easily get damaged when the booth collapsed. This one of the Squire's made an excellent second string. As a matter of fact, it was the one he used."

"And the collapse of the stall would be easy enough to arrange," I said. "It was quite a good way both to get hold of the gun and to make it appear possible that Joe had got it; let it, and another one or two, disappear in the mix-up; and I expect it would also be easy enough to spread a little wholesome dread of the same thing happening to other stalls, and get the other showmen to close down early—especially with Gregory doing the heavy Arm of the Law, and the general atmosphere getting a bit hectic. It wasn't a bad scheme.

And of course it was he who planted the gun—the show gun—in Joe's cherry tree."

"Of course."

"Why do you suppose he used the Squire's, after all?"

"I imagine because the bolt he picked up fitted the Squire's gun better than the other. You remember, it was a bit loose in the one from the booth. He could have found another bolt, no doubt, to fit the show one—there's stacks of bolts about—but why bother, when the one he found first fitted the Squire's gun exactly?"

"Why, indeed?" I agreed. "And then, after it was all over, I suppose he buried the Loxley in the wood—just a temporary hiding-place, which Tom Nokes saw him use—and later took it out and planted it in the shed. Not a bad idea. If the first gun wasn't found in Joe's tree the chances were that the second one would be found in the Squire's shed—both on the premises of 'suspects.'"

"Not bad, was it? And, I say, wasn't it bold of him to produce the child, and all those documents and things, when he knew all the time that the papers disproving his story, and practically proving him to be a murderer, were still hidden somewhere in the house!"

"Wasn't it? And I only thought that he'd stolen the papers he produced. I never thought of another set. . . . He really almost deserved to win. Suppose Inspector Grier, or I, had found those papers? Yes, he was bold enough. One thing, though—why, when he first burgled that room, did he get into the bed?"

"Lydia again, I expect—that remark of hers to Joe about Mrs. Harrington insisting on always making her own bed. I expect he thought that that indicated that she had a strong reason why no one else should touch it; and, you know, it would be the safest place, if you had prying maids—or even were suspicious of maids. An inquisitive housemaid might pry into your desk or your drawers, but she'd see quite enough of beds without unmaking and remaking an extra one on the off-chance of finding something that she didn't even know existed. Besides, it's an instinct to hide things in a bed. They say it's the comfortable feeling of having them at hand night and day. So I expect he thought that these papers would be right in the bed, and lay on it, either to see if he could feel a little lump, or to see if he could spot any secret *cache* (such as there actually was) which could be reached from the bed. And I've no doubt, from the postscript to that statement of Mrs. Harrington's, that she did keep them in the safe over the bed at one time, and then, when she thought that Celia had seen it, transferred them to the box on the dressing-table."

"And the other night—the night he turned out the light . . ."

"He'd given up the idea of the bed. He'd tried the little safe by then, you know, and found it empty; so he concluded that she'd put the things somewhere else. The tapping you heard must have been him trying the other furniture, or the walls, for hollow places. It's lucky you have these premonitions—instincts—whatever they are—that give you warning and wake you up at the critical moment."

"Yes," I said modestly, "and which also lead me to suspect a criminal when I don't even know for certain that such a person exists. You remember that I said X was the murderer when you and Stephen merely jeered at the idea of the existence of an X. I'm seriously thinking of taking rooms in some select London district and taking to detecting for my living."

"You're far better where you are," he said, half seriously.

"Oh, why? Think how tame life will be after all this. There'll be nothing to live for except seeing our solutions verified when Lagardi's brought to trial." (By the way, they were—all of them.) "We shall simply vegetate."

"Well, wasn't that exactly what you wanted to do only a few days ago? When you said how happy we used to be before—"

"Before we had Societies and Guilds and District Visitors. Yes, I did. Oh, of course, I don't mean a word of it! Ringshall's the only place I ever want to live in. We'll soon settle down and be as we used to again. . . . Not quite, though. I suppose there'll be marrying and giving in marriage—Celia and Stephen will be all right now that the Squire can give her a decent *dot*—though I hope they won't marry entirely on that—and Lady Gervaise will, I suppose, after a decent interval, become the third Mrs. Harrington. What a difference!"

"And I shouldn't wonder if there's another one or two," said he contemplatively.

"Lydia and Joe have already done it—or so you say. Who else is there?"

"Well—there's you—and me."

"I'm thirty-nine," I reminded him.

"What about it? I'm forty-two—very nearly."

I'm not going to go on with that part. You can fill it in yourself if you're interested in these things. But we're going to be married in September, and Celia says she'd known it for months. And I needn't say anything more about the Lagardi man, though I wish I could describe his pursuit and capture. I can't, because I have no first or even secondhand knowledge of it, and I haven't put in anything in this account that I didn't get at least at secondhand. He was found guilty, of course, and has gone to his account. And Inspector Grier has, I believe, earned immense kudos over the whole affair. I am extremely glad of that. I couldn't have borne it if it had been the Walrus.

NOVEMBER JOE

DETECTIVE OF THE WOODS

H. HESKETH-PRICHARD

MURDER
IN A WALLED TOWN
KATHERINE WOODS

THE LAST TRUMPET
A HUGH RENNERT MYSTERY

TODD DOWNING

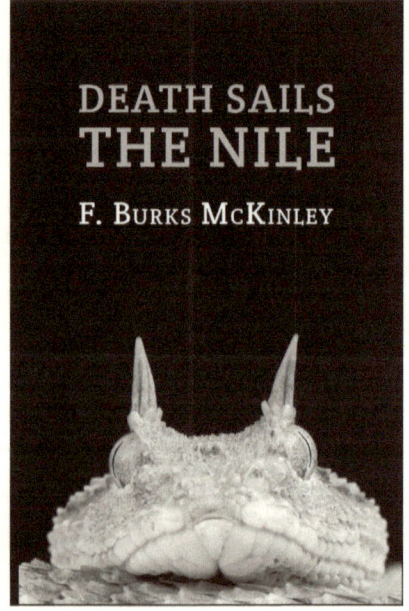

DEATH SAILS THE NILE
F. BURKS McKINLEY

Coachwhip Publications

CoachwhipBooks.com

FEAR OF FEAR

FLORENCE RYERSON
COLIN CLEMENTS

MURDER IN THE FAMILY

NICE PEOPLE MURDER

Mary Hastings Bradley

3 DETECTIVES

FEMMES AUDACIEUSES

MERWIN · SOMERVILLE · FOOTNER

DEATH DOWN EAST

Eleanor Blake

Coachwhip Publications

CoachwhipBooks.com

THE
MYSTERY
OF THE
FOLDED
PAPER

HULBERT
FOOTNER

The
Hollow Tree
Mystery

MADELON ST. DENIS

VIRGINIA RATH

FERRYMAN,
TAKE HIM ACROSS!

No Face to
Murder
EDITH HOWIE

Coachwhip Publications

CoachwhipBooks.com

THE QUINNY HITE
MYSTERIES

CHINESE RED · HERE LIES THE BODY

RICHARD BURKE

I'll Hate Myself in the Morning

Murder on the Left Bank

Elliot Paul

MURDER'S COMING

GRAVE WITHOUT GRASS

BY
DONALD CLOUGH CAMERON

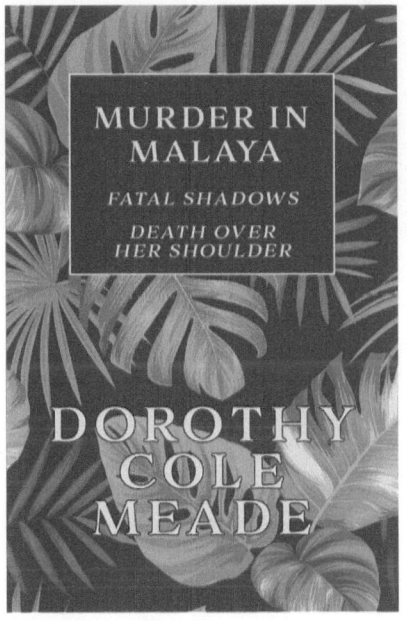

MURDER IN
MALAYA

FATAL SHADOWS

DEATH OVER
HER SHOULDER

DOROTHY
COLE
MEADE

Coachwhip Publications

CoachwhipBooks.com

MURDER
A LA
MODE

ELEANORE
KELLY
SELLARS

CLASSIC RED BADGE PRIZE MYSTERY

MURDER
ON THE
BLUFF

ESTHER TYLER

MURDER
BY JURY

MURDER
ON THE
APHRODITE

RUTH BURR SANBORN

LADIES
IN BOXES
GELETT
BURGESS

Coachwhip Publications

CoachwhipBooks.com

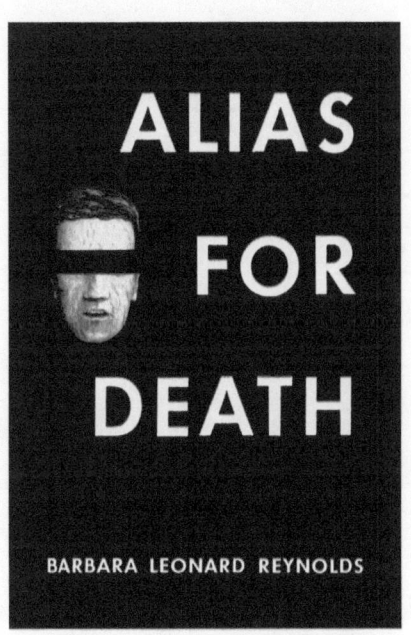

ALIAS
FOR
DEATH

BARBARA LEONARD REYNOLDS

THERE IS
NO RETURN
THE ADELAIDE ADAMS MYSTERIES
ANITA BLACKMON

Jack Dolph

MURDER
MAKES
THE MARE GO

FEAR
CAME
FIRST

VERA KELSEY

Coachwhip Publications

CoachwhipBooks.com

MURDER AT DRAKE'S ANCHORAGE

E. LEE WADDELL

MURDER AT THE KENTUCKY DERBY

CHARLES PARMER

MURDER ENDS THE SONG

ALFRED MEYERS

3 DETECTIVES
MURDER ON THE RAILS
WHITECHURCH • THORNE • TORGERSON

Coachwhip Publications

CoachwhipBooks.com

THE FIRES AT FITCH'S FOLLY

KENNETH WHIPPLE

DRESSED TO KILL

Emma Lou Fetta

GRIMM DEATH

THE GROUSE MOOR MURDER

JOHN FERGUSON

Coachwhip Publications

CoachwhipBooks.com

THE STUDIO
MURDER MYSTERY
THE EDINGTONS

THOMAS KINDON

MURDER
IN THE
MOOR

THE MAY DAY MYSTERY

OCTAVUS ROY COHEN

MURDER
AT SEA

RICHARD CONNELL

Coachwhip Publications
CoachwhipBooks.com

SHUDDERS

DESIGNED BY
CYNTHIA ASQUITH

DEATH IN THE DUSK

Virgil Markham

THE SEVEN BLACK
CHESSMEN

John Huntingdon

DEAD
WEIGHT

ADDISON SIMMONS

Coachwhip Publications

CoachwhipBooks.com

www.ingramcontent.com/pod-product-compliance
Lightning Source LLC
Chambersburg PA
CBHW032143010726
47494CB00002B/335